WARTIME BRIDES

LIZZIE LANE

B
Boldwod

First published in 2012. This edition first published in Great Britain in 2021 by Boldwood Books Ltd.

Cover Design by Colin Thomas

Cover Photography: Colin Thomas

A CIP catalogue record for this book is available from the British Library.

Paperback ISBN 978-1-80415-886-9

Large Print ISBN 978-1-80415-886-9

Hardback ISBN 978-1-80415-881-4

Ebook ISBN 978-1-80415-881-4

Kindle ISBN 978-1-80415-880-7

Audio CD ISBN 978-1-80415-887-6

MP3 CD ISBN 978-1-80415-884-5

Digital audio download ISBN 978-1-80415-878-4

Boldwood Books Ltd
23 Bowerdean Street
London SW6 3TN
www.boldwoodbooks.com

To my mother and all those of her generation who rebuilt their lives and told me their stories.

1

Edna stared. It was sitting there on the hallstand between a tweed jacket and a beige trench mac. A parcel – a third parcel – had arrived!

The sender's address was printed in the top left-hand corner, name, street and town. Finally, it read Mississippi, USA.

'Don't even think about opening it!'

Her mother's voice pierced as sharply as the pearl-ended pin she was presently stabbing into her hat.

'I wasn't,' Edna lied. She felt a hot flush creeping over her cheeks. 'I was just thinking.'

The sharp-featured Ethel Burbage rounded on her daughter and wagged a bony finger threateningly before Edna's eyes. 'Well, stop thinking about what's past, my girl, and think about your future. THAT's all that matters!'

She went back to adjusting her hat. 'What time did you say Colin was arriving?'

The question had already been asked last night over Spam and mash and this morning over a thick slice of bread fried in beef dripping. Edna swallowed a wave of revulsion at the memory of the grease congealing on her tongue. The war might be over but rationing certainly was not.

'The train pulls in at twelve,' she repeated for the third time.

She could see it in her mind's eye. Full of steam. Full of men. And herself standing on a smoke-filled platform waiting for Colin.

As she fastened her coat buttons, the clustered stones in her engagement ring blinked up at her. Three years since he'd slipped it on her finger and she had promised to wait for him. Today she must present herself at the station, smile, and pretend to be the same girl who had seen her garrulous, dependable fiancé off on that other train that had taken him to his ship and ultimately to the Far East.

'Better catch the eleven o'clock bus then. I did hear something about an unexploded bomb being found in Victoria Street. Poor old Bristol.' Her mother's tone softened for the briefest of moments. 'The heart's been torn out of the old place.'

Edna reached for her woollen gloves. I want time to roll back like the lid on a tin of sardines, she thought and sighed heavily. That was the trouble with time. Nothing had the power to roll back the weeks, the months and the year or so that had changed her life. All she had to remind her of that time was the arrival of these parcels, the third of which her mother loomed over like a guard dog over a fallen villain. Only *she* was that villain, the one who had done wrong.

'He didn't say much about his injuries in his letters,' Edna blurted suddenly.

Her mother tilted her hat a little more to the left and pushed it there firmly. 'Then they can't be very bad, can they? Nerves I expect. Shell shock they used to call it in the Great War. Give him my regards, won't you.'

'I will.' Edna sighed meaningfully in the vain hope it would convey to her mother exactly how she felt. 'But I certainly don't know what else to say to him.'

'There's no need to tell him anything.'

Edna's frail hope vanished. 'I suppose not.'

She made a meal of pulling on her gloves, as if the task required far more concentration than it needed. In her mind she rehearsed what she would say, edited the first words, rehearsed them again, then altered them some more. What if her tongue refused to lie? *I had an affair with an American GI and I had a baby.* She imagined the look of shock that would greet this announcement.

'There's no suppose about it,' her mother snapped, at the same time briskly brushing whatever specks, imaginary or otherwise, had dared to settle on the square-rigged shoulders of her everyday grey coat with the astrakhan collar. 'Don't even *think* about telling Colin. Poor lamb. After all he's been through.'

Edna nodded guiltily. As her mother never tired of reminding her, she had let her down. Only the fact that her liaison had happened at a distance saved her reputation. She'd been in the ATS manning the searchlights on the outskirts of Liverpool. Jim had bumped into her – literally – at some time before going on duty in the early hours of the morning when the blackout was at its worst. They'd become friends. She'd told him about Colin. He'd told her about the girl he'd left behind. They'd fallen into silence, the way people do when they suddenly realise they're attracted to each other. They were feeling the same way, thinking the same things. They were two lonely people, he far from home, she a shy girl thrust into a wartime job that she hated from the depths of her soul. They both longed for the war to be over and, in the meantime, they became more than friends. She'd tried to explain, but her mother had been mortified. During the last months of her pregnancy Edna had stayed with an aunt in North Somerset, just a short ambulance ride to a cottage hospital where she had been parted from her baby. For the sake of appearances it was two weeks or so before she came home.

Ethel's no-nonsense heels tapped on red and brown linoleum then softened as they reached the front door. The parcel was gripped tightly beneath her arm.

'I'll get this to Mrs Grey,' she said, 'and she'll get it to the orphanage. Thankfully she knows when to keep her mouth shut. But mark you, I'm going to write to him when I get back and tell him not to send things here any more. He can send direct to the orphanage or to Mrs Grey if he wants, but not here.' She held up a warning finger. 'But on no account are you to write to him. Understand?'

Edna nodded silently, her eyes averted now from the offending sight of the parcel and all the memories it resurrected.

Tears had threatened all morning. Only being occupied with buttering bread and laying out the table for Colin's welcome home party round at his mother's house had helped keep them at bay. His family, of course, knew nothing of her fall from grace. Everyone had been told she'd been off doing war work. But now she had to face him and pretend nothing had changed. It wasn't going to be easy.

Her mother forced a strained smile. 'Well, go and get yourself looking nice for Colin. He is home from fighting a war you know.'

The door slammed and Edna was alone.

'Does Daddy know we're going to meet him at the station?' asked Janet Hennessey-White, who was nearly fourteen and considered herself almost a woman and reckoned she would be once the freckles that covered her nose had melted away.

'No, darling. He doesn't.' Eyes bright, lips twitching with an excited smile that narrowed and broadened dependent on what she was thinking, Janet's mother, Charlotte, tried to stop her hands from shaking as she tidied her hair and arranged her hat. She couldn't stop chattering, her voice bubbling with girlish excitement. 'It was purely by chance that his old CO rang to wish him good luck and then realised he'd got the wrong day. He was going to surprise us, now we're going to surprise him.'

'What's a CO?' asked Janet.

'Commanding Officer, stupid,' snapped her younger brother Geoffrey who was eleven. He had followed the war with great enthusiasm and now seemed instilled with all the knowledge of any armchair general four times his age. 'I told my friends that my dad was an officer and that's why it took him so long to come home. He had responsibilities I said. That's why he wasn't around and their daddies were.' He frowned threateningly. 'I'll show them!'

Janet held her head saucily to one side. 'But they didn't believe you because THEY'RE stupid and YOU'RE too stupid to realise they are!'

Geoffrey's dark blue eyes sparked with anger. 'Destroy!' he shouted.

Janet yelled as the toy dive-bomber swept down the length of his arm. One wing of the wooden toy tangled in his sister's hair.

'Geoffrey!' Charlotte threw him a warning look though her voice remained calm. 'Please behave yourself, darling.'

'Mother! Tell him!' shrieked Janet.

Belief that the day could only be perfect flew into fragments. Charlotte took hold of her son by the shoulders and pulled him towards her. Janet aimed a punch but missed.

'Janet! Don't do that!' cried Charlotte, hating the fact that she had to shout and aggrieved that her children could still argue on such a special day.

After untangling the toy plane from her daughter's hair, she tossed it into a brown moquette armchair – David's favourite chair as a matter of fact. Soon he'd be there again, smoking his pipe just as he used to. The thought was fleeting but caused a smile to flutter across her lips.

Geoffrey struggled. Charlotte held him tight. 'Let me straighten your tie.'

'It won't straighten,' he said attempting to step away from her ministrations but being promptly tugged back again.

'Scruffy and crooked suits you,' said a triumphant Janet.

'It won't take a moment,' said Charlotte. 'And after that you can pull your socks up so that they're both level.' She glanced down. 'But wash your knees first.'

'I have!'

'Not well enough.'

'He's too weak to turn the taps on,' crowed Janet. Her mother wagged a warning finger. 'Janet!'

'He hates washing,' said Janet hunching her shoulders as she swung away. 'I need the lavatory,' she said suddenly.

'But you've already...' Charlotte began. Then a knowing smile came to her face as she watched her daughter skip off into the hall and up the stairs to the bathroom. The door slammed overhead. And that's the bolt going across, thought Charlotte.

Suddenly she was filled with a mix of trepidation and wonder. Janet was growing up, but not enough for the tube of bright red lipstick Charlotte had found hidden behind the medicine bottles and had thrown away.

Probably given to her by some spotty-faced GI, she thought wryly. God, how quickly children were growing up nowadays, thanks to the war. But thank God it was over. Perhaps things would now get back to normal – whatever that was. It was hard to remember what was normal before 1939. The children had been smaller, David had been home, and there was enough of everything if you had the money to pay for it. No rationing! What a luxurious thought!

'Ouch!' said Geoffrey. 'You're strangling me.'

'Sorry,' said Charlotte and proceeded to loosen the tie, just as she used to do for David when she had inadvertently slipped into a daydream.

As she patted the tie flat and straightened Geoffrey's shirt collar, she glanced at the pre-war photographs sitting on top of the piano. Shots of the family at the seaside, the children on their first bikes, Janet on a pony, the children as babies. Eventually her gaze rested on her wedding photograph. She smiled sadly. So long ago. A different world. Then she looked at the photograph of David in his army captain's uniform, taken before he departed for 'somewhere in Europe'. He'd looked so different, so distinguished, yet he'd still been the same man beneath. She didn't doubt that he still was, but she had heard sad stories since working at the Marriage Advisory Centre. Some men had been drastically changed by war. But not David, she thought. Too strong. Too level-headed.

'Come on Geoffrey,' she said brightly, as the sound of Janet's footsteps dragged down from one stair tread to another. 'Let's go and meet your father. And remember,' she said, her voice taking on a more serious tone as Janet re-entered the room, 'he's been through a lot, so if he doesn't seem like his old self at first, don't worry. He soon will be.'

'Of course he will,' said a confident Janet, unable to contemplate him being anything other than the Daddy she remembered, willing to give her anything it was in his power to give – perhaps even lipstick, she thought hopefully.

Charlotte noticed her hands were shaking again as she picked up her kid gloves, which were finely made and honeycomb yellow. 'Most people are bound to be affected by war. We certainly were.'

'He won't be. He's an officer,' said Geoffrey as if that explained everything.

* * *

Polly always took great care to look smart. Her preference for wearing black and white certainly helped, and it went so well with her blonde hair and bright blue eyes.

Gavin, her Canadian sweetheart, had said it was the first thing he'd noticed about her. He'd also said he liked girls who were slim and had boyish bottoms and feminine bosoms. And he'd also said he loved her and that he would marry her and they would leave for Canada together once the war was over. Another train was due at Temple Meads railway station at noon. This time he just might be on it.

She took out her powder compact to check whether she needed a touch more lipstick. If Gavin did arrive on the train she wanted to look her best. So much depended on it. Going to Canada meant escaping rationing, bombsites, and the dreary poverty she'd known most of her life. The idea of living in Canada or the USA had filled her mind ever since the friendly invasion of the early war years. They were so different and glamorous, so representative of everything she'd ever adored on the movie screen. She'd adopted the word 'movies' since the Yanks had arrived. Discontentment with her own lot had set in and she'd made a vow that she would marry a man in uniform, but not one from her own country. The British Isles had been invaded by big men from a big country and nothing would ever be the same again.

She closed her eyes and said a swift and selfish prayer. 'Please God let him be on this train. If he's not, he's had his chips!' She opened her eyes, then had a second thought and closed them again. 'And don't expect me to be responsible for my actions. I'll be downright irresponsible in future if you don't help me now!'

Carrying her peep-toe suede shoes under one arm and her clutch bag under the other, she crept on stockinged feet over dull brown linoleum. First open the inner door. The deep blue and ruby-red glass of its upper half threw pools of colour onto the varnished walls dull as dried out shoe polish. Despite her being careful the door creaked on its hinges.

Polly stopped and took a deep breath. Even though she'd set her mind on going to the station, she still had a twinge of guilt about leaving without telling Aunty Meg. She glanced down the passage to the door that opened onto what remained of the back of the house. Unlike the rest of the street, Aunty Meg's house only had two bedrooms. The third bedroom had been blown off by the blast from a bomb in an air raid. 'No sense of direction,' Aunty Meg had shouted skywards at the time. She was right, of course. The bombers had been aiming at the goods trains that sat in the shunting yards beyond the brick wall at the end of the back garden. Garden was really too grand a name for something that was little more than a yard. Potatoes and cabbages grew weakly through the stony soil and Christmas poultry clucked impatiently in a makeshift coop.

She sucked in her breath as her feet met the cold lino. Pausing she bent down and slid her feet into her black suede court shoes. So far, so good. But her luck didn't last.

Aunty Meg came in from the scullery just as she reached for the front door. Polly blinked guiltily.

Meg shook her head and tutted like she might at a small child. 'I take it you're meeting the twelve o'clock train.' Polly tightened her grip on the door catch. Her eyes met those of her aunt. 'Don't tell me not to go,' she said with a determined jutting of her chin. 'I have to see if he's on it, for Carol's sake as much as for mine. He might be, he just might be. I meant to ask you to look after Carol until I get back, honest I did. You will do that, won't you?'

Meg's jaw stiffened. For the briefest of moments Polly thought her aunt was going to shout at her, tell her she was making herself look cheap and she should have more pride. Perhaps she should.

But she couldn't ignore the desire that gnawed inside her. She had a dream to pursue and nothing would shake her from her path.

'You could have asked before sneaking out,' snapped Meg. She tucked her hands behind her apron and under her breasts. A formidable stance, but Polly wasn't fooled. Meg was soft hearted. The round-bodied, caring woman that Polly had lived with since her parents' death sighed resignedly and lowered her eyes. There was no doubt in her mind that Gavin wasn't coming back. He'd either got killed or had flown straight back to Canada, but she couldn't condemn Polly for hoping.

'Get out of it,' growled Meg, 'before I change me mind.'

'Thanks.' With a jaunty air that she always got on a day when a troop train was due, Polly was off.

Meg stared at the closed door before wiping her eyes with the blue gingham apron that was almost a dress because it crossed over her breasts and tied at the back. How many trains had Polly met in the hope, a fainter hope now after twelve months, that her Canadian would be on it? How many more would she still meet until she finally gave up and admitted to herself that she would remain unwed and her child fatherless?

Men, even nice young men like Gavin, a squadron leader at only twenty-five years old, did foolish things before they went overseas to do even more foolish things. Who was to know he didn't have a family already back home in Alberta or Manitoba or wherever it was? All over the country, men from overseas were being repatriated. No questions would be asked when they got home as to whether they'd left any dependents behind.

The sound of crying drifted in from the backyard where Carol was lying in a pre-war pram that had a deep body and small wheels. Meg would have liked a new one for the baby, but Polly had told her there was a waiting list. Besides, married women got priority, or at least it seemed that way.

Time for Carol's feed, thought Meg with a sigh, and turned back to the scullery door, dragging her slippered feet over the cold floor and wishing she could do more than she'd already done for her niece. If only Polly's parents were still alive. She especially missed her own sister, Marian. John, Polly's father, had died of TB and Marian had been in an air raid shelter at the aircraft factory where she'd worked which had taken a direct hit. She had been another casualty of war. But, Meg thought with a sigh, there were a lot of casualties in war, and not all of them were left dead or injured, just hurting.

2

The minute hand on the station clock that hung over platform nine was just approaching five minutes to twelve. The smell of soot mixed with the dampness of steam exhaled from engines called Bristol Castle, Truro Castle, or any other castle with West Country connections. The grey, pungent clouds rose only as far as the iron beams, where they hung like a brewing storm before gradually escaping into the sharp blue beyond.

Temple Meads Railway Station was showing signs of wear. Wartime neglect had left paint peeling like crisp skin and, although signs bearing the station's name were being re-erected after their long absence during hostilities, they looked dull and tired as though they'd just been roused from a long, dust-laden sleep.

Already the platform was crowded with people. The waiting families were herded like cattle behind barriers by railway personnel who informed them they had to stay there until the train came in. A few grumbled. After two, three, even four years, they still had to follow orders.

Privations aside, there was bright expectancy lighting the faces of most of those waiting though, like the station, many of them looked shabby unless their means went beyond wartime clothing coupons or they'd acquired friends in the US Army.

Charlotte Hennessey-White was one of those whose clothes, although pre-war, were of a quality made to last. They had been bought with David's encouragement on the day after war broke out. They'd driven to Castle Street in the centre of Bristol, parked just across from the Dutch House, a fine old seventeenth-century black and white timbered building whose upper storeys hung over the street like a benevolent frown. Despite some people insisting that the war would be over by Christmas, David had not been convinced. He had been generous, purchasing clothes for her and the children. She felt close to tears as she remembered asking him why he wasn't buying clothes for himself. With a wry smile he had answered, 'Because the government will be supplying me with all I need for the duration.'

Bittersweet as it was, she cherished the memory of that day. And memory was all it was now. Castle Street was no more and the Dutch House that had survived three centuries and Edwardian demolition plans to widen the road was gone. Only ash and rubble remained.

David had been right about the length of the war and he'd been right about being needed. As a doctor he was called up almost immediately.

She parked the car, her hands trembling with excitement so that she was barely able to lock the door once she had unloaded Janet and Geoffrey. It was as though there were no bones in her fingers or as if they had minds of their own.

David was coming home! David was coming home!

The words were like the lyrics of a song running through her head, the music spilling into her fingers, making her drop the keys. And all because David was coming home! It was like being eighteen all over again and meeting him for the first time. But it's only been two years since you last saw him, she told herself. Just two years!

She paused, closed her eyes and took a deep breath. What could she say? What would he say? Would he have changed that much since his last leave? He had seemed a little strained back then compared with pre-war, but was she really remembering how he had been? It was difficult to say. Nineteen thirty-nine seemed so long ago. September had been a russet-red season when they had walked and talked more than they had for a long while. They'd snatched moments to discuss with nervous excitement what might happen, how the gas masks smelled of something lately dead and how small the Anderson shelters seemed. But none of it had been as important as just touching and talking. It seemed as if each minute was snatched in lieu of a future when they would be apart, perhaps for ever. Suddenly Charlotte was overwhelmed with a great feeling of relief. He'd been one of the lucky ones. Her legs felt weak. Solid objects in the world around her seemed to wobble and blur around the edges. She closed her eyes and leaned against the car.

'Thank you God,' she said quietly. 'Thank God he's safe.'

Her moment of gratitude was swiftly shattered. 'Noooo!' Geoffrey, then a scream of car tyres. Her eyes snapped open and she turned sharply. 'Geoffrey!'

He was standing at the kerb, one foot in the gutter. The wooden aeroplane was wedged under the front wheel of a gleaming Bentley and the driver was looking peeved rather than upset.

'Let me get it,' she heard someone say. 'There. It's not broken.' The young woman who had spoken and now handed Geoffrey back his toy looked vaguely familiar.

'Geoffrey!' Charlotte ran to him, grabbed his shoulders and angrily spun him round to face her. But her ire was short lived, overwhelmed by excitement and anxiety. *Please. Don't spoil this very special day.*

She took a deep breath. 'Geoffrey!' Gently she held him by the shoulders and manoeuvred him around until he faced the young woman. 'What do you say to this kind young lady?'

'Thank you,' Geoffrey muttered sheepishly, eyes downcast and his chin resting on his tie.

'I'm sorry, but today is a day for us all to remember,' Charlotte said apologetically, aware of the excitement in her voice but curiously unable to control it. 'Geoffrey's not usually so careless. It's just that his father's coming home today. I think all three of us are far too excited.'

'I suppose you are, ma'am,' said the young woman, already moving away as the unmistakable discomfort of class deference came to her eyes.

Charlotte immediately felt that pang of regret she always did at times like these, that yearning to reach out and explain that she was no different from her. Show me who you are without fear or shame, she wanted to say. She had seen that look on the faces of people she'd helped in the Marriage Advisory Centre she'd been working in during the last two years. Before that it had been the WRVS. Marriage guidance had been available before the war but had been promptly disbanded on its outbreak. Then, as men went fighting overseas and long periods of separation and loneliness ensued, the service was rapidly re-formed. Charlotte found she was a natural at giving help and advice.

She offered her hand, judging that the young woman would consider it impolite not to take it. 'My name's Charlotte Hennessey-White,' she said. 'How do you do?'

'Edna Burbage,' answered the young woman.

Charlotte held on to her hand a little longer and said, 'He's very fond of that aeroplane you know. I got it locally from a man who serves on an aircraft carrier. Apparently he made it in the lull between battles.' I'm prattling, she thought and, although she wanted to continue and tell Edna that she was more excited than the children that her husband was coming home, she was an adult and was therefore expected to control herself.

To her surprise, Edna's gaze went straight to the little plane as if it were very familiar to her, but she had only just been reminded of it.

'I got it in Nutgrove Avenue near Victoria Park,' Charlotte went on.

Edna smiled a little pensively. 'I know. I saw you there. The man that made it is my fiancé. I was round visiting his mother.'

'Well,' said Charlotte in a very slow and thoughtful manner, 'that is a very strange coincidence.'

Edna frowned then smiled. 'He's coming home on the midday train. His name's Colin Smith.'

'That's the man!' said Charlotte, her pent-up excitement endowing the exclamation with more enthusiasm than it deserved. 'Look,' she went on, determined to overcome Edna's initial discomfort. 'Let me buy you a cup of tea. You did save my son's answer to the Luftwaffe.'

Edna hesitated, eyes shyly downcast. 'Well, I didn't really do anything.'

'But we could talk about Geoffrey's Christmas present for this year. I dare say your fiancé – Colin did you say? – must have plans to continue with his talent.'

Edna smiled. 'I don't know, but it is a possibility.'

Charlotte, pleased with herself for making such a useful suggestion, added, 'I do hope you don't mind me saying, but you should do that more often.'

Edna attempted to blink away her confusion. Her cheeks reddened.

'Smiling,' Charlotte explained. 'The war's over. You can do a lot more smiling from now on.'

She meant it. In that small moment when Edna had smiled, her brown eyes sparkled and her nut-brown hair seemed streaked with the richer tones of French brandy. Edna had problems, Charlotte thought, and made a mental note to offer her help if required. Offering help to other people came naturally. Taking advice herself was something she rarely had to do.

They walked into the station and got their platform tickets together, Charlotte bubbling with excitement, her eyes bright, her cheeks flushed, and Edna, apprehensive, her hands shoved deeply into the oversized patch pockets of her plaid, three-quarter-length coat. The children chattered and squabbled at their sides and the two women exchanged looks of understanding that held the seeds of friendship.

'I wish I could be as calm as you about all this,' said Charlotte. 'I mean, a woman of my age feeling like a silly sixteen-year-old...'

Her voice trailed off. Crackling and buzzing came from overhead, a sure sign that something was about to be announced over the loudspeaker system.

'The train's late,' said Edna before the station announcer had the chance to say anything.

Sure enough they had a thirty-minute wait before the train was expected. Frozen points according to the information crackling from the overhead speakers.

'I can believe it,' said Charlotte wrapping her fur a little closer around herself. Then, seeing Edna's envious look, she wished she'd worn something less ostentatious.

'Would you like that cup of tea?' Edna asked, taking up Charlotte's earlier suggestion.

Charlotte was just about to say that she would pay before real-

ising that could hurt Edna's pride. 'I could certainly do with one,'
she said with a smile.

The buffet was crowded but they managed to squeeze into a set
of rickety wooden chairs that surrounded a table by the window.
Smears of whitewash and the remains of sticky tape on the panes
testified to the fact that it hadn't been that long since a blackout was
in force and shattered glass from exploding bombs was a real
danger. But at least they were in the warm. Despite it being a fine,
dry day and the sky a summer blue, the air was raw with the crisp-
ness of December.

Cream distemper was flaking from the walls and brown painted
doors were scuffed and scratched from thousands of service boots
and mountains of kit bags. Despite the drab neglect, someone had
made an effort to be seasonal. Faded paper chains straggled across
the ceiling, their tattiness relieved here and there by a single sliver
of tinsel. Obviously the decorations were of pre-war vintage but the
very fact they were there at all heralded the hope that things were
returning to normal.

Tea was served in big, ugly cups that had chips around the
rim. The liquid itself was weak but palatable, although the
woman in charge of the sugar allotted only one spoonful per
person.

The children stayed outside, squashed against the barriers,
sniffing the soot-laden air, and watching the giant, black engines
steaming in and out of the station.

Charlotte took a sip of tea then looked out of the greasy
window.

'Peace,' she said plaintively. 'Is it possible that we've got so used
to war that we won't be able to handle peace?'

'My mother said it's a new beginning,' said Edna, her gaze
following Charlotte's to the smoky world outside the buffet room.
'She said the war made us do things we wouldn't have ever dreamed

of doing before. It made the world unreal.' She blushed, wishing she hadn't said it. Her guilt showed too easily.

Charlotte turned to look at her. 'Do you believe that it's a new beginning?'

Edna looked nervously down into her cup. 'I don't know. It might be for us, but I don't know how the men will view it. They must have got used to living dangerously, giving orders and taking orders and all that.' Charlotte felt for her. She shook her head. 'But how wonderful not to take orders, not to have to duck flying bullets and explosions and goodness knows what else.'

'It's the most thrilling time so I've heard, that moment when you think you are about to die,' said Edna.

'I've heard that too,' said Charlotte recalling the words of Doctor Julian Sands, a psychiatrist at the hospital. On one or two occasions she had turned to him for advice when dealing with some of the more difficult relationships resulting from the war. 'Some get such a thrill from being that close to death that they can't help courting it, daring it to try them again. The adrenalin flows. It becomes like a drug. They have to have it. They have to risk their lives, but they also risk the lives of others in the process. Some view them as heroes. Others as maniacs.'

* * *

'Hello again,' said the ticket inspector as Polly showed him her platform ticket. 'Definitely on this train, is he?'

'That's what it said in his letter,' she lied, her smile broad enough to convince anyone that she was telling the truth. 'I don't suppose the train is on time?'

'Oh ye of little faith!' said the beaming inspector, who'd been called back in from retirement to fill this post back in nineteen forty-one but was likely to be put out to pasture again now that a brace of more able-bodied men were coming home. *And thank God for that!*

'Trust to the Lord and the railways,' said the ticket inspector.

'Blasphemy!' snapped the woman standing immediately behind Polly's right shoulder.

Polly exchanged a quick smile with the inspector before moving to the platform where she would wind her way through the crowds waiting at the barrier until the train came. Once it had come, she would walk up and down looking for the familiar uniform that represented a dream she was desperate to fulfil.

Gavin had not been her first Canadian airman. There had been Pierre before him. His colleagues had called him Snowshoe because he was from some small place in the Rockies and knew how to trap and fish in the Canadian wilderness. He had been a tail gunner on a bomber that had been saddled, like a lot of others, with the job of bombing the enemy without the benefit of fighter protection. He'd told her he would marry her when he got back from his last mission.

Even now, after falling in love with Gavin, she could still remember how dry her mouth had been that day as she waited for Pierre to return. She had wanted to burst with happiness because he was so big and strong and was going to take her to a new place that was bigger than Europe and untouched by war. With mounting tension she had watched as his plane banked over the airfield, last of a force of twenty-one, not all of which had come back. But his plane had. With mounting excitement she had watched it land, then suddenly spotted the holes in its wings, bits of metal hanging like ripped skin from its main body.

As the plane swerved its tail round to face her, she saw the place where the tail gunner's turret should be. Instead of the usual bubble of glass there was nothing except a gaping hole. It was as though someone had drawn a tooth and made a mess of it. Her heartbeat had seemed to slow to a monosyllabic dirge. Snowshoe was gone and it hurt like hell. So she partied and threw herself into being the bubbliest blonde, the one with the loudest laugh, the most raucous singing voice. *Gather ye rosebuds...* But in her case it was men she had gathered and she didn't care who knew it. She didn't care what anyone thought of her because life was for living and young men were dying and who knew if she mightn't die too. So what was the point of being a little Miss Goody Two Shoes and waiting for the bomb to drop on her? Besides, she still had her dream to achieve.

She thought she'd found her dream when she met Al Schumacher. He was coarsely built with hands like shovels and pink cheeks.

'I farm with my folks,' he'd told her. 'In Kansas.'

'Is that in Canada?' she'd asked him.

'No way!' He'd sounded insulted. 'It's in the good ole US of A!'

Good enough, she'd thought, and they'd got on really well and got really close and, eventually, he'd asked her to marry him and she'd said yes. He'd even given her a brass ring as temporary confirmation that she was engaged to him. As a warm glow spread over her, he had slid it onto the third finger of her right hand. That night under cover of the blackout, she had felt the hairs of his chest against hers, his hands exploring her body as he mumbled sweet words in her ear. He'd also told her how it would be in Kansas and how his mother would be pleased to see he'd married a girl from the old country. 'Well, almost the old country,' he'd added. 'It's Europe, ain't it? What's in a name?'

She hadn't bothered to enquire further because his bulk was slamming the breath out of her and he was breathing heavily in her ear. Even if she got pregnant it wouldn't matter because Al was going to marry her and she was going to live in Kansas.

But Al got shot down. One of his friends swore he saw his para-chute open. Another wasn't so sure.

Her dream stayed with her, but it was six months before she got serious again. That was when she'd met Gavin.

Her legs were getting cold so she rubbed one against the other in an effort to keep her circulation going. She glanced at the clock then looked towards the end of the platform, willing the train to arrive and for Gavin to be on it.

Suddenly a shout went up. 'The train's coming! The train's coming!'

An engine whistle screamed and a cloud of smoke appeared just beyond the link that crossed over the bridge which, in turn, crossed the river.

Under pressure from the pushing crowd, the barriers were hastily removed. People surged like a wind-driven tide towards the edge of the platform, expectant, excited, and willing to risk falling onto the rails rather than lose their place at the front of the milling throng.

'Keep back! Keep back!'

The shouts of the railway guards and inspectors fell on deaf ears. They were like Canute before the tide, only this sea of people was far more determined than the North Sea could ever be. The winds of war had at last blown themselves out and people were tired, glad it was over, and hopeful for the future.

Piles of khaki, navy and air force-blue uniforms, interspersed with the grey pinstripe of demobilisation suits, hung from carriage windows and doors, jostled by more men behind them jammed into the packed carriages.

As the train slowed, the men's eyes searched the crowds of turbans, feathered hats, and hair curled especially for the occasion with the aid of heated irons and water reinforced with a precious spoonful of sugar.

Eager hands like tentacles sought the smooth metal of handles, doors swung open, and men piled out onto the platforms to outstretched arms welcoming them home. The noise was thunderous, far too powerful to be drowned out by the crackling loudspeaker that attempted to announce the train's arrival.

Polly, her eyes searching the windows as the men burst out from gaping doors, started to walk briskly along the edge of the platform, uncaring that she pushed embracing couples aside, her tears blinding her to how they might be feeling, how much they might have been missing each other.

'Gavin! Do you know Gavin?' she said, grabbing what she recognised as a shoulder adorned with the insignia of the Royal Canadian Airforce. The surprised-looking Canadian shook his head briefly before being engulfed by a pair of feminine arms clothed in the sleeves of a leopard-skin jacket.

Polly pushed on determinedly, oblivious to bumps from shoving arms, angry glares and shouts of protest.

She tried to gain more height by jumping in an effort to look over the heads of the crowd just in case she had missed him. People were like a sea around her, pushing, shoving. Shouts of recognition eddied around her from those on the platform, from those on the train.

There were other shouts too.

'Stop pushing!' she heard someone shout. 'The handle's stuck!'

'Watch it!' shouted someone else.

The shouts were ignored. Although those in front told those behind not to push, the urge to get off the train and as far away from war as possible was too strong.

The door sprang open across her path. She screamed as the bottom part hit her solidly in the stomach sending her flying against the side of the carriage. One leg slid away from her and plugged the gap between the carriage and the platform. She felt her shoe slide off her foot.

'My shoe! Where's my bloody shoe!'

A bevy of voices commented on her plight. 'Oh God!'

'Is she all right?'

Faces, legs and uniforms formed a barrier around her. Hands reached to help her to her feet.

'Make room,' someone said in a commanding voice, 'let me through. I'm a doctor.'

A tall shadow leaned over her. Its owner bent down and began examining her leg. There were definitely bruises, definitely abrasions. She winced as the helping arms pulled her clear of the gap. A numb burning circled her ankle.

Suddenly the crowds and those gathered round were just too much. 'I'm all right,' she said and looked back at the gap and her bare foot. She was still minus a shoe.

'I'll be the judge of that,' said the man who claimed to be a doctor. 'Can you move your ankle?'

She nodded at the top of his head as his cold fingers carefully manipulated where a rip in her stocking gave way to grazed flesh. 'Yes,' she said.

He straightened. She was surprised how tall he was. 'Nothing broken, but I think it's badly twisted.'

Polly looked down to the gap between the platform and the wooden step beneath the open door.

'My shoe!'

'Don't you worry, luv. I'll get it for you once the train's moved out,' said a young navy rating whose frizz of ginger hair stuck out like a halo from under the round hat he wore.

'There!' said the doctor, who wore the uniform of an army officer with the ease of someone used to being well groomed. 'That's the Navy for you, always at the ready. No wonder they've got a girl in every port. Good for you, son.'

The rating beamed. 'Pleased to be of service to the young lady, sir,' he added, perhaps a little tongue in cheek.

The doctor shook his head. 'Not sir, son. Doctor will do.' He spread his arms to either side of him, shrugged and smiled. 'I opted to hang onto the uniform by virtue of the fact that it fitted me far better than the suit I was offered.'

'I know what yer going to say,' said the rating, his cheeks as pink and round as polished apples. 'It was for an average man of five-feet-four with a thirty-eight-inch waist. Been there myself, sir.'

'Forty-two-inch I shouldn't wonder, judging by the way it kept sliding to my ankles,' laughed the doctor. 'We'll be over in the buffet. Can you deliver it there?'

The rating saluted at the doctor and winked at Polly. 'I don't want no tea,' Polly began. 'I just want me shoe so I can do what I gotta do and go where I gotta go!'

'I'll thank you to listen to my good advice,' said the doctor, his tone and the fact that he cupped her elbow in his hand and guided her towards the buffet leaving her in no doubt that he was used to giving orders and used to having them obeyed. 'I also owe you free consultation at my surgery.'

Polly hobbled as she looked up at him. 'Why's that then?'

For a brief moment he looked sheepish. 'My fault,' he said brusquely. 'I pushed open the door without looking.' Once his apology was out, his chin was up, his head high. He's like a hawk, she thought, with that hair swept back severely from his forehead, that straight nose, but most of all, the alert eyes that searched ahead and to either side of him.

Polly was just about to say that it was understandable. But she didn't get another chance to say anything. The pressure from the mix of men and waiting relatives was too great to resist. It was like a river trying to filter into a drainpipe. Some of the men were in uniform and others already in demob suits, but all were thankful to have survived. They were eager to get home and get on with their lives and nothing was going to get in their way. She was pressed against the doctor, standing on one leg, her bare foot held slightly off the ground. One moment his arm was around her, the next it was gone. The press of bodies had eased.

'Darling!'

There was a sudden flash of fur coat, expensive earrings. The woman wore a matching pillbox hat perched at a jaunty angle. Good stuff, thought Polly. Pre-war and bought in somewhere like Castle Street before it got blasted to hell.

A veil of stiff black net shaded the eyes that now closed in ecstasy. A tear rolled down one cheek, yet the red lips were smiling, teeth showing shiny white before he clamped his lips to hers and they clung together like magnets.

Two children glanced briefly at her but their interest was short lived. Smiling hesitantly, they eyed the man who now embraced their mother. He was obviously their father.

'How I've missed you!' the woman exclaimed, hugging him tightly and laying her head against his shoulder before turning to the children.

'Children! Say welcome home to your father.'

Polly sensed he was as nervous as they were. He watched them silently as they stepped dutifully forward, paused, then threw their arms around him.

Family business, thought Polly as he clung to them, and started to ease away. She felt like an interloper and, although she only had one shoe, she preferred putting up with the coldness of the platform in order to get to the buffet as quickly as possible where the rating would return the missing one to her.

But she wasn't forgotten. The doctor turned round, the look in his eyes similar to those she'd seen on a dozen service personnel when they spotted a 'looker' like her.

'Wait,' he said. 'We've still got to wait for your shoe.'

Frowning, his wife turned to him then to Polly. 'Her shoe?'

'Look, there ain't no need to worry about me...' Polly began.

His arm stayed around his wife's waist.

'A modern day Cinderella, my dear.' As he went on to explain what had happened and made introductions, his wife's expression became more sympathetic.

'So I decided we should have tea while we wait for her shoe to re-emerge. Then perhaps we could drop you off somewhere,' he said turning to Polly, his expression a picture of gentlemanly courtesy.

'Well, seeing as me shoe might be in two pieces, I'll accept yer offer,' said Polly with a toss of her blonde hair. 'That'll get the neighbours talking.'

'My word,' said Charlotte with an excitable laugh. 'I've already had tea with Edna and I must warn you that it's very weak and only lukewarm.'

'Edna? Do I know her?' asked David Hennessey-White.

Charlotte slipped her arm through the crook of his. 'No, but you must meet her. She's engaged to the man who made Geoffrey's aeroplane, you know, the one I had a terrible job getting hold of last Christmas. He's on the train today as well.' Her head bobbed enthusiastically as she searched the crowd for her new-found acquaintance. 'There she is,' she said, her face as excited as a child's with a new toy because she had her man back on her arm. She waved her kid-gloved hand. 'Look! There!'

Along with everyone else, Polly looked towards a girl with shoulder-length dark hair wearing a three-quarter coat with patch pockets. She could be pretty with a bit of makeup and some decent togs, she thought, but why's her face so pale and why is she looking down at the ground?

'Lost something, has she?' she said in a careless, offhand way.

'Edna!' called Charlotte and frowned. 'Surely she can hear me.'

As the crowd around Edna slowly fell away, husbands with arms around wives, children bouncing high on the shoulders of fathers they had never seen before, Charlotte's hand fell slowly to her side and her smile melted.

'Poor girl,' whispered Polly and really meant it. No one else said a thing. Silently they all took in the scene.

Edna's fiancé was still in uniform, medals shining on his chest, his hands resting on the enamelled arms of the wheelchair. Like ill-wrapped parcels the remains of his legs stuck out rigidly before him ending where his knees used to be.

3

'WELCOME HOME COLIN' shouted a bold banner across the front of number 56 Nutgrove Avenue. Despite the fact that it was a cold day, an avenue of blue sky and a winter sun had tempted everyone, thickly cocooned beneath layers of Fair Isles and tweed coats, to join the party.

Cheers went up and a host of union jacks were waved ferociously as Charlotte's car pulled up with Colin aboard. It had been her suggestion to give them a lift. Polly had also been encouraged to come while David and the children waited for her shoe to be retrieved from under the railway carriage.

'It will give the children and their father time to get re-acquainted,' Charlotte had said to Polly and Edna, with all the confidence of someone who knows how to handle people.

Colin wound down the window and waved his hand just as vigorously as the many tight fists that were waving the flags.

'Mum! Dad!'

'Colin!' His mother's voice was shrill with emotion, her eyes brimming with tears.

His father raised one hand and wiped behind his glasses with the other.

Neither of them allowed their gaze to linger on the iron chair securely tied to the car's rear. In mute understanding they looked at each other, mother biting her bottom lip for a moment, father's Adam's Apple rising and falling as he digested the truth. Then he sprang forward.

'Son!' he said as he swung the car door open.

A confused murmur ran through the crowd of would-be revellers. Glassy-eyed they gathered around the tables, waiting for the word to be given that Colin was home and, despite his injuries, ready to enjoy himself.

Edna clutched at her stomach as she saw the disbelief, then the hint of pity that crossed each parent's face before they buried their feelings beneath an avalanche of determined joviality.

'Son!' said Colin's father again, reaching to shake his hand before diving through the car door and enveloping his child in a hug desperate enough to break bones.

For a moment she thought she saw Colin's shoulders quiver and was convinced he was crying. But when his face reappeared, he was looking into his father's eyes and laughing in the same way as he always had.

'Hirohito couldn't get rid of me that easily, father, and neither can you. Here I am. Home again, home again, jiggity jig!'

Two men manhandled the wheelchair. Colin's father lifted his son gently and set him into it. Edna wanted to cry at the pain of it all. But Colin wasn't crying and neither would she. No one would, until they were alone and night had fallen and no one could see.

'Well, let's eat some real food!' shouted Colin. 'I've been waiting for this. Edna?'

'I'm coming. Just a minute.'

She let them take over. Relatives and neighbours pushed his

chair towards the tables, where they all fell to hiding their pity and their tarnished joy at his return in the pleasure of over-eating, a rare phenomenon during the last few years. Colin's father, a red-faced man with sandy hair and horn-rimmed glasses, had sacrificed one of the pullets he'd been rearing out back. The bird's plump breast gleamed like gold and, just to confirm how special the occasion was, little frills of red, white and blue paper rustled around its naked ankles.

'Wonderful!' Colin shouted as a leg was ceremoniously torn off and handed to him.

Edna turned to Charlotte and thanked her for the lift. 'My pleasure,' said Charlotte and affectionately patted

Edna's arm. 'We've stuck together in war, now we've got to do the same in peace.'

Handbag swinging on her arm, she marched off, entering the throng of people and talking to them as if she'd known them all her life. She was like an iron butterfly, floating among them with ease, yet all the time influencing them with words of wisdom that weren't always called for.

'She's very nice,' Edna said plaintively.

'She's bloody nosy,' Polly added with far less amiability.

'Still, it was kind of her to give me and Colin a lift.'

'Are you still going to marry him?' Polly asked.

The question took Edna unawares. Her mouth dropped open. 'Of course! Nothing's changed,' she blurted.

Polly shrugged and cockily tilted her head sideways. 'With him do you mean, or with you?'

Edna felt her throat go dry. She didn't answer.

'You don't have to you know, unless, you know,' she jerked her chin at the spot where Edna's stomach hid behind her coat. 'Unless you've got to.'

Edna felt a hot flush creep over her face. 'Certainly not.' But for a brief insane moment she wondered if Polly had heard rumours. Perhaps someone had questioned her time away or had seen her with Jim.

Polly grinned. 'No need to blush, sweetheart. You wouldn't be the first respectable girl to get caught out like that.'

Edna muttered something about she would never have been that stupid. Polly didn't seem to notice.

'Tell you what, Edna. How about you and me meeting up for a girls' night out? Your bloke wouldn't mind. Well, can't see 'im minding much. Nice bloke basically. I can see that.'

'Perhaps,' said Edna.

'Just the two of us,' Polly went on, then shoved a sharp elbow into Edna's ribs. 'Don't want old posh pants there spoiling things, do we?' She nodded towards Charlotte who was overseeing the serving of a group of children with bowls of jelly and paste sandwiches.

Edna nodded. 'I suppose so.' But she had reservations. No doubt Polly was fun to be with, but she sensed she was also selfish.

At that moment Charlotte came back with the air of someone who'd just issued battle orders to a detachment of Home Guard. 'That's that done!' she exclaimed. She began to rummage in the deep confines of her pigskin handbag which, Edna noted, was a perfect match to her shoes.

Charlotte enthused, 'I did so enjoy being with you today. Let me give you my address and telephone number.'

She pushed a piece of paper into Edna's hand. 'Besides,' she added with a gleaming smile, 'the rate Geoffrey is going on with that aeroplane, it'll be in bits shortly and I shall have to buy another. I really would like another for Christmas. I do hope Colin can oblige. Now you will get in touch, won't you?' She gave no one the chance to refuse. Perfectly plucked eyebrows arched above calm grey eyes. Her mouth, still shiny red with lipstick, smiled expectantly. A reply was called for, but only in the affirmative. Charlotte, Edna thought, was not the sort to take 'no' for an answer.

Yet Edna liked her. Charlotte really did mean what she said. She smiled up at her, Charlotte's height and refined features making her more aware of her own lack of stature and her moon-shaped face. 'Of course I will.'

With a flurry of fur coat, Charlotte got back into her car and started it up. Polly slid into the passenger seat.

Edna waved as she thoughtfully watched the black saloon go off down the hill that would eventually connect with St John's Lane. She glanced down at Charlotte's address. Clifton! She might have guessed. High above the Avon Gorge where the river ran sluggishly to the sea. And high above the rest of us, she thought with an amused smile as she curled her fingers over the piece of paper, meaning to throw it into the gutter where it would rot away with what remained of the autumn leaves. But she stopped herself from doing that as a thought came to her. Mrs Charlotte Hennessey-White lived in an elegant Georgian crescent and was wealthy enough to own a car. And yet Edna had the distinct impression she was lonely. That was why she was so involved in doing good works and suchlike. Either that or she was plain nosy and liked interfering in other people's lives. Why else would she bother with the likes of her?

Just when she was thinking about joining Colin and putting on a brave face, a shadow fell on the pavement and across her feet.

'You didn't let the cat out of the bag, did you?' Ethel Burbage's eyes darted over the buzzing crowd just in case anyone was more interested in what she was saying than in the homecoming Colin. 'Imagine what people would think. And the embarrassment it would cause to your father. Well, his job at the corporation does depend on a respectable reputation you know.'

'I didn't say anything,' Edna replied, swallowing the guilt she always felt when her mother reminded her of what she had done. 'Colin's lost his legs,' she added softly.

'I know. It's very sad.' She sounded genuinely concerned. But Edna knew her mother well. Even now she was thinking how best to turn even this dire situation to advantage. At last she said, 'Then he'll be glad you've waited for him and isn't too likely to listen to any gossip.'

'What gossip? No one knows.'

She tapped her arm with a hard bony finger. 'No. And you've me to thank for that, my girl. But I have to say, even if he does find out, he's in no position to be too choosy. After all, who else is going to marry a man with no legs?'

Except a fallen woman, thought Edna, and felt her face flush as it always did when her mother hinted at what she was and what her son was. But she wouldn't dare voice her thoughts.

Eyeing the laughing crowd who were gathered around Colin, listening as he told them stories of his 'heroic' exploits, Edna asked her mother the same nagging question she asked every time one of the parcels arrived and was forwarded on. 'How is he?'

The reply was terse. 'He's being well taken care of. That's all you need to know.'

But it wasn't all she needed to know. Much as it might hurt, much as it might threaten her own good name, Edna made herself a promise that she would go to see her son herself. Colin need never know.

4

It was her husband's first night home and Charlotte was feeling far more apprehensive about his return than she'd expected.

The children were in bed. David had insisted they go at eight o'clock although Charlotte had told him it was a little too early. Then she'd recognised the glint in his eyes, and felt a pink flush warm her cheeks as she remembered the feel of the black hairs of his chest against her bare flesh. But her personal needs were secondary to those of the children. At present they were in awe of this man who they only half remembered as someone they were supposed to respect and even love. Charlotte told herself that it was just a case of getting used to him again. He'd been away and seen goodness knows what horrors. Some of those images he must have brought home with him. His eyes were bright rather than warm and she sensed an unfamiliar tension in him. She told herself not to be silly and forced herself to be jolly. She asked him about Polly, the girl at the station, and the fact that she'd been in his arms before she'd got there. It was only meant to be a joke, yet his looks had darkened. She had laughed and told him so and he calmed down, yet she sensed the tension had not gone away.

Because of this, she decided not to question his orders. He was her husband and they were together for the first time since his last leave in nineteen forty-three.

'Is he really my daddy?' Geoffrey asked when she tucked him in and kissed him goodnight.

'Of course he is,' said Charlotte.

Geoffrey bit his lower lip, which he always did when he was confused or slightly nervous. 'I don't want him to kiss me goodnight. Not yet. He's not going to, is he?'

It was a bit like discovering a time bomb in Paradise. Everything was supposed to be perfect once the war was over.

She managed to smile and spoke as reassuringly as she could. 'Not tonight anyway. He has only just come home from overseas and he is terribly tired.'

Closing the door of Geoffrey's room behind her, she turned towards her own bedroom. David was standing in their bedroom doorway, his shirt undone, his cuffs hanging loose. Despite his casual appearance, he still looked smooth, every inch the professional.

'Aren't they a little old for you still to be kissing them goodnight?' He sounded impatient. It wasn't like him.

Charlotte forced herself to remain calm, to pretend that it was nineteen thirty-nine again and he'd just come home from his consulting rooms on the edge of Durdham Downs.

She smiled as if everything was exactly as she'd expected it to be. 'They're still children,' she said brightly, averting her eyes from the clenched jaw and the unfamiliar darkness she saw in his eyes. 'I'll just settle Janet down. It's been an exciting day for all of us, darling.'

He stared at her as though she had spoken in a foreign language and for a moment a sickening tightness gripped at her stomach.

What was the matter with him? He'd never had so brusque a manner before. The moment passed. With a grunt, he turned and disappeared into the bedroom. Give him time, she told herself. He just needs time.

Janet was looking out of her bedroom window. 'It's strange to see lights in the windows,' she said.

'Into bed,' said Charlotte, pulling back the bedclothes. 'The war's over, your father's home and there's a new world in the morning.'

Janet continued to stare out of the window. 'I think I preferred the old one even though it was pitch black at night.'

'Only because it included Betty Grable, red lipstick and drooling American soldiers.' Firmly but gently, Charlotte took her daughter by the shoulders and guided her towards the bed with its walnut headboard and dark pink eiderdown. Janet looked at her mother wide-eyed with innocent surprise, then sighed and pulled the bedclothes high over her head. Charlotte heard a muffled 'They were fun', before she turned off the light and closed the door.

Taking a breather outside her daughter's room she nervously patted the mane of chestnut hair she was so proud of and David had always admired. It was piled into a crocheted black snood, fastened with ivory pins adorned with butterfly wings. Butterflies were far more abundant in her stomach, tickling her insides and sending nervous shivers down her spine. '*Don't be so foolish,*' she said to herself. '*He's your husband. Nothing's changed. Absolutely nothing.*'

So far they had not talked about the action he'd seen. She had decided to let him do the talking all in his own good time. For now it was down to basic things.

Like a virgin on her wedding night, Charlotte made her way along the landing, her footsteps soundless against the pastel pinks and greens of a Chinese runner and her heart hammering in her chest.

She had expected David to be in bed, or at least to be waiting to take her into his arms. Instead he was looking into the top drawer of a serpentine chest and taking out items of her underwear, her stockings, her briefs, and her slips. She closed the door behind her and, puzzled, leaned against it and managed a tight smile.

'What are you doing, darling?'

He turned round, a pair of sheer nylon stockings hanging from both hands. 'Where did you get these?'

She laughed, walked across the room and took the stockings from him and bent down to put them back in the drawer. 'I was one of the lucky ones. I had friends in the right...'

His hands were suddenly like claws on her shoulders. He spun her round to face him.

'American friends! I heard about them. "While you British are fighting, the Americans are taking care of your wives!" That's what German radio told us.'

As he shook her, her carefully prepared hairstyle fell out of its confines and tumbled about her shoulders.

'You've got it wrong!' she said through clenched teeth, mindful not to wake the children. 'My friends were Americans in the Red Cross and they were women!'

Her legs felt weak. He was glaring down at her, his eyes wide, his pupils seeming a different colour from how she remembered them; not dark brown any more, but burgundy, almost red.

'I hope you remembered your marriage vows!' he growled.

Not one blink. She held his glare although her legs were weak and her mouth was dry.

'Of course I did!' Her voice was low but emphatic. She stared into his eyes. There was no need for her to say more. She wouldn't –

she couldn't – ask him the same question yet it was there, waiting to be asked, waiting to be answered. In that moment she wanted to turn back the clock and be alone with the children again. Perhaps he guessed what she was feeling.

'You're my wife,' he blurted as if that explained everything.

He cupped her face in his hands. His kiss was hard on her lips, his need of a shave prickly against her skin.

Despite the fact that he had almost accused her of being unfaithful, she had to forgive him. He'd seen sights no civilised man should ever see. So she returned his kiss.

'You're my wife,' he said again, his tone low and demanding.

'I am,' she said, then bit her lip with shocked surprise as he tore at her dress. There was a series of popping sounds as all the buttons down the front snapped off or tore away from the material.

She tried to make for the bed, but he grabbed at her wrists and pushed her back into the alcove at the side of the fireplace.

'I want you here.'

'No! We always...'

She winced as he slammed her back against the wall. She froze, unable to move because she could hardly believe that this was her husband and she was allowing him to do this. But what else could she do? For now she had to bear it. That's what she told herself as he pulled her breasts from her bra and ripped the crotch of her briefs to one side.

He grunted as he thrust himself into her. She tried to pretend that it wasn't happening. She squeezed her eyes shut, turned her head away and lay her chin upon her shoulder. She put up with it – but only for tonight she vowed. Only for tonight.

She lay in the darkness afterwards, a chill gap in the bed between his body and hers. What had happened to make him behave like this? She turned and gazed at the outline of his body against the meagre light filtering in from the arched street lamp out in the crescent.

Physically her husband was home, but part of him was still among the dead and dying in the midst of a bloody battle. What had he seen there to make him take her like that? How could a professional man, a doctor, change so much?

It had once been Charlotte's ambition to be a doctor herself, to escape from the society circuit already allotted to her by birth.

Unlike David, born in Bath to a family who owned a sizeable estate on the outskirts of the city, she had been born in Kensington, daughter of a high-ranking civil servant who had been knighted at the end of the Great War and accepted into the echelons of higher society.

Charlotte had gone to a girls' boarding school where it was noted she was a good organiser possessing maturity beyond her years. Her height, her grey eyes and her beautifully arched brows gave her a serene look. It was to her that the girls came to air their problems with parents, teachers, lessons and, most of all, with the emotional problems that all young girls have.

Being wise to herself as well as for others, it occurred to her that she enjoyed this sort of thing so it seemed only sensible that she should enter some sort of career where she could put those skills to some use. That was why she'd considered becoming a doctor. In her final year at school she applied for the famous teaching hospital, St Bart's, but to her horror was told that there were fewer places for women than for men. To some extent, even in the twentieth century, women were still regarded as an eccentricity in the medical establishment, and the few that were accepted tended to be blue-stockings who had already fought their way through university.

Her parents were greatly relieved that her dream was never realised. Working for a living was not what they had planned for her. They wanted her to be a debutante not a doctor. Besides, she didn't need to earn money. The family had plenty. It seemed everything was against her, but Charlotte was not the sort to sit back, look pretty, and wait for Mr Right to come along. The same friend who had told her how to apply for a teaching hospital now asked her if she'd like to do hospital visiting in connection with WRVS and the Red Cross. Charlotte accepted and thus found herself listening to people's problems, medical and otherwise.

Pouring out endless cups of tea, reading to those who'd recently had eye operations, pushing wheelchairs, and even comforting those who'd just been told their loved one was dead. It was all grist to the mill.

It was at Bart's that she'd met David, a star even as a young doctor about to take his finals.

He was the epitome of what a doctor should be – tall, dark and handsome with a wonderful bedside manner. Women were drawn to him. Even when Charlotte was on his arm, she was aware of admiring glances and easily able to guess at the fantasies occurring behind the lowered lashes.

Strangely enough, she'd never felt jealous. On the contrary, she'd been pleased that others admired the man she loved. It made marrying him seem all the more worthwhile.

Their marriage had always been good, even after the children had come along and his private practice in Bristol became ever busier. His partners took over his workload when he declared his intention to go to war. He needn't have gone. Doctors, of course, were a reserved occupation.

A regency house in Royal York Crescent, Clifton became their home. On Sundays, in that far-off peacetime, they had walked on Durdham Downs, a vast expanse of grassland bequeathed to the city by wealthy benefactors. From there they would gaze in awe at the Clifton Suspension Bridge, nearly one hundred years old and spanning the three-hundred-foot drop of the Avon Gorge. The children had kept her busy, and although David had been adamant that they should attend boarding school he relented when she threw a tantrum that was completely out of character. To his mind children attending day school was at least worth his wife's happiness though, unknown to him, she still had trouble finding enough *useful* things to do to fill her days. The war had changed that. She hadn't told David all that she had done and all she intended to do. She had, of course, outlined some of her activities in her letters, but not all, just the things she thought might lift his spirits and let him know she was doing her bit.

Even though she had been beside herself with excitement at the thought of his return, she had feared telling him that she intended pursuing a career, the roots of which had been put down in the war years.

Now he was home and she wasn't sure she knew him any more. In the drabness of a December dawn she watched him sleeping and tried to remember how he would have reacted to her plans before the war. It would have definitely caused a scene but he would have attempted to understand. She knew that much. But how would he react now? He had got used to giving orders, to being in charge. And he expected those orders to be obeyed. The horrors he'd seen on the battlefields could only be guessed at. But at least he was physically fit. Perhaps the fact that he had ravished her was purely because he had only just arrived home. She squeezed her eyes shut and wished it were so. He's not been with a woman for a long time, she told herself.

* * *

In the morning she presumed she was the first up and was just about to go along to the bathroom when she noticed that a draught was blowing up the stairs. Leaning over the mahogany banister rail, she saw that the front door was ajar. The bathroom would have to wait. Either someone had got in or someone had gone out. It had to be one of the children.

The garden was shrouded in a damp mist that made greens look grey and left the stoutest of plants limply hanging their heads.

She shivered, wrapping her dressing gown tightly around her while deciding who had found it necessary to venture forth at this hour.

Her daughter was prime suspect. Janet was young and her enthusiasm for young American soldiers had known no bounds from the first moment they'd given her gum, chocolate, and then stockings as her tastes and her looks developed.

GIs were encouraged to rise early by sergeant majors who took pride – and sadistic pleasure – in tipping men out of warm beds and into a damp dawn. But there weren't too many of them around nowadays. Those that weren't mopping up in Europe and the Far East were waiting for ships to take them home.

'Geoffrey?'

There was no reply so she took a look in the hall cupboard. She sighed once she'd worked out which coat was missing and to whom it belonged.

'Geoffrey!'

She closed the door and went back into the kitchen where Mrs Grey, a woman with a jolly red face caused by acne rather than accident, was putting the kettle on and sorting out breakfast.

'I saw 'im go out,' she said. 'Said he had something to sort out.'

'I see.' Boys always had something to sort out – conkers, cricket, swapping cigarette cards with one of the other boys in the Crescent.

She went back into the kitchen. There was enough to think about without worrying about her son. In the hope of easing her anxiety, she began checking Mrs Grey's shopping list for the week but her mind wasn't really on it. How could it be after last night?

Although she looked good, she certainly didn't feel it. She ached all over and already purple blotches were rising on her inner thighs and on her back.

The items on the shopping list jigged up and down like a conga of madly dancing matchstick men. And all waiting in queues, she thought with worn amusement. One thought above all others predominated. What David had done and why he had done it. Had she done or said anything to deserve it? She didn't think so. She couldn't have!

Wrapped up in her own confusion, she didn't hear Mrs Grey asking her a question until she repeated it.

'I said, how's Doctor Hennessey-White? Glad to be home, is he?'

Charlotte put down the pencil she had been chewing, forced a weak smile and nodded, her chin dropping a little lower each time she did it. 'He'll be fine given time. It takes a while to get over a war.'

'Oh yes!' Mrs Grey exclaimed knowledgeably. 'When my George came back he didn't speak to me for three months. Just stared out the window he did. Stared and stared and stared. What he was seeing, I just don't know. And when he finally snapped out of it and I asked him what he'd been thinking about, he looked at me as though I was mad. "What you talking about?" he said. Didn't remember a thing you see. Didn't want to remember!'

Funnily enough, what Mrs Grey said did make Charlotte feel better. Give David three months and he'd be right as rain and she'd be fine too. Of course, there was still the small matter of her intended career, but she convinced herself that things would be fine. She imagined the scenario in her mind, he taking her out to dinner to make up for his extraordinary behaviour, and she taking advantage of the opportunity to outline her plans for the future – *her* future. Again she became aware that Mrs Grey had said something and had had to repeat it.

'I said I thought I heard someone going up the stairs.'

'Geoffrey!' Charlotte marched towards the kitchen door and reached for the handle. Before her fingers had touched it there was a bellowing cry from upstairs then a scampering of feet.

She opened the door in time to see half a dozen of Geoffrey's friends running down the stairs, sprinting past her and out of the door. Geoffrey brought up the rear. Charlotte grabbed him.

'And what have you been up to?'

His face was flushed and his eyes were wide with fear. 'I wanted to show them that I had a dad too.'

Charlotte, aware that a curious Mrs Grey was loitering behind her, looked at him in disbelief. 'You showed them?'

He nodded.

Mrs Grey began to laugh. 'Imagine! The doctor waking up and seeing all them eyes looking down at him.'

Charlotte had to control her amusement until after she'd given Geoffrey a shake. 'Don't you dare do it again. And you'd better apologise when your father gets up.'

Only after he'd been told to get into the bathroom and wash his face did she allow herself to laugh.

'That'll cheer Doctor Hennessey-White up,' said Mrs Grey as, still chortling, she turned back towards the kitchen and the precious egg she'd just cracked into a cup. Charlotte decided to brave taking her husband's breakfast up on a tray. What Mrs Grey had said made sense. His son's pranks had made David laugh before the war and there was no reason why they shouldn't now.

She went up the stairs, opened the bedroom door, then stopped dead in her tracks.

'David! No!' Her hands shook and the crockery on the breakfast tray rattled. Her heart didn't want to believe it, yet her eyes took in the set of his jaw and the unearthly gleam in his eyes.

'Where is that little swine?' David growled, his brows knitted in a deep, dark frown. 'It's time the little bugger got some discipline. I've been away too long and you've been too soft with him.'

'David, you can't!' With sinking hope for what might have been, Charlotte froze as David slowly wound the end of a leather belt around his fist.

5

Gavin hadn't come home and Polly was not going to put a hold on her life because of that.

She was not tall but jutting out her chin like an aggressive prize fighter gave her a determined look. And that was certainly how she was feeling as a few days later she marched towards the bus stop, the rabbit-skin collar of her black coat turned up against the chill evening air.

Gavin had not been on the train and her mind was made up. She had given both him and God this last chance and both of them had let her down. Now it was up to her to take care of her future. If he couldn't take care of her and Carol, then she had to find someone who could. But the chances of fulfilling her dream were lessening. She had to act quickly.

Time was ticking away. The war in Europe was over and the American and Canadian troops were going home as fast as the job could be done.

'And what good is that to me!' she muttered as she marched along. Soon there would be no more GIs left in Britain and her chance to escape to something better would be gone.

After some persuading Aunty Meg had agreed to look after Carol even though she had taken care of her for most of the day. But Polly had been resolute.

'I'm too young to be stuck in with a kid for the rest of my life!'

'You should have thought of that earlier,' said Meg.

Polly had avoided her aunt's eyes and bolted upstairs where she slid into her favourite dress, a long-sleeved black number with a white satin collar and matching cuffs. Her friend Mavis was waiting for her at the bus stop.

Mavis was at least five inches taller than Polly, dark-haired and slim enough to fit into Polly's clothes if it wasn't for the fact that they'd be far too short on her to be decent.

'Brass monkeys tonight, innit,' Mavis stated, shrugging her shoulders and nestling her chin further inside the old fox fur whose rigid claws rattled like dry bones each time she shivered.

Polly grinned and nodded at the glazed eyes and black nose of the dead fox. 'Must be. Killed 'im dead for a start.' They laughed. A bit more gossip and a bit more banter and Polly's thoughts about Gavin were forgotten. Her determination to find a suitable replacement was not.

There were about twenty people waiting at the stop by the time the bus came. Cigarette smoke mixed with steamy breath, a few coughs, and raucous laughter from single men just returned home and intent on getting drunk to celebrate the occasion.

Mavis nudged Polly. 'They're looking at us. I quite fancy 'im in the grey suit.'

Polly glanced quickly then just as quickly looked away. 'They all got grey suits, stupid. Demobs! What the bloody 'ell do we want with them?'

Smirking, Mavis continued to give them the eye. 'Control yerself,' said Polly, grabbing Mavis by the sleeve and pulling her onto the bus.

'Goin' to take us out then, girls?' one of the men shouted as they got on behind them.

Mavis looked over her shoulder and giggled.

Polly grabbed hold of her arm and dragged her inside the bus rather than going upstairs where they usually sat. 'Polly!' Mavis protested. 'I wanted a fag. And I ain't got a light and they...'

But Polly was adamant. 'Don't be so bloody common!' She plumped herself down on a side seat and averted her eyes from the lecherous crew of ex-soldiers who had to go upstairs with their half-finished Woodbines.

'I ain't common. It's just that I don't want to be left on the shelf.'

'And them upstairs suit you, do they? Well you're easily pleased. Now me, I want something better I do, somebody that talks nice and got clean fingernails.'

'You've 'ad it! Gavin ain't come back.'

Polly pouted her full red lips. Mavis was exasperating because she was telling the truth. 'Then I'll find someone else.'

'They'll all be gone 'ome before long. Then what?'

'Then I'll hitch up with a decent sort in this country, one that can give me a bit of class in the world.' Before Mavis had a chance to interject that she wasn't likely to find one with Carol in tow, she said, 'Now let me tell you about these posh people from Clifton that I met down at Temple Meads. A doctor 'e was. Even gave me a private appointment so he could examine my ankle.'

Mavis giggled. 'Just your ankle?'

Polly threw her a superior expression and batted her eyelids. 'My ankle got hurt, and 'e reckoned it was his fault for pushin' the door of the railway carriage open too quick.' She went on to explain about Dr Hennessey-White, his wife, the children, and the poor soul named Edna meeting her disabled sweetheart from the train.

'I don't think *I* could marry 'im,' said Mavis, sheer horror written all over her face.

Polly shrugged. 'Depends on the injuries I suppose.' She smirked suggestively. 'Can still 'ave children, can't they? Ain't as though anythin' too vital got shot off.'

The Cat and Wheel, conveniently situated next door to the Bear and Rugged Staff near the spot where Bristol Castle used to be, dated from a time when no one grew much above five feet two judging by the ceiling height. Already crowded with off-duty servicemen and girls like Mavis and Polly, all out to celebrate peace in Europe and in the Far East, too. What walls could be seen were the colour of milk chocolate and the ceiling was stained dark ochre by years of cigarette smoke. Dark eyes scrutinised them as they entered. Polly paused then stepped forward.

'GIs!' Polly exclaimed.

Mavis nudged Polly. 'They're all Negroes.'

'They're all that's left. Must be their turn tonight. Still GIs ain't they?'

Anyone, thought Polly, as long as they were from the other side of the Atlantic. The colour of their skin was of no consequence.

'Hi, gorgeous,' said one.

The two girls nudged and smiled at each other. 'You or me?' said Polly

'Me of course,' said Mavis and dug her friend in the chest.

It was a nice feeling being surrounded by a horde of uniforms again.

'Can I get you a drink, honey?'

The black GI who had asked the question was broad shouldered and bull necked. He had little hair and deep eyebrows and narrow lips set in a sombre straight line. Surprisingly, it was Mavis he seemed to be interested in. The attraction of opposites, thought Polly, who accepted half a shandy from him. Mavis, being Mavis, angled for a gin and orange.

'So why ain't you gone home?' asked Polly.

'Cleaning up to do in Europe,' he replied. 'Most of us belong to the Field Hygiene Unit.' He saw Polly's puzzled expression and explained. 'Dead bodies. We go along and clear up after the fighting's moved on or after the death camps have been cleared. This is our last party before going home. Hallelujah!' he finally exclaimed, raising his drink as high as he dared. His head was already buckled up to the ceiling.

She didn't press the point. Just the thought of the things she'd seen on Pathé News was enough to turn her stomach.

The tobacco smoke that hung like a pall between people's heads and the ceiling suddenly whirled as a current of fresh air swept in through the opening door. Like a lot of others, Polly looked to see who had come in and instantly felt a tightening in her stomach. The grey pinstripe suits, the Woodbines held at the corner of thin, grim mouths. She recognised the men from the bus and sensed immediately there was going to be trouble.

With unconcealed arrogance, they pushed their way through the crowd of American uniforms, disdainfully slapping shoulders, glaring their intentions rather than asking if they could be allowed to get to the bar.

Polly nudged Mavis. 'Looks like trouble.'

Mavis eyed the blokes from the bus. To Polly's disgust she smiled, patted her hair, and made it obvious to a weak-chinned individual with pale blue eyes that she had appreciated his earlier attention – definitely more so than that of the man she was with.

'I think I was here first,' said the pale-eyed young man, the shoulder pads of his demob suit moving independently of his flesh due to the fact that it was at least two sizes too big.

Polly swallowed nervously, put her drink down on the counter, and grasped Mavis's arm.

'Time to go, Mav.'

'Oh, I don't think so,' simpered Mavis, her gaze firmly fixed on the scrawny specimen who squeezed himself purposefully between her and the GI who had bought their drinks.

Strong brown fingers and a broad palm folded over the other man's shoulders and for a moment Polly imagined she was seeing bones being crushed. Yet she couldn't hear anything breaking. Then she almost laughed when she realised why. The shoulder pads again. But her amusement was stifled by the fear of imminent violence.

She nudged a knee into Mavis's shin. 'Let's go.' There was no response.

'I think I was here first, buddy,' said the GI, his twang typical of the American voices she'd heard since a few months after Pearl Harbor.

'You're wrong,' said the guy with the big suit, his back to the American.

'No way, man,' said the black man in a thoughtful and meaningful way. 'I can prove I was first here 'cause I bought that drink there.' He indicated the gin and orange sitting in front of Mavis.

The man in the demob suit reached nonchalantly for the drink. 'Well, it's gone, ain't it?' With that he flung the contents of the glass into the GI's face. Droplets flecked the black man's forehead and trickled down his cheeks. His mouth straightened into a grim line. A breathless hush fell over the packed bar as all eyes turned to the trouble spot.

Polly could almost smell the blood lust, young men aching to prove who was Cock of the Walk.

'Cool it!' someone said. Another brown hand stayed the arm of the man with the liquid running down over his face.

It won't last, thought Polly. She'd seen it before all too often, one man supposedly backing down, then turning back, lashing out with a fist or a broken bottle, and all hell letting loose.

She grabbed Mavis's arm. 'Come on! Let's split.' Her exclamation, borrowed from the friendly invaders, had no impact whatsoever on moony-faced Mavis.

'No! I wanna stay,' and, to Polly's disgust, like an oversized eel Mavis wriggled out of her grasp, her eyes shining with expectation.

'You bitch,' Polly said under her breath. 'Opening them wide for the bloke that gets bashed the most are you! And I don't mean yer bloody eyes!'

For a moment Mavis looked hurt, but it didn't last long. She was positively beaming because two men looked about to fight over her. Well, Polly was having none of that. All right, she had her own dreams, perhaps even mercenary intentions, because she wanted to live in North America or at least get a bloke who could give her something better than she had. And loose morals were something she'd acquired herself during the war. But she didn't hold with setting one man against another and she certainly had no intention of being the centre of a brawl.

'Well, I'm off,' she snapped indignantly. She paused to give Mavis a chance to change her mind, but her friend's attention was elsewhere.

Polly slid away from the bar. 'Excuse me,' she said, pushing her way through the crowd who were slowly pressing forward, sensing that there was more to come.

'Calm it down, lads, or I call the MPs!' shouted the landlord from behind the safe confines of the mahogany counter.

There was no doubt in Polly's mind that things were not going to calm down. One war was over but another war was brewing, only this time it was between individuals, one black and one white.

Although she loved uniforms, she hated fighting. Small as she was, she pushed the door with one hefty swing of her right arm and sent it crashing back against the wall outside.

'Hey!'

The door rebounded and to her embarrassment, she realised

someone was standing immediately outside it and she'd hit him.

'Oh, sorry, chum,' she apologised, and was going to rush on when she thought of her own accident at the station and the Samaritan who helped her earlier that day. She turned to see a tall figure with dark eyes and coffee-coloured skin.

'Are you all right? Have I hurt you? I didn't mean to. Really I didn't, it was just that there's a fight about to start in there and I hate blokes fighting. I just can't...'

She narrowed her eyes against tears of anguish that threatened and pushed her shoulder-length hair into a confused mass on top of her head. The man stayed oddly silent. His hand covered the lower part of his face.

'You've squashed my nose,' he said.

Frowning, she craned her head forward in order to see better.

She immediately felt contrite. 'Oh no,' she said, her own hand covering her mouth in embarrassment.

Above the dark hand a pair of velvet eyes looked down at her. 'I don't think my nose will ever be the same again. Look,' he said as he took his hand away. 'See? Have you ever seen such a flat, fat nose?'

For a moment the sound of his voice took her by surprise. His accent was subdued, his tonal inflections incredibly refined, especially for a black GI. She'd only heard white officers from well-heeled backgrounds talking like he did. Most of the blacks talked like the slaves in *Gone With The Wind*, or at least, that was the way it sounded to her.

She eyed his nose and although it wasn't small, she didn't think it really looked that bad. Still, how did she know what it usually looked like?

'Look yer, I'm truly sorry, really I am! I ain't got no money to get it put right, but I do know a doctor,' she said, suddenly remembering David Hennessey-White and the piece of paper he'd given her on which he had scribbled the address and telephone number of his consulting rooms. She unzipped the brass clasp on her handbag and rummaged for the piece of paper the doctor had given her. 'If you could go there, or if you could ring.' She glanced up at him sheepishly. 'That's if you've got a telephone of course. Though you would, wouldn't you, back there on the base I s'pose.'

He glanced at the pub door, from behind which shouts of violence could be heard. 'Well, perhaps it wasn't entirely your fault. After all it was a pretty dumb place to stand and smoke, wasn't it? But,' he said stepping forward and cupping her elbow in his hand, 'let me take you away from all this. Besides,' he said, glancing at the door again, 'I've fought enough battles to last a lifetime.'

Normally Polly would have protested. Prejudice was not a word that she easily recognised, but she'd always thought herself a bit too good to go 'mucking about' with a Negro, even one in uniform. But most of the others had gone home and there wasn't much choice.

She let him take her arm and guide her towards the Tramway Centre, where the winds of war had left piles of rubble and twisted metal in its wake.

He told her his name was Aaron.

She said, 'That's nice.'

They ended up in a pub called the Llandoger Trow near the Old Vic in King Street, a place nearly as old as the Cat and Wheel where they'd been earlier, but larger and packed with a variety of service personnel and civilians. Perhaps because it was next to the waterfront and had catered for sailors of many nations in its time, all manner and colour of people were noisily drinking, smoking and talking while someone in the background belted out 'Roll Out the Barrel' on an upright piano.

Aaron found a cast-iron table and two stick-fine chairs near the piano and left Polly there while he fetched the drinks. Claustrophobia had never been a problem in Polly's life, but all the same she found herself wishing that he would hurry back and cause a break in the crowds so she could at least see the bar. The only place it did break was around the bumbling piano player, who she watched with mounting fascination. Sometimes he played with only one hand, his other lifting a pint pot to his mouth, the tune shaking as much as his fingers.

By the time Aaron got back, the pianist's singing voice had deteriorated to a garbled hotch-potch of made-up verse and broken-up words. Polly began to giggle.

'That guy ought to be hanged for crimes against music,' said Aaron and shook his head despairingly.

There was a sudden lull in musical rendition – if it could be called that. Polly took the opportunity to talk.

'Where are you from?' she asked.

'Not from round these here parts, missy,' he said shaking his head, his accent a comic parody of most of the Hollywood blacks she'd ever heard.

Her cheeks dimpled. She was enjoying herself. 'I know you're from America,' she said, 'but where? You're not from Alberta are you?'

He looked stunned. 'That's in Canada! I'm from the United States of America, ma'am!' and he stood up and saluted her.

A few around raised their glasses and laughed before their attention went back to the pianist. Two patrons, tired of his drunken renditions, were trying to remove him and asking for someone else to play. The pianist was holding onto the iron-framed instrument with as much tenacity as a drowning man clinging to a piece of driftwood.

Aaron shook his head and they exchanged an understanding smile. 'I'm from Boston actually. I'm a graduate and when I get back, my father insists I recommence my law studies. He's determined I'm going to be a lawyer.'

'Blimey!' said Polly and took a swig of her gin and orange to quell her surge of excitement. A lawyer. Well, hadn't she hit the jackpot? And her a mere counter hand in Woolworths before Carol had come along. She'd never expected him to be that. Snowshoe had lived in the back of beyond and didn't seem to have a recognisable profession. Gavin had worked in a canning factory, and Al Schumacher had been a farmer's son. 'Fancy being able to do something like that.'

He looked at her almost angrily then looked away as if regretting it. 'Being able to do it is one thing. Wanting to do it is another.'

She frowned. What was he getting at? Didn't he realise how lucky he was to get that sort of an education? 'So you don't want to be a lawyer?'

He smiled and looked at her sidelong, his fingers tapping impatiently but tunefully on the marble-topped table. His gaze went back to the piano where a woman with the figure of a pre-war cottage loaf was trying to tap out a few notes and singing in a high-pitched voice that fell off more keys than it hit.

'I want to be an entertainer,' he said getting to his feet, the shadow of his tall, well-built frame falling over her like a velvet curtain.

The crowd nearest the piano had obviously had enough of having their ears seriously abused. 'Get off, missus!'

By the time Aaron's shadow fell over her, she'd given up the fight.

'God 'elp you!' she shouted before sliding off the stool. 'This load of shit don't appreciate good music!'

The crowd roared. Aaron smiled at her good-naturedly. 'Sure, damaged ear drums are a sign of the times, ma'am. Must be the sirens that did it.'

Another roar of laughter went up from those nearest the piano.

Fascinated, Polly watched as Aaron sat down on the stool, unbuttoned his jacket and rolled back his cuffs. He seemed so confident, so sure of himself. He was not her kind, and yet she found herself being drawn to him, intrigued by his elegant self-possession and exotic difference.

A low murmur ran through those nearest the piano. Hostile eyes waited to see if this singer, too, needed to be shown the door. Polly said a silent prayer for him. But she needn't have worried. As his fingers met the keys the low murmur fell stone dead.

He sang 'As Time Goes By'.

Humphrey Bogart and Ingrid Bergman: everyone in that bar was remembering them, reliving their fear and their love. Every single person was swaying and humming or softly singing the words. They had an empathy with all those people stuck in a bar in *Casablanca* because they'd been through a war too and, by hell, they hadn't been acting. But they were also moved by the way Aaron was caressing the keys, making the music and singing the words they knew so well.

At the end the crowd clapped and cheered. Encores were shouted for, drinks were bought and forced upon them both, although Polly noticed that Aaron drank sparingly.

''Ere! You got something against them drinks, Yank?' asked one pink-faced, grey-haired old chap, a checked cap slapped flatly on his head.

Aaron smiled and gave the man a friendly clap on the shoulder of his worn, grubby jacket. 'I wish I could keep up with you old timer and I don't want to appear ungrateful, but...' he patted his stomach. 'Got it in the guts over in Italy. But if you and your pals can help me out drinking all this stuff...'

The old man nodded in instant understanding. 'Don't you worry about that, my boy,' he said, his gaze falling to the drinks, his tongue licking his lips as he absentmindedly slapped Aaron's broad back. 'Glad to oblige,' he said.

Polly was impressed. 'Did it hurt a lot – what you said about getting it in the guts in Italy?'

Aaron looked serious. 'It certainly did.' He leaned closer to her. 'Do you know, I spent so much time in the John the battalion commander thought I'd deserted.'

A tic of a smile lifted one side of his mouth. The penny dropped.

'Do you mean you had Delhi Belly?'

'If you mean were my guts in turmoil from some goddam germ I picked up, the answer's yes, though I did see my fair share of action to start with,' he added, suddenly defensive in case she thought he was the sort that shirked his duty. 'And I got involved with some other stuff and got shipped back here instead of straight home.'

'Oh!' said Polly and wondered what crime he had committed. He certainly didn't seem the criminal type. She desperately wanted to ask him what the reason was but was sure he would give her one of his leg-pulling answers. The moment was lost, drowned in the demands of the other customers asking him to belt out 'Chatanooga Choo'. 'And don't spare the horses, lover!' shouted the woman with the cottage-loaf figure, her wide hips gyrating and her fat legs kicking as Aaron played honky-tonk.

Polly joined in, clapping and singing in time with the tune, her blonde hair tumbling over her face as she danced the jitterbug with a lanky sailor, his long legs spiralling out in all directions like the arms of a skeleton windmill. Aaron can't have done anything very dreadful, she thought to herself as she skidded around the floor. If he had he would be under arrest, wouldn't he? Unless he was facing trial, or unless he'd escaped.

Haphazardly, because she was moving so fast, she tried to study the flurry of faces as she was whirled, thrown over a shoulder and slid along the floor. White, pink, brown and black, plus shades in between. This truly was an international alliance. Everyone was enjoying themselves and no one was interested in fighting.

Polly eyed Aaron dreamily and imagined herself in slinky satin, looking every inch the glamour girl in a dimly lit American nightclub – just like Rita Hayworth – when suddenly someone tapped her on the shoulder.

'Polly?'

She looked up and came face to face with Edna.

'Oh!' she said, without thinking. 'You're the one with the fiancé.'

Edna winced. 'Yes. Edna,' she said, realising that Polly probably remembered her fiancé more readily than her name by virtue of his injuries. 'We're having a night out – me and Colin that is. Care to join us? It was Charlotte's suggestion. She's been in constant touch since the other day and gave us a lift down in her car. Wasn't that kind of her?'

'I suppose it was,' said Polly looking expectantly for the tall, elegantly attired woman who made her feel more envious than anyone else she'd ever known.

'She's not here,' Edna added, realising that Polly was looking for her. 'She's picking us up at ten o'clock. She's out collecting sewing for one of those things she does.'

'Oh!'

'I noticed you were sitting by yourself,' Edna went on. 'Would you care to join us?'

'I am with someone,' said Polly, nodding towards Aaron and studying Edna's face for her reaction. She'd automatically expected her to look shocked, even to withdraw her offer when she saw she was with a black man. Instead a strangely wistful look came to her eyes.

'He's very talented,' she said softly.

Polly, suddenly full of pride to be with such a man, got to her feet and stretched to her full, diminutive height. 'Reckons he's going to be a musician.' Then she followed Edna to the table where Colin was sitting patiently in his wheelchair.

'Hi there!' he shouted.

Edna explained to him about Aaron and what his intentions were after the war.

'Best of luck to the bloke,' he said raising his glass. 'It looks as though I'm going to be a toy maker if that Charlotte Hennessey-White has her way. First an aeroplane for her lad and now a battleship.'

'You could make one for me,' Polly said quickly, unable to control her need to outdo or, at least, equal Charlotte. 'A wooden horse? Could you manage a wooden horse? It's for my niece,' she lied, and didn't bat an eyelid. She rarely admitted to having a child.

Colin agreed. 'And what sort of future have you got planned out, Polly?'

Now it was Polly's turn to look wistful. Her eyes fixed on Aaron as she answered. 'All I want to be is someone's wife in a place as far away from here as possible.'

Unseen by Polly, Edna and Colin exchanged knowing glances. They hoped it wasn't Aaron she had in mind. Like Edna, Colin knew that the American army practised a colour bar. There would be no wedding bells for a mixed marriage, but neither of them could bring themselves to mention it.

Polly insisted on leaving before Charlotte turned up, using the excuse that she had promised not to be late tonight. She couldn't really explain how uncomfortable she felt when Charlotte was around. It just hurt to see those beautiful clothes and that perfectly coiffed hair.

Polly introduced Aaron before they left. He offered her his arm once they were outside the door.

'She's a brave girl sticking by her guy like that,' Aaron said softly.

Polly pouted. 'I suppose so. She doesn't have to. Anyway how do you know for sure that there wasn't someone while he was away?'

Aaron shrugged.

'I know her kind,' Polly went on. 'All strawberries and cream but deep down she's boiling like a kettle.'

'You're cynical,' said Aaron squeezing her arm. She returned the squeeze. 'And you're gorgeous!'

He went on to tell her he was going to play music on Broadway one day.

'I've heard of that,' she said. 'I saw it at the pictures. Is that really what you're going to do?'

God, he thought, but these English dames were easy to impress. He never referred to them as Limeys.

The clippie on the bus they were travelling on chose that minute to clip their tickets. 'Next stop Old Market,' she said curtly, her eyes glancing at Polly before giving Aaron her own superior look as though she were looking over a prize stallion and finding it not quite what she was looking for. She sniffed and reached for the next seat.

'Fares please,' she said, moving down between the two rows of seats.

'My stop,' said Polly getting up.

'I'll walk you home,' said Aaron and as he got up and his full height towered over her, she felt too overwhelmed to refuse his offer.

As they turned into York Street she became aware of net curtains twitching as the sound of their footsteps reverberated between the Victorian terraced houses that squatted meanly on either side of the road.

Polly bristled. How dare they? At least she was single. There were married women in her street who had not always sat home alone while their husbands were away fighting.

She glanced up at the bedroom windows of Aunty Meg's house. No lights were on and there was no sound of crying. Carol was sleeping. Hopefully she'd stay that way. She didn't want to tell Aaron about Carol – not yet anyway.

'Can I see you again?' he asked. 'Tomorrow?'

'Why not? I'll meet you outside the Llandoger where we were tonight,' she said quickly. She didn't want him to pick her up from the house. Mentally she weighed up the cost of the bus fare against the opportunity to be the wife of a GI. 'I've had a lovely time,' she said in her most sultry voice, her blue eyes wide and purposely appealing.

He smiled. His lips came down to meet hers.

Some girls she'd known had said that the black blokes were over-sexed, more so even than their white counterparts and, on the whole, better lovers. In a way she had expected him to reflect that, hard kisses, feverish fumbling around her breasts and even up her skirt. But he did none of those things. His kiss was warm; the hands on her shoulders were gentle. A thrill ran through her. She really wanted him and pressed her body against him in an effort to let him know.

To her surprise he stepped back. 'Goodnight. I'll see you tomorrow.'

His footsteps echoed between the twin rows of brick houses. She didn't put her key in the door until the sound had melted away. Once inside she slumped so heavily against the wall that a lump of damp plaster slid out from behind the wallpaper and cascaded to the floor. 'Be still,' she said to her heart. It totally ignored her and continued to beat wildly.

She reached out and ran her hand down over the front door and imagined in the darkness that he was still there, big and broad above her. Perhaps this was the one who would fulfil all her dreams. He was the last of a great army and would soon be gone. In order to go with him she would do anything, anything at all, and woe betide anyone who upset her plans.

6

Meg sighed in defeat when Polly explained to her why she wanted her to look after Carol.

'It's free. Can't refuse if it's free, can I!' Her blue eyes flashed and she tossed her head so that her hair slapped around her cheeks.

Meg had no argument to offer. If all it took was the price of a bus fare, she had to let it be. She pursed her lips to prevent herself calling Polly a selfish little cow. Her patience was wearing thin. Nowadays when the neighbours made snide comments about her niece, she didn't always stick up for her as readily as she once had.

She tilted her head and viewed Polly from a sideways angle. There was no doubting she was pretty in a brazen kind of way. Blondes always were. 'Are you sure it's only yer foot he wants to take a look at?'

Just like Mavis, thought Polly. She stuck her hands on her hips, her elbows forming acute angles. 'Just my ankle, Aunty Meg. Besides, there might be something else in it seeing it was him that did me the injury. Compensation like.' She twigged Meg's speculative raising of eyebrows. 'I mean money.'

Meg snorted slightly before throwing in one last dig. 'Not going to cost him much time anyway. It's not hurting is it? Haven't seen you limping for days.'

Those last words came back to Polly as she walked past the rank of detached stone houses in Park Row, Clifton. With self-conscious swipes at a few cat hairs that had transferred from Meg's black moggy to her coat, she trotted on. Every now and then she glanced at the high bay windows and wondered if anyone watching would judge her as being a visitor to Dr Hennessey-White's house. Naa, she thought. Definitely a servant; that's what they'd think; a skivvy to tidy up after the likes of the doctor and his snooty wife. And what a posh cow she was with her fine fur coat and that wisp of veil over her face. And those children! Too good to be true, they were.

The house was bigger than any she'd ever entered. Bay windows as broad as they were high reflected the grey sheen of the winter sky. A brass plaque stated the doctor's name. Polly marvelled at the size of the house, tilting her head back as she looked up four storeys. At that time she didn't know that only the ground floor was used as a surgery. The upper floors were divided into apartments, an investment David had made for extra income and his old age. She didn't know he lived within walking distance in Royal York Crescent.

Before knocking, she looked around her at the neat lawn, the swept drive and the ivy-covered walls that surrounded the garden. What a difference to York Street where the door opened straight onto the street and the walls at the rear provided a feeble barrier between the houses, the shunting yards, and the incessant noise of goods trucks being pushed backwards and forwards.

As she stood at the gate a man in a tweed overcoat and a trilby hat with the brim pulled over his eyes stared at her. She stared back, briefly wondered what he thought of her, then smiled broadly and slipped him a saucy wink. He dashed off.

She glanced after him and burst out laughing when she saw

him looking back at her over his shoulder instead of where he was going. So engrossed was he, that he walked slap-bang into a lamp-post. Seeing the funny side of something made her courage return. So did her limp. What was the point of going to see a doctor if there was nothing wrong with you? So the limp returned, a little more pronounced than it had been before.

Mentally she prepared herself to keep things believable. 'The right ankle,' she muttered as she pushed open the door. 'The right ankle,' she explained to the receptionist after the woman had looked her up and down then checked with the doctor that he really had an appointment with a woman named Polly Chandler.

The right ankle, the right ankle! Again and again the words ticker-taped around in her mind. Telling right from left had never been her strong point. No matter how often she repeated which was which, lapses occurred.

'Please take a seat, madam. Doctor Hennessey-White will be with you shortly.'

The chair was almost too good to sit in – certainly better than anything she'd ever come across.

The receptionist kept her eyes discreetly fixed on the paperwork in front of her. No conversation there. Polly took in the details of the room.

Thick rugs, high windows, great sweeps of brocade curtain, and all for a waiting room. The urge to throw her shoes off and bury her toes in one of the rugs was overwhelming. But she didn't have time to get too comfortable or too bored.

'Miss Chandler. So pleased to see you again.'

His voice mesmerised her. His palm was warm against her hand.

'Steady, doctor. Hurts like hell, you know.' Just to add believability, she staggered slightly against him.

'My dear, I can't apologise enough.'

He guided her through a pair of double doors and closed them once he'd sat her down in a winged armchair that owed nothing whatsoever to utility in its design. Scrolls of dark wood and cabriole legs framed the deep red plush upholstery.

'Is this old and worth a bit?' she asked, her fingers playing over the polished wood in the same way as a child might. 'Or is it just old junk to tide you over?'

He had been half way back behind his desk, but at her words he stopped, turned and faced her, his arms folded across his chest. She looked up fully expecting to see amusement in his eyes. She saw it on his lips, but there was a different expression in his eyes, something there that she could not quite comprehend.

'Five hundred pounds,' he said in a calm but firm voice.

'That's what it's worth?' Amazed, she glanced towards a second chair. 'That for the pair, is it?'

He shook his head. 'And there's this too,' he said as he pulled forward an equally well-upholstered footstool. He patted at the back of a chair. 'Now. Let's take a look at that ankle.'

I like the smell of this place, she thought, as she placed her foot on the stool being careful to do it slowly, gently as if it still hurt like hell – which it didn't.

Dr Hennessey-White sat in the chair opposite her. 'Remove your stocking, please.'

He didn't look at her when he said it. She hesitated, briefly wondering about his intentions before remembering that doctors were not quite the same as real men. Their profession didn't allow it.

She reached up under her skirt, slid the button out of the back suspender and the farthing out of the front one. Damn it, why hadn't she thought to fix a new suspender onto her corset before coming?

She coloured slightly, keeping her eyes downcast and clutching

the farthing in her hand as she rolled her stocking down her leg
and away from her toes.

Her foot was in his hands. She gasped. 'Always cold,' she said.
'Doctors' hands.'

He frowned. She sensed his disapproval.

'Cold hands, warm heart,' she added with a light laugh. 'It
seems fine now,' he said letting her foot go and sitting straighter in
the chair. 'I wouldn't have thought you'd be limping at all by now.'

Polly thought quickly. 'It was a long walk from the bus stop. I got
off at the wrong one.'

'Well,' he said slapping his thighs before getting to his feet. 'I
should think another one or two days and you can go back to work.'

'That's a laugh! What work?'

The mocking in her voice seemed to make him stand more
rigidly, almost as if she'd shoved an iron bar up through the back of
his coat. He looked genuinely concerned. 'You have no work?'

She shook her head ruefully. 'Everything bombed. Canteens
overflowing with staff taken on during the war and not wanting to
be put out now. Not much work at all for cooks. Not even assistant
cooks. Though I'd take anything, mind you. Shop. Factory. Even
thought about learning to type.' She refused to recognise her role in
Woolworths as merely that of a counter hand. She always meant to
be a cook but people always wanted experience and she had none.

Dr Hennessey-White looked thoughtful. Polly dived in. 'Do you
know somewhere that's taking on?'

The enthusiasm in her voice seemed to jerk him quickly out of
his thoughts. 'Not canteens, no. But neighbours of mine could do
with some help. Their cook's son has come home complete with a
new wife. Italian I believe. They've moved in on her, the wife is
expecting a child and the woman wants to be at home with them.
Would you be interested? Good family. Respectable.'

'Oh I am!' Polly exclaimed, hardly daring to believe her luck.

'I'm talking about the family you'd be working for,' he said.

'Oh, doctor, I'm so grateful,' she said, uncaring that her skirt was half way up her thigh as she struggled to fix the farthing back into the broken suspender.

Again he looked at her strangely, as though he was planning something. But she disregarded it as one of those things. She could bring out the worst in men as well as the best.

'I'll be in touch,' he said as he escorted her to the door. And no funny business, thought Polly.

She was taken by surprise. Just as he reached for the door handle, the flat of his hand gently slapped her bottom.

She gasped. The dirty man! Then she wondered what his wife would think if she knew. Well, Polly Chandler knew how to handle the likes of him!

She sang all the way home, her step lighter and her limp non-existent as she swung off the bus and marched up York Street, mindful that the curtains were twitching and imagining their disappointment to see she had no one on her arm.

The smell of the plush consulting rooms – and the smell of the doctor – stayed with her. What made it so attractive? Suddenly it came to her. Money. Both Dr Hennessey-White and the place smelled of money and both were irresistible.

* * *

Meg was rocking backwards and forwards on the settee, a sleeping Carol cradled in her arms.

She looked up as Polly breezed in, flung her hat to one side and hooted with laughter because it landed on top of a Victorian urn of riotous colour with ornate handles that stuck out like perforated ears.

'I've got a job!' she cried. 'Well, almost!' she added spreading her arms and twirling round because she really was feeling she could almost fly.

'I thought you went to the doctor's.'

'He knows someone who wants a cook.'

Meg beamed. 'Glory be! You could have a job for life doing something like that.'

Polly stopped twirling. 'It's only until I marry Aaron and go off to America.'

A disconcerted look came to Meg's face. 'Has he asked you?'

'I'm going to ask him.' She glanced warily at Meg. Her aunt returned her gaze.

'You haven't known him long and you haven't told him about Carol yet, have you?'

Polly shifted her gaze. 'No. But I will when I'm ready.' She'd been out with him almost every night, meeting him at one of their favourite pubs or outside the Kings' Picture House. Although she'd allowed him to walk her to her front door that first night, she'd been lucky that Carol hadn't cried and she didn't want to scare him off just yet. Since then she'd only let him walk her to the end of the street.

'I'm late,' she said, as she reached for a comb and shook a lipstick from her handbag.

'I know,' Meg blurted. 'He called in a few minutes ago. I told him to...'

Polly turned sharply, her heel digging into the threadbare carpet so that it swivelled around with her. 'You didn't tell him about Carol did you?'

'No! I didn't. She was out back asleep, but I did tell him to...'

'To go! You told him to go! You don't like him, do you? You don't like him because he's black!' Polly was livid. She hardly heard Meg trying to explain. The only words she heard were something about the chip shop.

'I don't hold nothing against him,' Meg shouted after her. 'Think of your daughter, you hard little bitch!'

Polly slammed the door behind her. Meg shouldn't have said that. She had no right...

Her daughter's disturbed whimpers turning to a loud wail drifted out into the street where the sound of the slamming door had set the curtains twitching at number twenty-eight directly opposite.

Polly's head jerked in that direction. Mrs Gardiner! The cow!

She poked out her tongue. 'Where do you think you are? The bloody Hippodrome? Think I'm the star turn, does you? Nosy cow!'

But no matter her daughter's crying, no matter the fact that Meg had lost her temper and – yes – made her feel like dirt, the urge to be with Aaron and have the chance of a better life was too much to resist. She ran off down the road.

The noise from the shunting yards muffled the sound of her flying feet as she ran over the uneven paving slabs of York Street then skidded around the corner onto the cobbled surface that ran all the way down the 'Batch' and into Midland Road.

Meg's words rang shrill in her mind, yet still her urge to find Aaron was too strong to ignore. He had stepped out of the night and into her life so recently, and yet she felt she had known him far longer than that. Perhaps it was because he reminded her of those other GIs – Government Issue, that's what it stood for. And he represented a general mix of those that had gone before. He had the uniform, the size, the glib way with words, just like all the others. But he had something else. Aaron was not just the person she saw on the surface. It didn't all come bursting out like it did with a lot of the other guys. There were deep emotions; anger, hate, pride and passion. They were all there but coated with a warm, calm and cultured surface. Far above her experience, but intriguing all the same.

Nothing distracted her as she ran, not wolf whistles from lonely men, or the catcalls of the whores who seemed to think they had first call on anything in trousers. Just sluts. That's all they were; no one important enough to make her slow down. No one and nothing could be that important.

As dusk fell, the last dray of the day was returning to Georges' Brewery at the bottom of the Batch, the heavy shires snorting, their chests and flanks foaming with sweat. Polly heard them, turned her head and saw the fear in their eyes as their ironclad hooves slid on the glistening cobbles.

Keen to get home, the driver had let the brake off. Big backsides of big horses were not enough to keep the empty vehicle from swerving to one side and pulling them over. She'd seen it happen before, one horse, perhaps both, going down and lying with their chests heaving, perhaps with a broken leg, just waiting for the shot to the head that would put them out of their misery.

And here it was again. Would the fools never learn?

The dray was slap-bang against their rears and gradually their legs were splaying out from under them.

Going hell for leather and keen as mustard to get to Aaron, she still had time to shout out exactly what she thought. 'Put the bloody brake on, you rotten sod!'

A hand sign, not unlike the one Churchill was so keen on giving, yet with a completely different meaning, was accompanied by a suggestion that she should 'fuck off!' Polly slowed, her fists clenched, her brow heavy with anger. She stepped into the road and was just about to return his abusive language with some of her own, when the piercing sound of a police whistle stopped her in her tracks.

Just fifty yards further down the Batch, the unmistakable gleam of silver against blue serge shone like a saviour in the middle of the road.

A shouted order and a raised hand closely followed the sound of the policeman's whistle. The brake on the dray was pulled on, the wheels screeching like the cry of a scalded cat. The worst was over. Still snorting white foam down their flaring nostrils, the horses came to a halt.

Polly caught the driver's eye, grinned and returned the hand gesture he had given her earlier. 'Now who's fucked you rotten...?' She didn't finish her sentence. Somehow she knew he was there standing behind her. His presence was tangible even before he spoke. Perhaps she could smell him, his uniform or even his maleness.

'That was quite a performance. Great horses.'

At first she didn't turn round. She merely smiled and closed her eyes, letting the sound of Aaron's voice wash over her like the hoppy, yeasty, smell of warm beer when it's just coming up to being fully cooked. The only time she liked beer was when the steam was rising from the chimneys of the brewery, the smell like a wet blanket lying all around.

She eyed the scene before her. A few other people had gathered round, shouting up at the driver and daring him to get down from his perch.

She said, 'I don't like people who are cruel to animals. I don't like any kind of violence, especially now. Think we've 'ad enough of it, don't you?'

When she turned to face him he was smiling down at her and shaking his head. 'I would have thought that judging by the size of them horses, ma'am, they'd be quite capable of looking after themselves!'

She laughed at his 'field talk' as he called it. Reaching out she fingered the buttons of his tunic as though she were some shy virgin from a home where they read the Bible on Sundays and never went to pubs and dances. 'You're pretty big yerself but I bet you could do with some looking after.'

He caught at her hand, his fingers wrapping tightly around hers. 'Are you offering?'

She raised her eyes slowly to his face and paused before she spoke. 'Do you believe in love at first sight?'

His lashes were incredibly dark, she noticed. What was he thinking when he smiled like that? It was such a secretive smile, yet confident as if he were a captain and not merely a corporal.

'Let's walk.'

He took her arm and slid it through the crook of his. It made her feel small, sweet and fragile. She fitted well enough into the first description, but no one, once they got to know her, ever considered her sweet or fragile.

'Madame. Allow me!'

'Thank you kindly, sir.'

As they walked the warmth of his body seemed to permeate his clothes: her clothes. She wanted to look at his face, to study the colour of his skin, the shape of his nose and the arched curve of his upper lip. Holding that urge in check was torture, but when the moment came and she did look...

Oh, the shivers of delight! Blood raced through her veins, thudded at her forehead. It was all so crazy, her wanting to marry a Yank and see the world, and him popping up like a genie from a bottle, a big dark genie as exotic as anything she'd read about in the Arabian Nights.

It had been such a short time, but now she found herself wanting him to want her as other men had wanted her – and had her. Past sins and old guilt were irrelevant now. This man was becoming more important than her dream. The raw excitement of being with him, of seeing other people's eyes follow them, some disapproving, only heightened her desire. If he didn't marry her, if he didn't take her with him... The thought was terrifying. Not only would she be disappointed, like the war itself, it would change the whole of her life.

They continued to walk arm in arm, the recently re-lit street-lights throwing amber pools across their path. We must look like an old married couple, she thought. She grinned.

'What's so funny?' Just like him to notice.

She shrugged and looked into his face, her eyes just above the level of his shoulder. 'I was just thinking how funny we must look together.' He blinked. She knew what he was thinking. 'You so tall and me so small,' she lied. If he did take it that she had been refer-ring to the difference in their colouring and their cultures, it was all to the good. How could she tell him she was imagining them married? And how could she tell him that she could imagine them in bed together, feel his bronze flesh hard and demanding against her own, his lips crushing hers.

Then it was he who shrugged, the shoulders of his uniform smartly falling back into place the moment his body did. 'Makes no difference. All the same lying down.' Polly stifled a giggle. 'I suppose you're right.' He hadn't guessed at her plans. They hadn't changed. Not really. But the picture of them in bed together stayed with her, him broad, brown, and stretching the full length of the bed from head to foot, and her, just filling in the gap between his shoulder and his ankles. Delicious! She shivered with excitement. 'Short or tall, it doesn't matter at all!'

They walked down through Old Market where a queue was forming outside the Kings' Picture House. *Mrs Miniver* was showing – yet again. Inquisitive eyes followed their progress.

Polly pretended she did not see. Prejudice between fellow coun-trymen, albeit of different colours, was difficult to understand. Hadn't they been fighting against that sort of thing?

Eyes straight ahead, they walked around what remained of the

damage where the tramlines used to be. Buses had taken over once
the twisted metal had been cut away and the bomb craters filled in.
One chugged past now.

'Whore!'

Polly jumped and looked quickly up. It was shouted from a top
deck window. All she could see was a pair of arms, the glow of a
lighted cigarette hanging from the narrow opening.

Anger quickly replaced shock. 'You...!'

Aaron's hold tightened on her arm. 'Let it be.'

An indignant stiffness held her bolt upright. 'Did you hear what
he called me?'

He looked away from her when he nodded. He didn't want her
to see the look in his eyes and, in a way, she didn't want to see.

'Sticks and stones,' he said in a level voice. 'It's nothing.'

Polly took a deep breath. Swallowing insults was not something
she found easy. Taking another deep breath because she was
shaking with anger, she stopped and Aaron stopped with her.

'Got a fag?'

'A cigarette? You?'

He was right to be surprised. He hadn't seen her light up before.
Smoking had been almost taboo since having Carol – and less
money. She'd sworn to Meg that she'd ditch the habit. But hell,
tonight she'd sworn *at* Meg.

'I need one.'

He let her arm go and dipped into his pocket. 'You okay?' he
asked as he flicked a chromium lighter.

'I will be.'

'This place something special?' he added, looking about him as
she cupped her hands around the flame, her hair falling forward
around her face.

Blowing the smoke away like an exasperated sigh, Polly
looked around her. They were in shadow, although a shaft of light

shone from between ill-fitting curtains drawn across lop-sided windows.

'The Pied Powder,' she said. 'It's an old pub.'

'That's an odd name.'

'I suppose it is. I think it's foreign.'

She bent her head, glad he couldn't read her expression. Like a cat fouling a flowerbed, the man calling her a whore had spoilt her thoughts. Just for the briefest of moments, it was easy to tell him she didn't want to see him again.

It was as if he read her thoughts. 'You don't have to keep seeing me, baby, but hell, it would sure hurt if you didn't.'

The feel of his hands on her shoulders made her straighten. Once she looked up into his face, the moment passed.

'That man...' she began.

'Jealousy,' he said.

'Of me?'

'Of me. I bet you had plenty of guys before the war. What were they like?'

His question surprised her and for a moment it seemed that her tongue had stuck to the roof of her mouth. Pillars supported the gable of the fourteenth-century market inn above them. Looking out from there and over to the shops opposite for an answer proved fruitless. Did she really have to admit to going out with delivery boys, men from the brewery and some from the docks? And what about Snowshoe and all those other Canadians and Yanks that she'd known?

'Just local boys – guys,' she corrected herself.

'So why me?'

She started to walk again. He offered his arm. She took it and all the affection and desire she'd felt before flooded back over her.

He kept his eyes facing forward. She sensed he was either playing with her or testing her – for whatever reason. But she hugged his arm that bit closer. He'd know then that she meant what she said.

'You're good looking.'

'Because I wear a uniform?'

'It's a nice uniform.'

'And what else?'

'I like the way you speak.'

'I suppose you mean my accent. Is it because I'm an American that you care for me so much?'

Polly bit her lip. Had he guessed that she wanted to be a GI bride like all those others and sail away across the ocean? 'It's not just how you speak, it's what you say. And you can play the piano,' she blurted.

'Yes indeedy!' he laughed, showing his teeth and waving his hands like wings at the sides of his face.

That Negro thing! He was doing it again! She grabbed hold of him, spun him round to face her. 'Stop acting the fool!'

His laugh was loud, but she sensed it was self-mocking, even self-pitying. It stopped when he saw the look in her eyes. His smile softened as he looked down into her face. Polly caught her breath. Something special had passed between them. It couldn't be put into words. It was more like a path had been opened and she couldn't stop her feet from running along it.

This was the moment she'd been waiting for. She reached up and cupped his face in her hands, his skin velvet soft against her palms. She ran each thumb gently, so very gently, along his lashes, his brows and the line of his nose.

Night air turned her breath white. If it hadn't she might almost have believed that she was not breathing at all. Her chest felt so tight. This was a precious moment, a unique moment. All those other times had been with Yanks. This time she was with Aaron. This time she felt a fluttering inside that she had never felt before.

Her eyes dropped to his lips. They were almost the colour of plums just before they turn properly ripe. Mouth slightly open, she lifted her chin and closed her eyes as his lips met hers.

The warmth in his body seemed to flow into her mouth, down her throat. Becoming part of him and his place, wherever that was, mattered more than anything else now. And him becoming part of her and what she was – that also was important. She wanted him to enter her world and she thought hard how best this could be achieved. Something ordinary, something so undemanding that he couldn't possibly refuse.

'What are you doing for Christmas?'

He looked surprised. 'Nothing special.'

'Christmas dinner at my place then.'

'Sure.'

So simple! So easy! She could hardly believe she had achieved so much in such a short time.

There was no need for him to pull her into the shadows. Their thoughts and their bodies acted in unison. Rushed breathing, rushed caresses, hasty fumbles born out of a passion that was not the result of the fear of dying, not like it had been during the war. This was a mutual passion born out of mutual desire. Neither resisted. Neither protested that it shouldn't be.

As far as Polly was concerned there was no time to lose. Tonight she had been going to ask him to marry her. But the New Year would be soon enough. Having him to Christmas dinner would be adequate compensation.

Meg's reaction was something she would think about in the morning. Considering what Aaron would say when he found out she had a daughter did weigh a little heavier. But tonight wasn't the time to tell him.

* * *

Aaron caught the last bus that would take him from Bristol City Centre to the POW camp, which was nine miles distant and surrounded by ploughed fields and green pasture.

The bus crawled along at the same snail's pace as in the blackout and the passengers rolled together like set jellies as one pothole followed another.

There was little to see out of the window except tired terraced houses and half-empty shops, some highlighted by street lamps, others dark and faceless.

Muffled against the chill of a dampening December, more and more people crowded on at each bus stop. Even those seated downstairs who didn't have cigarette smoke to contend with coughed and sneezed.

From experience, Aaron sat on the side seat nearest the platform. At least there he could still breathe some fresh air and not the damp smell of woollen coats that had once upon a time been a blanket on a bed. Make do and mend they called it. He admired their resilience. No wonder the southern black boys had felt so at home here. They'd lived like it for most of their lives, not like himself, coming from Boston with a father in a good job and a mother who'd vowed that all her children would go to college. All the same, he hadn't been entirely untouched by prejudice and, after coming to Europe and seeing what he had seen, he knew his life would never be the same again.

There was also Polly to think about. He had tried not to care about the women he had met over here. But Polly was different. At first he'd thought her flighty, perhaps even a little hard-bitten regardless of her pronouncement that she hated violence. But tonight that thing with the horses caused him to reconsider. She had guts. She had integrity and a lot of affection to give. He smiled at the memory of what they had done in the shadows. The feel and smell of her body would remain with him for a very long time. To his own surprise, he found himself almost wishing their relationship might have a future. Of course it couldn't.

After only three stops the bus was crowded and it was standing room only out as far as the platform.

'Church Road!' shouted the clippie in the desperate hope that someone might get off and she'd have more room to squeeze between the tightly packed bodies.

Instead, three men attempted to get on, two in civvies and a US sergeant from the camp, a man that Aaron had as little to do with as possible. He bowed his head. Staring at his hands was preferable to being seen by that man.

'Full up!' shouted the clippie, her arm shooting out so fast that the flat of her hand nearly landed splat on the sergeant's face.

The civilians groaned and stepped back. The sergeant grabbed the clippie's arm. 'Come on, honey. I'm a war weary soldier in need of his bed – any bed, come to that. How about it?'

She shook her arm free. 'Don't fink you can sweet talk me, you bloody Yank!'

His arm shot out. He grabbed her tie. 'Now look here, sister...'

Aaron straightened. The sergeant's name was Noble, though he rarely lived up to his name. He was a bigot, a liar, a moron. A pig of the first degree who could make life hell if anyone dared cross him. Self-preservation battled with Aaron's chivalrous ideas. But if no one else stood up for the woman, he'd have to step forward.

He glanced out. Nothing was moving, including the bus.

'Come on soldier, there'll be another bus along in a minute.' It was one of the two civilians who'd been denied a place on the platform. Both men got hold of Noble's broad shoulders and pulled him backwards.

Relieved, Aaron sighed. 'Damn the other bus!'

Civilians shrugged aside, Noble swung one leg onto the platform so that the clippie was pressed tight against the small window where Aaron rested his arm.

A babble of noise broke out further down the bus. Others near him grumbled about wanting to get home and eyed his uniform as if he were as awkward a customer as the bull-necked sergeant.

In war he had sensed when an attack was imminent and he had to face the enemy in unavoidable combat. That was how he felt now and, just like in battle, he knew he had to face it head-on.

Just a moment was all it took. At the same time as wishing he'd caught an earlier bus, he looked over the clippie's shoulder. Sergeant Mickey Noble was looking right back at him, instant recognition and an equally instant resolution to get back to camp written all over his face. Aaron knew immediately what was coming.

Noble stabbed his finger at the glass that divided them. 'There's a black riding on a white man's bus sitting in a white man's seat! My seat!'

Aaron looked down at his hands. He couldn't count the number of times this sort of thing had happened. If it wasn't a bus it was a taxi or a train seat or the very fact of daring to be with a white girl in a country with no colour bar. It was an incongruous gesture mirroring a similar thought, but he couldn't help shaking his head and grinning. It was fifty-fifty as to what would happen next.

The clippie pushed at his chest. 'Get off of my bus!'

Although looking surprised at the outburst, Noble stood rigid, his brows a straight line above his beetle black eyes. 'That nigger should be giving me his seat!'

Suddenly the clippie seemed to swell to twice her size. 'Well, he bloody well ain't, is he? This is my bus and we'll 'ave none of that nonsense!'

The two civilians at the bus stop grabbed Noble from behind so he couldn't help but topple backwards. A man got up from a seat and pushed through to form a barrier with another man out on the platform.

Noble was left struggling on the pavement, the two civilians, obviously veterans of boot camp themselves, holding onto him.

As the bus moved off, the clippie held onto the pole at the rear and leaned out at an angle. 'And if I see you again, even if I 'aven't got one bloody soul on this bus, I ain't letting the likes of you on it!'

A cheer went up.

'Bleeding 'ell, your mate's enough to make anybody swear,' she said to Aaron as she squeezed by.

Laughter rippled from one end of the bus to the other.

Aaron grabbed her arm. 'He's not my mate,' he said quietly.

'No,' she said, 'he's a bastard!' She left him open mouthed.

'Any more fares please!' she shouted, then, 'Move yer ass. Let me get through.'

Aaron stared down at his hands again, wishing he was back home or at least with the same guys he'd been with when he'd first volunteered to fight for his country. As the bus rattled on he thought about when he'd had sergeant's stripes. They'd lasted until he'd said outright what was in his mind, that the US High Command were a bunch of hypocrites. He had accused them of something they had no wish to face up to. Why was the US army a segregated army when it was fighting a war against a race that regarded itself as superior to all others? Could someone tell him what the difference was?

No one could, so he'd lost a stripe and got himself a beating plus relocation as a guard to a Prisoner of War camp.

'I'm sure them Krauts will appreciate having you there seeing as there are not too many Jews around these parts!'

Some guys had thought it funny. They'd laughed, but he hadn't cared. He'd thought he could handle it. And he would have done, too, if there'd been other black guys there. Instead, he was alone among whites. He had a room on his own, he ate on his own. The civilian staff that came in intermittently were his only respite, they and the prisoners.

The main bugbear was Mickey Noble. He was mean as a rattlesnake with just as small a brain, except for his memory that is. Noble, like an elephant, never forgot a perceived wrong.

7

It was the Saturday before Christmas and Edna was alone when another parcel arrived.

For a while she stared at it, longing to rip it open and fondle its contents. She also longed to write to him, but simply didn't have the courage.

When she could no longer face the parcel or her own cowardice, she reached for her coat and rushed out of the door.

She was going to marry Colin. Her son, Sherman, was going for adoption. Everything would be for the best and Colin need never know.

She ran down the avenue, her tears under control by the time she reached Colin's house. Charlotte's car was parked outside; no doubt she was once again checking on the progress of the toy Colin was making Geoffrey for Christmas. Well, that was fine. She could do with the company of someone who always seemed brave and able to cope with everyone else's troubles.

Charlotte beamed at her the moment she entered the room. 'Edna, darling. Look at this. Isn't it wonderful! And how very sweet of you to name her after me.'

Balsa wood painted battleship grey, her details picked out in blackboard paint with a brush from a child's pre-war water-colour set, the Royal Navy destroyer *Charlotte* sat in a russet sea of chenille tablecloth on the dining table. 'The only thing is, I thought I asked you for another aeroplane,' Charlotte continued, her gloved hands folded tightly in front of her so her fur coat stayed firmly shut to the neck.

'I figured boys are like men, Mrs Hennessey-White, in that they like a bit of variety!' said Colin from the confines of his wheelchair, which had become a useful part of his toy-making since he could wheel it between each project he was working on.

Edna wanted to tell Charlotte that paint was hard to come by, unless you knew someone with access to army or navy supplies.

'I see that I am not your only customer, Mr Smith,' Charlotte went on. Her eyes took in the wooden horse awaiting its wheels, the submarine, and a brick trolley, all painted in the same battleship grey, the horse with black spots added, the submarine with detail, and the bricks with black spots and stripes. 'Goodness, a real Santa's grotto.'

'That's it. Santa's got a sleigh and I've got one with wheels on,' said Colin, his grin seeming to split his face in half and his hazel eyes bright with childish pride.

'But he hasn't got any reindeer,' said Edna with a sheepish grin.

'Which is just as well, 'cos it saves me picking up the poo!'

Edna felt her face reddening. The good-humoured but courteous Colin who had gone to war now cared little what he said or who he said it to. 'Colin!'

'Edna!'

This was another aspect of his recently acquired behaviour – aping an exclamation or, sometimes, an action. 'No!' he said suddenly, pushing hard at the wheels of the chair and wheeling away to the end of the table. 'I'm not tall enough to be Santa, thanks to the Japanese navy. I'm more like one of his workshop elves.'

He laughed as he said it, but Edna was not fooled. His description was painfully apt. At present he vaguely resembled some goblin workman, dressed as he was in a knitted blue jumper that had stretched in the wash, was rolled up at the sleeves and almost covered what remained of his knees.

'You have very skilled hands,' Charlotte said as she picked the boat up. 'I advise a lot of war veterans on how best to manage on their pension or what to do about setting up in business or in some sort of hobby. Do let me know if you need any extra assistance. I'm sure I can find the funding for you to take your skill further. I can probably find the customers too, though from what I see here,' she said, nodding at a can of navy issue paint with an amused smile on her face, 'you appear to be doing quite well without any help.'

Her face shone with enthusiasm. She's like a lighthouse, thought Edna. The point to rush to when you were tossed in a storm. If only I had her courage. She wondered whether to tell her about the parcel and about Sherman. Perhaps her determined confidence might rub off and she'd bravely claim her child. But then, what would she tell Colin? And could she cope with hurting him?

Charlotte bent to pick up the boat. It was then that her coat fell open and the scarf around her neck came adrift.

'Mind you don't lose it,' said Colin.

Charlotte put the boat down and retied the scarf hastily. It was the first time Edna had ever seen her look embarrassed and she wondered why.

'I must be going,' she said hurriedly and immediately turned to leave.

'Ten shillings and sixpence!' Colin shouted over his shoulder from the confines of his wheelchair.

Charlotte stopped in her tracks, her face flushed even more. 'Oh my goodness! I'm so sorry.'

She put the wooden ship back down on the dining table and unclipped the silver clasp on her tan leather bag.

Once the money was jingling in Colin's palm, Edna saw her to the door. It was raining outside.

'Silly me! I haven't brought an umbrella,' said Charlotte.

Both women stared for a moment at the drizzle falling from an iron-grey sky. It was hardly rain, more of a mist that left droplets shimmering on dead stalks and the crisp remnants of autumn leaves.

Once she'd regained her usual confidence, Charlotte asked her when she was getting married.

Edna blushed. 'As soon as we've saved enough what with a dress and a going-away suit.'

'My dear! I can offer you a most wonderful opportunity. The Red Cross is holding a Christmas bazaar and jumble sale at the Shaftesbury Crusade mission hall. It's just off Old Market so there are buses. I can assure you the most wonderful clothes will be available. I have begged everyone I know to dig deep into their wardrobes and donate for a good cause. Now,' she said, a pink glow warming her cheeks, 'I won't take no for an answer. And,' she added, leaning closer as if imparting the most wicked of secrets, 'I will ensure that something is put aside for you. Will you come?'

Edna thought about what her mother would say.

Charlotte continued, her face gleaming with almost missionary zeal. 'There are good wool suits, some from the best fashion houses in London. Hats, shoes, handbags and dresses from Liberty.'

Edna had never heard of Liberty but didn't let on.

Fully expecting Colin to be pleased at her news Edna went back into the room. Her jubilant expression froze on her face. Her fiancé sat very still in his chair, looking down at his hands. He wasn't whistling or singing like he usually did when he was working or about to start doing so.

She told Colin all about it. 'I won't go if you don't want me to,' she said, automatically surrendering even before challenged, a matter of habit after living with her mother and father.

'Up in Clifton, is it?'

Relieved that he seemed unconcerned, Edna nodded vigorously even though it was being held in Old Market, not Clifton at all.

'You go, girl.' He pointed his finger at her, a mischievous quirkiness playing around his lips. 'That's where all the Conservatives is and, if my old mum is telling the truth, Conservative jumbles got better quality chuck outs than Labour 'uns!'

Eyes shining, Edna clasped her hands together. This was her old Colin, the old common sense side by side with his chirpy sense of humour. Overcome with relief, she dived to his side and threw her arms around his neck. 'You're a right card, Colin Smith! And there was me thinking you were going to say I wasn't to go.'

'If Mrs Hennessey-White says you can find some frilly bits and pieces to wear on our honeymoon, it's to my advantage, ain't it?'

He grinned and lifted his eyebrows in a scandalously suggestive way that made Edna blush but also smile primly.

'Poor woman,' Colin went on. 'Can't help feeling sorry for her, can you?'

Edna almost burst out laughing. 'Sorry for her? With a house in Clifton, her children at a posh school, and a cook and a cleaner to do her housework! Lucky, I'd call it!'

Colin shook his head and his earlier frown came back. 'I wouldn't treat you like that.'

Edna frowned. 'Like what?'

He looked wistfully towards the window. The buds and flowers of a cream net curtain hung between the mellow cosiness of the room and the rank of bay villas on the other side of the street. Edna was not at all prepared for what he said next.

'She's got red marks around her neck. I think she's got problems.'

* * *

It was Mrs Grey's day off so Charlotte made breakfast. She could have got Nellie in, an amiable woman who came in to do the cleaning on occasion. But she didn't want anyone else entering her world. It wasn't the same as it had been and, in a strange way, she needed to keep it to herself until things were sorted out.

She needed to keep herself physically busy while she brooded on David and the frightening violence he'd shown towards her. Her hands shook slightly as she took the food into the dining room.

Light, whitened by an overnight frost and further frosted by sheer white nets, poured into the room from the floor to ceiling Georgian windows. Despite the warm reds of Turkish carpets and the gleam of richly polished wood, the room felt cold.

As though they're all made of ice, Charlotte thought, eyeing in turn her husband, her daughter and her son.

Cutlery moved from plate to mouth, cups were raised from saucers and replaced. The sounds tinkled like hollow silver bells.

If only David would take an interest in them like he used to. If only Geoffrey chattered like he used to, and if only Janet lolled over her father's arm as he read his paper, unafraid of rebuke, revelling in the fact that she was his little angel. But nothing was like it used to be.

But it will be! It has to be!

Perhaps her husband needed help of some kind. But what and who would give it? No. He'd be all right. He'd surely be all right.

'More toast?' Even to her own ears the sound of her voice seemed an intrusion.

It hurt to hear the mumbled 'No thank you, Mummy' from her children, less hurtful to hear it from David who was reading *The Times*, a familiar action that had survived the war unscathed.

Charlotte poured him more coffee and buttered him more toast. It was subservient in a way, but small favours were what women had to do if they were to get what they wanted from their menfolk.

She turned to the children. 'We might as well get on to school then, children.' She glanced nervously at David, afraid he might notice it was a little too early. 'Goodbye dear,' she said kissing him on the head. 'I'll clear the dishes away when I get back.'

Heart thumping, she started to follow the children to the door where she intended to remark that they should kiss David goodbye. After all, he was their father.

She gasped as David grabbed her arm. 'Just a minute.'

'The children...' she began, flustered because she was half-afraid he might guess where she was going after dropping them off. Working outside the home, whether voluntary or otherwise, was still a bone of contention between them. So far she had always been there in the mornings, at weekends and when he got home. He was assuming she had obeyed him. She had not.

Geoffrey and Janet were already at the door. Geoffrey looked nervous, his chin resting on his tie while he eyed his father from beneath a heavy brow. Janet looked openly defiant, her eyes wide and her pupils large and staring; *as if she's trying to understand him – and remember how it used to be.*

'Get your school things and wait for your mother by the front door,' said David without relinquishing the grip on her arm.

'David, they'll be late.' She made the effort to smile. Inside she was all nerves.

'Well, they won't be for much longer. I've decided that it was a bad move to have them educated at a day school. It's a hard world out there and they have to be prepared to face it. I think the time has come for them to board.'

'Boarding school?'

Charlotte's worst fear! Her children snatched from her loving, responsible bosom and thrust into a cloistered atmosphere where self-reliance was paraded as a virtue simply because it was the only option available to the lonely souls left there.

'The best education for life, my dear. I went through it. And so did you. Can you honestly say it did you any harm?'

As she looked down at his hawk-like features, the dark, deep set eyes, the black hair that slicked flatly back from his high forehead, memories of schooldays flooded back. Cold mornings rushing to wash in even colder water, the smell of chalk mixed with that of sweaty hockey boots and stale cooking, and the dark varnish plastered on Victorian rafters that made you feel you were trapped in some subterranean prison. A rabble of girls who might or might not get on together, who might be homesick, lovesick, or just sick of trying to prove they had some worth. Adopting an air of confidence, of making an effort to appear above it all, had drawn others to her. In helping them she had also helped herself. Yes, it had made her stronger, but it was an experience she had no wish to repeat.

David was still talking. 'And if they are at boarding school, you won't need the car, my dear. You can be a full-time housewife and spend all your time looking after me.'

'The car?'

She thought of all the things she depended on the car for: the orphanage, the Red Cross fund-raising sales, going off to give advice at the Resettlement Centre. And soon, she'd be going out to the POW camp to help those imprisoned readjust to a new world, wherever theirs might be.

'But how will I go shopping?' she blurted.

'You can telephone. That's what it's there for. You can have it delivered.'

'But what about clothes shopping, things for the house...' She was almost screaming, an entirely different Charlotte from the one everyone was used to. Any excuse! Anything to stop him doing this.

'You can do it at the weekend. I'll take you and the children whenever any of you need anything.'

'That means depending on you every time I go out of this house,' said Charlotte.

The newspaper slapped down loudly on the table. His fingers dug into her arm. 'I am the master in this house, Charlotte. Please understand that, my dear. My word is law!'

She hardly saw the road ahead as she drove the children to their individual schools. Stark trees grew at regular intervals on either side of the road. They seemed to shiver as if they were trying to run away. It might have been the wind. It might just as easily have been her shivering.

Both schools were good. Both took boarders as well as day pupils, she thought, with a sudden flash of hope. But she knew deep down that David wouldn't countenance that. In some odd way since coming back from the war, he wanted to make them all suffer. Either that or he wanted to control their lives, utterly and completely.

The children were as subdued and silent as she was. Geoffrey's school was first. He looked glum as he climbed out of the back seat.

'Be a good boy,' Charlotte said, making an effort to sound as genuinely cheerful as she always did.

'Yes, mother.'

Although she offered her cheek for the usual kiss, he ignored it and, like Shakespeare's schoolboy, crawled like a snail towards the school gates.

'Will we really have to go away to boarding school?' asked Janet once they'd arrived at her school.

Charlotte managed a smile before turning round. 'Nothing's settled, darling. You may not have to go at all.'

Janet scowled as she tugged her satchel out after her. 'I wish he'd never come back from the war. I wish he'd died!'

'Janet!'

The door slammed behind Janet, who did not look round. Charlotte sighed and gripped the steering wheel. It was hard to accept what was happening to her family. One thing she did know was that it had started on the day David had come home from the war. He was redefining his role in their world, redefining their role in his.

So far he had accepted that the work she was doing for the Red Cross and the Marriage Advisory Centres was still important, what with all the displaced persons and disordered family lives. But soon he would put a stop to it. She would be forced to relinquish this separate life she had so enjoyed while he'd been away. She understood what Janet was feeling because she felt a little of it herself. But it was no use dwelling on it. Today she was off to the POW camp out at Pucklechurch, a village on the edge of the city. The Red Cross was doing its best to repatriate German prisoners. There were papers to be filled in and collated, relatives to trace and permissions to gather. Europe was in turmoil, its cities flattened and millions dead. A shifting population drifted across each country searching for those they had once known.

The guard who scrutinised Charlotte's pass card was American. 'Carry on, ma'am. Adjutant's office is on the left-hand side.' He saluted her smartly as she pulled away and drove past the raised barrier.

The office was housed in a brick Nissen hut with a curving green tin roof that vaguely reminded her of the protective tunnels they used down in Cheddar to protect growing strawberries. Much smaller of course, but the same shape.

She and the family had spent a week's holiday in Cheddar before the war. She smiled when she thought of it: such a happy time for all of them.

'Delighted to meet you,' said the adjutant, an English officer who politely removed his cap and dusted off the chair he pulled out from beneath the desk. 'Hope this will do for you. Best we can offer, I'm afraid.'

'It's fine.'

'Tea?' he asked raising his eyebrows.

'Love one. Milk and one sugar.'

'Well, I'll go off and get you your cuppa while you see your first appointment, if that's all right with you.'

She smiled, said her thanks, set her brown leather briefcase down on the desk and took out the papers she needed. There were six prisoners of war to see.

'Morning, ma'am,' said the American corporal who escorted the first prisoner in. She was surprised at his being black, the only black man she'd seen in the whole camp. Throughout the war the American army had been noticeably segregated, the 'Jim Crows' being mostly used for supply, transport, and entirely black infantry battalions.

The prisoner, a thin man with a five o'clock shadow and heavy eyebrows, looked her up and down. She avoided his eyes and, for the umpteenth time that day, wondered if the navy blue suit with the peplum waist had been the right choice. After all, it wasn't as though these men had been cut off from women altogether. It had been explained to her before being assigned that these men were used to mixing in the community, helping on local farms and repairing local roads. Since VE Day they'd even been allowed to go to the pub.

'Do you have to stay, corporal?' she asked with a smile.

'That, ma'am, depends on your German.'

What a fool! She stopped herself from blushing but could have bitten off her tongue. Why had she presumed him to be merely a prison guard?

'I'm sorry. Most interpreters have been officers.'

'I almost used to be.'

She wondered at his reply and sensed the bitterness in his voice. None of your business, Charlotte, she told herself. You're here to do a job. She turned to the prisoner.

'Then let's continue, shall we? Now,' she said, smiling across at the prisoner. 'Your name, please?'

As promised, the tea came in at the same time as the next prisoner. The adjutant brought in both.

'You've met Corporal Grant, I see,' he said as he set the cup and saucer down. 'Everything all right, is it?'

She sensed what he was really asking her was did she mind working with a black man.

She smiled broadly. 'The corporal has been of immense assistance. Thank you.'

'Then I'll leave you to it.' He nodded at them both, tilted his cap then exited. The corporal glared after him before instructing the prisoner to sit down. For the first time she noticed that the flesh around one of the corporal's eyes was slightly darker than the other. There was also a graze on his right cheek. Had he been in a fight?

After the second prisoner had exited there was a gap before the third prisoner made his entrance.

'Tea, Corporal Grant?' She found a tin mug in the drawer of the desk. He nodded.

'Do you take sugar?' she asked.

'Everything, ma'am.'

She glanced up at him. 'Mrs Hennessey-White will do. I'm only a Red Cross worker, not a queen.'

He laughed and she managed to smile more broadly than she had all day. David was someone she'd left at home that morning and would return to later this evening. In the period in between she felt lighter, more alive and in charge of her own life.

'How do you feel about helping our ex-enemies get home?' she asked.

Corporal Aaron Grant swallowed his tea and shrugged. 'I don't feel aggrieved with them if that's what you mean. A few are real Nazi types but most are just ordinary men, dragged from their ordinary lives and told to go out, kill and get killed. All most of them want to do is get back to their homes, their factories and their farms.'

'So you don't hate them.'

'No.'

Charlotte sat back in her chair and folded her arms. 'They were pretty brutal towards the Jews.'

A serious expression came to Aaron's face. 'Moral victories can be used to jog consciences and there sure are a lot of them need jogging back home.'

Feeling suddenly uncomfortable she looked down into her tea. 'I hope you're right. You sound as if you're going to be a lawyer when you get back home.'

He shook his head and his face softened. 'A musician. I want to be a musician.'

'Have you a family back home?'

'If you mean am I married, then no. But I do have parents and two sisters. And before you ask, there's no lonely girl back there waiting for me. If there had been, thanks to Uncle Sam and Adolf Hitler and the length of this war, she'd probably have given up by now.'

'Lonely for you too, so far from home. Have you met anyone here?'

His whole face tensed. 'What's the point?'

He has met someone, she decided. No one could sound so bitterly frustrated unless something like that had happened.

She checked the details of the next prisoner: Josef Schumann, place of birth, Hamburg, date of birth, 12 March, 1910. She heard him enter.

'Are you the woman from the Red Cross?' His English had only a slight accent. Charlotte looked up in surprise. He had broad shoulders, a lean frame. Blue eyes looked boldly into hers and he held himself ramrod straight, the epitome of what a German officer was supposed to be. His service record stated that he used to be a U-boat commander.

Aaron got to his feet. 'This is Mrs Hennessey-White,' he said to the German. He turned back to Charlotte. 'You won't be needing my services with Joe, so if you don't mind...' He held up a pack of Lucky Strikes. Charlotte nodded and, as the door closed behind him, the tall German with the lantern jaw and the dark blond hair sat down. His smile was sardonic. As if we're all fools, thought Charlotte. She decided not to like him.

'Our corporal gets a bad time,' said Josef before she had asked him her first question.

'He's a well-educated man.' She knew she sounded defensive.

'I have watched them. They give him a bad time.' He tapped at his eye and cheekbone. 'If you know what I mean.'

She knew what he meant all right. But his attitude intrigued her. Was he merely playing a game or was he genuinely concerned at the way Corporal Grant was being treated?

A laconic grin seemed to drift over Schumann's lips. It was as though he had seen most of what the world had to offer and didn't think much of it. He didn't stare, but she got the impression he missed nothing.

She asked him to confirm his name, date of birth and his address.

'If it's still there,' he added with a shrug of his shoulders. 'I hear not much is left of Hamburg.'

Charlotte willed herself not to show any remorse for what her country had done to his. 'Nor Coventry.' It was out before she could stop it.

He seemed to ignore her comment. 'My parents used to have a bakery. I remember the smell of the bread drifting up into my bedroom around five o'clock in the morning and the bustling and banging from down below. I doubt if it's still there now.'

'Are you married?' she asked quickly, in an effort to quell the guilt she felt at his loss.

'I was. She's dead.' He stated it in a matter-of-fact manner as if no emotion was attached to the event.

'I'm sorry.' She stopped herself from asking how she died. It was irrelevant. All she was supposed to do for the Red Cross was to collect particulars and fill in the forms. They would do the rest over in Germany. But he made her feel uncomfortable. His eyes seemed to look straight through her.

'Before the war. Typhoid. And you?'

'Me?' His sudden question surprised her.

'Did your husband come home?'

She looked down at the forms as she nodded, pen in hand. 'Yes. Yes, he did.'

'He's not the same, is he? He never will be, you know. None of us ever will.'

Suddenly she felt an angry flush spread over her face. What right did he have to pry into her private life?

She gripped her pen with both hands and got to her feet. 'We're here to deal with your life, not mine!'

He was slower getting to his feet and when he did he towered over her by at least five inches. 'Have some more tea.' He nodded at the pot. 'Tea cures everything, doesn't it?'

He was mocking her. She felt her cheeks reddening and clasped them with both hands. Angry tears pricked her eyes. Her problems with David, especially when she was alone with him at night, suddenly seemed too much to bear. She took a handkerchief from her handbag and dabbed at her eyes. As she raised her arms the silk scarf she wore around her neck dislodged and slid to the floor. Josef picked it up.

He said nothing as he handed it to her but his gaze dropped to the latest bruise on her neck. The hostility left his face. Her eyes met his. Her voice was low, as official as she could make it. 'I have all the information I need. You can go now.'

He hesitated. 'I'm sorry,' he said.

This was just too embarrassing. She was here to help him! He was the one with problems, not her. At least, that was what she told herself.

She felt sure he would have lingered if it hadn't been for the return of Corporal Grant.

Josef left. Grant was perceptive. 'Are you all right, Mrs Hennessey-White?'

'Of course.' She swiftly retied the scarf around her neck. 'Let's get on, shall we?'

It was getting dark when she left, far later than she'd meant to. Luckily, she'd arranged a taxi for the children and Mrs Grey had promised to put in an appearance. But she had to get home before David.

Shadows fell across the uneven concrete surface where she'd left her car. The trees stirred slightly, their few remaining leaves floating like dislodged wings into dark puddles. One particular shadow seemed to be following her. She quickened her footsteps then told herself she was a fool to be frightened by childish terrors.

Her heels tapped a light constant beat. A heavier tread echoed her footfall. Boots! A man was following her.

'I am sorry about what I said earlier.'

She recognised the slight accent and spun round.

'I had no business upsetting you like that. Please accept my apologies.'

He came close to her. For a moment she was afraid, but in the chill glow of a nearby light she saw the sincerity in his face.

He shook his head, looked around him, up at the sky, down at the ground. 'All I want is to go home. We have all been injured by this war – all of us.'

'Thank you,' she said as she opened the door of her car.

'But you will be back?'

'Yes. I have more prisoners to see. The Red Cross needs all the help it can get.'

'Then I will see you again. When I do, I will make my decision whether to stay in this country or not.'

Charlotte stared at him. 'Stay here?'

'The adjutant says I can do this if I have nowhere to go back to.' He grimaced.

His face stayed with her all the way home. At first she had made up her mind to dislike him. Now she was not so sure. He seemed sensitive.

On the whole she had had a good day. This was the sort of work she was good at; listening, collating information, rebuilding people's lives. How could David not see that she was needed? It was women like her that would help the likes of Josef Schumann rebuild their lives. But how could she persuade David of that?

* * *

It was Charlotte who brought Polly the news that her husband had decided to give her a job at his own consulting rooms doing a bit of cleaning and a bit of office work – just general filing and answering the telephone. Charlotte beamed like a Cheshire cat as she prattled on about it. Polly had merely listened, smiling all the time though her teeth ached and she longed to tell Charlotte to shut up. Of course David was going to give her a job. She'd seen the look in his eyes when she'd protested that she didn't mind a bit of cooking but she'd always wanted to work in an office. Of course he didn't want her to be a cook in someone else's place. Of course he wanted her close to him. He'd try it on of course, but she could cope with that. Anything was better than going back into Woolworths.

'I could also do with some help at home. Would you object to sleeping over now and again when my housekeeper isn't available to do breakfast?' Charlotte asked, noticing the empty fire-grate in the front room at Aunty Meg's house. There was no doubt that Polly needed the money.

'I don't think that's a problem,' Polly replied.

Not a problem. Of course it wasn't a problem! Things were pretty comfortable where she was. Meg looked after her as well as looking after Carol but it was downright suffocating at times. A bit of a change, she told herself, was as good as a rest.

Things were looking up all round, she decided. Aaron was coming to Christmas dinner! The knowledge skipped as merrily through Polly's head as her feet did once she had stepped off the bus from Clifton. She had completed her first day at Dr Hennessey-White's consulting rooms. All she had done was clean a bit, write in a few notes and speak in as good an accent as she could to the patients she happened to bump into.

It was the best job she'd ever had, but she still told herself it was only temporary. Once she was married to Aaron she would give it up and move to America.

The bus had hardly moved away from the stop before a loud bang echoed around the tired streets.

A bomb! It was the first thing that came into her mind. Yet it wasn't loud enough and there was not enough vibration.

She ran along York Street, aware that the frontage of number 14 was better illuminated than usual. Light from bedrooms as well as front rooms shone from square paned windows and out into the street.

Shouts and hoots of laughter seemed to erupt from every house along the street. It couldn't be a bomb!

The outside door was, as usual during the day, wide open above the stout brass step.

She dashed in, calling out for Meg as she ran over the bare linoleum floor, but there was no answer, though she sensed movement somewhere out the back of the house. Polly glanced into the front room as she passed. No one was there. In the back room she stumbled over a pile of blankets, then steered a course through bundles, boxes and battered brown suitcases. They obviously had visitors. But who were they?

The yard seemed full of people, though it could only hold about six people fairly comfortably. They were all bent over, scrabbling at piles of something on the ground, gathering them up in their arms and tossing them into a cardboard box next to the clothes post.

Carol was sleeping in her pram in the scullery. It was a wonder she could sleep at all through this hullabaloo, thought Polly.

'Aunty Meg?'

A face lined with age but brightened by good providence looked up.

'Look,' said Meg, holding up a bunch of bananas as if it were the crown jewels. 'Bananas!'

Just as she spoke, there was a lot of shouting from the shunting yard at the back, voices full of Christmas spirit, definitely of the bottled variety.

Another bang was followed by another shower of the yellow-skinned fruit flying over the wall.

'Can you really eat them?' piped up a small voice. Polly recognised Alfie, her cousin Hetty's eldest boy.

And there was Hetty and there was Bertie, her old man, and the youngest kid, Stephen.

Meg told him he could.

'What are they doing 'ere?' Polly asked aggressively. 'And I don't mean the bloody bananas.'

'The landlord wanted them out,' Meg replied.

Polly couldn't believe it. 'They're staying 'ere?'

Meg folded her big arms across her ample breast and nodded. There was a warning look in her eyes. Polly ignored it.

'There ain't room. They'll 'ave to find somewhere else.'

Meg's expression darkened. 'Now look 'ere, my girl. They need someone and somewhere – just like you did.'

'All right Poll?' shouted Bertie as he and Hetty and the kids dived in among the new crop of free fruit.

Polly stormed off, purposely hammering the stairs up to her room and slamming the bedroom door. Then she saw that it wasn't her room any more. Her single bed was gone, replaced by a double bed squashed into the space between the dressing table and the wardrobe. She grimaced. No room to swing a bloody cat. She guessed the two kids would be joining Carol in the other room. That left her squeezing in with Meg on the single which, she surmised, was now cluttering up the front room.

Folding her arms, she gazed out of the window at the busy gatherings in all the backyards along the street. Bananas hadn't been seen since before the war.

She hadn't yet told Meg she'd invited Aaron for Christmas dinner. Another mouth to feed, but spam, chocolate, and silk stockings from what remained of US army stores would make it worthwhile. But she couldn't mention it with Hetty around. When she'd announced she was pregnant with Carol, it was Hetty who had looked down her nose at her as if she were some kind of tart who opened her legs for anybody. Unmarried mothers weren't quite nice, not even in a rough area like the Dings. A black boyfriend wouldn't be acceptable unless he became a husband. And even then...

Polly pulled the curtain across and immediately the scene outside the window ceased to exist. Yes, she knew what Hetty would say. 'Second best is all a girl like you with a kid can hope for.' And that was how she would view Aaron, as second best because he was black.

I'll never stick it, she thought to herself. Why the bloody hell did they have to come here? The place wasn't big enough. Then she thought about Charlotte's suggestion of staying in Clifton overnight. Suddenly it looked an attractive alternative.

* * *

Charlotte preferred to forget Christmas. Throughout the war years she had enjoyed the smells, the treats, even the tawdry trimmings. This year should have been more magical, the first of a new peacetime, but it didn't work out that way.

Hopes of trying to alter David's mind about sending the children to boarding school died with the old year. Amid tearful farewells the children were shipped off to boarding schools. The house echoed to memories. Silence lay heavily, even in the shards of sunlight where dust motes danced in mockery of her sadness.

She fingered the note in her hand. David had stood over her

while she'd written it. His presence had made her hand tremble but the words were still legible. The New Year already felt empty. No children, no job – or there wouldn't be once she'd handed the note over.

'Mornin', Mrs Hennessey-White.'

Charlotte looked up. It was Polly. 'Oh. I forgot it was Mrs Grey's day off. Thank you for stepping into the breach.'

Polly smiled. 'Glad to be of service, Charlotte.'

Charlotte smiled back as she got to her feet, though she felt slightly uncomfortable. On meeting Polly at the railway station it had seemed fine for her to call her by her Christian name. But to have a servant or employee of her husband call her that, seemed slightly strange. Imbued tradition, she thought wryly and went to the table to pick up her briefcase.

'Right, I'm off,' she said as she reached for her gloves – pale blue suede to match her dark grey suit. She didn't wait for Polly to say anything. There was too much on her mind.

'Cheerio!' Polly called.

Charlotte was too preoccupied to hear. If she had she might have avoided the hostility she instantly aroused.

Polly was already out of sorts with Hetty and her family moving in. Hetty made a point of putting her down. Now Charlotte had done the same thing. She grimaced at the door. 'Stuck up bitch!' Inside she wished with a passion that they could change places.

8

Josef was waiting for her at the main gate, his lean frame braced between two silver birches.

Her sensible side told her not to look in his direction. Even so she could feel his eyes following her. So be it. He'd be her first appointment of the day.

As it turned out Aaron Grant took that favoured spot. He was waiting for her by the hut door and opened it as she approached.

'Can I speak to you?' he asked.

Trouble clouded his eyes and she noticed a muscle twitching in his jaw. She also noticed a fresh bruise on his forehead.

'Of course you can.' Charlotte set down her briefcase and tried not to look at the crisp white note among all the other bits of paper she had in there. There was time for that later.

'You don't mind talking to me, do you?' Aaron asked.

'I'm here to help. You've got as much right to speak to me as anyone else.'

He looked down at the floor, hands shoved in pockets. 'I wouldn't count on it.'

Charlotte gestured to him to pull up a chair and studied him as he swung it towards the table. He was a big man, perfectly suited to military uniform, even though he was only a corporal. And yet she judged he was worth more.

She sat down and faced him. 'How can I help?'

Again and again he folded and unfolded his fingers over his knees. He looked at them thoughtfully. 'I want to get married.'

He said it softly, slowly, as if they were the most precious words in the world.

'You're old enough to do that without parental consent I take it?'

He nodded and nervously licked his lips. 'The problem is that she's one of yours – English.'

Charlotte laughed and allowed herself to relax. 'Lots of British girls have married Americans.'

A sardonic smile came to his face as he shook his head sadly. 'No black American soldier is allowed to marry a white girl, Mrs Hennessey-White. Only white men are allowed to do that.'

Charlotte tossed her head. 'Don't be ridiculous.'

He shrugged, his smile unchanged. 'Takes some believing don't it, Mrs Hennessey-White. Makes you wonder what we've been fighting for, huh?'

Charlotte hesitated to comment because she really did not believe him. It was just so unfair. 'I'm sure there must be a mistake.' Feigning concentration she fixed her eyes on the paperwork set before her and vowed to find out if it was true.

Aaron nodded silently as he got to his feet. 'Shall I send in your first appointment?'

She got the papers out of her briefcase. 'Please do.'

As she'd expected, Josef Schumann was first. She smiled up at him as if he were just another displaced person in need of help. He smiled back at her knowingly, with a look in his eyes that seemed to be asking her a question. *What are you going to do about it?* She remembered the scarf slipping from her neck and the pitying look he had given her. He knew her secret and it unnerved her. She put on a brave front.

'I've found your family. Your parents are in Potsdam. It appears they moved in with an uncle there after Hamburg was bombed. This is the address.' Without looking into his eyes she slid a note across the table on which someone at the Red Cross central sorting office had scribbled an address.

For the first time she sensed just how badly he was hurting inside. Now it was she that looked at him, mentally asking, *How are you feeling?* Potsdam was in the Russian sector, but he didn't refer to that.

'What about my sister?'

Charlotte delved into the pile of paperwork she'd set out before her.

'Erica?' she said, screwing up her eyes better to see the faint carbon copy of a piece of paper headed Export Visa Application. Her mouth went dry, making it necessary to clear her throat before she replied. 'She's applied to marry. An American soldier according to this.'

Josef smiled wanly and shook his head. 'First we fight. Then we...'

His eyes met hers. She blushed and looked away. 'I'm sorry,' he said. 'It's all so ironic.'

It wasn't easy, but she did manage to regain her composure.

'You told me last time that you were thinking of staying here. Is that idea still in your mind?'

The smile came back to his lips and the knowing look to his eyes. 'Certainly. I believe that the fact of my family being in the Russian sector would help. Of course it would also help if I married a British girl.'

'Yes. So I understand. Is that a possibility?'

There was no doubting the meaning in his look. 'If the right woman came along and was free to marry.'

Don't blush! Charlotte hid her discomfort by studying the mass of carbon copies, scribbled messages and stencilled notes sat before her.

'These things take time,' she said curtly. 'It could be a year before we get round to repatriating you. Things aren't good in Germany. Agriculture is destroyed. Food is scarcer than it is here and that's saying something!'

Josef got to his feet, all six foot of him towering over her. 'Nature provides. Isn't that what you English say?'

'What?' she stared at him, puzzled.

'I have a present for you,' he said, turning and making for the door. He returned with a brace of rabbits hanging from each hand. 'We are allowed to go out snaring some extra food. Sometimes it's pigeons, this week it is rabbits.' Charlotte got to her feet. 'But what about you?'

'Wednesday was a good day for hunting. These are extra.'

For the rest of the morning she worked like a robot. She did everything she was required to do with automatic precision but her thoughts were anything but precise.

The same officer who had taken charge of her induction on the first day brought lunch of cheese soup and raisin cake on a tray.

'British fare?' she asked him, her eyebrows raised after surveying the food.

'Afraid so,' he replied. 'Just as the camp is a mix of British and American, so is the food. Can't say I've come across cheese soup before. And hopefully, never again.'

She smiled and pushed the pile of official documentation to one side and, with an uneasy heart, added the white envelope containing her resignation. 'I'd like to see the commanding officer this afternoon. Would that be possible?'

'He's a busy man but I dare say I can swing something for you. I'll come back later if I manage to fix it. All right with you?'

'Yes,' she replied and although she knew the officer was waiting for her to invite him to stay, she bent her head and dipped her spoon into the uninviting off-white soup. However, she was grateful to him for getting her an appointment. The CO was a thickset man with a shiny head and small eyes. REUBEN M. COHEN stated the wooden plaque on his desk.

With gentlemanly politeness, he rose from his seat as she entered and came from behind his desk, offering his hand.

'Mrs Hennessey-White! Great to meet you. Please. Take a seat.' He was full of typical American warmth.

She did as ordered.

'Coffee? Tea?'

She shook her head.

He rested his backside against the desk, folded his arms and looked down at her. 'Ask me for whatever you want. Anything! Anything at all! If we haven't got it I promise I'll get it for you. okay?'

She smiled and nodded her appreciation. 'I have a question to ask.'

'Ask away.'

'Is there a law forbidding a Negro soldier from marrying a British girl?'

'Ah!' His jaw dropped slightly. 'I take it you mean there is.'

As if putting a barrier between her and the question, he went back behind his desk and sank heavily into his chair. 'In twenty-three of the states of the union, mixed marriages are forbidden.'

Charlotte eyed him accusingly. 'This isn't the United States, Commander. This is Great Britain. Those laws don't apply here.'

Cohen sighed heavily and clasped his podgy hands on his belly. 'Sure, this guy, whoever he is, could marry under your law. But as a serving soldier he'd need his commanding officer's consent and that would not be given. They'd end up having kids of mixed race. We have enough of our own mongrels in the States, Mrs Hennessey-White, without importing another batch.'

A flush of anger warmed Charlotte's cheeks. It was all she could do to stay sitting, to stay unflustered. 'We've been fighting a war against that sort of thing. I find your statement objectionable.'

Cohen leaned forward. 'Statement of the American Senate. No mixed race kids, period!'

Outraged, she sprang to her feet. 'So what was the damn point of it all! What was the point of millions dying for a cause!'

Too angry even to say goodbye, she stormed out, slamming the door behind her so hard that his nameplate became dislodged and rattled to the floor.

And his name's Cohen, she thought, as she made her way to her car. A Jewish name. Ironic, Josef had said. He was right.

Josef was leaning on her car. 'You forgot your rabbits,' he called as she made her way towards him. He held them high, floppy little bodies tied by their ears.

Words of thanks didn't come easily because her mind was preoccupied. All the hopes and dreams of a world at peace were turning into a nightmare. Rights and wrongs were not as clear-cut as the voices of leadership had led her to believe.

She was aware of him watching her, silently assessing her mood. 'There's a pub in the village,' he said suddenly. 'Too early yet, but perhaps, one night – a Tuesday or Wednesday maybe, at about seven.'

'Perhaps.' She secreted the game in the boot of the car then sat herself at the wheel. 'And I will be out again,' she blurted decisively. 'I'm bringing civilian clothes, things to make life a little easier for you while you wait to go home.'

'Wherever home happens to be,' he said solemnly.

'I must also see Corporal Grant again. I went to see the CO about him. He was not helpful.'

Josef's face darkened. 'You shouldn't have done that.'

'But someone had to do something,' she blurted. 'It's not a hanging offence, is it?'

'Not for you. But it could be for the corporal.' The way he spoke turned her blood cold.

He noticed her concern and rested his hand on hers. 'I will keep watch over him – as much as I can.'

She had no doubt of his capabilities and couldn't help but smile. But she'd seen the bruises on the corporal's face. It was worrying.

The car engine roared into life as her eyes met his. She saw warmth there, the sort she'd once seen in David's.

'I'll be seeing you,' she said softly and put her foot down on the accelerator, her heart racing in time with the engine.

Back in his office Reuben Cohen telephoned the guardhouse. 'Send Sergeant Noble into me will you? And then after that I want to see Corporal Grant.'

He reached into his humidor, a stupid gift from his wife shaped like an elephant – so he wouldn't forget her. As if he could! Women. They were all fools. He didn't like the natives coming in, demanding this and that and then storming out of his office. Grant was to blame. Had to be. And because of that he'd arrange for Sergeant Noble to give him something to remember him by.

* * *

Charlotte changed into a green dress of soft silk and pre-war length for dinner. She and David were going to dine in the great hall of the university's medical school, a glimmer of pageantry to light the drabness of real life. She spent time over her hair, added a touch of perfume and told herself over and over again that if she were overly pleasing at dinner, David would forgive her for not giving in her notice. After all, he'd got his way with regard to the children. And what would she do at home all day without them?

She decided to tell him while there were plenty of people about. He couldn't get angry then, could he? No doubt he would be angry but, hopefully, by the time they got home, he would have calmed down.

He'll understand, she reassured herself. He'll understand.

* * *

Edna felt her life was on tramlines and she was completely incapable of getting off to freewheel around on her own. On her way home from work she thought how best she could ask her mother the address of the orphanage where Sherman was. The child was now three months old and she badly wanted to see him, but up until now his whereabouts had remained a closely guarded secret.

It was her mother who had taken the child from the hospital where he'd been born and made the arrangements with the orphanage. She had cried bitterly, pleaded to keep him a little while longer, begged to know where he was, but her mother had stood firm.

'You've the rest of your life to think of,' she'd snapped. Ethel Burbage was a ramrod of determination and lack of emotion. All her life Edna had allowed herself to be moulded into whatever her mother wanted her to be. Each time she had tried to have a night out with the factory girls, or attempted to buy something outstandingly frivolous or deliriously sexy, her mother had come down on her like a ton of bricks. And a nauseating sensation of shame and fear came over her every time she tried to pluck up the courage to demand to know where Sherman was.

Only when she'd joined the ATS and had manned the search-light had she enjoyed some measure of freedom. It had been hard for Ethel to check whether her daughter had been on duty or not, and it was then that she'd met Jim and discovered a freedom she'd never experienced.

But once she'd got pregnant, her position had reverted to what it had always been. She was almost a prisoner. Not so much in her own home, but in the sense that the things she did had to mirror the things her mother would do in a similar situation.

There was no question of her not marrying Colin. Her mother had ordained that it should be so and the sooner the better. Basically, the case was that she had to marry where she could and as quickly as possible, just in case the truth came out. And in the meantime her child would remain in a faceless institution until, perhaps, someone came to adopt him. In the meantime she'd been told to get on with her life.

Her job typing invoices at the tobacco factory was hardly exciting but, as her mother kept telling her, it was far superior to working on a factory floor or being a shop girl. She was in the office and a better class of person worked there.

Colin had been kept very busy before Christmas, making toys to order from any bits of wood he could get hold of. He'd saved all the money he'd earned, insisting they'd need it if they were to marry in May as planned. 'No one wants toys in January,' he said, 'and my pension won't get us very far.'

It was a Tuesday night when she came home from work and another unwelcome command from Ethel.

A note was jammed in the letterbox. It said,

We're at the Smiths for tea. Join us there.

Her mother's writing. No please. No thank you.

When she got to Colin's house, both sets of parents were sat in the front room. Colin was in his wheelchair. He looked up at her as she entered, said hello, but both his voice and his smile were stiff. There was a look in his eyes that told her something was troubling him.

Despite it not being her house, her mother pointed to a chair. 'Edna! Sit down there and we can tell you what's been done.'

Colin's mother passed her a plate. 'Have a sandwich, dear. I'll pour you a cuppa. One sugar or two?'

'One,' said Edna swiftly, still wondering what was going on. She immediately turned back to her mother. 'What's been done?'

'The wedding arrangements.' A smile swept across her mother's face and stayed there stiffly like a warning. 'Now don't worry about a thing.' She glanced at Colin's parents who were looking decidedly uncomfortable. 'We're sharing the costs between us all. We've arranged the church, the reception and the wedding cars. You can wear my wedding dress. It's still good as new and you're about the size I was then. Then Gladys and I,' she said indicating Colin's mother, 'will go into town and choose some material for the brides-maids' dresses.'

Edna trembled with dismay. 'But I want to choose my own!'

The plate clattered to the floor along with the untouched sandwich.

Her usually meek and silent father dared to open his mouth. 'Now, now, Edna, if you don't like it...'

'She's got to like it!' interjected Ethel. 'Ungrateful little madam!' She sprang to her feet. 'Me and your father are willing to foot the bill along with Gladys and Fred here. You should be grateful, you should. In fact, you should be down on your bended...'

For once she found the courage to protest. 'No I shouldn't! It's my wedding. I want to organise it myself. I want to choose my own wedding dress, my own bridesmaids' dresses. I want to do everything myself!'

Her mother took up a threatening stance directly in front of her and wagged a finger in her face. 'Now, you look here my girl...'

'I'm going home!' Edna spun towards the door. It wasn't in her to fight and she didn't want to stay. Her mother grabbed her arm. 'Oh no you don't!'

Colin rolled forward. 'Leave her alone! If you don't leave her alone and stop yer bickering there ain't going to be any wedding!'

Everyone turned to Colin. Edna took advantage of the opportunity and ran out of the room, tears stinging her eyes. Back in her mother's house, she slammed the outer door behind her and leaned against it, squeezing her eyes and clenching her fists. Her anger was just too much to bear.

Slowly she opened her eyes to the oppressive browns of the hallway. Even the coats on the hallstand were shades of brown or beige, flecked wools or tweedy jackets. There was only one bright spot, one hint of brilliance. Like snowdrops peeping through the winter ground, an opened letter lay on the floor. It looked as if it had fallen out of the envelope.

Edna picked it up, her heart skipping beat after beat as she read the heading:

Muller Orphanage

And it wasn't that far!

She read the letter. It thanked her mother for the generous contribution of baby clothes she regularly made to them. Generous! It wasn't her being generous. It was the last thing she could ever be.

Because of her anger her first thought was to screw up the letter and throw it to the floor.

Think! Think ahead!

She wanted to see her baby. She wanted to know if he had his first tooth, how big he'd grown and whether he looked like his father. After memorising the address, she put the letter back where she'd found it.

In the solitude of her own bedroom she wrote the address in her diary then flung herself onto the bed and wished she was dead. What a mess she'd made of her life. A secret baby, marriage to a man with no legs, an act her mother was determined to make her go through regardless of whether she loved him or not. But everything had changed suddenly. There was now a chance that she could see her baby.

That night in the twilight realm between waking and sleeping she dreamed of her wedding; Colin in a suit with ribbons tied around the empty legs of his trousers, roses festooned all over his wheelchair. And herself, cheeks red, eyes wet, walking down the aisle wearing her mother's wedding dress that had been out of fashion since nineteen twenty-two. Rationing was still in force but that didn't mean she shouldn't have some choice.

Colin was waiting for her at the end of the street on Wednesday night. Although his chair was designed for pushing, his arms were still strong enough for him to propel himself forward by turning the extra rim he'd made and connected to his wheels.

'The worker returns bearing gifts,' he said merrily.

'How did you guess?' She managed to return his smile and tossed him a five of Woodbines – free issue for the week. They started walking – or at least she did.

'At least you're no sacrificial lamb.'

She frowned. 'What do you mean?'

'You refuse to be led to the slaughter. All that organising going on behind your back. And I didn't help.'

'What good's a mere man against my mother?'

When their laughter had died away, Colin came to a halt and

took hold of her hand. 'You don't have to go through with it you know. I would understand.'

She looked down at him. A mixture of guilt and hope swept over her. He'd given her a chance to escape but in her heart of hearts she knew she couldn't take it. Her son and his father had both been taken away from her. Colin was all she had left. Would the day ever come when she could tell him about Sherman?

She bent down and kissed his forehead. 'I've made my decision about marrying you. I'd also like to make my own decisions about the wedding.'

Colin visibly relaxed. 'It won't be easy. Your mother likes getting her own way.' He paused suddenly and snatched his hand away. 'Here! Does that mean you'll end up just like her when you're older.'

'I hope not!'

'Hope the kids don't either,' Colin added.

Edna's smile froze as she remembered the dark hair and coffee-coloured skin of the child that had been taken away, his chubby hands and his even temperament.

'No. I don't think they could be,' she replied, and hoped Colin didn't notice the tremor in her voice.

* * *

There were over one hundred guests at the reception to celebrate the homecoming of a number of top doctors in the Bristol area. The university dining room thronged with lately returned combatants, their faces a little more strained than before the war and their suits sharply cleaned and pressed for the first time since hostilities began.

David was exuberant. His natural charm was at full strength as he greeted old acquaintances and basked in the admiration of those who had not seen as much action as he had.

Only when they started asking him more in-depth questions about his escapades, particularly the more social side of his service, did his face stiffen and his voice sharpen.

'I hear Cairo is a beast of a place,' said one old surgeon, a very large whisky in one hand. 'Beastly things happen there.' He tapped the side of his nose. 'If you know what I mean.'

Charlotte, filled with apprehension, placed her gloved hand on David's raised arm. She felt the muscles harden. 'Can you get me a drink, darling? I'm terribly thirsty.'

The old surgeon, whose tongue was rapidly running out of control, turned to an equally elderly colleague who had no doubt spent his uniformed existence no further south than Surrey.

'Take no notice of him,' said a pleasant voice close to her side. 'His imagination is prone to run riot occasionally.'

'I won't,' she said, smiling as she turned to face the speaker. Her smile froze.

The speaker's mouth was crooked, his skin purpled and severely dimpled by burns. Eyelids as smooth and immobile as plastic seemed tautly stretched across his eyes.

'We've all been through a lot,' he said in a gentle voice. 'Even those who stayed in Blighty were under a fair amount of stress.' He nodded in the direction of the old surgeon who was now extolling the licentiousness of a Cairo he himself had never visited. 'He's glad he didn't go abroad but embarrassed about it.'

'My husband was sent to the Western Desert,' Charlotte said, once she'd got over the shock of his face. 'Then he was transferred to Singapore.'

'Not a healthy place to be.'

She asked him, 'Where were you when the war ended?'

'Hamburg,' he answered.

'Really?' He must have seen her puzzlement and went on to explain.

'I'm not a Jerry. I stayed behind with the wounded at Dunkirk and was promptly marched off to a POW camp.'

'Is that where you...' Charlotte began. She felt embarrassed asking.

He shook his head. 'No. As a doctor I was sent to Hamburg when the blanket bombing started – Americans by day, RAF at night. I got caught in a firestorm. Still, marvellous what they can do nowadays, isn't it?'

At that moment David came back with her drink. The disfig-ured surgeon shook hands and exchanged pleasantries before drifting off.

Charlotte watched him go, feeling sadly inadequate and extremely grateful. What were her problems compared to his? Her own, personal domestic bliss had gone with the war. That man had lost a lot more. So why should she be frightened of telling David that she was not giving up her Red Cross and counselling work? She took the plunge.

'I didn't give my notice in,' she blurted, sounding braver than she actually felt. 'I want to continue.'

His face seemed to turn to stone.

Charlotte took a deep breath. 'I don't care what you say, David or what you do. I have to have some purpose in life and without the children...'

'Ah! So we're back to that,' he growled.

Charlotte glanced round at the assembled crowd. How long would it be before someone realised that one of their most eminent members was arguing with his wife?

'David!'

The intervention of another old acquaintance saved the day. For the rest of the evening an uneasy truce held. It wasn't until they were in the car driving home that the storm finally broke.

She knew it was going to happen the moment he turned onto Durdham Downs and toward the sea walls that bounded the cliffs along the Avon Gorge.

'Please, David,' she began, her stomach tightening with fear. She had recognised another of his mood swings and guessed what was coming next.

He switched off the engine. His hand stung her cheek and there was a slight click of neck bone as her head went sideways.

She willed herself not to cry, instead she fought, not caring what anyone might say if they saw a bruise on her face or her neck. But David was devious. So far no one had noticed a thing – except Josef.

'You are my wife and will do as I say!' he snarled.

His hands were around her throat. Her head was bent back as his alcoholic breath smothered her face.

'I'm not your slave!' she managed to say.

She struggled, clawed at his hands as they almost choked the breath from her body. Just when the whole world seemed to fade into night, his hands left her throat. 'You're mine!' he mumbled against her ear as his hands tore at her clothes and he pushed between her legs. 'You do as I say and don't you forget it!'

There was a ripping sound as the silk dress was torn from knee to waist. She cried out as his fingers ripped at her underwear and bruised the soft flesh of the inside of her thighs.

An odd thought occurred to her. If it had been anyone else this would be called rape. But this was her husband and in law there was no such crime.

* * *

Polly held the door open for them when they got home. Just lately she'd started staying overnight, glad to escape the overcrowding down at York Road now Hetty and her lot had moved in.

'Let's have a nightcap,' David shouted and strode purposefully to the study. Charlotte followed unwilling to cause a scene. Aware that Polly's eyes were following her, she grasped her coat firmly so that it wouldn't fall open and expose the fact that her clothes were ripped to shreds.

Once the door was closed he started on her again. 'Don't defy me, Charlotte.'

'David. There are a lot of people needing help nowadays.'

'It doesn't have to be from you.'

She raised her voice. 'But I want to help! What else is there for me to do all day alone in this house.'

David swigged back the gin he had poured and threw the tumbler onto the floor.

'Women like you!' he growled.

Uncomprehending, she frowned. What did he mean women like her?

'I saw a woman like you destroy a good man. A very good man. And all because he took pity on her life behind a wall. But they're right you know, those Libyans. Women should know their place, then there would be no problems.'

Polly's ear was close to the door and her sympathy was entirely with David. What the hell was the matter with Charlotte, the silly cow! What *she* wouldn't only give to pack in work and stay at home all day with someone to come in and clean and cook and do all the nasty domestic things she particularly hated.

'Woman don't know when she's bloody alive!' She whistled as she went up the stairs to the yellow distempered room at the back of the house, a cool oasis from the haphazard arrangements at York Street.

Christmas with Aaron had consisted of walking through the city centre, dodging the piles of rubble and twisted metal, all that remained of Bristol's old tramway. It hadn't mattered that there was no Christmas dinner. Anyway, all Meg could provide was a small chicken and a Christmas pudding made of breadcrumbs, saccharine and any bits and pieces of fruit, including discarded orange peel, that she could find.

As it turned out Aaron brought food from the base, slices of tinned turkey meat and Christmas cake flown in from the States but had declined to enter the house and stay for a meal.

It had suited Polly. 'Don't blame you now Hetty and all 'er kids 'ave moved in,' she said, as the noise of children shouting, laughing and crying spilled out into the street. One of them had been Carol.

She'd left the supplies with Meg and marched off with Aaron. So far she had avoided mentioning the fact that she had an illegitimate child. There was plenty of time yet.

Number 14 York Street was now severely overcrowded. Hetty and Bertie slept in Polly's old room, the kids were in with Carol, and she'd been expected to share a bed with Meg in the front room downstairs. It wasn't that she didn't love Meg. She was a good woman. But blimey, there had to be a line drawn somewhere.

Never mind, she said to herself with a smug smile as she took off her dress and hung it on a hanger on the wardrobe door. You've got a date with Aaron on Friday and you know damn well that he's going to ask you to marry him.

Stripped down to her brassiere and bloomers, she stretched her arms wide and did a quick twirl. 'Look out America! Here I come!'

9

Rain spewed from gutters and gurgled down drains.

Polly hopped from one foot to another. Her shoes were sodden, her hat was limp at the edges and a decorative feather flopped over one eye.

'Great George', the bell in the university tower that could be heard all over the city, confirmed eight o'clock. Aaron *had* said seven-thirty.

There were lots of excuses for him being late. Perhaps the bus had broken down. Perhaps he'd got extra duties.

Two off-duty sailors strolled by, eyed her up and down and slipped her the wink.

'Fancy a good time?' one of them said.

She tossed her head. 'Not with you I don't.'

They shrugged and strolled off. At one time she'd have decided to forget her absent date and go and enjoy herself. In the case of Aaron she found it impossible. What if he found out she'd been drinking with other men? He wouldn't kill her or hurt her. She was pretty sure of that. But he would be upset, she just knew he would.

Funnily enough she would be too. He meant too much to her to spoil it now. He was her passport to a better life.

So she stood and waited some more. Great George struck nine.

'Damn the bastard!' she muttered under her breath. Spirits low and coat wet, she turned to go home.

She headed for Old Market, not caring that more water filled her shoes and ran down her neck. Head down, she barged through the crowds coming out of the Kings' Picture House and would have charged onwards if she hadn't met an obstruction.

'Polly?'

She recognised Edna and Colin, whose wheelchair she had unseeingly barged into.

Wary that they'd ask her where she'd been, she got in first. 'Hello. Been to the pictures then? Good, was it?' She nodded at the billboard advertising *Brief Encounter*. 'I hear it's romantic. Is that right then?'

Colin smirked wickedly. 'Saucy more like! Love between two married people, who aren't married to each other. Hanky panky!'

Playfully Edna smacked his shoulder. 'Colin!'

'There's been a war on,' Colin protested. 'Lots of things happened that shouldn't have happened and straying off the straight and narrow ain't nowhere near the worst of it.'

Edna ignored his comment and asked the question Polly had been dreading. She hated being stood up, no matter what the reason. 'Have you been anywhere nice?'

'Working,' Polly said brightly. 'You know I do a bit now for Charlotte and David, don't you?'

'Doctor and Mrs Hennessey-White?' Edna never could get used to calling Charlotte by her first name. 'I haven't seen her for a while.'

'Still busy with her Red Cross stuff and all that. Don't know why she bothers though with the house that she's got and the money he makes. Give me half the chance and I'd change places with her like a shot!'

'She likes helping people,' Edna said, and couldn't help sounding defensive. Charlotte was a bit of a busybody, yet she was basically kind-hearted.

'Care for a drink?' Colin piped up suddenly. 'So long as we can find a pub with a wide enough door to get me and the old Wells Fargo express through the door!'

Polly thought about refusing but then thought of the conditions back in York Street. God, if she'd known that swine wasn't going to turn up she'd have stayed overnight up in Clifton. At least it was quiet and there was no doubting that David Hennessey-White appreciated her being around. Never mind. She'd just been offered an alternative.

'Love to!' she said.

Because the Stag and Hounds dated from medieval times, its door was wide enough to take a horse and trap.

Colin was an avid collector of trivial information, and imparted some of it to Polly and Edna as they went in.

'Stables used to be out the back so they brought the horses through here. And the pigs for slaughtering out back. Nobody was too fussy in those days.'

Polly wanted to say you haven't met Bertie and Hetty. They're not too fussy either. But she held her tongue, took off her hat and shook the water out of it.

Colin bought the drinks. Polly had a small stout, Edna a port and lemon.

Colin made himself comfortable behind a pint of beer and explained how the staff in the Kings' Picture House over the road had carried his wheelchair up the stairs then set him down in the front so he had the best view in the house. Edna sipped her drink quietly. Polly did the same and as she did so noticed a man at the bar was looking over at them.

He didn't look like a local, mainly because his suit was well cut, and his trench coat looked to be a genuine Burberry.

Well, so what? she said to herself. You're spoken for. Remember?

She dragged her gaze away from him and asked Edna and Colin about the wedding. They said it was set for May. Edna looked a little strained as she said it. 'You'll have to come,' she said.

'Couldn't keep me away.'

'I've asked Charlotte and the doctor to come too,' said Edna, her eyes shining brightly.

As if they're bleeding royalty, thought Polly.

She then made her excuses to go to the ladies. When she came back out she wasn't surprised to be apprehended by the well-dressed man she'd seen standing at the bar.

She folded her arms and looked at him defiantly. 'Whatever's on yer mind the answer's "no"!'

'You rate yerself too highly, my love. All I wanted to know is whether that bloke you're with lost his legs in the war?'

Slightly abashed, Polly unfolded her arms. 'Oh! Yes. He did.'

'Poor sod. I thought so. Wouldn't be offended if I bought 'im a drink would 'e? Only I know the pension ain't much and jobs for the likes of 'im are just about non-existent.'

Polly couldn't help getting defensive. 'He's not an idiot, you know! He can make toys.'

He slid his hat to the back of his head. 'Can he now! Well that's interesting.'

To her surprise he went straight to their table. Polly followed.

He thrust his hand in front of Colin's chin. 'How do you do, chum. Billy Hills is my name and I'd like to buy you a drink.'

Colin's jaw hardened. Somehow Polly knew he'd respond like that. He might not be whole but he certainly had his pride.

'I don't need charity!'

'And I don't give it,' replied Billy Hills as he pulled a chair up to the table. 'Get the drinks in, girl,' he said pushing a ten-bob note into Polly's hand. 'I want to talk business.'

Both Colin and Edna seemed entranced by the time Polly got back to the table. Billy Hills was still talking.

'Now it's goin' to be a bloody long time, 'scuse me language, until the big toy makers get back into production, specially the Jerry ones. Good toys they used to make. But even British producers went over to war work. Torpedoes instead of train sets, you might say.'

Polly set down the drinks and offered Billy the change. 'Keep it, love,' he said without even looking up at her.

Flash, she thought. He's trying to impress me. I don't care what he said, he's fancying his chances.

They were still in the Stag and Hounds at closing time. But not once did Billy Hills try it on. She was only slightly disappointed. Just as she'd guessed, he wasn't local. He was from Bedminster on the south side of the city near the tobacco factories, a fact he was imparting to Colin and Edna and saying how useful it would be seeing as he didn't live too far from them.

She didn't concentrate too much on the rest of it. He wasn't her type. Okay for money but had no class. Bit of a wide-boy in fact. Besides, Aaron could offer her America. No one else could offer her that.

But she was worried. Why hadn't he turned up? What had happened to him?

* * *

'You can come shopping with me.' It was Saturday morning and Ethel Burbage was already plunging the pearl-ended pin into the crown of her dark brown hat. Her voice was as firm as her grip.

Edna made an attempt at rebellion. 'I thought you were going to play whist at the Baptist Hall afterwards?'

Whist was the last thing Edna wanted to get involved with; middle-aged men and women, all concentrating on a game that seemed to her to hold little excitement.

'You can walk on back with some of the shopping.'

Edna became aware that her mother was looking at her quizzically.

'You're looking happy. Blooming in fact. Is there something you think I should know about?'

Edna blushed. 'No! Of course not.'

She knew what her mother was referring to. Had she and Colin gone too far. They hadn't. It was just that Billy Hills had made them a certain proposition and it was like the answer to their prayers. On top of that she now knew where her baby was. All she had to do was plan how to get to see him.

They walked into East Street, Bedminster, a busy thoroughfare of shops, buses and factories. It was a lively, noisy place.

Next to the public toilets and the London Inn were the street traders. Barrows were piled high with beetroot, potatoes, cabbages, and mountains of swede, the latter used in some of the most stomach-churning recipes ever invented. The thought of those meals caused her almost to envy the skewbald horses that drew the carts, their muzzles permanently enclosed in feedbags that looped around their ears.

Greengrocer, butcher and baker; they went to each one, mostly standing outside in the queue, ration book at the ready.

The conversations going on around them were about continuing shortages.

'Rations! I thought the war was over.'

'Swedes don't come in ships. Plenty of those around,' said a woman with no teeth, a fag hanging out of the corner of her mouth.

She wore a checked woollen scarf over a head bristling with metal curlers, her appearance enough to frighten off a battle fleet!

For five years the conversation had altered little. Edna was glad when they at last got to the Baptist Hall.

'Take these.' Her mother gave her the heaviest two of the four bags. 'I'll see you later. Make sure your father's been fed by the time that I get back.'

The bags were heavy and although she could have made her way home straightaway, she didn't. Thinking of Billy Hills and his offer to Colin made her light on her feet.

Her step grew even lighter as she approached a turning just before Sheene Road where a bomb had destroyed a building and the bombsite had been cleared by virtue of the black marketeers. Even before she got to it she could see the crowd of people and hear Billy Hills shouting out the prices of the goods he sold from the back of an old van.

'I've got plans,' Billy had told them. He'd also informed them he had a dicky heart which was why he'd not been accepted for active service. It was an old excuse but they needed his help so they chose to believe it.

Her eyes met Billy's as she walked past and she fancied he gave her a barely perceptible nod. She smiled. Her mother wouldn't approve of him. His clothes were too good, his eyes too quick and too dark. But he seemed like a fairy godmother to her.

Her spirits were high so she walked further than she had intended. She passed the police station, which vaguely resembled a small, square castle, crossed Bedminster Bridge and went up Redcliffe Hill where the Tudor-style spire of St Mary's parish church stood sentinel over the muddle of old shop roofs. The rich aroma of good food steamed into the air as she passed the faggot and pea shop, its bow front hardly changed since the seventeenth century.

Edna licked her lips, but it wasn't food she was looking at. On the left-hand side was a wonderful shop with curved glass windows to either side of its wide doorway and a central glass-covered podium from which a plaster bride stared out at the world.

Gorgeous wedding dresses adorned each of the side windows. They were far beyond her price range of course, but if Billy could do all he said he could, she might at least be able to get enough ration books together for a bit of decent material and make a copy.

Beautiful, she thought, as her gaze swept over gowns that seemed part of another world, one that had existed before austerity and blackouts. They took her breath away. She pressed her palm flat against the window and could almost imagine she was touching them.

I can just imagine myself dressed in that one there, a veil over my face and Colin standing...

Her thoughts stopped there. Colin would never be standing at her side. He would be in a wheelchair for the rest of his life.

A strange coldness seemed to take her over. Her hand dropped to her side. For all her married life she would go to bed with a man with no legs. Images of what those hidden stumps might look like had so far been kept firmly at bay. But one day soon she would have to confront them – or not marry him.

Her spirits dropped. Her fears grew. She cared for Colin. She knew she did. But did she love him or was it merely pity she was feeling? On top of that there was her shame and guilt, which her mother had used to make her keep her vow to Colin.

Absorbed in her thoughts, she didn't see the door swing open or the smart woman dressed in a brown suit with black velvet detail who came out carrying two large bags. 'Edna! Now don't tell me! Which one are you going to have?'

'Mrs Hennessey-White – Charlotte!' said Edna swiftly correcting herself before Charlotte did.

'Lovely, aren't they?' said Charlotte, her voice mellow with admiration.

Edna turned her face back to the window. 'I suppose they are.'

'You don't sound very convinced. Having problems?'

'Well...' Edna began.

'I see. Pre-marital nerves. I think you need a heart-to-heart talk with a long-married woman. How about a cup of tea?'

Charlotte looked as if she wouldn't take no for an answer.

'That would be lovely,' said Edna. And it would. She wasn't going to say anything silly. Just have a cup of tea. The teashop door had an old-fashioned bell that jangled on a coiled spring as they pushed it open. A waitress zig-zagged through the closely packed tables to get to them.

Charlotte ordered. 'Tea for two. Biscuits would be nice if you've got them.'

'Certainly, madam,' said the waitress. 'But we only have digestives. Is that all right, madam?'

Charlotte told her it was.

They took a seat by the window. They could watch the new double deckers crawl up past the ornate Victorian tram supports that had once carried the electric wires and now merely stood like leafless plants in the middle of the road.

The tables were covered with white cloths. Brass bits and pieces hung from the walls and the white crockery clinked pleasantly around them. Sugar lumps were not left in a dish on the table. Two were supplied in each saucer when the tea arrived at the table.

'That's why I ordered biscuits,' stated Charlotte with an amused grin. 'One lump for the first cup of tea. One for the second. The biscuits make you believe you've used more than that.'

She proceeded to pour.

'Now, Edna. Tell me what you're so worried about.'

Edna felt Charlotte's eyes on her as she pushed the cup and saucer across the table.

'Well... it's difficult.'

Charlotte leaned closer and in a low voice said, 'Is it about the first night? Is that it?'

Staring into her tea, Edna shook her head. 'No. It's nothing like that. Not really.' She sighed, not wanting to tell anyone because, in truth, she hated hearing the words herself. But wasn't it only fair – both to herself and Colin – that she question her motives? A second opinion could be very helpful.

'I feel confused,' she blurted, her hands grasping her cup tightly. 'Am I marrying him for the right reasons? He's changed. I've changed.'

'Oh!' Charlotte said it softly, as though she understood completely.

'I hope I love him. I care for him. I know that. But do I love him enough to marry him or is it merely pity?'

Charlotte looked away, silently readjusting the yellow scarf she was wearing. Edna assumed she was thinking her own thoughts, probably feeling thankful that her husband had returned from the war unscathed.

Charlotte cleared her throat. 'Did you love him before he went?'

Edna nodded, looked down at the soft brown of the milk-starved tea, her hands clasped nervously together. 'He's always been around. We'd both always taken it for granted that we would marry. So did our parents. But so much happens in war, doesn't it?'

It was hard to finish an outpouring once it started, but Edna knew it had to happen. She'd tell so much, but she couldn't, mustn't, tell all.

'Just me being silly I suppose,' she said with a nervous laugh. 'But I want to be sure.'

Charlotte patted her hand. 'Of course you do. Is there anything else you want to ask me?'

Edna shook her head. 'Have you bought some lovely things?' she asked, in an effort to turn the conversation in a different direction. She nodded at the carrier bags nestling at the side of Charlotte's chair.

'Bits and pieces,' said Charlotte, delving into one of the bags and bringing out a bundle of muslin, cotton, silk and linen scraps. 'The bridal shop gave them to me. I'm setting up a little sewing group to make baby clothes for one of the orphanages.' A watery look came to her eyes. 'Not that many of them are true orphans. Most are put up for adoption or otherwise by girls and women with no men to support them. Some of the mothers are unmarried and wanting to restart their lives. Some are married and in a hurry to get the unwanted child out of the way before the husband comes back from the war.'

Edna felt the colour drain from her face. In her hurry to appear unaffected by Charlotte's statement she reached swiftly for her cup, clumsily hit the handle and sent tea into the plate of biscuits.

She sprang to her feet. 'I'm so sorry!' Charlotte called for a waitress and apologised.

Edna offered to pay for her clumsiness. Charlotte was having none of it.

'My treat,' Charlotte said once they were outside after having had a second cuppa and a fresh plate of biscuits. 'Can I give you a lift?'

Edna's first inclination was to refuse. From across the road the bells of St Mary Redcliffe pealed merrily, announcing that another man and woman had promised to love, honour and obey. According to the church clock it was twelve-thirty, just enough time to get back in time for her father's midday meal. 'I'd be very grateful,' she replied.

Charlotte did most of the talking on the way home. Edna sat almost tongue-tied, thinking about what Charlotte had said and the name of the orphanage on the letter she'd found earlier that week.

'We get a nice little bundle of clothes together before I take it to the Muller Orphanage. So if at any time you have some free time and don't mind doing a bit of sewing – especially once you're married – I'd much appreciate your help.'

The moment Charlotte said the name of the orphanage, a window opened on Edna's life. Providence! First she'd found the letter from the orphanage and at last knew where her child was. Now Charlotte was offering to take her there.

'I'd love to!' she said with honest enthusiasm. 'I'd really love to.'

* * *

Charlotte glanced in the side mirror and watched Edna striding to the front door of the house in Nutgrove Avenue. Strange how she'd gone so pale back there in the teashop when she'd mentioned the orphanage and the babies. Strange too how much colour had now come back to her cheeks. *A dark horse.* Was it possible that Edna had more than one reason for having second thoughts about marrying Colin?

She unwound the window and sighed heavily as she made her way through the Tramway Centre, which had now gone over completely to buses. She wound it up again as the yeasty smell from Georges' Brewery flooded through the window.

The engine slowed as she hit the uphill gradient of Park Street. She didn't mind. Going home was not something she wanted to do quickly.

* * *

It was a long journey to the prisoner of war camp at Pucklechurch and if Tommy Adams hadn't offered her a lift on the back of his motorbike, Polly would never have got there before noon.

A brisk breeze was blowing, reddening her cheeks and sending her hair flying.

'I won't be long,' she called over her shoulder as she made her way to the guard post.

The American guard on duty did a second take. Cows outnumbered blondes in Pucklechurch and those women that did live roundabout had more muscles than sophistication.

'I want to talk to Aaron Grant.'

The guard purposely turned his back. 'He's not here. Goodbye.'

Polly drew herself up to her full height. 'You ain't looked.'

He turned back to face her. His smile had disappeared. 'What's he to you?'

When she'd first got off the motorcycle he'd looked at her appraisingly. Now he regarded her with contempt.

'I'm his fiancée!'

The guard outside exchanged looks with another man who stuck his head up from behind a glass partition.

'Send her in here, private.'

The guard moved aside. Polly brushed past, deliberately sticking her elbow out at an awkward angle so it caught him fair and square in the ribs.

The American sergeant sitting at the desk flung his pen down as she entered but did not get to his feet. 'Sergeant Noble. At your service. And what can I do for you, little lady?' He did not smile.

'I want to see my fiancé. We've got things to discuss.'

'Have you now?' His tone was overly sarcastic. 'And what kind of things might that be?'

Polly held her head high. 'Wedding plans!'

The sergeant smiled and shook his head some more. 'Not with

him you don't. He's been shipped back to the States and I can cate-
gorically state here and now that there ain't no way you and him are
ever going to be married!'

Polly couldn't believe the cheek of the man. 'What the hell's it
got to do with you?'

'Blame Uncle Sam, little lady, but don't blame me.'

'But he can't be gone. Not without me; not without saying goodbye.' She knew she sounded hysterical. But hell, she had every right
to be.

The sergeant started to turn his attention back to the buff-
coloured folders on his desk. 'The US army judged it best in the
circumstances.'

Polly stood her ground. 'I want to speak to someone in charge.'

The sergeant looked amused. 'The commanding officer is a little
busy at the moment. Now if you'd care to leave my office...'

Still Polly didn't move. 'Then tell me who I can talk to.'

The sergeant picked up his files and shuffled them like a pack of
over-sized playing cards. 'Have a talk to the Red Cross lady.' He
fingered a piece of paper in front of him. 'Her name is Mrs
Hennessey-White. She's the one who brought a certain matter to
the CO's attention.'

'Charlotte!' Polly could hardly believe it. Charlotte had broken
up her romance. Charlotte who had seemed to be her friend.

She walked silently back to where her lift was waiting, her eyes
flinty hard and her heart like lead. Everything she had dreamed of
sharing with Aaron was no more than a fantasy.

Despite the breeze stinging her face on the way home, Polly
boiled with anger. How dare Charlotte interfere! She had no right!
Supercilious cow!

What was it with these classy broads that caused them to stop
the likes of her from getting on in life?

Jealousy! Just sheer jealousy!

Well, she'd be having a word with her when she got to work on Monday. Mrs Grey was back and doing Sunday. But she'd be there on Monday regardless, you bet if she wouldn't!

Josef Schumann watched as Polly re-mounted the motorbike. He badly wanted to tell someone of what he suspected had happened to Corporal Grant. But he had no real proof. Falling down a flight of stairs could be as fatal to a German prisoner of war as it was for a soldier who had stepped out of line – and far easier to get away with.

10

Sunday evening. The house was completely empty.

David had left for a BMA conference in London. The Government was intent on bringing in a national health scheme for the benefit of all, but the BMA was sceptical of how it might benefit their members. Their private fees would be affected, their standard of living reduced, went their argument.

Charlotte was glad of the respite. Tonight she would be alone. Inevitably, her thoughts turned to Josef. She'd seen him a number of times now. On the last occasion he'd appeared anxious, as though something was weighing heavy on his mind. She had found herself desperate to know what was wrong but he wouldn't tell her and wouldn't say why.

There was undoubtedly something special between them. It was like an electric current, unseen but dangerously powerful. At times she could almost guess what he was thinking about her. Sometimes it made her blush. For the most part it made her want to hug him.

Go to the pub. He asked you to.

The thought came unbidden, but instantly goaded her into

action. It was a fine evening, chilly but promising spring just over the horizon.

She drove out through Kingswood and across Syston Common. Timid greenery was just starting to push its way through. Seeing it and smelling it cleared her head of ugly things like husbands who were not quite as they had been.

She passed the POW camp and made straight for the pub, parking her car on the road outside.

She paused at the door. Her head told her she was being a fool. Her heart told her that caution was the sensible refuge of the emotionally infirm.

In one swift movement she reached out, then, having second thoughts, curled her fingers into her palm. What if he wasn't there? What if he was with some of the others and people saw them? What would they say?

Swiftly, before her head again ruled her actions, she pushed the door open.

The lounge bar was a place of dark brown woods and Windsor chairs. It was easy to imagine it in times gone by, men straight from hunting sitting in here, church-warden pipes clenched between uneven teeth, cheeks red from too much port. Drinks were served through a small hatch roughly cut into an expanse of stained panelling.

He saw her before she saw him. At first she blanched visibly. He was with some of the others, each with a pint in front of them. He got up when he saw her and walked over. There was no doubting his pleasure.

'Charlotte.'

He'd taken to calling her that on the last few occasions they'd met.

He repeated her name as though enjoying the sound of it and the way it rolled off his tongue. 'Charlotte. Can I get you a drink?'

She nodded, then realised her mistake. 'Let me! Please! Take this.' She handed him two half crowns. She looked up at him and said in a low voice, 'You haven't much money. If you buy it I won't drink it.'

He thought about it for a moment, then smiled and nodded.

She watched him walk to the bar, unable to take her eyes off him.

He came back with the drinks. 'How did you know I'd be here on a Sunday night?'

She shook her head. 'I didn't.' She felt herself blushing.

'We all need to get away some time. I'd certainly like to! But...' He laughed and shrugged helplessly. She laughed with him.

Their conversation consisted of questions about each other's lives – small things really; childhood, favourite things, hopes for the future, all the things that matter as two people get to know each other better.

He also told her about being a submariner, the close confinement of life in a metal can lurking beneath the waves, watching for enemy merchant ships. She found it hard to equate this man with that life.

He seemed more at ease than when she'd last seen him. She wondered what had been troubling him and asked him outright.

He looked swiftly away. 'Nothing I can do anything about.'

She didn't push the point but sensed intuitively that it had something to do with Aaron.

Time seemed to fly. 'Another drink, Charlotte?'

The way he said her name sent a thrill down her spine. David used to make her feel like that in the days before the war. Now he only scared her. The fear of what he might say if he found out she'd been drinking with another man, and an enemy at that, made her spring suddenly to her feet.

'I'd better be going.' She made for the door.

Josef returned the glasses quickly to the bar then followed her out. 'You can't escape them,' he said once they were outside.

She stopped by the car, a thudding in her head. 'Escape what?' The blush on her cheeks seemed to spread over her body.

He came closer and ran his hand up and down her arm. 'Your emotions.'

She took a deep breath. 'I'm married, Josef.'

'But not happy.'

'He's just got back from the war. It takes time to readjust.'

Josef sighed. He hung his head mournfully and leaned against the car. 'If ever. Everything that has happened to us is now part of us. It wasn't just buildings that got knocked down.'

'There's a lot of rebuilding to do,' said Charlotte resolutely, refusing to acknowledge that he was referring to people's lives.

'Charlotte,' he said, taking her face in his hands. 'For the rest of our lives we will reap what those terrible years have sown. Do not expect things to return to what they were. They won't. Not ever.'

She braced herself, sure he was going to kiss her. But instead he sighed and leaned back against the car, a melancholy figure who suddenly looked smaller than he actually was.

The old Charlotte, the one who had taken on the troubles of her school friends, now took over.

'This won't do! We should be feeling glad to be alive. It's almost spring. I could see it everywhere as I came across the common. I can show you if you like.'

'It's too dark.'

'Then you can smell it,' she said in the sort of voice she'd used when she was head girl and out to boost morale. 'I insist.' She unlocked the car door. The journey proved silently expectant.

There was a moon hanging low over the common, the grass touched silver by its magic glow.

They opened the windows. Charlotte still encouraged. 'Breathe it in.'

'You're right,' he said. 'It does smell of spring and we should be grateful for all the precious moments yet to come.'

She took another deep breath before she realised that he was looking at her as he said it and not at the view. She would never recall the exact way it happened but the next moment she was in his arms. His kiss was gentle yet full of passion. His arms were strong and her nipples hardened as he clasped her tightly to his chest. Yet she felt no shame at such a physical reaction. She wanted him.

His voice was low against her ear. 'Charlotte, you give too much of yourself and your advice to everyone else and keep none for yourself. Stop living other people's lives and start living your own.'

His words struck a deep chord within. Suddenly she didn't care about being married, about David and what he wanted. All that mattered was feeling safe and having a moment for herself.

Time flew. By the time she'd dropped him back at the camp it was ten-thirty. By the time she got home it would be gone midnight. Not that it worried her. There was no blackout any more. Lights twinkled from isolated cottages in the countryside around her and from the city that sprawled like a sequinned counterpane at the bottom of the hill. It was as if the world had awoken from a deep sleep.

She hummed to herself most of the way and manoeuvred her way through the Horsefair, where little remained of what used to be. There was talk of a new shopping centre where the old one had been. Huge stores would replace the select dressmakers, tailors, haberdashers and tobacconists, or so she'd heard. Sad really. There had been much pleasure in such variety.

Her elation abated the minute she turned into Royal York Crescent. It had all but disappeared once she'd parked the car and approached the front door.

The shadow of the house she had once loved fell over her like a black cloak. There were no lights burning. Neither Mrs Grey nor Polly was needed because David was away at his BMA meeting. She sighed, grateful she didn't have to face him. She was alone; at least she thought she was.

A movement, something in the shadows beneath the portico where the moon did not shine, caught her eye. The movement became a figure. Charlotte paused, heart thudding, mouth open.

'Who's there?'

The figure moved forward. 'Mother?'

She couldn't believe it. 'Janet! What are you doing here?'

Janet sounded close to tears. 'Where have you been, mother? I've been waiting for you. I needed you.'

Charlotte threw her arms around her daughter. 'Oh Janet! If I'd known...' Her words trailed off. Thinking of where she had been and with whom made her feel guilty. 'Come inside, dear.' With one arm around her shoulder, she guided her daughter into the house.

They settled in the warmth of the kitchen, with large cups of cocoa. Charlotte ignored the fact that sugar was still scarce and ladled two spoonfuls into each cup.

Janet told her in no uncertain terms how awful school was and how she had no intention of returning. 'You have to tell Daddy not to send me back, Mummy. You have to!'

Tell Daddy. It sounded so easy. It probably was to a child. Shoulder a trusted adult with the responsibility and things would be sorted out. If only it were so!

Charlotte stared into her cocoa, feeling guilty. Tonight had been too good to be true. Janet's homecoming had brought her back to earth with a bang.

* * *

Mrs Grey decided to come in on Monday morning so by rights Polly should have been acting as assistant receptionist at the surgery. But Dr Hennessey-White wouldn't be back until Tuesday and there were no appointments to deal with except over the phone. The truth was she hated paperwork and Marjorie, who'd styled herself chief receptionist, seemed to find her plenty of filing to do.

Despite Marjorie's protests, Polly excused herself and made the short walk from Clifton Park to Royal York Crescent. She had a job to do.

Mrs Grey was standing at the kitchen door when she arrived. 'What are you doing here?'

'None of your bloody business!' Polly retorted as she flounced on through, her usual smart self in a black suit updated by Aunty Meg who had sewed on white collar and cuffs.

She tried the drawing room first. No one. But she halted a moment to take in the tasteful colours of pistachio green, pale pink and dark beige. It was the sort of colour scheme she would have chosen if only she was getting married and setting up a home of her own.

The softness of the colours did nothing to quench her anger. The feeling of having been robbed of a future was like a fire within her that flickered then raged as each perceived slight was thrown on to it.

She swept on down the hall. The door to the study was closed but she heard voices. Without knocking she barged in.

Charlotte was standing in front of the window, an elegant picture in a yellow twinset and a fitted grey skirt that matched her eyes.

Polly gritted her teeth. *So perfect!* Well, she'd soon fix that!

'I want to talk to you!'

Charlotte looked at her daughter before looking back at Polly.

She looks a wreck, thought Polly, spotting the dark lines beneath Charlotte's eyes. But she felt no pity. What's she got to be wrecked about? And what's the brat doing at home?

'I want to talk to you now! In private!'

She purposefully threw Janet a dismissive look. Charlotte took her cue. 'Wait outside a moment, Janet. We'll continue our talk later.'

Both women watched as Janet walked out of the room and shut the door behind her.

'My daughter's unhappy,' said Charlotte in a wistful voice.

Polly swung round immediately, her eyes blazing. 'She isn't the only bloody one!' She took a step forward. 'Now let's get this straight, Mrs bloody Hennessey-White, you and nobody like you has got any rights interfering in my life.'

Charlotte frowned and took a step back. It pleased Polly to see her do it. 'I don't know what you mean.'

Polly, liking the feeling of power she'd suddenly discovered, took another step towards her. 'YOU!' she said, pointing her finger full into Charlotte's face, 'made sure that me and Aaron never got permission to marry. YOU got him shipped back to America!'

Charlotte blinked in surprise. 'What?'

'You 'eard! Me and Aaron Grant were going to get married. He might not have said so, but I knows we were. It was understood. Then you interfered.'

Charlotte slumped onto a chair. 'You've got it wrong! Aaron told me he wanted to get married and I went along to see his commanding officer. I'm sorry, Polly. I was only trying to help.'

'You lying cow!' said a scowling Polly, her finger still wagging in Charlotte's face. 'Just do me a favour, missus. Don't do me any favours. I don't know what the bloody 'ell you said to 'im but you've gone and bloody ruined my life!'

As the words echoed around the room Polly stormed out, her fists tightly clenched, her jaw aching.

It was enough that Charlotte had slumped into a chair with a shocked expression on her face. It was enough that Polly had stated exactly how she felt. But if Charlotte thought that was the end of it then she was very much mistaken. Polly wanted revenge. If Charlotte had denied her a better future overseas, then she would find a man in this country who could give her what she wanted, no holds barred!

* * *

Edna and Colin told no one about the house Billy Hills had offered to rent them in Kent Street. It was small and had a shop front, which meant stepping straight out into the street, but there was an extra room downstairs which they could turn into a bedroom.

'Easy for getting the chariot in and out,' Colin said when they first took a look.

'I'm glad it suits you,' Edna replied.

'I meant the pram for the kids,' he said lightly. 'Them two bedrooms upstairs are going to get pretty full pretty damn quick, you know.'

Edna smiled bashfully and felt a warm blush seeping over her face. Time was running out and she had to go ahead with the wedding. Backing out now would break a lot of hearts. And still she hadn't managed to get out to see Sherman.

'I'll have my workbench here, my jig here, and my stock of wood just there,' Colin said, rolling his chair around the room as he pointed out each position. 'And there's plenty more room for wood out the back. No, I can't see any drawback, can you, my love?'

My love! The words sounded different coming from Colin than

from anyone else. It was a typical Bristolian form of address. But from him it sounded special.

They fell silent, each thinking the same thoughts. Colin spoke first.

'So, when do we tell the dragon?'

'She thinks we're going to move in with her.'

'Like hell we are.'

'She'll be upset.'

'I don't care. It's my wedding, my marriage, and you'll be my wife. The fact that I get her as a mother-in-law is a cross I have to bear. Bloody big one though, innit?'

Edna laughed and threw her arms around his neck and kissed him on the back of the head. His funny moments obliterated any second thoughts. She loved him then. It was hard not to.

Thoughtfully she rubbed her cheek against his. 'What if we were to go on honeymoon – and not come back?'

'Edna. Even though Billy Hills is flogging every toy he possibly can from the back of his old van, our money don't stretch to a honeymoon, unless you fancy a day trip to Weston.'

'But we don't have to tell her that. We can tell her we're going for the week, that Billy's really come up trumps. And in the meantime we'll furnish the house and get it just as we want it. Billy will help. I know he will.'

She looked down into his eyes. Weston-Super-Mare for a day then a home of their own. 'What do you think?'

A slow smile crossed his face. 'I think she'll steam right up and burst like an old kettle when she finds out.'

Behind Edna's happy smile one nagging thought still remained. Somehow or other, despite the wedding, she had to contact Charlotte, start making the baby clothes, and find an opportunity to get to the orphanage. She would have to explain why but Charlotte was a person she felt she could trust.

* * *

How, she didn't know, but somehow Charlotte managed to persuade Janet to go back to school. She drove her there, one eye on the speedometer and one on her watch. It was imperative she was back in time for dinner so that David never suspected that his daughter had absconded from school. Mrs Grey had been sworn to secrecy.

Coming back she got caught in the tide of people coming out of the tobacco factories and wished instantly that she'd taken the other route over Clifton Suspension Bridge.

It wouldn't have been so bad if the factory girls had stuck to the pavement, but there were so many of them, buddies arm in arm, that they spilled onto the road and took no notice whatsoever of bicycle bells or car horns.

* * *

Edna was hurrying along, head down. So much seemed to happen before a wedding. Besides her mother fussing and fidgeting with all the things *she* thought her daughter should have, neighbours had handed small home-made presents to her. It was also a foregone conclusion that the girls in the office had collected and would either present her with a purse full of money or buy her something they thought she surely needed like towels or flannelette bedsheets.

The main thing on her mind at the moment was the discussion she'd had with her mother last night regarding her wedding night.

'Screaming would be best, or if you can't manage that you can at least cry. The one thing you've got in your favour is that he's not a complete man what with having no legs to steady himself with.'

Edna's mouth had dropped open. Her mother had said all this without showing the slightest embarrassment or emotion.

It was a cruel and foolish thing to say. Edna could have cried then and there. Instead she'd stormed from the room, past her father who sat snoring with a newspaper over his head, a cold pipe by his side. He'd always been merely a shadow that drifted along behind her mother. Now she pitied him.

A crowd of laughing girls from Woodbine production elbowed her off the pavement. As she stepped out into the road a car horn honked loudly. In response she skipped back on again, then realised someone was calling her name.

'Edna!'

She immediately recognised the voice and turned round.

Charlotte was hanging out of the window. 'Can I give you a lift?'

Edna's spirits lifted. This was exactly the person she wanted to see. 'I'm glad I saw you,' said Edna once they'd got the small talk about the weather out of the way. 'There's something I wanted to ask you. It's about helping make the baby clothes.'

'Oh, I didn't think you'd have time for that until after you're married. You are giving up work, I take it?' said Charlotte, sounding her horn indignantly at every fresh-faced young factory girl that stepped into her path.

'I don't know that I can afford to. Not yet. Not until Colin's got established.'

Charlotte gripped the steering wheel and glared angrily at the intransigent crowd. Edna had never seen her so tense before. Talking seemed to help; the more she talked the more her grip loosened.

'I can bring some material and patterns for dresses and romper suits over to you. I leave it to your own common sense to use any feminine material for dresses and only cotton for romper suits. Boys will be boys even when they are babies! Get out of the way will you! Stupid girls!' The last comments were directed at yet more factory girls who seemed to tumble out of the door like heaps of porridge oats.

Edna smiled at the thought of baby boys acting tough. It was exceptionally piquant to imagine because her son was one of them.

'I think I can manage.'

Charlotte became thoughtful. The tyres squealed as a gap opened in the crowd and she urged the car forward. 'I think it would be a very good idea if you came up to my house now and collected it. The material and patterns have all been divided into carrier bags so it won't take a minute. Have you time?'

'Yes,' Edna replied and had the distinct impression that Charlotte visibly relaxed. Oh well, she thought, everyone has to have their off days.

As they entered the hall of Charlotte's house, David Hennessey-White strode purposefully out of the drawing room. Edna barged into the back of Charlotte as her friend stopped quickly in her tracks.

'David!'

Edna sensed her nervousness.

Charlotte did her best to hide it. 'You do remember Edna don't you, darling. You remember her fiancé...' She did not finish the sentence. She did not need to. Colin and the day at Temple Meads Railway Station were easily remembered. The tight expression David Hennessey-White had worn when he came out of the drawing room was replaced by a warm smile but there was a dead look in his eyes.

'Of course I remember. How are you, Edna?'

Edna shook the proffered hand.

Charlotte stood close to his side, her voice oddly cajoling. 'Darling, I was doing some shopping at a market garden near Long Ashton and got caught in the crowd coming out of the tobacco factory. I saw Edna and suggested she come up here to collect one of the orphanage bags. She's going to make some baby clothes.'

He smiled. 'Very commendable of you, Edna.'

She smiled stupidly and nodded towards the floor. There was something of the snake about his voice. There was no harshness, just a slippery charm and a bland smile that never altered. If he was hoping to charm her, he had failed miserably. He frightened her.

Charlotte dashed off to get the carrier bags as promised. Still smiling, David asked her about the wedding. 'The fourth Saturday in May.' Edna glanced towards the door Charlotte had disappeared through. She made an effort to stop being nervous. 'You are both invited.' She prayed that Charlotte wouldn't be long.

Her prayers were swiftly answered. Charlotte returned with a carrier bag in each hand. She was smiling broadly and with almost as confident an air as on the first day they'd met. She held up the two carrier bags, a mischievous gleam in her eyes. 'I've brought you two. I'm sure that will keep you busy.'

'As dinner is an hour away, I insist on giving you a lift home,' said David. Edna thanked him but wished Charlotte was taking her.

Face flushed, Charlotte handed him the keys. She seems relieved, thought Edna, and as the string handles of the carrier bags bit into her fingers, it occurred to her that she'd been used. The material and patterns could have been delivered at any time. But Charlotte had needed her as some kind of excuse, perhaps a defence.

11

Charlotte was arranging daffodils in a tall blue vase. David gathered up his papers and put them in his briefcase. There was an uneasy peace between them after her late arrival home last night, but she hid her discomfort, hoping that today she would see some glimmer of the old David.

In the past she had used her superior strength and confidence to help others with their problems. Now she had the problems and couldn't bear to unload them on someone else. It was against her nature. So she concentrated on other things. Giving out good advice and being generous to other people made her feel especially good.

That very morning she had received a letter of thanks from Edna. She smiled at the thought of Edna's face when she discovered the six yards of white silk, the lace and the strips of seeded pearls she'd crammed into one of the carrier bags.

I'm using it to make my wedding dress, as if you hadn't guessed.

Which was exactly what Charlotte had intended. She was grateful for having bumped into Edna on the day she'd taken Janet back to school. Her presence had saved a lot of awkward questions being asked. David would not know about Janet running away from school unless someone told him.

There was a knock at the door and Mrs Grey entered. 'I've finished packing your case, Doctor. It's out here in the hall.'

'Very good.' David fastened his briefcase and straightened.

'These conferences are getting ever more frequent aren't they?' said Charlotte, trying her best not to sound relieved that he was going away.

'They need to be!' snapped David. 'Most of the BMA are opposed to this National Health rubbish. We have to fight it or see our incomes cut to unmanageable levels.'

Charlotte didn't mention that she'd read something about it and didn't think it was that bad an idea – with some reservations of course, but it was basically sound. But David rarely listened to her point of view nowadays. She resigned herself to being submissive. 'Whatever you say, David.'

'I'll see you when I get back.' He gave her a quick peck on the cheek. In times past he would have held her close, run his hands down her back. The warmth and affection between them would have been almost tangible. But it wasn't like that any more.

Charlotte stared after him thoughtfully. He hadn't mentioned anything more about her going out to work. He'd actually been more amenable over the past few days, absorbed in fighting a new idea that he might have embraced in pre-war years.

Majorie the receptionist had developed a heavy cold on the Tuesday when Dr Hennessey-White was due back from conference. Although Polly was mainly there for domestic and menial office work, she had done enough reception duties to manage by herself.

'Don't worry, Marge,' she said in a put-on voice as common as any she knew. 'I'll look after things.'

Majorie had looked at her with dread. 'You can't talk to patients like that!'

Polly grinned. She loved putting it on just to upset the older woman whose bun was tight enough to stretch her skin, and her glasses as thick as milk bottle bottoms. She went on, 'Oh I won't, Majorie darling. I will speak very slowly so I don't drop my aitches or stick "l"s and "r"s on the end of everything.' This time she spoke with as much refinement as she could and Marjorie sighed with relief.

The afternoon went well. Polly made an effort to be very solicitous to patients, and although David was surprised she was there he seemed pleased to see her.

At the end of surgery she knocked on his door and asked him if it was all right to lock the outer door. The dropdown leaf of the cocktail cabinet was open and he was pouring himself a large whisky. It wasn't the first time she'd caught him drinking.

'Yes please,' he answered.

When she went back into his office he was pouring himself a fresh whisky. Any humble employee – such as good old Marjorie – on seeing him drinking so heavily, would have retired discreetly, but not Polly. She had a destiny to achieve. Besides, she'd seen the way he had looked at her on the day she'd pulled down her stocking and he'd examined her ankle.

Smart as ever in another of her made-over black and white outfits, she sat herself down in one of the armchairs and seductively crossed one leg over the other.

'A gentleman would invite a girl to join him.'

A hard, surprised expression came to David's face. For a split second she thought he was going to show her the door. But slowly a smile spread over his face. Never met anyone so bloody cheeky, she thought, cocking her head to one side like an inquisitive sparrow.

She beamed as he handed her the well-filled tumbler. 'Bottoms up!' She took a large swig. The amber liquid warmed the back of her mouth and seeped into her brain. This was good!

'I appreciate you stepping into the breach at such short notice,' he began.

'Don't mention it.'

'So what have you been up to?' David said as he sat himself in the chair opposite her. He meant in reception that afternoon, but she wasn't going to leave matters so mundane.

'Well, besides working for you I've been planning my future. But it's not always easy. People get in your way, don't they? Especially busybodies who like to buzz about thinking they're helping people when they're really only being plain nosy.'

A knowing look came over his face.

Thinking about Charlotte, thought Polly, which is exactly what I meant him to do. Never before had she felt as angry towards anyone as she did towards Charlotte. Everything about her was suddenly hateful. Charlotte's clothes, Charlotte's lifestyle and, most of all, that confident smile, that air of superiority, added up to everything the upper class was and she wasn't. She disliked her for that alone, but she hated her for ruining her chances of a new life in a new world.

He drained his glass. She followed suit.

'That's a lot of whisky for a woman,' he said, frowning with disapproval.

Polly raised an eyebrow. 'Now, now, Doc. You weren't thinking you could out-drink me, were you?'

He looked at her steadily as though he was making up his mind what to do about her. Then, as if a decision had been reached, he took her glass and poured her another.

'Do you enjoy working for me?'

She said she did because she knew it was what he wanted to hear. But oh, it would have been so much better if she could have married Aaron and gone to America. Remember what you promised yourself, said a small voice in her head.

If you don't get a better life over there, then you'll aim for one over here. Oh yes. She remembered all right. And as she did, she smiled at David over the top of her glass.

He was talking about when they'd first met. 'At least it makes amends for me pushing that door open so quickly and knocking you down.'

She laughed, partly as a result of the drink and partly because she had made up her mind to hurt Charlotte just as Charlotte had hurt her. Her skirt slid up and exposed a lot more leg. David noticed. She did not adjust it. Instead she caressed the soft velvet of the chair. At the same time she kept her eyes fixed on his. 'I loved this chair the first time I saw it,' she said.

'I remember.'

You're remembering me in it, stocking off and your hands all over my foot, perhaps thinking of running them up my leg, under my skirt.

He got up, his hands shaking slightly as he poured himself another drink.

I'm right, she thought, and smiled smugly to herself.

He said, 'I would have thought a good-looking girl like you would be married by now.'

She joined him, leaned her head on his shoulder and sighed. 'My sweetheart got killed in the war. No one can understand what it's like. I feel so sad at times. So lonely.' She silently congratulated herself. The lies rolled off her tongue so easily.

She looked up into his face. Something was different. His expression had changed. There was a slackness to his jaw, a vacant look in his eyes.

For a moment it frightened her. She thought about leaving but her desire for revenge forced her to stay.

You should leave, said the voice of reason. He's happily married and there's two children to think of.

That was it! Charlotte was happily married and had two children along with everything else that she had. Why should Charlotte have it all and not her?

Hurt and confused, she forced herself to stay, her anger overwhelming her good nature and common sense. She knew men well. Even before his lips met hers she knew he was going to kiss her. She'd known plenty of servicemen just like him, far from home and in need of female comfort. And that's what David was, home from the war, yet in his mind he was still there, tasting something he had not tasted before.

* * *

It was a weekday when David went off to another BMA meeting and Charlotte breathed a sigh of relief. It was only when he was not at home that she became anything like her old self. When he was there she behaved the way he wanted her to, did everything he wanted her to. It was like walking on eggshells. She trod softly, silently, and hardly spoke unless she was spoken to.

His obsession with fighting the government's new health scheme occupied his mind. The fact that she still had her car and was still involved in various projects, paid and unpaid, was overlooked.

On the drive out to the camp, she thought about Polly and her anger. She had never meant for Aaron to be shipped out and she had no idea that it was Polly he was talking about marrying. She resolved to see the commanding officer and see if there was anything to be done.

A sergeant she didn't know, white, greeted her and informed her that it was now his task to organise the prisoners' appointments for her. He had shiny hair and an air of arrogance. 'My name's Sergeant Noble,' he said, and asked her if there was anything he could do. She had the distinct impression that he didn't think she had any right being there. Probably the type that thinks all good Germans are dead ones, she thought. But she was not the sort to let herself be bullied by him.

She pulled herself up to her full height which, bearing in mind her high heels, meant she was almost looking down at him. 'Yes. I would like to see the commanding officer before I start. Take me to him now.'

'I'm sorry, ma'am,' he said, openly smirking and shaking his head as though she were little more than a child. 'But Commander Cohen is a very busy man and...'

She slammed her briefcase down. 'Then I'll wait outside his office!'

She strode resolutely to the door, the heels of her tan court shoes beating a strident tattoo as she did so. The sergeant followed.

'This is US territory and you've got no right...'

This was the last straw. Charlotte stopped so abruptly that he almost collided into her when she turned.

'This is *my* country, sergeant, and I have every right! If you want to make an issue of it, please put it in writing. But I would warn you that I know some very influential people in very high places!'

His skin paled to the colour of unbaked bread.

Pleased with the result but giddy with anger, Charlotte marched on.

Outside the commander's office she smoothed her green jacket firmly over her hips and realigned the mink fur collar. She meant business.

After knocking, she walked right in.

'Mrs Hennessey-White!' he got up from his chair as she entered, his expression amiable but condescending. In his right hand he held a large cigar. 'Please,' he said, indicating with a wave of his hand, 'sit yourself down.'

She shook her head. 'I wouldn't feel comfortable.'

His amiable expression froze, like some cartoon character when the film's broken down.

'Mrs Hennessey-White. Please tell me, have I done something to upset you?'

'When I was last here I spoke to you about Aaron Grant and his wish to marry. I now understand he's been shipped home. Might I ask why?'

As he studied her he drew on the cigar. A pall of smoke floated up and hung between them.

'Best for him. Best for the army. Fraternisation of non-white combatants is something we couldn't control in your country. But we sure as hell don't have to put up with the result of these liaisons. I take it the girl is pregnant. They usually are.'

Charlotte knew that Polly was no saint. And she hadn't thought to ask her whether she was expecting. But she wasn't going to give Colonel Cohen the satisfaction.

'No!' she said vehemently.

'I'm sorry,' he said. 'But rules are rules.'

'And laws are laws. You are subject to British law as well as US law.'

His expression crumpled then hardened. 'Grant was a member of our army, Mrs Hennessey-White, not yours. It's none of your business.'

She went on unabashed. 'I'd like his address, or does that belong to the army too?'

He glared at her, his eyes no more than chips of hard glass in a face now glistening with a thin layer of sweat. She sensed he was searching for some way of refusing her request. But he couldn't do that. He knew without her saying that she would go above his head.

And indeed she would. For her own self respect as much as for anything else, she felt compelled to put things right between her and Polly.

'I'll have to write and ask his parents' permission to let you have that.'

It was a small hope and a very small triumph, but she felt she had achieved something.

She told Josef later. 'I feel awful about it. Polly blames me.'

'There's nothing you can do. Anyway, in one way it is for the best. At least it happened now before there was a child.'

'As far as I know,' Charlotte interjected, unable to control the anger she felt at such bigotry, such hypocrisy.

She went prattling on about the hypocrisy of men fighting a war against those who killed because of race or religion. Only when she fell to silence and Josef did not respond did she realise that he was sitting very quietly, his gaze fixed at the door directly in front of him.

'What's the matter?'

Still with his gaze fixed on the door, he rubbed his hands together.

'I have decided to go home as soon as I am allowed.' She hadn't expected this.

'But I thought...' She got up and stood behind his chair, her arm trailing around his shoulders. Briefly she glanced outside the small, square window, desperate to be close to him yet concerned that their behaviour should not be observed.

She knelt at his side then reached up and touched his cheek, a slight stubble rough but enticingly masculine beneath her finger-tips. 'What is it, Josef?'

He too looked out of the window but not, she guessed, for the same reason. 'They made us watch a film today about war crimes.'

He turned back to look at her. His eyes were moist.

Charlotte had been hurt both physically and mentally since David had come home. Now she was hurting more. She didn't want him to leave.

'I would have thought you would be put off going home. If you stayed here I could arrange...'

He clasped her hand between his. 'It would be easy for me to stay here. But I have to go back. Don't you see that? I have to make amends.'

They drove silently to the village pub after she'd seen her last appointment.

'It's going to take some time to arrange your repatriation. You do know that?' she said, as they sat at a rough oak table with their drinks.

He nodded and folded his hand over hers, the gesture hidden by the tabletop.

'You say I can get a job in the meantime. Perhaps on a local farm or something.'

But I want you with me, not stuck in the country.

Her mind searched for a solution. An idea came to her.

'Do you like children?'

His mood lightened. 'Are you propositioning me?'

'Be serious, Josef...'

'Yes.'

'Then I think I might be able to arrange something.'

He seemed pleased but she could tell that something was troubling him.

'Everything will work out terribly well,' she said brightly, as though she were talking about a netball game result rather than the course of their lives.

'I was not thinking about me,' Josef said haltingly and suddenly rested his head in his hands. 'I'm wondering if you really will get Aaron's address.'

'I fail to see why not!'

Josef stayed silent and in that silence she sensed there was something about Aaron he was not telling her.

* * *

Edna approached Colin's mother about making her wedding dress. Gladys had a sewing machine in an upstairs room and was sympathetic to the fact that Edna did not wish to wear her mother's old gown.

'Remember, the bridegroom's not supposed to see it before the big day,' she said, as she bustled about the room pulling pins, scissors and tape measure into Edna's easy reach.

'There's no chance of that,' said Edna and could have bitten off her tongue. Colin would never climb the stairs again. 'I'll lock the door,' Edna added in an effort to repair the damage.

Mrs Smith's face brightened a little. 'Good idea. Now I'll leave you to it.'

Edna did indeed lock the door. But it was the baby clothes for boys she got to work on first, her fingers feverishly cutting out the tiny garments. It was boy babies she was interested in.

By the end of one week she had made four outfits, mixing silks with cottons and blues with yellows. The material for her wedding dress remained in the bag.

Colin asked her to go and see Billy Hills with him. There was a whole box of aeroplanes, horses on wheels and pull-along dogs, all painted and ready to sell. Besides, they had to make the final arrangements about the house. There were curtains to be measured and furniture to be bought. Although she longed to be elsewhere, Edna went along with the plans.

The furniture was strictly utility and bought on coupon. A bedroom suite was a must. A dining suite would also be useful but a three-piece suite might have to be second hand – if at all obtainable.

For Colin's sake, Edna gave her all to the plans. But the baby clothes – washed, ironed and sitting in the paper carrier bag – still filled her mind. Charlotte had said that she would collect the garments, but Edna had her own agenda. She wanted to deliver them herself. A weekend was out of the question. Her time was taken up with Colin. In the time she wasn't with him, her mother's eyes followed her everywhere as if she were fearful she might run away before she got to the altar.

Much as she disliked doing it, she made up her mind to take a day off work. On return the next day she would feign illness as the excuse. She'd had little time off since joining the firm and it shouldn't be a problem.

On Wednesday of the following week she dressed as though she were going to work, wearing her grey dress, tweed coat, and a red and gold patterned scarf. She'd taken the carrier bag from Colin's house the night before and hidden it behind the laurel bush that grew against the front wall.

Taking care not to leave until her mother was hanging out the washing, she rushed out of the door, retrieved her parcel and made her way towards the park entrance.

There were no railings or gates to stop her from using Victoria Park as a short cut. Park railings were early casualties of the war, taken away to boost the metal mountain that was needed to make guns and shells.

The trees were in bud and a mist promised that the day would turn warmer. But Edna hardly noticed a thing. Instead of turning off in the direction of the tobacco factories, she carried on to St Luke's Road, a long sweep of terraced houses that would take her towards the railway station and the city centre.

There were no buildings between the station and up Victoria

Street. Here and there were gaping holes and danger signs. Young sappers with the worried faces of old men were overseeing the removal of twisted and blackened beams of buildings that had stood for centuries and were now no more.

She caught a bus in the city centre that would take her up Muller Road to the orphanage, which bordered Stoke Park and an area known as 'the Duchesses'.

Orphanages were not something Edna was familiar with, except that when older people talked of them they seemed to lump them together with workhouses. She had never wanted to think of her baby's home that way. In her mind she had imagined him in a place of bright colours and warm people. As she stood outside the iron gates and looked up the drive at the grey Victorian edifice before her, she wanted to cry. How could her mother have put her baby in a place like this?

Concern for her child gave her the courage to step forward and make her way to the front door, a large, wide opening surrounded by solid grey stonework.

The entrance hall had high ceilings and a shiny brown floor. The windows stretched from ceiling to floor and had wooden shutters on the inside.

Her footsteps echoed around her.

A woman in navy and white who she presumed to be the matron greeted her.

'Mrs Hennessey-White sent me,' she blurted, knowing it was a lie but determined to be let in. 'I've got some baby clothes,' she added, raising the bag she carried.

'That's very kind of you, my dear.' The matron looked at her quizzically. Edna wondered if she really believed her or was the shame of her wrongdoing stencilled on her brow forever. 'Shall I take them?' The matron reached out her hand.

Edna swung the bag behind her back. 'I've come a long way. I took the bus,' she blurted. 'If you don't mind, I'd like to see the babies.'

The woman looked surprised and for a moment Edna was sure she was going to be sent packing with or without her donation. Her heart felt like lead.

'I don't see why not,' said the matron. She called to a passing nurse. 'Sister Ruth? Take Miss...?'

'Burbage. Edna Burbage,' Edna replied, hardly able to believe her luck.

She felt as though she were in a dream. The pristine surroundings blurred into softness simply because she was feeling warm all over. Sister Ruth led her into a colourless room where wooden cots were ranged around the walls. Some of the babies were crying. Some lay quietly, eyes following the newcomers as they moved around the room.

'Are they all boys?' Edna asked and feeling stupid for doing so.

'No.' Sister Ruth indicated a nameplate on the side of a cot. 'Their names are written here, boys on blue paper, girls on pink.'

Edna's heart went out to the round, little eyes looking expectantly up at her, the soft little faces of those sleeping. But one cot above all others caught her eye. The name '*Sherman*' was written on a piece of blue paper.

'Most of the children are half-caste,' sniffed Sister Ruth. 'All of the girls, of course, are unmarried. That's how dependable Negroes are, I suppose.'

Edna was not listening. Her eyes were fixed on the cot and the name she knew so well. Hardly daring to breathe she approached and looked down at her son. His eyes were open and so was his mouth. He was the one crying the loudest.

'Sherman!'

The bag of clothes fell to the floor. Before Sister Ruth could stop her she leaned over and picked up the child wrapping him tightly to her body, his little head resting on her shoulder. The crying stopped immediately as he made sucking sounds against the shoulder pad of her coat.

Sister Ruth rushed over.

'Miss Burbage! You have no right doing that! You're spoiling him.'

'He needs me,' whispered Edna, her eyes filling with tears. 'He needs me.'

'Put him down or I'll get Matron and you'll never be allowed in here again!'

The last comment hit home. She had to come here again. She just had to.

'There, there,' she cooed, rocking Sherman tightly against her until his eyes were almost closed. Slowly and gently she lowered him back into his cot and tucked the bedding around him.

'He'll be all right now,' Edna said softly and her heart ached fit to break. But she determined that she would visit again. No one would stop her from doing that.

Sister Ruth was too busy to tell Matron what had happened. She was the sort who administered the necessities of life but not the love. The incident was forgotten. It was Matron who remembered the young woman with the intense expression and the carrier bag when she did her rounds. Thoughtfully she slid a baby's name card out of the receptacle to reveal his mother's surname. This one said *Potterton*. It rang no bells. She did the same to the name card of the next baby along. This time it revealed the name Burbage. She smiled. Sherman's mother had come looking for him, unmarried no doubt. I wonder how much she'd sacrifice in order to have him back, she thought?

On the following day at work Edna was called to the supervisor's office. He was a middle-aged man who rarely entered the typing pool except to complain about errors or ogle a new recruit who he might be able to do favours for – given the right incentive. The girls called him The Groper.

He had the neck of a giraffe and looked at her stiffly. 'Do you have a note from your doctor, Miss Burbage?'

Edna tried to be brave. 'No. I'm sorry. It was only a day and I thought...'

'You're not paid to think, Miss Burbage. You're only an invoice typist. I do all the thinking round here.'

Yes. And we know what about.

She tried not to show what was in her mind.

'I'm sorry,' she said again wishing the floor could swallow her up.

'Well so am I, Miss Burbage.' He lit a cigarette, drew on it and almost spat the smoke into the air. 'I hear you're leaving us soon anyway. Is that right?'

'I'm getting married. But I don't want to leave. Not right away.' She was worried. She couldn't afford to leave and live on Colin's money, not until Billy Hills got more orders for toys.

Teasing young women was another of the 'Groper's' favourite occupations. 'Well, I don't think we can keep you on once you're married, Miss Burbage. As far as I'm concerned you're taking liberties with the company having days off without a bona fide medical note.'

It was too much to bear. The threat frightened her. She sprang forward, palms flat on the desk. 'I can't afford to give up work, Mr Gordon. Please reconsider!'

A slow smirk crossed his face. Yes, he would reconsider. She could see it in his face.

'In this office after work and we'll discuss it further.'

For the rest of the day Edna's fingers refused to hit the right keys. Groper Gordon was only part of the problem. The other lay more heavily on her mind. She could still see Sherman's eyes looking up at her, feel his wet little lips sucking against her coat. If only she had the courage to do something about it. But she wasn't courageous. Her mother had seen to that. Even now, she was afraid of what she would say about the dress she was making and the house Billy was letting them have. But in her heart of hearts she knew that owning up to Sherman would be the hardest thing of all. Could she ever bring herself to tell Colin about her son and what would his reaction be? No! It would do no good. She couldn't do it.

12

Polly held her head high as she made her way down the Batch towards York Street. The workers from Georges' Brewery were coming in the other direction, a host of clogs clattering on the old cobbles like a herd of horses.

The men divided and lifted their caps as she passed by. The women eyed her enviously and muttered disparaging comments. They cut no ice but only served to make her hold her head that bit higher.

It had been two weeks since she'd last called in at York Street and she hadn't stayed long. Carol had been howling her head off on that occasion and Hetty's two had been arguing over some cardboard cut-outs that Meg had probably made.

Bertie had been sat shirtless in front of the fire, his thin arms poking out through the sleeves of his vest. He was reading the paper and barely acknowledged her as she entered except to say, 'Put a bit of coal on the fire while yer up, our Poll.'

She glared at him. 'Too busy, are you?'

'He's thinking about work,' Hetty had explained.

'Yeah,' said Polly. 'Strikes me he's doing more thinking about it than actually doing it!'

A row had erupted and Meg had got upset. Better to stay away for a while, she'd decided, until things calmed down. Not that she needed much persuading. York Street was a place she wanted to leave behind. Clifton was where she wanted to be, and if no man other than David was available then so be it.

So far she had been the perfect tease – just so far and no further. Yet at times his dark looks and deep voice had scared her. She could sense his anger and wondered how far she could go before he refused to take no for an answer. At those times when he didn't scare her, she felt guilty about playing fast and loose with another woman's husband, but she reminded herself of Aaron and felt a little better.

She acted now both as his part-time receptionist and nursing assistant, though God knows she had no experience of either. But she knew how to make the patients, especially the men, feel at ease. It was a natural flair.

As she lay in the yellow-striped room with the fresh and airy smell, she could almost forget where she'd come from. The only thing she couldn't really forget was Carol. It wouldn't be long before Meg was sending her a note to come and visit her child. She sighed and wished she'd planned her life differently, then went out and caught the bus.

Mr Long the greengrocer was still in the street, his horse-drawn cart slap-bang in the middle of the road. York Street was his last stop of the day. There, he usually shifted what was left of the vegetables for knock-down prices because he was in a hurry to get home and not have too much unloading to do when he got there. His old horse certainly looked ready for bed. It hung its head, its eyes drooping as a troop of fruit flies buzzed busily around its ears.

Meg was standing with the other women, her apron spread out

in front of her as Mr Long took his scoop off the scales and rolled the potatoes into it.

Polly shouted a greeting to her and smiled.

Her aunt looked straight at her then, without saying a word, she went tight-lipped into the house.

Polly took a deep breath. Meg was not pleased with her. She recognised the signs. Adapting to another life had been so easy!

Polly wrinkled her nose as she entered the passageway that led out back to the living room and the scullery that, according to Meg's description, wasn't big enough to swing a cat in.

When it had been only her and her aunt in the house, the place had never smelled of old cabbage and dirty washing. Since Hetty and her brood had moved in, this had changed.

Polly could see that things had got worse. Lines of wet washing were festooned across the kitchen. Steam was rising out of the old copper that sat in the corner. Dishes were piled in the sink and two pans were boiling away on the stove smelling of onions and pork cuttings.

Aunty Meg's sleeves were rolled up to her elbows. Her arms were red and sweat glistened on her face. Despite looking utterly exhausted she stood glaring at Polly as though something weighed heavily on her mind. Through the open door, Polly could see her daughter's pram moving as she kicked her legs and arms. She promised herself she'd go out and see her in a minute.

'Where's Hetty?' she asked.

'She's upstairs lying down. She's not feeling well,' answered Meg.

Polly was astounded. 'And left you to do everything? Well, that's a damned nerve!'

Meg rounded on her, face reddening, arms waving. 'Nerve is it! And what about your nerve! When was the last time you saw that child of yours? She's growing up! She needs her mother. Why haven't you been home?'

'I've been working!' She said it sharply, quickly. If she allowed herself to feel guilty or ashamed she might cease to continue on the path she'd planned.

'I can see that,' said Meg looking her up and down. 'New coat and shoes is it? And where did you get that hat?'

'Cast offs! Just cast offs!' It wasn't quite true. David had given her money. He'd actually thrown five-pound notes across the desk at her and told her that he had no use for money, and that if the government had their way he'd soon have no money at all.

He'd frightened her, shouted at her to take it, his eyes blazing. She'd done as he'd asked, fearful that to disobey might only increase his anger.

Before coming here she'd felt good, but Meg was a reminder that she was far from perfect. She flounced out of the back door and made for Carol's pram. If she didn't already know it, she might not have believed that this was her baby. She was much bigger, sitting up and chewing on a crust of dry bread. Had it really been that long since she'd seen her?

'Carol?' She blinked away her tears as the child looked up at her and smiled – as she might at a stranger who she quite liked the look of.

She unfastened the leather harness that held Carol in her pram and lifted her out. She was wet and she took her inside to change her. A small voice in her head told her that it was the first time she'd done such a mundane thing for a very long time.

Polly heard the soft flap, flap of Meg's slippers as her aunt came into the living room. She was sitting on the settee, with Carol lying flat kicking her legs. She felt Meg's eyes boring into the back of her head.

Meg said exactly the words she was dreading. 'I can't go on

looking after her for much longer, Polly. You're going to have to make other arrangements.'

'I can pay you more,' Polly offered and wished that David was her husband. Then working and having Meg to look after Carol wouldn't be a problem. But David was married. So far she hadn't given in to him. But she knew she had to if she had any chance of taking him from Charlotte. She swallowed the guilt and again reminded herself, as she had many times before, that it was Charlotte's fault Aaron was no longer around.

Meg was not going to let it drop. 'It ain't no use to the child. It's her mother she wants and a proper home.'

Carol was sitting up now playing with the brass clasp on Polly's patent handbag. Polly touched her daughter's cheek. 'I will get you a proper home, Carol. I promise I will.' She turned round to face her aunt. Meg was frowning and eyeing her suspiciously.

'I can't have her with me at the moment, Aunty Meg, what with the job and all that. But I'll give you a bit extra until I can sort things out. I'll get me and Carol a better home and be out of your hair before long. I promise.'

As she got to her feet and smoothed her coat, Polly saw a questioning look in her aunt's eyes and immediately guessed what she was thinking.

'It's a proper job, Aunty Meg, and my employer's a very nice man.'

Meg picked Carol up from the settee, handed Polly her bag and gave her a knowing look. 'That's what I'm afraid of.'

* * *

'Not finished yet?' said Colin's mother to Edna, who was turning the sleeve of her wedding dress beneath the foot of the sewing machine.

'I'm frightened of making mistakes,' Edna explained. Her future mother-in-law nodded understandingly and left the room.

Edna's own mother had not been half so understanding. She'd stated in no uncertain terms that she was insulted by her daughter's refusal to wear her own wedding dress. When Edna had explained about the new material Charlotte had given her and Mrs Smith's offer of her sewing machine, she was doubly annoyed.

'What's wrong with my sewing machine? Not good enough either?'

Eventually she'd simmered down. Her main aim was still to ensure that Edna became respectable. She would be married and unassailable by man or gossip.

As Edna fed the material beneath the machine, her thoughts kept returning to the orphanage.

Sherman. His name lay softly on her mind. All through the night his eyes looked up at her, begging her to cuddle him to her breast. His frantic cry filled her worst nightmares.

Some people at work had commented that she wasn't as happy as a forthcoming bride should be. But how could she tell them why, and what good would it do anyone if she did. Colin would not want to marry her and she would have no security to offer her son, no home, no income. All she could hope for was to marry Colin, help Charlotte with her sewing circle and, hopefully, see her baby now and again when she went to deliver the finished clothes to the orphanage. But in time someone might adopt him and the prospect filled her with fear.

Groper Gordon posed another problem. She had not gone along to his office after work as requested. If she lost her job now things would be really hard for her and Colin. And yet she could not possibly contemplate 'being nice' to the balding office manager in return for keeping it. All the same she badly wanted to see her son again. Perhaps Charlotte could help.

The following day she left the canteen and was back in the typing pool just before two. No one else had rushed to get back – except Groper Gordon.

'I want to see you, Miss Burbage,' he called across to her.

Her stomach turned to lead as she got up from her chair. He stood close to the door as she entered the office. His arm swept around her and she heard the unmistakable click of a key being turned.

Edna pressed herself against the door, her hand frantically searching for the key.

He stood close up against her. She couldn't move. Then he smiled and brought out the key, dangling it in front of her eyes, taunting her with the closeness of it and with his power to withhold it from her.

'Now, there's a naughty girl. You didn't come along and see me last night, did you? And just for that I'm not going to give you the key.'

'Please,' she said, glancing swiftly over her shoulder, praying someone might pass. 'Everyone will be back from lunch soon.'

'They will indeed, young lady, but they know better than to come in here especially when my door's locked. They know I'm busy when my door's locked.'

Edna knew he spoke the truth. Whispers of what he did behind the locked door circulated around the typing pool.

'Mr Gordon. Please let me go.'

His face came close to hers. She turned her head to avoid the smell of stale tobacco on his breath.

'You'll have to show me you're really, really sorry about not coming along to see me. I mean it. Really, really sorry.'

His mouth was like warm tripe on hers. The hand that held the key groped for her breast.

This must not happen!

She would not give in! She would not let him take advantage of her no matter how important her job was.

As she pummelled his shoulders with her fists, she brought up her knee. Groper doubled in agony. The key fell on the floor.

With fumbling hands she opened the door, then, trembling with emotion, she ran to her desk, gathered her things and, without stopping to punch her card into the time clock, bolted from the building.

Myriad thoughts whirled round her brain as she fled towards East Street and the bus stop. All she wanted was to get away, but not home. She needed to talk things through with someone. She needed to tell them about Sherman and her fears about both his and her own future. The only person who had willingly listened to her problems was Charlotte.

The bus stop was near the Clifton Suspension Bridge and it was only a short walk from there to Royal York Crescent. When she saw the imposing height and opulence of the Hennessey-White residence, she paused on the black and white tiled step and bit at her knuckles. Did she dare to knock just like a visitor of Charlotte's own social standing?

Taking a deep breath she tucked her red and gold patterned scarf into her pocket and patted the lapels of her jacket. Somehow the image struck her as smarter.

A middle-aged woman with a pock-marked face and an easy smile answered the door.

Edna gathered up all her courage. 'Is Mrs Hennessey-White in?'

The woman shook her head. 'I'm afraid not. You might try at the doctor's consulting rooms though. She might just have popped in on her way back from shopping.'

Edna thanked her and asked directions.

It was a short walk from Royal York Crescent to Clifton Park. Again she had to ring a doorbell before gaining entry; nothing like the doctor I go to, she thought. This time it was Polly who answered and her appearance almost took Edna's breath away. She looked smarter than she'd ever looked before and more refined, almost a lady.

'Gosh, Edna,' said Polly in a low voice, smiling as she leaned close to Edna's ear. 'What are you doing here? Not in the club are you?'

Edna felt herself blushing. 'I wanted...' She couldn't say any more. The events of the past few weeks had finally caught up with her. Raising her hand to her head, she slowly closed her eyes and fell forward into Polly's arms. When she came to she was lying on a couch, her coat and hat to one side, the buttons of her blouse loose over her breast. David was examining her.

'You fainted,' he said as he smiled down at her.

Polly came to his side carrying a glass of water. 'Here, drink this.'

Edna did as she was told.

'Now,' said Polly before the doctor could ask her anything. 'What did you want Charlotte for?'

David raised the back of the couch just as Edna began to cry.

'Nothing can be that bad,' he said showing sudden signs of impatience.

'It can be for working girls,' said Polly daring to push him roughly to one side. Her action earned her an angry look. She chose to ignore it. She could handle him.

Something inside warned Edna not to mention the baby clothes. If she did that she might tell them about Sherman and she wasn't sure Polly was entirely trustworthy. Instead she swore them to secrecy between her sobs and explained only about her boss and what he wanted her to do in exchange for not sacking her once she was married. 'I have to stop him, or make sure I can get another job. I thought Charlotte could help me,' she explained.

David straightened and stood back to leave Polly to it. With cool fingers she brushed Edna's hair back from her face. 'What a rat! I've got a good mind to go down there and give him hell myself.'

David lay his hand on Polly's shoulder and pushed her firmly to one side. 'No need to, my dear. I think I might be able to help. I do know some of the management there. Leave it to me, will you?'

'Thank you.' Edna blinked. It struck her that David and Polly were far friendlier than she could ever be with her boss, Mr Gordon. Not that she'd want him to be that familiar with her.

They insisted on her having a cup of tea before allowing her to leave. Even after she'd managed to persuade them that she was all right Polly escorted her to the door.

'I'll tell Charlotte you were asking after her,' she gushed, her cheeky smile and bouncing blonde hair far removed from the secretaries Edna was used to at the tobacco factory. Most of them were austere with stiff hairdos, stiffer backs, and wire-rimmed glasses.

It wasn't until she got to the bus stop that she realised she'd left her scarf behind. Clothes were scarce enough as it was without her losing such a nice item. Sighing with frustration but telling herself not to panic, she ran back to the consulting rooms, hating to disturb such a busy man from his duties but too fond of her scarf and short on clothing coupons to leave it behind.

She clasped the lion's head knocker but did not use it. The door opened easily beneath her hand. A hybrid smell of polish and anti-septic drifted out. Typical, slap-dash Polly, she thought, so anxious to get back to her work that she hadn't locked it properly.

The reception area was just off the hallway, an elegant room of cream walls, parquet floors and Indian rugs. It was empty. Suddenly aware of low voices, she went over to the double doors of the consulting rooms. The voices got louder. She formed a fist, was just about to knock, then paused. The door was ajar slightly. She peered in through the gap and immediately wished she hadn't. Her hand flew to her mouth. Suddenly she felt sick. Polly and David Hennessey-White were wrapped in each other's arms. The bodice of Polly's dress hung open exposing white flesh above a cream satin brassiere. David Hennessey-White was panting like an animal over her shoulder.

13

As the bride prepared to leave the Baptist church hall to get changed and depart for her honeymoon, Charlotte gave her a hug and whispered, 'Wonderful dress, darling.' She would have let her pass there and then, but Edna held her arm. Charlotte beamed broadly, anything rather than look with pity at her and Colin. Her smile faltered slightly when she saw that Edna was looking at her in exactly the same way.

'This is my new address,' she said with a brighter expression. She slipped a note into Charlotte's hand. 'Bring me some material and I'll make some more baby clothes. And I'd love to have you visit.'

They exchanged knowing looks. Charlotte ached to think how Edna must be feeling. Most brides were too wrapped up in their wedding day to think of anything or anyone else. Obviously Edna was not one of them.

'Your chariot awaits you!' Colin cried, coming up behind his bride in his wheelchair. Laughing, Edna fell into his lap. Charlotte waved and Edna waved back. Was that concern she could again see in her eyes? Wedding night nerves, Charlotte thought with a knowing smile, and remembered their conversation in the little teashop on Redcliffe Hill.

As she moved away, a woman in a royal blue suit and a squat hat with a bunch of brown leaves at the side gave her a tight smile and a sharp jerk of her head by way of greeting. Edna's mother, if she remembered rightly. There was a suspicious look in her eyes.

In an effort to avoid holding a conversation with the woman, she deliberately turned her back and looked around for David. For a moment she couldn't see him and half wondered whether he'd left without telling her. Quite honestly, it had surprised her that he'd agreed to come in the first place. But he'd surprised her a lot lately. The aggression he'd shown since coming back from the war was not so frequent. Instead there were long silences, periods when he would stare into space or act as though what she did and whether she was there or not were of no consequence at all. But every now and again he would explode. On such occasions she had managed to avoid the slaps to the face but not the bruises to the body.

Eventually she saw him talking to Polly, who was wearing a black and white check suit. A black pillbox hat sat at a jaunty angle on her blonde head, its veil almost reaching the end of her nose.

Just like the one I wore when I met David off the train. Oh well, isn't copying the sincerest form of flattery?

Polly's smile was utterly bewitching. Her chin was down slightly but her eyes were looking up at David in a childish, teasing fashion.

Almost like Janet flirting with those young GIs, thought Charlotte. If I didn't know better...

The thought was carelessly flung aside as a smartly dressed man with the look of a spiv brought two glasses of brown ale to Polly's side. The spell was broken. David took one of the drinks and thanked him. Polly adopted a rather bored expression, looked around for diversion and spotted her. Her lips smiled but there was malice in her eyes.

Polly held her head high and sashayed over, red lips smiling and teeth shining white.

Charlotte could read people. Despite Polly's body language, there was no doubting the look in her eyes.

'Charlotte! Nice dress old Edna was wearing. I hear you gave her the material. My, but you're such a saintly person. I could never live up to it myself.'

'It was the least I could do,' said Charlotte and couldn't help but get the feeling that she was being belittled.

'Well, I ain't a saint nor a nun,' Polly went on. She winked at the two men. 'I'll always be wicked. Can't help it. Can I, Billy?'

The last remark was addressed to the man she appeared to be with.

'This is Billy Hills,' David said. He went on to explain how he sold the toys that Colin made. Charlotte listened. At the same time she noted the change in both Polly's speech and clothes. The latter were certainly of a higher quality than she'd worn before. When they'd first met, her Bristolian dialect had been thick enough to cut with a knife, 'r's and 'l's added to the ends of words and 'aitches' dropped all over the place.

'An' he'll be back in business come Monday,' said Billy, who made no attempt to hide his origins. He in turn went on to explain that the bride and groom were only going to Weston-Super-Mare for the day and that they were retreating to their new home immediately after that. 'It's a nice 'ouse,' he said. 'Even got a little workshop at the front. Suits Colin a treat. Nice it is. Real nice. His parents know all about it. But no one's told 'er mother.' He grinned cheekily. 'In fact, nobody dares!'

'What a wonderful idea,' said Charlotte, visibly warming to him. Billy, she decided, might be a rough diamond worn smooth, but he had a good heart. 'This is the address, isn't it?' She rummaged in her pocket and brought out what she thought was the piece of paper Edna had given her.

Suddenly Billy looked awkward. 'Yeah!' he said quickly, glancing at it then looking swiftly away. 'Looks like it.'

Polly's next comment surprised her. 'How would a bloke from the gutter like you know what "nice" is? You don't even know how to read and write.'

With an aching heart Charlotte noticed the pain in Billy's eyes and the faint flush that rose to his cheeks. She touched his arm gently. 'I think it's very kind of you,' she said. 'I also think you're very brave.'

He looked puzzled. 'Brave?'

Still with her hand on his arm she nodded in the direction of Edna's mother. 'I wouldn't like to be responsible when she finds out.' She smiled and Billy smiled with her.

Later that evening she wondered what had brought about the change in Polly's clothes and the softening of her accent. Oh well, she thought, I can't blame her for trying to better herself, and David was letting her do more work in the office, mostly filing and making tea, so he'd told her. But there was also a new hardness to the young woman. Polly had been overly sarcastic at the wedding, commenting that poor Billy Hills could neither read nor write.

Not my business, she said to herself, but of course everyone's business was Charlotte's business. It wasn't until later that she took out the piece of paper she'd shown Billy on which should have been Edna's new address. It wasn't. By mistake she'd pulled out a dry-cleaning ticket. So it was really true. Billy could not read.

When they left the wedding reception, David and Charlotte made a detour up through Old Market in order to drop Polly off in York Street.

Without turning the hallway light on, Polly watched them drive away, the red car lights brightening as they paused at the junction with Midland Road.

There was a soft click as the light was turned on. Aunty Meg stood there in a dark red dressing gown, the cord hanging loose, the front edges clutched together with her hands.

'Another man friend?' Meg asked with a hint of disapproval.

'Doctor Hennessey-White and Charlotte, if you must know,' Polly retorted. 'They went to the wedding too. Nice do it was. Fancy a cup of tea?'

Ignoring the disbelief on her aunt's face, she swept into the kitchen. The pipes hammered as she filled the kettle under the single cold tap before slamming it down on the gas and striking the necessary match.

Aware that Meg's eyes were on her, she hummed nonchalantly as if unaware that her aunt did not entirely approve of her lifestyle. She well knew how to disarm her. 'Did Carol go down all right?' she asked, warming her hands on the pot as she waited for the tea to brew.

Meg nodded. 'She always does. You'd find that out if you were home enough.'

'I have to make a living for us both. And I'm doing quite well. I'm a receptionist now, not a skivvy. I don't need to live in—.' She paused, thinking quickly. There would be times when she wanted to be away. 'Only when Mrs Grey's not available.'

'Oh yes,' said Meg accusingly, plumping herself down in a chair and folding her arms in front of her. 'And you get paid enough to go out and buy clothes in Park Street stores, do you? And don't try and tell me you bought that frock you're wearin' off some spiv on a bombsite corner!' Polly turned and cocked her head as she always did when she had a ready-made answer. 'It's one of Charlotte's cast offs. She's very good to me like that.'

'And I s'pose it's her that brings you home in the early hours of the morning.'

'Billy brings me home.'

'In that van? Don't make me laugh. I know the difference. I've heard that car before. What are you up to, Polly?'

Polly pulled in her stomach. She hated lying to Meg who'd been good to her, but what she did with her life was her business. She decided to lie.

'Charlotte sometimes gives me a lift if I attend one of her charity functions. She asks me to help out now and again. She is a friend as well as my boss's wife.'

Meg's expression remained unaltered. Polly put on her brightest smile. 'Here, drink your tea,' she said handing her the cup.

That night she shared Meg's bed and pretended to be asleep until her aunt was snoring gently beside her. Then she opened her eyes and smiled smugly into the darkness. Sooner or later she wouldn't have to put up with these cramped conditions, this low class way of living, not if she played her cards right.

* * *

The ground floor rooms of the house in Kent Street had pine panelling to waist height, all painted in the hideous brown varnish so beloved of the Victorians because it didn't show the dirt.

Cooking was done on a cast-iron range, which sat in the fireplace like a fat black spider. This room was to serve as both kitchen and living room. The shop was at the front and the bedroom was sandwiched between the two. Up above were two more rooms, both with bare board floors and devoid of furniture. The lavatory was at the end of the garden and a tin bath hung on the outside back wall.

It was less than Edna was used to but she loved it all the same. 'I'll make it look like a palace,' she had promised Colin. And she'd done her best to do that. Net curtains hung at sparkling windows. The furniture was old, the chair stuffed with horsehair and covered in leather, the table of well-scrubbed pine and scarred from the blows of many a carving knife or meat cleaver.

Colin removed all his tools to the new house, swearing his parents to secrecy and to ignorance once the truth was disclosed to Edna's mother.

The shop in which he could now both make and display his toys was warm and welcoming. At one side was a stack of empty shelves. 'They'll all be packed with stuff by Christmas,' he stated with confidence. And Edna believed him.

Despite the fact that Sherman was still on her mind, she was enjoying setting up her own home, being able to do what she wanted without her mother lurking and looking, asking questions with her eyes that Edna did not want to answer.

But all the same she knew her need to see Sherman again would not go away. No matter if, for some reason, she were never to see him until he was fully grown, the need would still be there.

On their wedding night she had cried. As they'd made love to suit Colin's physical shortcomings, she had wanted to roll back the years, to obliterate the fact that Adolf Hitler had ever lived. Things might have been so different. But her tears were not just about their love-making. It was also about bravery, guilt and the need to be loved. Would she have chanced telling Colin about Sherman if he hadn't had his legs blown off? Perhaps so; somehow a man uninjured by war seemed more capable of coping. But then, if there'd been no Hitler and no war there would have been no Sherman and, despite everything, she was glad he was alive. If only she could find the courage to tell Colin all about it. But she couldn't.

* * *

'Last item on the agenda, but by no means least, a vote of thanks for the continuing supply of clothes for our children.'

The speaker, Mr Nathaniel Partridge, lately of the Provincial Bank, now retired and Chairman of the Trustees of the Muller Orphanage, looked directly at Charlotte who was sitting to his left. 'Mrs Hennessey-White, do keep up the good work.'

The assembled trustees, matrons wearing fox furs and large hats, retired professional men, bankers, clergymen and military, clapped politely. Charlotte returned their fixed smiles and murmured the expected 'thank you'.

'Hear, hear,' said one of the elderly trustees whose hat, despite it being late May, was trimmed with fur rather than flowers.

'If I may speak, Mr Chairman...'

Mr Partridge nodded. 'Indeed, Lady Garribond.'

Full of her own self-importance, Lady Garribond got to her feet. 'I do hope Mrs Hennessey-White can continue to organise the making of baby clothes until such time as they are no longer needed. Until such time, in fact, that the flood of unwanted babies becomes no more than a trickle.'

A Major Rawlings interjected. 'Indeed, let us hope we can get most of these babies adopted – by suitable people of course.'

Assent ran around the room.

Job done, Charlotte shuffled her papers and prepared to leave, intending to see Josef before she did so. He was employed as groundsman now, tending lawns, trimming trees and doing general maintenance work that included looking after the swings, slide and roundabout in the children's play area. She was feeling well satisfied with what she was doing and grateful for the trustees' vote of thanks. Not such a bad lot, she thought – until Lady Garribond spoke again.

'Those that can be adopted will be. We have to bear in mind

that a lot of our charges are half-caste. The fathers ran out on their white victims and left them literally holding the baby.'

A few tittered at Lady Garribond's tasteless joke.

Charlotte turned to stone. She could not believe her ears. She'd always known that a number of the trustees were less than charitable when it came to the morals of everyone except their own class. But Lady Garribond's statement was simply outrageous. Slamming her briefcase down hard on the shiny oval table at which they were sitting, she sprang to her feet. All eyes turned to her.

'Lady Garribond! Your ignorance of the situation is unforgivable! Few of those women were victims. If anyone left them and their innocent babies high and dry it was the Allied High Command. Now it is up to us to pick up the pieces without prejudice towards either class or colour!'

'Well!' Lady Garribond's hand flew to her chest as though she were having a heart attack. Charlotte half expected her to call for the smelling salts. But she didn't. 'An apology! I want an apology!' she shouted in a shrill voice.

Pearl drops set in marcasite danced angrily in her ears as she threw a warning glare at the chairman. He winced visibly but stood his ground. Hard to do, Charlotte thought, with a woman whose face was as dour as Queen Mary's on a very dismal day.

'Mrs Hennessey-White?' The chairman looked up at her questioningly and, although his expression was suitably austere, she detected an amused twinkle in his eyes.

Charlotte shook her head. 'No. I cannot apologise. Might I suggest, Lady Garribond, that you make some enquiries before we next meet? You might very well find yourself apologising to me!'

After a curt goodbye Charlotte made her way to the matron's office. Matron was as wide as she was high and politely got to her feet when Charlotte entered.

Matron glanced at her watch. 'Meeting over already?'

'Yes,' said Charlotte, annoyed with herself for losing her temper as much as for Lady Garribond's remark. 'I'd like to see the children. Would that be possible?'

'Of course it would.' Matron, her face flushed permanently red and her bosom thrust forward like a song thrush, smiled and nodded, almost as if she had an inkling of what had been said. It was a well-known fact that she did not always see eye to eye with some of the board members.

Charlotte asked her what things they were short of.

Matron informed her.

'Nappies, of course. I don't expect them all to be of best quality terry towelling but it would certainly be nice if they were. And blankets. Clothes, of course. The little darlings will keep growing.'

They both chuckled warmly.

Charlotte liked Matron. She did her job well and efficiently, her emotions seemingly under control. But she guessed she had a soft centre. A moment of weakness and her life and home could become crowded with other people's children.

'I take it your car boot is as loaded up as usual,' said Matron.

Charlotte nodded. 'I spent all yesterday afternoon collecting from my sewing ladies.'

'One of them made a personal delivery a while back.'

'Really?'

'I didn't catch her Christian name. But her surname was Burbage.'

Charlotte frowned. 'Burbage? I do know a Burbage. Are you absolutely sure about that?'

Matron crooked her finger and beckoned Charlotte over to a cot and a sleeping child, his skin coffee gold against the crisp whiteness of the pillow.

'She was particularly interested in this little chap.'

Charlotte gazed down too and smiled. 'I don't blame her. He's beautiful.'

Matron clasped her hands beneath her ample bosom, breathed a large sigh and shook her head. 'She picked him up, cuddled him to her body and was hard pressed to let him go.'

Charlotte's eyes met hers. Even before she dropped the bombshell Charlotte could see it coming.

'You think she knew the child?'

Silently Matron removed the name 'Sherman' to reveal the surname of the child's mother. Charlotte felt a huge lump rise to her throat. She remembered a Saturday morning on Redcliffe Hill when Edna had told her that she thought she might be marrying Colin for the wrong reasons. Her heart went out to her. If the secret got out her marriage would be over. She'd be ostracised by those who thought ill of a girl who'd 'got into trouble' and, worse, with a black American. For the rest of her life she would always wonder where her child was and whether she had married Colin out of affection or pity – pity for him and for herself.

After making the excuse that she needed to get some air before unpacking the car, Charlotte strolled through the grounds making her way to where a plane tree spread its waving branches. Just before she got there she heard children laughing to her left beyond a thick privet hedge. She turned off in that direction and came across the play area. She remembered it as being pretty basic; metal swings, slide and roundabout all painted in a dull green.

Children were playing on the apparatus provided. There were two new additions from the last time, she noticed. Four children were playing in a sandpit made from a series of old logs formed into an oblong perhaps eight feet wide by four feet deep. There was also a wooden climbing frame, made from a cut-down tree, gnarled branches meeting at the top like the bare bones of a wigwam.

In among the children was Josef, directing some not to push, rubbing the grazed knee of another, and listening to the sob story of one little girl who appeared to have lost her shoe.

She stood transfixed. He loves this job, she thought to herself. So ironic, the German submariner who had participated in the sinking of goodness knows how many ships. Yet he couldn't have been happy doing that. After seeing him with these children she was sure of it.

Suddenly he looked in her direction. She smiled at him expecting him to come dashing to meet her. Instead he dealt with the five-year-old Cinderella, finding and refitting her shoe. Even after he'd done that the child continued to hold on to his hand, her brown eyes looking up at him adoringly.

Slowly both he and his follower walked towards her. 'You seem to have settled in,' she said. At the same time she took an apple from her pocket and handed it to the child.

A lock of hair hung damply over his brow. He pushed it away, his blue eyes brightening as he smiled. 'I think I have found my vocation,' he said with a light laugh. 'Children's entertainer – like Mickey Mouse.'

The child, more enamoured of the apple now, ran off. They both watched her run, her brown legs kicking out behind her.

'So many victims of war,' Josef said softly.

Like my children, thought Charlotte. Exiled to boarding school because their father went to war as an ordinary Dr Jekyll and came back as a version of Mr Hyde. Their absence still grieved her although Janet's letters seemed happier than they had been.

'Have you thought any more about going home or staying here?' Charlotte asked hopefully.

Josef looked away, supposedly staring at some far-off trees.

'Yes.'

'And?'

Even before he turned back to her she knew what he was going to say. And she didn't want him to go! It didn't matter that children surrounded them or that prying eyes might be peering out of the orphanage windows. The urge to throw her arms around him and beg him to stay was overwhelming.

Then he asked a question. 'Are you going to leave David?'

It startled her. She looked down at the ground. 'I can't. Call it old-fashioned, call it a sense of duty. I can't do it.' David was less amenable, less patient than he had been. But it's the war she told herself, unless there was something I never saw, something so deeply buried it took a world war to bring it to the surface.

Josef reached for her and squeezed her arm. 'I admire you, Charlotte. You are right. A marriage should be for ever.'

She laughed. 'At least you think so. I'm afraid there are a lot of people who think otherwise nowadays. The divorce rate has gone through the roof. And if you ask people why, they just say, "It's the war you know".' Her own words caused her pain. Wasn't that where she lay the blame for her own marriage?

The silence hung between them. She wanted to prick it as if it were a balloon, say something to lighten the depression that suddenly hung like a weight around her shoulders. Although she wanted him to stay and knew beyond doubt he wanted that too, she also knew what he was asking her. He wanted her commitment and somehow, no matter how violent David was or had become, she couldn't bring herself to leave him. If she did, her whole life would change. A divorced woman. And the children... she knew only too well from her work with the marriage counselling service how the children of divorced or separated parents were treated.

Her thoughts depressed her. She was thankful when Josef broke the silence.

'Mr Partridge had a talk with me. He congratulated me on the sandpit and the climbing frame I built. We spoke about Germany and the rebuilding programme. He asked if I'd thought about being an engineer.'

'Had you?'

Josef shook his head and smirked. 'I raised bread, not buildings. And I was involved with an organisation that assisted the families of submariners. I explained that to him. He seemed impressed and promised to see if he could find something where I could work with people.'

'There's a lot of rebuilding happening here,' said Charlotte with unconcealed enthusiasm. 'A lot of buildings in Bristol were destroyed. Some of them dated back to the beginning of the fifteenth century.'

'Buildings are easily rebuilt,' said Josef plainly, then he took a deep breath and looked up at the sky. 'It's going to rain. I'd better get the children inside.'

Like a shepherd tending his flock or some latter-day Pied Piper, he led the children inside where the nurses and voluntary helpers took charge.

Once he'd attended to that, he ran through the rain with her and helped unload the clothes and bedding from the boot of her car. As they both grappled with the bags and bundles, their arms and thighs brushed together momentarily. The smell of the wet rain permeating his clothes and running down his skin invaded her senses. Something crazy had happened to her since that night on the common. Something more was happening now. It was like stepping onto a moving staircase and finding it impossible to stop. She wanted to keep his company.

She took the first step in one almighty leap. 'How about going to the pictures tonight?'

For a moment there was a questioning look in his eyes.

Was he going to say no? Suddenly she felt a fool. 'That would be nice,' he said.

* * *

They saw *Blithe Spirit* and linked hands. Despite the antics of Margaret Rutherford who was playing the medium, Madame Arcati, Charlotte found it hard to concentrate. Relaxing was something she did little of. She was always involved in organisations, doing things for other people. I do so little for me, she thought suddenly, and wanted things to be different for once.

The feel of his arm pressing against hers was oddly sensual. It made her think of what it would be like to kiss him here in the darkness, to have him wrap his arms around her and nuzzle her neck like he had that night on the common. Instead he watched the film. She watched too, wishing Madame Arcati would vanish in a puff of smoke along with the audience and everyone else in the building. Tonight she wanted more than the closeness she'd encountered on the common.

It was raining quite heavily when they got outside. The windscreen wipers squealed as they swept the raindrops from the screen. Streetlights made the road glisten, an effect strangely missed during the blackout years despite the rain. She'd never regarded any of it as exciting before. Perhaps it was the hypnotic swish of the wipers, perhaps the darkness or even the lights. Whatever it was, she did not want to let this night pass without making it truly memorable.

A tremor of excitement passed through her as she thought about things, the thoughts seeming to hang on each sweep of the wipers.

Can you really do this?

Remember you're married.

Remember he's an enemy prisoner.

Remember he's going home.

You may never see him again.

All is fair in love and war. But it wasn't. David had come back a changed man. Josef was leaving her to go home. Some piece of him must stay, even if only as a memory.

She knew what she wanted to do, but how to proposition a man? She'd never done it before. As if in answer to a prayer the engine spluttered suddenly.

'Oh no!'

'Do we have a problem?' asked a concerned Josef.

'Petrol! I thought I had enough. In fact I did have enough to get to the orphanage and back. But not twice in one day.'

'Can we get some?' asked Josef.

Charlotte shook her head, aware that her throat was dry and her hands were shaking. Lying wasn't a habit of hers. 'Not at this time of night, I'm afraid. No garage is open much beyond six o'clock and, besides, I haven't got my ration card with me.'

'Perhaps I could walk or grab a lift. I have heard the others at the camp used to do this.'

Silence prevailed as Charlotte summoned up the courage to take a step that she knew, deep down, could lead to all sorts of complications.

'There's no other thing for it. You will have to stay the night.' She said it quickly, resolutely, leaving herself no time to change her mind.

Although her gaze was fixed on the road ahead, she knew he was looking at her, trying to read her face, to see exactly what she meant.

'What about your husband? He may not like this.'

'He's at a conference. They take up a lot of his life at the moment. It's all to do with this National Health Service thing the Labour government wants to bring in. The doctors are banding together because they fear they may end up overworked and underpaid.'

'Too bad,' said Josef.

'That you won't meet him?'

'No. That the doctors feel threatened by radical ideas that will benefit everyone.'

They lapsed into silence. It was almost tangible, as if the thoughts and desires of each were reaching out to the other. At least, that was what Charlotte wanted to believe.

The door squeaked loudly as it jerked open. She entered the darkened hallway, Josef two steps behind her. The light switch was to her right but she made no attempt to reach for it. If she did switch it on perhaps both Josef and her intentions might disappear like a dream.

'Charlotte?' His chest was warm against her back.

He hugged her and kissed the nape of her neck. 'You will have to lead me to where you want me to be.' Perhaps it was the accent: his voice thrilled her. She led him to the bedroom.

Guilt was banished by passion. With each caress, each step of arousal, her body took over her mind. Every part of her tingled with sensation. He fondled her breasts, ran his fingers down her spine and caressed her belly. Even before his hand was between her legs, there was no turning back. For the first time in a long while she climaxed and afterwards held him tightly to her, unwilling ever to let him go.

She drove him back to the orphanage the following day.

He was strangely quiet. She wanted to ask him whether it was anything to do with last night. Did he regret it? She didn't think so. Leave it to him, she thought, and that was what she did.

Just before he left the car he rummaged in his right hand pocket and brought out a piece of paper and unfolded it. It looked as though it had been ripped from a much larger piece.

'Corporal Grant's address,' he said emphatically. 'You must write to him.'

They were too close to prying eyes to kiss, so instead she

watched him walk away and wondered why he had waited until now to give it to her.

* * *

It was the weekend immediately after the wedding and Colin and Edna were settled in the house. Billy was outside knocking like crazy upon the door. Colin opened it, Edna right behind him.

'I've got it all,' said Billy, gesturing at the handcart on which were stacked all the remaining items from Edna's parents' house. 'Like you said, Edna, yer ma was off shopping and only yer old man was there. He was helpful enough about you having yer stuff but shaking in his shoes about what yer old lady would say when she got back and found you weren't living with them after all.'

Edna shivered as she contemplated the storm that was to come.

Colin squeezed her hand and turned to Billy. 'Nice of you to push that old cart around here in those nice clothes.'

Smiling broadly, Colin gave Edna's waist a quick nudge and pointed to the two young adolescents sat next to the wheels.

'Take the Mick if you like,' said Billy, 'But I had to be there just to make sure they pushed it properly,' he said with a grin.

Once the two lads had unloaded and been paid half a crown each for their labour, Edna offered Billy a brew.

Billy glanced swiftly at his wristwatch and Edna did too. It looked German and had probably been traded with some soldier lately demobbed. 'I don't think so, Edna my love. I'll be seeing you.' He turned away immediately, and was marching off down the street, shouting at the two lads to push quicker before they got a clout from him and he got a load of abuse from Edna's mother.

Edna exchanged looks with Colin as Billy marched swiftly away.

'You know what this means,' said Colin. 'Your mother's on her way!'

Edna felt her face freeze. For the rest of the day she was all at sixes and sevens.

It was mid-afternoon when the expected storm arrived. She wore a pinched expression, had her hat pulled down firmly on her head and her handbag tight against her body. Like a tame shadow, Edna's father limped quietly behind. 'Come on in,' Colin said brightly. 'You're quite welcome.' Edna stood behind him and the wheelchair.

Mrs Burbage glowered. 'Well, that's a nice way to treat your mother!'

'That ain't right? Why's that then?' Colin's face was a picture of innocence. 'You're our first visitors,' he lied. 'You're the first to know. Stepped into this a bit lucky, didn't we just. Straight back from our honeymoon and into this. Couldn't be better.' He didn't elaborate on the fact that they'd only been to Weston-Super-Mare for one day. 'So there was no point in going back to you first,' he went on blithely, 'and anyway, as you can see, I've got room to move and to work in this place. I can honestly say I'll be able to keep your daughter in the style to which she's accustomed. Ain't that right, Edna?'

He took hold of her hand and clasped it tightly to his shoulder.

Perhaps Colin's presence gave her strength. For the first time in her life Edna found herself holding her mother's gaze. 'Would you like some tea and cake while you're here?' she asked, her voice trembling slightly.

Her mother said she would take tea.

The conversation remained stilted, Edna's parents stiff. The worst part of the visit was showing them around the place and, worst of all, her mother helping her wash up while Colin showed her father his tools and the toys he'd made so far.

'At least you're married,' her mother said. 'I suppose that's something to be grateful for. But I would have liked to know direct that you had a place of your own and not have some errand boy tell me.'

'I thought Dad told you?'

'Don't be cheeky. You know I don't mean your father. Them barrow boys; that's who I mean.'

'I'm lucky to have a house. There's plenty that have only got a couple of rooms or only one room,' said Edna. Having the house made her feel happy. It even made her feel more at ease with her mother than she had at any time in her life. But the feeling didn't last.

'Yes, you are lucky. You threw your respectability aside when you had a black man's baby. It was a good job Colin came back like he did. Losing his legs didn't give him much choice and you didn't have much either.'

As her mother marched off back into the shop, Edna slumped against the sink. All her courage seeped away. She wanted to cry but she also wanted to scream. Up until her parents' visit she had really felt that they were rebuilding their lives. A house, the start of a business and her continuing to work until Colin, his work and his pension, could keep them. She'd also been thinking a lot about Sherman and how and when to tell Colin. Now her mother had made her feel utterly shameful. She had made it plain that no other man would have wanted her anyway.

14

Damage done to Temple Meads Railway Station during the blitz was being repaired and the smell of new paint mixed with that of coal tar. Along with the rest of the city, the pride of the Great Western Railway was being rebuilt. Charlotte wore a blue dress sprinkled with white daisies. Her hat was white and matched her peep-toe shoes. Once she'd bought her platform ticket she raced down the underpass and up the steps to platform five. Janet and Geoffrey had left their respective schools for the August holidays and had met up at Salisbury station. They would both be on the same train.

The train was late. Charlotte eyed her watch then glanced towards the cafeteria. Don't bother, she told herself. The tea will be weaker, the bread greyer and the butter non-existent. Rationing had got worse not better.

The train pulled into the station, steam growling from beneath the iron wheels and hissing from valves beneath the boiler.

Her heart began to pound. She was looking forward to seeing her children again. This was going to be the best August ever. There was every chance that David would agree to the children not having to go back to school. They could get day places again locally. It would be so much better for everyone, especially for Janet. The school had forgiven her for running away and David had never found out.

Charlotte sucked in her breath when she saw Janet. She looked slimmer, taller, and there was a new confidence about her. Geoffrey seemed full of bounce. She kissed them both.

'Are we going to Devon?' asked Geoffrey.

Charlotte was amazed and slightly hurt that he hadn't thrown his arms around her. Just his age, she told herself. Janet seemed more self-contained and Charlotte was worried. Her children had been away only a short time, but in that time they'd grown away from her. Was this what David had meant when he'd said that going away would do them good? 'Are you looking forward to going to Devon, Janet?' she asked brightly, determined to raise their spirits as much as she could.

'I don't mind.' She continued to stare out of the open car window at the people walking by, men in shirtsleeves, women in summer dresses, pushing prams or carrying shopping.

Dust rose from bombsites presently being cleared. Eventually new buildings would rise from the ashes of the old. But it would take a long time. Traders had set up shop from handbarrows or old vans on those sites that had been cleared. One particular van caught Charlotte's eye. A man in a smart suit stood at the back of it shouting out prices, his arms gesticulating. Billy Hills! Like a marionette he didn't stop moving, wooden aeroplane in one hand, toy car in the other. She opened her window a little wider and stopped.

'Buy now, ladies. I know we're only in August, but don't leave it till November to buy for Christmas. Make sure you've got more than an orange an' an apple in the little chap's stocking this year. Make sure you've got more than that in the old man's stocking though, won't ya?' He winked as he said it and a titter of restrained amusement ran through the crowd. Most were women.

She was just wondering whether to drive on or get out and say hello, when a sleek Bentley pulled up and a large man got out. The crowd divided as he pushed his way through. 'I want a word with you,' she heard him say to Billy.

'Are we going home?' Geoffrey grumbled.

Charlotte wound the window down further and strained to hear.

'Just a minute.'

Their conversation was none too clear.

Afraid that Billy was about to find himself in trouble, Charlotte got out, determined to put in a good word no matter what.

The man crooked his finger and Billy bent low.

'I'll take these,' said the man and immediately took the wooden toys from Billy's hands.

Not at all sure what she would say or what she could do, Charlotte followed the path cleared by the man from the Bentley, her head high and her jaw jutting firmly. 'Billy! I was just passing by. We met at Edna's wedding. Remember?'

Both men stared at her, Billy with a smile of recognition and the other man with a warning frown.

'Am I interrupting something?' she said looking from one man to the other and back again.

'No. Not at all. Mrs Hennessey-White, ain't it?' said Billy, his smile widening. 'Nice to meet you again.'

He tipped his hat slightly. The man from the Bentley followed suit but in a far more formal fashion. He knew a lady when he saw one.

Charlotte looked meaningfully at the big man, fully expecting him to introduce himself or depart. He ignored her and kept his gaze fixed on Billy.

'My name's Lewis. I want to see you at three thirty tomorrow afternoon. You know the address, don't you?'

Billy nodded. With one toy tucked under his arm, the other dangling from his hand, the man departed. Billy's eyes followed him all the way back to the sleek machine he'd arrived in.

'Worth a few bob that,' he said and whistled low.

Charlotte wondered about Billy. Good-hearted he might be, but she wasn't entirely sure he was honest. Billy was doing very nicely and had probably been trading on the black market all the way through the war.

'He seemed very insistent on taking *Colin's* toys,' Charlotte said, emphasising the fact that the toys were Colin's.

'Yeah. Certainly got a bee in 'is bonnet about them,' said Billy. He grinned and looked suddenly bashful. 'Seen anything of that Polly then?'

Charlotte considered. 'Not since the wedding. Have you?'

He shook his head a little sadly, then sighed and looked away. 'Oh well. Better get on. Got to make some butter to spread on me bread! Ladies and gentlemen,' he shouted as he climbed back onto the back of the van. 'Do I 'ave some bargains for you. Spam! Spam at knock-down prices.'

Charlotte got back into the car. Whatever Billy was up to with the big man and the toys, she hoped Colin wouldn't be the loser for it. She put it from her mind. Her children were home and they would have a lovely summer holiday together.

'I shan't be coming to Devon with you,' said David that evening at dinner. 'I'm busy at the practice and also have to be in London for some of the time.'

'I'd like to go to London,' said Janet. 'I hear you can still get decent clothes there if you know where to look.'

Charlotte smiled. Janet had sensed her father was in a good mood.

'You are going to Devon with your mother and brother, Janet. *I* am going to London!'

Charlotte noted Janet's crestfallen expression. 'We shall go shopping in Brixham,' she said.

'I suppose it will have to do,' said Janet and sighed. 'I'm not going shopping. I shall play with my boat. Or swim. Or play cricket. Anything but go shopping,' said Geoffrey.

Even David managed a forced smile.

Charlotte felt happier that night than she had for a long time. Perhaps things with David really were getting better. They were like a family again. But at the back of her mind there was Josef and a wonderful night when the only person to benefit from her action was herself.

Later she put on her favourite nightdress, a satin, bias-cut affair that was formed around the bust and edged with Nottingham lace.

As David used the bathroom in the next room along the landing, she brushed her hair and dabbed perfume behind her ears. I don't look like a long-married woman, she thought to herself as she studied her reflection. There are a few lines, but not enough to worry about.

Thinking about wrinkles made her study the grey eyes that looked back out at her. They sparkled. Perhaps it was the lights. She looked at the room beyond her reflection. The bedside lights were on. The bedclothes were spread neat and tidy over the matrimonial bed. Yet Charlotte wasn't seeing them. For a brief moment, she saw herself with Josef's naked arms entwined around her shoulders, his mouth on hers. Her thoughts left her tingling as a hot flush seeped from her face to her neck.

Why had she done it? All through the war she'd been faithful to her absent husband. Many had not been. Why had she left it until now?

She hadn't seen Josef alone for over a month. Unless it was a trustee meeting, she only delivered the baby clothes on a Saturday afternoon with Edna. She'd told herself it was best that way. And Edna was always desperate to come. So far Charlotte had not spoken to Edna about Sherman. She had her own problems and they were in her own life, in her own bedroom.

Again she fixed her eyes on the bed and shivered with pleasure. The memory of what she had done would be there each time she eyed the green flowers that formed the centre of the satin-covered eiderdown. And each time she slid between the crisp cotton sheets she would feel his legs entwining with hers.

David entered. The vision melted. She forced herself to be cheerful and hoped her brightness did not seem brittle. 'Isn't it wonderful to have the children home, David?' At the same time she nervously dabbed more perfume behind her ears.

He grunted and pulled back the bedclothes.

Charlotte turned on her stool to face him. 'They miss us you know. Especially you, darling. I mean, you've been away so long,' she added hurriedly.

He sat on the side of the bed and took off his watch. 'I suppose so.' He looked tired. She hoped he was. Intercourse with him remained unattractive.

'I would like them at home again,' she blurted. 'Now that you're so much better...'

She froze. Judging by his expression it was the worst thing she could have said. 'Are you saying I've been ill?' He got up and walked towards her, stood between her and the bed, her and the vision of a different man, a different time.

'It's the war!' She said it quickly as if it would be enough to placate him.

Nerves taut, head erect, she sat on the stool, waiting for the blow, the slap to the face or the head. It still happened – occasionally.

'Get to bed, woman!'

Obedience was easy if it meant the blow wouldn't come. She got up and walked to the bed. He pushed her onto the eiderdown before she had a chance to pull back the bedclothes.

She turned her face away from him, unable to stomach the look in his eyes, the roughness of his hands.

Her mind screamed.

Why is he doing this?

She had told herself he was better, that the children could come home and things would be fine. Now she wasn't so sure. The soft satin she adored was ripped away from her body. When would the nightmare end? She told herself it would, that there was no point in telling anyone about it. It would pass. There was no need for anyone else to know. It was just the war and he was sure to get better in time.

* * *

Polly pushed open the door of The Swan With Two Necks, a small pub not far from Old Market. The smell of cigarette ash and stale beer spewed out to meet her. Once she'd coped with the sting of the smoke, she got her bearings and looked for Mavis. *For old times' sake*, Mavis had said when she'd seen her at the corner of York Street. But Polly knew it had to be more than that. What sort of trouble had she got herself into?

Once she could focus, she saw Mavis waving. She was sitting at a tripod table, the top of which was held in place with cast-iron Britannias at the top of each leg.

'I got you a half of bitter,' said Mavis indicating the brimming glass already on the table. 'Me purse don't run to a port and lemon.'

Polly grimaced. 'It'll do I suppose.' She looked around her. 'What did you want to see me about?'

Mavis grinned and nodded. 'It wasn't me that wanted to see you. It was 'im.' She nodded towards a table in the corner.

Polly recognised Billy Hills. 'What does he want?' Mavis stared at her. 'My, but ain't you the posh one. Can see you spend more time in Clifton than you do round 'ere.'

'Do you blame me?' said Polly as she got up from the chair. 'Who wants to stay around this dump?'

Mavis raised her eyebrows. 'Charmed I'm sure, but I ain't toffee nosed. I know my place.'

But Polly wasn't interested. She wished she hadn't come and had never expected to feel such an outsider as she did.

Billy stood up politely when she got to the table and pulled out a chair for her. Polly regarded him with undisguised contempt. What did he have to offer compared to a doctor with a private practice in Clifton? After all, he did fancy her, didn't he? This was what it was all about? 'I told 'er to get you a port and lemon,' said Billy, noticing the half of bitter she'd brought with her. 'She reckoned she didn't have the money.'

'Cheeky cow! She kept the change.'

He half got up and looked over to where Mavis had been sitting. Only an empty chair and an equally empty glass remained.

'No matter.' He turned back to her, his fingers tangling nervously together on the table.

Polly cocked her head, remained mute and waited for him to speak. What did the little squirt want?

Nervously he swigged at his beer. 'I met your brother-in-law, Bert, the other day. Asked if I was interested in some fags he'd got from a docker he knows.'

Polly went cold. Up until now she'd regarded herself as superior to the likes of Billy Hills. It was easy to be contemptuous of someone when you knew a bit about them. But when they knew a bit about you, well, that was different. But she stayed calm. 'So?'

'Well, 'e told me about the house being so crowded and you having a kid an' all an' bein' short of money...'

'I don't do favours!'

He looked visibly shaken. 'I didn't think you did. I weren't finking of anything like that, honest!'

Polly pursed her lips. She didn't want to be here. She never wanted to be in this neck of the woods again, and when she got hold of Bertie...

'It's just that...' Billy paused, looked up at her from under his bushy eyebrows then looked bashfully away. 'Well, I'm all alone an' I've got this house me old man left me. Used to be in scrap metal 'e did. Would have made a killing now, wouldn't 'e, with all they old tanks and stuff not wanted any more.'

Polly was getting impatient. 'What about this house?'

Billy licked the dryness from his lips. 'It's like this, it's a big house, too big for me. I need a housekeeper.'

'Now look here!' said Polly starting to rise, heads turning in their direction.

'No! No!' said Billy, his hand grabbing hers. 'It's not like that. It's all above board. Honest it is.'

Polly snatched her hand away. 'Oh, is it now?'

'I just want someone to look after the place, that an' provide a bit of company for me mother.'

'Your mother! What do you bloody take me for?'

Billy shook his head. 'Look. It's a big place, so if you're interested...' He searched her face for a reaction. Polly's expression didn't alter. Billy looked away.

'Sorry I asked. I just thought...'

Polly sprang to her feet. 'Well you thought wrong. I'm not a bloody housekeeper! Nor a damned skivvy! I'm a receptionist up in Clifton. That's what I am!'

She started to make for the door. Billy grabbed hold of her arm. 'If you want to think it over...'

Polly shook him off. It did occur to her to shout at him that he was nothing better than a pimp. The bar was crowded and it would have satisfied her ego no end. But as she turned to do that a sudden thought entered her head.

What if Meg insisted on her leaving before she was ready? What if she needed somewhere to live at some time? So she buttoned her lip and left the door swinging behind her between the fresh air and the fug within.

* * *

It was Saturday evening and there was smoked haddock for tea.

'Charlotte's going on holiday,' Edna said to Colin as she sliced bread from a dull grey loaf and spread butter sparingly.

'Thought she'd have took us with her,' said Colin jokingly. 'Blimey, what a let down! Where's she going?'

'Devon. They've got a cottage there.'

'I bet. Probably more like a mansion.'

Edna had already thought out what she was going to say. 'I'll be taking the clothes out to the orphanage while she's away. You don't mind, do you?'

'Do I have a choice?' he said at the same time as picking up the evening paper.

'No. Of course not.'

'Well, there we are,' he retorted with a laugh. 'I'm already a henpecked husband.'

Edna kissed him on the top of his head. He wrapped his arm around her waist and dragged her close. 'Now what was that for?'

'Because you're nice and Charlotte's nice.'

'Can't say the same for her old man,' said Colin. 'Not that I've ever met him but I have seen the bruises on her neck.'

'Of course you've met him. He was at our wedding. Remember?'

Colin let the paper drop to the floor. 'Oh yes. The one drooling over brassy Polly.'

'Colin! She's not brassy.'

'No,' he said. 'Not now she isn't. Wonder why?'

Edna blushed and turned away. During the next few weeks she intended broaching the subject of Sherman though quite how to do it she wasn't yet sure. But would Colin then think she was as common as Polly? She didn't like secrets yet they seemed to be piling up. David and Polly's intimate embrace was still clear in her mind. Would it be fair to tell Charlotte about it or fairer not to? It was a difficult decision and one she'd have to sleep on.

* * *

She was waiting for the bus to take her to the orphanage when Billy Hills drew up in his van.

'Wanna lift?'

She told him where she was going. It was a few miles further than he'd thought but he still insisted she hop in complete with her bundles and bags.

'It's a nice day for driving anyway,' he said, 'and everything's going my way.'

He whistled as he drove and Edna couldn't help wondering if he'd got anywhere with Polly. It was easy to see he was sweet on her. She made a point of asking him. He smiled secretively and tapped the side of his nose. 'Could be but then there's Betty. I said, 'ow would you like to move in with me and be me sweetheart, and Betty said...'

Edna's mouth dropped open. 'Betty who?'

'Grable of course!'

'Oh Billy.'

He leaned closer. 'There's something good in the pipeline for us all. I'll be up to talk to Colin about it before very long. An' you make sure you're there. It'll excite you. I know it will.'

The words flew over her head. As they pulled into the drive that led up to the front of the orphanage, Edna's eyes fixed on the door. Beyond that was her baby. He was in her mind more and more nowadays and it was affecting her work. Although Mr Gordon was behaving himself following a quiet word from someone higher up, he had pulled her aside to mention that she was making far too many mistakes. If she didn't smarten up he'd have to give her a written warning. She had promised to do better but it wasn't easy to forget your own flesh and blood.

The pristine corridor of the orphanage echoed to her footsteps. Sherman was ahead of her. Sherman would be glad to see her, his little mouth smiling and his eyes bright with excitement.

'Miss Burbage!'

Edna stopped and turned to face the wide bosom and small stature of Matron.

Matron nodded a greeting. 'Could you come into my office for a moment?'

Edna followed her in, the bags of clothes and other things bumping against her legs.

Matron closed the door behind her and bade her sit down. She herself sat in the chair behind a light oak desk. A dark blue blind was pulled halfway down the window behind her, making her vaguely resemble an overweight Madonna.

'Before I say anything else, Miss Burbage, I have to tell you that your secret is safe with me.'

Edna put down her bags and stared wide-eyed at the woman across from her.

'I recognised your name,' Matron went on. 'Even if I hadn't, I would have known Sherman was your son the way you held on to him.'

Edna stiffened. 'Does this mean you'll stop me seeing him?'

Matron looked thoughtfully at her hands. 'No. But you do realise that all these babies are available for adoption.'

Of course she knew! Fear squeezing her insides, Edna leaned forward, her fingers gripping the desk edge for support. 'But surely the white babies go first?'

Matron nodded. 'That's true. But Sherman isn't too dark. His day may come. Then what are you going to do?'

Edna shook with desperation. Adoption! She knew it was likely but had ignored it up until now.

'Until he does get adopted you can continue to see him. But I felt I had to point this out to you. It is likely that someone may offer and, remember, you did give your baby up for adoption shortly after he was born.'

Edna shook her head emphatically. 'No! No! I didn't. My mother made me do it. I didn't want to have him adopted!'

Matron sat back in her chair and shook her head sadly. 'You and a thousand others. Adolf Hitler has a lot to answer for.'

'His father wouldn't want it either!'

'How do you know that?' said Matron, then stopped. 'Ah! The parcels! I believe your mother knows Mrs Grey who works for Mrs Hennessey-White.'

Edna remembered her mother mentioning a partner with whom she played whist named Mrs Grey. But the parcels themselves were no longer important. All that counted was her son. 'Does he have to be adopted?' she asked.

The homely woman wearing the dark blue uniform and the crisp white apron came round and put her arm around her shoulder. 'That, my dear, is up to you. Is there any chance of you having him at home?'

'I've just got married.'

'And your husband doesn't know about him.'

Edna blew into her handkerchief and fixed her gaze on the floor.

He was awake when she went to see him.

'He's only just woken up,' said Sister Ruth. 'He must have known you were coming.'

Edna nodded through her tears and looked down at him. 'Sherman,' she said, softly reaching down and holding the downy soft hand in hers. 'I'm not very brave, and whatever happens you must believe it's for the best. Honestly it is.'

* * *

Although she tried to appear composed when she got back to Billy's old black van, he immediately saw her tear-stained face. 'What's the matter? Someone upset you?'

'It's all those babies,' sniffed Edna. 'All alone in the world and no one to care.'

Embarrassed by sentiment even though he was pretty much that way himself, Billy drove silently. When he did speak it was merely to remark on the bomb damage or to enthuse about what the city would look like in the future. But for the present it vaguely resembled the surface of another planet, the sort he'd seen pre-war in a film like *Flash Gordon*.

While he drove, Edna took the opportunity to tidy her face. 'You won't tell Colin I was upset, will you?' she asked in a small voice.

Billy shook his head. 'Not if you don't want me to. Any time you want a lift, just say the word. You know where to find me. Flogging from the back of the van, Bedminster first three days of the week, end of the week and weekends I'm down in the Centre.'

She thanked him and got out of the van. 'Would you like to come in for tea?'

Billy eased himself out of his seat and still looked neat and tidy despite having been driving a while. 'Better come in and explain I gave you a lift,' he said with a grin. 'Wouldn't want old Colin thinking we were up to something, would we!'

Edna laughed. 'Colin isn't like that.' They went inside the house.

* * *

Polly liked watching David drive. There was something sensual about the way his finely manicured hands handled the wheel and his thighs moved as he pressed the pedals. The scarf that Edna had left behind at the consulting rooms lay folded neatly on her lap but slid to the floor. 'You don't think she came back for it and saw us, do you? Only I thought I heard something?'

David shrugged. 'What could she say even if she did? If she does betray us, I can make things pretty difficult for her. She wouldn't want to lose her job. I think, from what I've seen of her, she is more sensible than that.'

His attitude made her feel uncomfortable. She told herself that all posh blokes were like that, but deep down she was questioning whether she really wanted to be with him. Aaron was someone she'd fallen in love with. There'd been strong physical attractions with the men she'd known before him including the father of her child. She felt none towards David. And then of course there was Billy to consider. Whether she cared to show it or not, she liked him. Although she was having trouble admitting it to herself, the idea of taking revenge on Charlotte by taking David was not as attractive as it had been. Sometime soon she would call a halt to the whole ugly situation.

'This turning,' said Polly a few yards before Kent Street. He turned the wheel. 'And this house.'

He stopped the car outside Edna's house in Kent Street. She had the urge to remark how small the house was, but who was she to make comment? A cobbled street of flat-fronted houses just off Midland Road was her real home, full of children and relatives she wished she didn't have.

She got out first and knocked firmly on the door. David followed. She was sure a few net curtains twitched as they stood there. In York Street she would have pulled faces and made rude signs for their benefit. But she was here with David and guessed that neighbours were admiring the car and the posh couple that had stepped out of it.

Polly smiled up at David and adjusted his tie. 'It's not straight,' she said.

'I'm not a child!' he said testily, and smacked at her hands.

Edna's mouth dropped when she opened the door. The sound of a machine, the smell of shaved wood and flying sawdust came out to meet them.

'Here's your scarf,' said Polly. Edna coloured up.

She knows, thought Polly. She was confident of Edna's silence. Edna needed her job.

Cocky as ever, Polly placed her hands on her hips and waited for an invite. Edna continued to stand there with her mouth open so Polly said it for her. 'Well, are you going to leave us waiting on the doorstep? A cup of tea would be nice, Edna.'

Colin was sat at a lathe, an oddly shaped piece of wood in his hands. He stopped, looked up as they entered and swung his chair round to face them.

'Oh! We've got visitors.'

'You remember Polly!' said Edna. 'She works for Doctor Hennessey-White – David – Charlotte's husband.'

Polly winced at Edna reminding her that David and the lifestyle he represented belonged to Charlotte.

'I'll make tea,' blurted Edna.

Colin blinked and, for a moment, Polly was convinced that he knew everything, was going to shout it out and show them the door. She'd forgotten how amiable he could be. 'You girls do that. I'll explain the ins and outs of toy making to the...' he paused, 'doctor here.'

'I'll help,' said Polly and threw Colin an angry look. He'd been about to say 'the good doctor' as people did, but had scowled and done otherwise.

Rather than suffer an uncomfortable atmosphere, she followed Edna into the kitchen. Old-fashioned as it was, its cosy warmth surprised her. The range was black and ugly, but its glowing coals seemed to give it life. An old dresser had been painted cream and was now festooned with crockery, mostly blue and cream-striped Cornish. The gaps were filled with old willow patterned meat platters.

Bloody hell, they must have belonged to Queen Victoria. I'd put them in the dustbin, thought Polly to herself, but didn't remark. Instead she turned to Edna and smiled cordially.

She looked Edna up and down as she bustled round her kitchen, a slim figure in a green woollen dress that she must have had for years. With an air of self-satisfaction she adjusted her collar and tightened her belt and said, 'You certainly are a capable little housewife.'

'I do my best. We haven't got much but it suits us fine. We haven't even used the rooms upstairs, what with Colin.'

Polly pretended not to notice that she was referring to the fact that Colin couldn't get upstairs unaided or, at least, not without difficulty.

'Well, that could work out okay. How many rooms are up there?'

'Two.'

'Two children at least then! Four if you double them up. Six if you triple! You look just the sort to suit babies. Ever had one, have you?'

A teacup smashed to the floor. Edna's face had been pink enough before. Now it was a much deeper colour. 'No!' she growled as she reached for a handle of the dresser cupboard.

I've hit a raw nerve, thought Polly, and although she would never ask outright, she wondered exactly how they managed in bed. She shivered the thought away. It wasn't her problem, thank God! Instead she looked down on Edna busily brushing the remains of the cup into the dustpan.

Polly smiled as she beheld the deep blush behind the pale brown hair. No need to worry. Colin must be up to the job if Edna's blush was anything to go by.

'Never mind,' said Polly. 'You can always adopt.'

She sauntered back into the shop where Colin had temporarily buried his hostility towards David and was enthusing about his toy making, explaining that although it was quiet now, it would be hectic by Christmas.

'Any bit of wood you come across,' he was saying. 'Any at all, I'd be most grateful. And paint. I can always do with paint. Mind you, Billy Hills provides me with a lot of stuff. Sells a few toys for me too an' all. You do know him, don't you? Oh, yes. Of course you do. You met him at our wedding. He visits here a fair lot.'

Edna came in and put a brown Bakelite tray of four cups and a plate of digestive biscuits down on the corner of a workbench.

David looked to Polly. 'Have I met him?'

'Yes,' said Polly quickly drinking the tea. 'I was with him at

Edna's wedding.' She glanced swiftly at her watch. 'Do you think we'd better go now?'

She ignored David's look of surprise and headed for the door. The last thing she wanted at this moment was Billy Hills turning up and laying her history bare in front of David. She hadn't uttered a word about Carol. Kids spoil relationships.

Head down, Edna bustled the tea things away quickly once David and Polly were gone. She didn't want Colin to see her face or stay around long enough for him to ask her questions about where she had left the scarf and why she had gone there. If she got to the kitchen door quickly enough...

'Oh no you don't!'

He'd got quick with the chair. Very quick. His fingers were around her wrist. The tea things rattled on the tray. 'He said you left the scarf at his place in Clifton. You didn't tell me you'd been up there. Is there something I should know?'

Despite having just drunk a cup of tea her lips were dry. She licked them but they remained resolutely the same.

It was difficult to look into his face. 'I was looking for Charlotte. I needed more material to make clothes for the kids at the orphanage. I thought it was the least I could do, seeing as she gave me that stuff for my wedding dress – and that suit she put back for me at the jumble sale.' Colin loosened his grip on her wrist – not that he held her that firmly anyway. He looked at her a little sadly and shook his head. 'I used to think you were too good to be true. Now I know I was wrong. You are too good, Edna, and I'll never understand why you married the likes of me.'

The tea tray landed on the floor, the crockery clattering and the teaspoons flying. They were of no importance. Edna threw her arms around his neck. Her eyes were full of tears because she'd suddenly remembered exactly why she'd loved him in the first place. Incapacitated as he was, he still put others first, generous to a fault no matter what. And she couldn't hurt him. She couldn't tell him about Sherman. Not yet. Not just yet.

She saw his hand reaching for the scarf and immediately knew he had a question to ask.

'You love this scarf. What happened to make you leave it behind?'

The truth could not be avoided. Even her silence would speak volumes – and Colin heard.

'I thought her and David were too friendly. Poor Charlotte,' he said hugging her as close as the wheelchair would allow.

* * *

Just she and the children: Charlotte told herself she was going to enjoy this holiday. Sea air was famous for clearing the head.

But duty came first. Before leaving she attended a Trustee meeting. To leave without doing so would have been irresponsible. As it turned out she was glad she did go. Lady Garribond actually apologised!

'I've never known that before,' said Matron who had overheard the mumbled words.

'Perhaps she's found a few skeletons in her own cupboard,' Charlotte remarked.

Matron smiled as if she knew something no one else knew. 'Bear in mind that she was a society belle when old Edward was king and you know what sort of man he was!'

'I've heard rumours,' Charlotte said. Edward VII had indeed frequented the city to see one or two of his lady friends.

'It doesn't hurt to remind the old what it feels like to be young,' said Matron, as if reading Charlotte's thoughts.

'Enjoy your holidays, Mrs Hennessey-White. Forget your duties and have a nice time,' Matron called, her words echoing off the glossy coldness of the corridor.

'Thank you.' Duties were the last thing on her mind.

What was it Matron had said about reminding the old how it feels to be young? And being happy? What about being happy? That's how Josef made her feel. She reminded herself that she was a married woman. Divorce was on the increase but it wasn't an option she wished to contemplate.

'No!' she muttered to herself. 'I have to try!'

The cool darkness of the entrance hall framed the view through the windows where her car sat baking in the bright sunshine. By the time she reached the door she was convinced that she could leave without wandering the grounds like a lovesick fool.

The sun was hot, the sky bright. She squinted and raised a white-gloved hand to shield her eyes. Once she was in her car the sound of the engine and the wheels turning on gravel would drown out her emotions. Once she was in the car she would be safe.

But there he was, leaning against it just like she'd seen him do before. And her heart beat faster.

If I rush past and don't look into his face...

There is nothing he can do to make me stay and talk to him, she told herself as she hurried forward.

'I've come to say goodbye.'

She stopped in her tracks and looked into his face. Those blue eyes, the kind mouth that smiled so casually and with such charm.

'Where are you going?' Her breath felt tight in her chest.

He shoved his hands in his trouser pockets – such a casual gesture, completely devoid of military pretension. 'Mr Partridge has located an organisation in Germany that places people wanting to work with charity organisations.'

'You specifically asked him for that?' It surprised her that he'd found something suitable so quickly.

He nodded just once and a tight slightly sad smile came to his lips. 'I want to do something towards rebuilding my country. Do you know how many orphans there are in Europe, in Germany alone?'

She shook her head. 'I dread to think.'

'Millions!'

She who had for so long been involved in charity work was suitably awe struck. Words stuck in her throat. 'When?' she whispered.

'One week. The eleventh.'

'That's halfway through our holiday. I'm going to Devon,' she blurted. 'The children are home from school' He placed his hands on her bare arms. His touch was warm and so unbelievably pleasant. A cool breeze played with the hem of her blue striped dress – so clean, so pristine. But she wasn't clean, she wasn't pure! She had sinned. But the straight and narrow was turning out to be a lonely road. Was it really so wrong to feel like she did with Josef? And could she resist sin? Or was it love?

His voice was irresistible. 'You will be at the station to see me off?' One fifteen. My train leaves at one fifteen.'

'I will,' she said, resolute that somehow she would indeed make her way back to Bristol and say goodbye to him on the same station she had welcomed her husband home from the war.

15

Toot! Toot!

Polly nearly jumped out of her skin. 'Very funny!' she said, hands on hips as Billy Hills' battered black van pulled in beside her.

Billy grinned. 'Wanna lift?'

'Again? Everywhere I go you seem to be going my way,' she said, standing as seductively as she knew how. Much as she liked to belittle him in public, she had to admit he was kind – and besotted, which automatically attracted her to him. She'd always liked men to be besotted with her. It made her feel like a film star.

'How's yer kid?' he asked, as she got in.

'Okay.'

She took her time, careful not to snag her stockings on the boxes of cheap china and bric-a-brac stored on the floor in front of the seat.

That was something different about Billy too. He didn't mind about Carol. In fact every time she saw him he made a point of asking how she was. Most men would run a mile.

'Off to the doctor's, are you? Odd thing to do on a Sunday night.'

She tried not to look guilty at his question. 'Mrs Grey's not well.

I'm doing the cooking while she's away.' Actually, she was worried. Mrs Grey being ill was very inconvenient. Charlotte was away on holiday with the children and, to put it mildly, she was afraid of being alone in the house with David. But she'd braced herself to do it. This was an opportunity to tell David that she had changed her mind about getting involved with him. Once that little problem was out of the way she was free to dally with whom she liked and, at present, she liked Billy.

There was a silence. She knew instinctively that Billy had been about to mention his need for a housekeeper again. Obviously he'd decided not to risk being told to sod off. Well, silence was all right with her. She had things to think about. Meg was getting on her back, keeping on about Carol needing a better home. Well, she was doing her best.

Billy spoke and broke into her thoughts. 'Beginning to look a bit tidier.'

They were crossing what used to be the Tramway Centre. Polly looked out at what was left of the old tram lines, now twisted bits of metal glowing softly red in what was left of the setting sun. Sunday silence lay over the scene like the curtain in the picture house, waiting to go up on the activity of clearing the roads and getting things moving again – really moving.

'Couldn't look any worse,' she said.

They drove up Park Street, where bomb damage had left gaps like broken teeth between buildings. The smell of old cinders and dust lay heavy on the evening air.

'Buses get up here easier than trams,' said Billy trying his best to provoke some response from her.

'Do they?' she said. A car would be better. Preferably chauffeur driven. That would be better. She sighed heavily and rested her head against the side of the van. She pretended to look at the damage and noticed the signs saying 'KEEP CLEAR – DEMOLI-

TION IN PROGRESS.' Just like our lives, she thought. Demolish the old and build up the new. If she didn't do something about David she could achieve just that. Only it would be Charlotte's life she'd be demolishing and goodness knows what would become of her own. She was sure that Edna had seen them and it embarrassed her. She was desperate to live it down and, besides, she wanted to leave the door open for Billy. Although he couldn't read or write, he had a mind full of ideas for making money. Life with him could be good.

He had given up trying to impress her and was staring at the road ahead. But he caught her looking and gave her a warm smile. She smiled back. She knew when a man wanted her.

Grand Victorian houses, some six storeys high, threw their shadows over the road ahead of them as the sun sank lower. Polly eyed them thoughtfully. Somehow they didn't seem quite so attractive today. Their reflections flashed by in the broad-paned glass of the wide bay windows. Lights were being turned on in high-ceilinged living rooms, curtains were being drawn. No looking in, no looking out, and suddenly it struck her how isolated the lives of the people that lived here seemed – even David and Charlotte. Was that why Charlotte threw herself into charity work and all that stuff?

They were at the end of Royal York Crescent. 'Stop here!' she said suddenly.

'Are you sure you've got to stay overnight?' Billy asked.

'Sorry mate, but there you are.'

She waved as she walked away but didn't look back, partly because she didn't want Billy to see the guilt in her eyes but mostly to avoid any accusation in his.

* * *

Sand, sea and brilliant sunshine. People were swimming again, children were building sandcastles, and others, like Charlotte herself, were sitting in deckchairs outside their gaily-painted beach huts. Granted the paint was looking a bit tired, but once the paint manufacturers went back into brightly painted colours instead of battleship grey or khaki, she'd get someone to brighten it up. She busied herself writing a letter to Aaron. It was difficult to know what to say. She mentioned Polly of course, and also thanked him for his assistance at the camp. After posting it air mail she expected to get a reply back in about three to four weeks.

Geoffrey was launching the boat he'd had for Christmas from off the rocks and into a pool.

Janet was slumped in a deckchair next to Charlotte, her face a picture of adolescent boredom.

Charlotte took off her sunglasses and squinted at the rock pools where some other boys had joined Geoffrey, pushing the boat from one end of the pond to the other. He seemed happy enough and she smiled. She turned to her daughter and frowned. Janet was obviously far from happy.

'Why don't you go for a swim?' she said.

'I don't want to.'

'Then why did you bother to put your swimming costume on, darling?'

'To air my body.'

Charlotte frowned more deeply. The cheeky comment called for a reprimand yet, somehow, she couldn't bring herself to do it. Childish rebukes didn't seem to suit her any more. Charlotte eyed her speculatively. Janet's eyes were closed, one arm tossed up behind her head. She was no longer a child. The light woollen swimsuit her daughter wore clung to curves Charlotte was sure were not there before last term.

'Then let's talk,' said Charlotte. 'You know your father is considering letting you stay at home and go back to your old school.'

Janet turned round to face her and opened her eyes. 'Mother, how could you be such a fool! Of course he's not! If you hadn't told him I ran away that day...'

Charlotte's jaw dropped. 'I never told him any such thing! And he's never mentioned that he knew...'

'Well, he mentioned it to me,' Janet said bitterly, before turning on her side so that Charlotte was left looking at her back.

Charlotte racked her brains. Mrs Grey wouldn't tell. So who else?

The answer came swiftly. Polly! Polly had seen Janet there.

She reached for her skirt and blouse. 'I'm off to the Post Office. I won't be long.'

Gripping the letter in her hand she made her way off the beach. The sooner Aaron confirmed her story the sooner there would be a truce between her and Polly.

* * *

'There you are,' said Billy.

Colin took the crisp notes Billy handed him.

'Twelve pounds, fifteen shillings and sixpence. Not bad for a month's work, is it?' Billy said.

Colin beamed. 'Not bad on top of my disablement.' He looked up at Edna and grabbed her hand. 'Keep us going, girl. Won't need your wages before long.'

Edna smiled weakly. 'I'll keep going as long as I need to. Once you're making millions I'll give it all up.'

They all laughed. No one there could guess that behind her smile Edna's heart was aching. Sherman needed her. She wanted to go to him again but the length of time it took to get a bus out there was unfair on Colin. She didn't like leaving him alone that long. But if Billy could give her a lift?

Billy stopped laughing. 'That's what I want to talk to you about. This bloke approached me down on the Centre and took two of your toys away.'

'You gave them away?' asked Colin with raised eyebrows.

'Sort of, free samples you might say. Anyway, he's come back.' Billy paused, obviously enjoying the looks of apprehension on their faces.

Edna broke first. 'What did he say, Billy?'

A wide smile spread slowly across Billy's face. 'He said 'e wants one hundred by Christmas.'

Edna clapped her hands. Billy would be calling in even more than he was at present. 'That's wonderful! Which one does he want?'

Billy looked from one to the other of them. 'One hundred of each.'

Edna and Colin's mouths dropped open as they turned and looked at each other.

'But we've got ten different designs now,' said Colin. Edna touched his shoulder. She was aware that he didn't always feel one hundred per cent. A man who'd gone through what he had couldn't expect to. But it was obvious that Billy had more to say.

'You need to employ someone,' said Billy. 'You can find someone, can't you?'

Colin said he'd think on it. 'In the meantime you'd better take that lot,' he said pointing to six more horses painted in dark pink with yellow dots.

'I'll help you,' said Edna, desperate now to get Billy alone so she could ask him one huge favour.

The back doors of the black van had oval windows, similar to the frames you used to get on Victorian pictures. The headlights had a brass trim. Billy kept them highly polished. It hadn't occurred to him that such gleaming accessories made the rest of the vehicle look positively decrepit!

'Billy!' said Edna breathlessly as he opened the back doors. 'I wonder if you can do me a favour once a week.' She glanced furtively towards the front door of the shop. Colin had not come out. It was sunny and something about sunshine made him depressed. Other people walked out in it. He didn't.

'Whatever you want, Mrs Smith, I'm only too pleased to oblige,' said Billy with mock civility.

'Charlotte – Mrs Hennessey-White – is away on holiday. I promised I'd take some baby clothes and things out to the orphanage but it takes so long on the bus and I don't like leaving Colin alone for too long. Do you think you could take me out there – if it's not too much trouble?'

'None at all! I'd be pleased to do it.'

'Billy!' She touched his arm. 'I don't want Colin to know. You won't tell him, will you?'

There was a questioning look in his eyes, almost as though he knew that there was someone at the orphanage she particularly wanted to see. She blinked but kept her courage.

'I won't say a word,' he said. Edna breathed a sigh of relief.

* * *

A plan flashed through Polly's head as she brushed her hair before the bedroom mirror in the lemon-striped room she had come to call her own. For days she'd been agonising as to the best way of putting a distance between them. Telling him she had a steady man friend was possible but not intense enough. She had to add something extra and she'd decided exactly what the extra would be.

The brushing slowed as she got the words clear in her head. She straightened, eyed her reflection and imagined it was David's. Once she was sure of what she had to say she cleared her throat.

'David. I have something to tell you. I have a man in my life, a steady man, and I'm having a baby!'

She shrugged. One more shot. As Aunt Meg always reminded her, there was always room for improvement.

She did as before, this time adding a swift lick of her lips. 'David!'

'Yes.'

His voice caught her by surprise. She had thought he was still in the bathroom. She turned round, her heart beating so loud it seemed to echo around her brain.

'I have something to tell you!' She said it quickly. Well, here goes! Look helpless. Look appealing. She took a deep breath. 'I think I'm expecting.'

Oh, but it sounded so puny. Expecting! What sort of word was that? She could have said it so much better... Regrets were irrelevant. All that mattered was that the colour had drained from David's face. His eyes were like chips of jet-black beads.

Polly got to her feet, put down the brush and clasped her hands in front of her. Her fingers seemed to tangle into a tight knot. Her nerves were tangled too. But she'd started this. It had to be finished.

'So I'm telling you to keep away from me, to leave me alone.' Her voice sounded weak, as if it belonged to someone smaller, less confident of her looks and abilities.

A nerve flickered beneath his eye as he clenched his jaw. 'We can get rid of it,' he said evenly.

Polly stared at him in disbelief. This was not the response she'd hoped for. 'Get rid of it! How do we get rid of it?' Her stomach ached. So did the knuckles of her clenched fists.

His smile was laced with sarcasm. 'I'm a doctor. Remember?'

Now it was her turn to feel the colour draining from her face.

The very thought of what he'd just suggested made her feel like fainting away. The idea made her feel sick.

'I can't believe you just said that.' Her voice was small. She sank back onto a stool. But Polly was not one to be weak for long. 'You're a monster!' she shouted as she got to her feet. 'A killer! And in cold blood too!'

His expression hardened. The glint in his eyes was like neon shining on sheet steel. 'Don't talk to me about killing. I've seen enough killing in the last few years to last me a dozen lifetimes! I've seen men screaming as their legs are blown from under them. I've seen them carrying their guts in their arms, hoping that I can do something for them. I've carried men from the battlefield as the guns fired around me, and when I've laid them down, thinking they're safe, I've found that I've been carrying a body that no longer has a head, his blood congealed with the dust and dirt upon my back.'

Too stunned to move, Polly listened. He sat down on the bed, his head falling forward into his hands. There was silence for a while before he began to sob, then wail. 'I don't want to do it again! I tell you, I'm not going back out there.'

There was silence again.

Polly took a step to her right, her eyes fixed on David. 'Don't order me to go back out there!'

His head was rolling in his hands.

'I can't take it, I tell you. Please listen!'

She flattened herself against the wall. 'I'm listening,' she said, but her words went unnoticed.

Slowly he got to his feet and just as slowly saluted. It was then that Polly realised it wasn't her he'd been talking to. He was back on the battlefield being told to go into the fighting and help bring in the wounded. But his nerves had cracked. She wondered what he would do next. Perhaps if she spoke firmly to him...

'David. Snap out of it will you! Come on. Sort yourself out!'

He turned his head slowly, his eyes darkly menacing from beneath a frowning brow.

She realised her mistake. 'Oh no,' she said softly and attempted to make her way along the wall to the bedroom door.

He came forward. She moved back, her knees weak, a cold sweat breaking out all over her.

'I swear to you I'll kill you before I ever go out there again, and once I've done that I'll go and kill myself. You'll never get me to do it again!'

Despite the fact that her legs felt like jelly, she managed to move sideways, and backed into the alcove.

'Leave me alone!'

His brow was furrowed, his cheeks were flushed. Spittle seeped from the corners of his mouth. She was in no doubt this was the face of a madman. He took another step, then another. He was close to her now, she could smell his sweat. Glistening like beads, it sprang on his forehead, on his cheeks, on his chin. He was going to kill her. She was sure he was going to kill her. Visions of Carol, Aunty Meg, Billy – even Mavis – flashed before her eyes. His shadow fell over her. There was nothing she could do. She flattened herself against the wall, waited for the first blow and after that felt nothing more.

* * *

The eleventh was only three days away. Changing her mind about going up to see Josef off at the station was something Charlotte did every day. Some days she determined to be the truly dedicated wife, loyal to her husband despite everything. On other days both her body and her heart ached for a man who had made her feel worthwhile as a woman. She couldn't just go back to Bristol purely to see him off. If there were some other reason to go back for a few days, that would be a different matter.

Suddenly, everything changed. It was mid morning. The children had been taken on a pony-trekking trip and she was sipping coffee in the chintzy cottage living room when the phone rang.

A cool breeze was blowing in through the open window, billowing the net curtains and gently caressing her hair. If she closed her eyes she could almost imagine it was the soft touch of someone's hand. So when the phone rang she was disinclined to leave the chair and her dream behind. But she did so. Perhaps David was joining them. With a pang of guilt she hoped that wasn't the case.

The phone sat in the wide window ledge behind the rose-patterned curtains. There was a window seat just in front of it and she made herself comfortable on it, curling her legs up beneath her.

'Charlotte?' The voice was only vaguely familiar at first. A memory stirred and gave him a name. Julian was an old friend from her hospital days and David's commanding officer in the army. Julian was the man who had phoned to tell her which train David was on when she hadn't even realised he was coming home.

'Mrs Grey told me you'd gone away on holiday with the children. I hope you don't mind, old thing, but I thought I'd take the opportunity to talk to you about David while you're alone. You do remember some of what I said on the day I told you he was coming home, don't you?'

Charlotte faltered. He was talking about an event that happened eight months ago. She tried to remember exactly what he'd said but couldn't. 'I'm sorry, Julian. All I remember is that my husband was coming home and I was very excited. We'd all missed him.'

A taut silence followed on the other end of the phone.

Then he spoke. 'How has he been?'

She had every intention of saying he was fine, but the hint of concern in Julian's voice caused her to pause. 'Well, I have to say he hasn't exactly been his old self.'

'Ah!' said Julian. 'Look, I don't like talking about things like this over the telephone. When are you back in Bristol? I could meet you there.'

'The eleventh!'

'I'll be at the Royal Infirmary. We've set up a post-depression research facility for returning servicemen. I won't tell you any more than that at the moment. We'll talk further when you get here. What time can I expect you?'

Josef was leaving at one-fifteen. She had to allow for the train being late. After that he'd be out of her life.

'Three o'clock?'

After putting the phone down, she sank thoughtfully back into her chair. What had Julian said to her when he'd first phoned to say David was demobbed? It seemed such a time ago, a whole lifetime. So much had happened. But bits of what he'd said that day started to come back. There was something about an incident and him being upset about a friend who'd been killed. But David had never mentioned this friend since he'd been home and he'd never appeared upset, only violent.

Because her reason for going back to Bristol had expanded, she packed an overnight bag. The morning train would get her into Temple Meads for twelve noon, enough time to snatch an hour with Josef before he began his journey home. Then she would make her way to the Royal Infirmary for her appointment with Julian. He'd sounded friendly but concerned, a true professional, and it worried her.

Mrs Peacock, the woman who looked after the cottage when it was empty and came to tidy and cook for them when they were in residence, was quite happy to look after the children while she was away. Charlotte gave her the phone number at home should she need to use it.

'Only in emergencies, Mrs Peacock. Don't let Geoffrey near it. He uses the telephone just for the fun of it.'

Is it selfish of me to be thinking more about Josef than I am about David, wondered Charlotte as she selected the right clothes to wear. Then she sighed audibly. David, his behaviour and his problems, would still be there long after Josef had gone. She owed this to herself.

The hat she chose was of navy blue straw with a thin bow at one side. Her dress was yellow, scattered with tiny navy blue dots. Shoes and handbag were chosen to match. The Great Western express ran through countryside rampant with ripened corn. Fat cattle grazed in grass that grew long enough to tickle their bellies. The first harvest of peacetime would shortly be gathered in. Unlike the cities, the countryside looked untouched by conflict. Everything seemed to be the same, or perhaps better than it had been.

Thanks to the land girls probably.

Exeter, Taunton, Bridgwater: As each city, town and mile was eaten up by the train, her stomach tightened. Bristol came closer and with it Josef and her appointment with Julian. The first she viewed with brittle excitement, the second with a hint of fear. Afterwards, she would make her way home to Royal York Crescent, find something light to eat, and take a long bath in a really wasteful amount of water. No rationing there any more! Later she would sleep in her own bed, completely alone. Mrs Grey would not be there because David was away at yet another of his BMA conferences. He was adamant that a National Health Service would never work, and called Beveridge, Bevan and the rest of them a load of lying thieves who he hoped would die in agony. It seemed a bit strong. But she hadn't argued. She might have done before the war, but David wouldn't have said such a thing back then.

There was a hold-up between Bridgwater and Bristol. For twenty minutes she sat there, fiddling and folding her ticket until it was barely recognisable. The conductor politely reminded her that she'd need it if she wanted to get out of the station without having to pay twice.

'Are we going to be long?' She tried not to sound impatient.

'Depends,' the conductor replied.

'On what?'

'On how long the cow takes to get off the line.'

'Good grief,' said another passenger in her compartment, his head suddenly appearing above a newspaper. 'It should not take terribly long to push a cow off the line. Surely your chaps can manage that?'

'Once she's finished calving it should be no problem at all,' replied the conductor politely. 'Then we'll move them both!'

The cow and her newborn took long enough. The train was running late. The prospect of missing Josef, after having dressed herself so carefully for their goodbye, was agonising. Impatience was not something Charlotte usually gave in to, but she did now. She was on her feet before the train pulled into the station. The wide leather strap that let down the window was weak. The window slammed fully open and a piece of leather came off in her hand. She threw the broken piece out to land among a cluster of yellow flowering weeds. Uncaring if her hair, her face or her hat received a smattering of soot from the puffing engine, she leaned as far out the window as she dared. Narrowing her eyes against the smuts and the smoke, she stared straight ahead searching for the face she wished most in the world to see.

'What platform for Portsmouth?' she asked a guard the minute she got off the train.

Case bobbing at her side, she dashed down the steps to the underpass, dodging businessmen in trilby hats and parents toting children with buckets and spades of painted tin, then through the underpass and up the steps to the platform. A train was in the station. People were hanging out, kissing or waving loved ones goodbye.

She ran the length of the train, then back again but couldn't see him. Where was he? Was this the right train? Was he sat in the corner of a compartment resigned to the fact that she wasn't coming?

Gasping for breath she stopped and stared again at that window, another, another and another, squares of glass filled by the faces of strangers.

'Can I help you?' asked a voice at her side.

She started. A man, obviously a railway employee, stood at her side looking up at her kindly.

'Civilians that end, ma'am,' he said pointing to the front of the train.

'I'm not looking for a civilian.'

'Oh!' The kindly expression disappeared. 'Oh! The Krauts are at that end,' he added and waved with casual contempt towards the back of the train.

She headed in that direction. Again she scoured the windows and met the disdainful gaze of some, the interest of others. Suddenly he appeared through the open window above a door, pushing his comrades aside, looking up and down the platform – looking for her.

'Josef!'

Grappling with handbag and case, she ran to him.

Josef reached for the door handle, his eyes never leaving her face. An MP's hand appeared on his shoulder. 'And where do you think you're going?'

For one brief moment she could see a fighting look in his eyes and was sure he was going to land a fist on the MP's jaw and get out of the carriage anyway.

'No! It's all right, Josef. Stay where you are.'

She rested her hands on the bottom half of the door. It trembled beneath her touch. The train was about to leave. The stoker would be throwing in more coal. The steam gauge would be rising.

'I expected you earlier,' said Josef, his hands covering hers.

'I wanted to be here.' She smiled and it almost felt painful. She let her luggage drop to the ground. 'Unfortunately a cow got in the way.' She laughed enough to stop herself crying.

He laughed too and nodded as if he understood completely. That's what she liked about him. She only needed to say the most minimal things. It was as though he could read her mind or had been there with her.

He patted her hands. 'We haven't much time. I'll write to you.'

'Please do.' Oh, why did she sound so lame? So polite: the sort of thing one says at tea parties. 'I won't forget you, Josef. You do know that, don't you?'

He nodded sadly. His hands tightened over hers as he leaned down, his hair falling over his eyes as his lips met hers.

Slowly, almost imperceptibly at first, the train began to move. Still their lips clung together. Charlotte began to move with the train. Breaking apart was so difficult. The train began to move faster. She kept up as long as she could. First their lips parted. Her hands dropped from his.

'Remember to write,' she called after him.

He shouted back, the wind beginning to ruffle his hair. 'Remember I love you!'

Time seemed suddenly to stand still. He said that! Why had he said it now?

She stood spellbound, with only her thoughts for company, until the dark brown rear of the very last carriage had disappeared from view. The rest of the world seemed suddenly to be of no consequence. She was like an island, surrounded by the hustle and bustle of a station in need of care and attention – just like her really.

The overnight bag might have been forgotten but an overhead loudspeaker crackled into life and brought her back to reality.

The train now approaching...

There was a clean handkerchief in her pocket. She blew into it and dabbed at her eyes. I hadn't planned to cry, she thought. Pull yourself together. He's gone and you've got responsibilities; in fact, you have a very full life. *Work is not enough*, said a voice from somewhere deep inside her.

Slowly she walked back to where she'd left her bag. The old railwayman who had pointed her in the right direction now looked at her with undisguised disdain. As she picked up her bag he leaned close to one of his compatriots and whispered something. Then he turned back and spat at her. It landed some way from her feet. 'German whore!'

She walked quickly on, unable to come to terms with what she'd just heard. Her face was on fire. Her breath was tight in her chest. A German's whore! Normally she might have responded, gone over to him and in her most cut-glass accent threatened to report him to his superiors. But a post-war world seemed more complicated than one at war. How long, she wondered, would it be before the open wounds were healed?

Edna knew she was in for trouble when her mother saw her driving through Bedminster in Billy Hills' van. She blamed herself for being so preoccupied with thinking about Sherman. Her mother always went shopping early on a Saturday morning in East Street, Bedminster. The queues for anything, whether it was rationed or not, were still horrendous. And all for tired vegetables, fatty meats or bits of offal, and bread that was greyer than it had been in wartime. But her mother usually came home with something a bit special. Most weekends there was meat of some sort, perhaps a rabbit or a few pigeons, all ending up in a pie. They'd never run out of sugar like some during the war though her mother had doled it out sparingly, as if it were the most precious thing on earth.

If she had thought about being seen she could have instructed Billy to take her to the orphanage by a more roundabout route. But it was too late. She'd face the music another day.

It wasn't easy, but she put her fears behind her when she got to the orphanage. Matron smiled at her as she handed her the bags of baby clothes and the warm blankets Colin's mother had taken to knitting from old wool.

Matron thanked her, then said, 'He's waiting for you,' and nodded towards the nursery.

Edna smiled back. Though still nervous about who might be waiting for her and what might be said when she got back, Sherman's smile helped her forget – at least for the moment.

He gripped her finger in his tiny hand as she looked down at him. His chuckles betrayed the presence of two more teeth. Edna felt her eyes turn moist. She so wanted to pick him up, to run out with him, go home to Colin and say, 'Look. This is my son.' But until she could find the courage to do that, she had resolved to resist picking him up. The temptation was too strong.

When it was time to go she retraced her steps along the echoing corridors. The sky had turned grey outside and the air hung heavy with the threat of thunder. Overhead lights hanging from long cords and subdued by the addition of white china shades did little to lift the gloom inside the building.

Outside she could see Matron standing next to Billy's van. She'd obviously seen her arrive in it. When she turned away from Billy her face looked troubled. Edna wondered what Billy could have said to cause that.

Matron stopped by the door looking a little embarrassed. She paused as if to say something, attempted to walk on then stopped again. 'Edna!'

Edna halted. What had Billy said?

'I'm sorry,' said Matron. 'I have just made a terrible mistake. Do forgive me.'

Edna frowned. Surely whatever she'd done couldn't be any worse than being seen by her mother in a van with Billy Hills?

'I presumed he was your husband and you had told him about Sherman. I'm sorry. I'm afraid I may have put my foot in it.'

Raindrops as big as pennies were falling when she got outside. Billy looked numb when she slid into the seat beside him. He didn't look at her but stared ahead as if the raindrops trickling down the screen had some dark secret to impart.

'Better get going,' he said at last and turned the key. The engine spluttered and sighed. So did Billy. 'Damn. Better get out and use the starting handle.'

As he opened the door, she grabbed his shoulder. 'You won't tell Colin will you, Billy – about Sherman I mean?'

He chewed his lip. At least he was thinking about it. But he didn't look at her. Not once. And that unnerved her.

'Billy?'

Billy shook his head. 'No. Course I won't. Bit of a shock though, I don't mind telling you. In fact, one hell of a bloody shock! Still,' he smiled ruefully. 'Not the first are you? Won't be the last either.'

As on all the other occasions he'd taken her to the orphanage, he dropped her off at the London Inn where the remains of vegetables and the odd bit of fruit from the barrows lay squashed on the ground. From there it was just a short walk to Kent Street.

They were in the parlour just behind the shop, her mother, father and Colin. She smiled at them nervously, her heart fluttering in her chest.

Her mother's lips were a taut mauve line. Her father was dutifully sipping his tea. But it was Colin's expression that worried her most. He looked at her furtively as though afraid of what he might see if his eyes lingered.

She managed to swallow the sandpaper dryness of her throat enough to say, 'Hello.' It sounded muted and unclear, like when someone turns the sound down on the wireless.

'Colin tells me you've been making baby clothes for the orphanage,' said her mother. Judging by the look in her eyes, there was no doubting what she really meant. That's where the parcels go. That's where your baby is.

'Yes.'

'Charity begins at home! That's what I always say! You should be making baby clothes for your own children, not other people's cast-outs!' As if to emphasise her statement, her mother slammed the cup and saucer back on the tray. 'You've been married since May. I thought you might have something to tell me by now!'

Edna felt her face getting warm. Oh, why did she blush so easily? Perhaps if she didn't do that she could find the courage to stand up to others, especially her mother.

She glanced swiftly at Colin. He had been looking down at the floor, but suddenly looked up and met her gaze. Usually he would have smiled and winked, aware that her mother was an interfering old bag who could cut deeper than a bayonet. For the first time she wondered just how much a child might mean to him. Unknowingly, her mother had touched a sore spot. Colin felt less of a man than he let on. A child, Edna suddenly realised, would make him feel more of one.

'Women shouldn't work,' said her father suddenly. All eyes went to him. It wasn't often he was given the chance to make a comment.

'Well, just for a change, I have to say that you're right, Cedric,' said Edna's mother. 'Women should be running a home, having babies and looking after their husband. Don't you agree, Colin?'

'Yes,' said Colin quietly and Edna felt that terrible guilt again.

* * *

Normally the departure of her parents after a fleeting visit left the atmosphere of their little house a lot lighter. But on this occasion it seemed that a void had opened between her and Colin. And all because of my mother, thought Edna and wondered if she'd said anything to Colin about Billy giving her a lift.

'I'll get us some food,' she said and started to make her way to the kitchen. Colin grabbed her wrist.

'Is there anything you want to tell me, Edna?'

She looked down at him, her lips parted and her tongue dry. She shook her head. Was this the time to tell him about Sherman? Had her mother said anything?

'Of course not.'

Slowly his hand dropped from her wrist.

'You don't regret marrying me do you, Edna? I mean, being as I am?'

'No! Of course not!'

Ordinarily she would have flung her arms around his neck and told him he was all she'd ever wanted. But even though he hadn't mentioned Billy giving her a lift, she knew without being told that he knew. Her mother had seen to that. Telling him about Sherman was becoming impossible.

* * *

Julian was kindness itself but nothing could detract from the awfulness of what he was telling her.

'I think he's verging on schizophrenia.'

Charlotte felt weak. It was as if someone had taken every bone out of her body. 'But he's a doctor.'

'We're not immune,' said Julian with a wry smile. 'I'm afraid one of the problems with medical men like David is that they're not very good at being patients. He didn't really show any signs of depression as such – at least – yet. Modern thinking is that a particularly stressful incident is at the root of the disease. Like so-called shell shock, it's not a physical thing. It's a mental thing, a locking up of the horror of certain experiences.'

Charlotte sighed. She'd taken off her gloves. Now she crumpled them up in her hands. 'So instead of showing signs of depression you are saying it has affected his personality.'

He nodded slowly, chin resting on his knuckles. 'I did try telling you when I phoned.'

She could barely remember what he'd actually said. The fact that David was coming home had been more important than anything else. She didn't comment but only thought about how shocked she'd been on his first night home. It had been like sleeping with a stranger and was no different now.

'You may find him acting completely out of character, not at all the nice person you knew.'

She nodded. 'I know.'

There was silence for a moment.

'Is there anything else you want to know?' asked Julian at last.

'Is he likely to...?' She failed to get the word out.

Julian filled in the gap.

'Suicide? It's a possibility. He's been traumatised by some event he witnessed or experienced. You've no idea what it is? He hasn't mentioned anything?'

She shook her head.

'I thought he might have by now,' Julian continued. 'But in

answer to your question, as long as the problem continues to stew inside him, there is every reason to believe that he could, eventually, do harm, either to himself or to someone else.'

Charlotte automatically raised her hand to her throat. How could she say out loud that he'd already done her harm? It seemed so disloyal somehow.

Julian offered her a lift home, but she declined. Much as he might be concerned for David's plight, she needed time by herself to think of what she could do. There was now no question of the children not going back to boarding school. They would be safer there.

The old Charlotte came into her own, the head girl and dormitory prefect who had gone out of her way to advise her fellow scholars, who had enrolled in the Red Cross at the outbreak of war and assisted in the orphanage and the Marriage Guidance Council.

It was up to her to save David from himself. Somehow she had to heal the festering wound in his mind. She looked wistfully out of the window as the taxi made its way up Park Street. Architects with rolled-up plans beneath their arms and builders were standing on the wide pavements eyeing the damaged buildings. Rebuilding was only at the planning stage and there was much to be done. Just as there was with David.

The first thing she noticed when the taxi pulled up outside the house was that the bedroom curtains were drawn. Julian's words rang in her ears. After telling the cab driver to keep the change, she dashed to the door, her fingers like jelly as she tried to get the key in the lock. Eventually she pushed it open and was in the hall, the door left wide open behind her.

Taking the stairs two at a time she dashed into the bedroom she'd shared with David all her married life.

He'll do things he's never done before – act out of character – it's like an anger festering inside – it has to come out.

The room smelt of perfume. Bottles, face powder, creams and sprays were scattered over the floor as if by a childish hand.

She felt sick, but not because of the spills. Polly's blonde hair lay on her pillow in her bed! Charlotte clutched at her stomach. 'Polly?' Polly didn't move.

A small cry escaped Charlotte's throat. Polly's eyes remained closed, and even though the curtains were drawn, Charlotte could see they were purple and puffy, the result of a series of blows. Her cheeks were red and bruised. One arm dangled limp and white from the bed, her hand almost touching the floor.

'Oh my God!'

Charlotte ran downstairs to the phone that sat on a table in the hall and swiftly dialled an ambulance. After that she dialled Julian and told him what she'd found.

Julian joined her later at the Royal Infirmary. 'Do you know where he is?' he asked.

She shook her head, aware of the concern in his voice but too numb to speak.

Julian paused, then nervously cleared his throat before speaking. 'I'll phone his consulting rooms. If he's not there, I'll have to phone the police. You know that, don't you?'

She nodded, afraid to ask him why the police because she knew what the answer was likely to be. It was such a short walk from their house to the Clifton Suspension Bridge. And from there it was such a long drop to the river and the road below.

He said nothing when he came back. She looked at his face. It said it all.

'You've phoned the police.' She said it in a matter-of-fact manner: no inflection, no emotion.

He patted her shoulder. 'They're searching the most obvious places.'

A small cry caught in her throat. Their eyes met in mutual understanding.

Charlotte found her voice. 'I have to be sensible about all this. There are reasons for David being like he is, goodness, after all that he's been through I have to give him time. And as for the prospect of him being unfaithful with Polly, well, what can one say. I would imagine she was the sort who had a wonderful time when the Americans were here. They brought glamour to her life. I suppose she thought David could do the same.'

She bit her lip in order to stifle her distress and voiced her next concern. 'If he is able, will he stand trial for beating Polly? Will he go to prison?'

Julian sighed. 'He needs treatment, not punishment. A lot depends on Polly. Apparently he chased her into your bedroom. She'd said something to him about the war and he went stark, staring mad – those are Polly's words.'

Charlotte sighed. David had gone to war and someone else had returned. She had borne it, told herself that in time he would heal. But having to face the prospect of infidelity was hard to bear, especially as she knew Polly and she worked for them. Now it seemed that there was nothing to be jealous about and, she had to admit, she had been jealous.

Julian's voice broke into her thoughts. 'Charlotte, you are a real brick, the sort of woman every man dreams of marrying. But you need to be less selfless. Doing good deeds should not be your sole occupation.'

Although choking with despair, she managed a brilliant smile. 'You're quite right, Julian. I should have more passion in my life. Do you think I should take a lover?'

Julian blushed and looked away. 'Now steady on, old girl...'

She slapped him on the shoulder and he almost jumped out of his skin. 'Don't worry, Julian. You're quite safe. I've already had passion in my life, but leopards don't change their spots. I was made to serve and I'll go right on doing that.'

He looked up at her with his mouth open.

She smiled down at him, thinking just how vulnerable people could really be when their Achilles heel is suddenly exposed. She knew Julian didn't care too much for women – not in a sexual way. 'We all have our wounds, Julian – and our secrets. I'm not a saint. Please don't treat me as one.'

She saw him blink and his jaw tighten and knew he understood.

* * *

Charlotte had been at her bedside. Polly remembered it clearly though what she had actually said to her was less clear. Something about David being ill. Mad more like it, she thought to herself. Well that was that! So what was she going to do now? She certainly couldn't go back to her job with him in Clifton. A factory? There was a fair selection; tobacco, chocolate or paper bags. Now which did she fancy?

Or there were shops. Working in a dress shop would be nice. Might even get some good gear she thought, with or without me ration card!

Aunty Meg made up the bed in the front bedroom for her when she came home. There was more room now because Hetty and Bert had been given a prefab out on a new estate at Brislington.

Meg explained what it was like. 'I went out on the bus with them to have a look. It's not a proper home. It ain't made of brick like these old places. It's made of metal and it all slots into place like a jigsaw. But it's got two bedrooms, a living room, a kitchen and a bathroom – all indoors! Ain't that marvellous?'

Polly agreed that it was. She didn't add that it was especially marvellous for her because their leaving meant there was more room in York Street, but she certainly thought it.

When Meg suggested that Carol should sleep in her mother's room, she didn't object. Although there was a cot in there, it looked far too small for the growing child, so Polly allowed her daughter to come into bed with her. She had a need to love someone, to cuddle a warm body close to her own and rain kisses on an innocent head. Because of this she began to get to know her daughter, to notice the way she wrinkled her nose, the fact that she had most of her teeth now and that she could get out of bed by herself and retrieve her potty from beneath it.

Once she was up and about, Meg allowed Billy to visit. Ever since she'd been home from hospital he'd knocked to see how she was, and when Meg told him off for hanging around outside the house, he waylaid her on the corner of the street when she was on her way to the shops. Polly still enjoyed teasing him. 'I'm taking Carol for a walk,' she'd say, always pretending that she was going out when he had only just arrived.

'I'll come with you,' he would respond with undisguised enthusiasm.

It never failed to surprise her that Billy offered to push the pram. She didn't know any man who would do that. And there was no asking questions about why she hadn't told him that she'd been alone in the house with David. He took it for granted that David had had some kind of brainstorm because of his wartime experiences. Plenty of people had been affected by it, some more so than others.

It was October and they walked down towards the Feeder Canal that connected the River Frome to the River Avon. Italian prisoners of war were repairing a part of the road that ran alongside it. The air was damp with mist, but streaked with shafts of watery sunlight.

'I've got a present for you,' Billy said suddenly. He reached into his pocket and brought out an easily recognisable tin.

'Powdered egg,' said Polly with little enthusiasm.

Billy's face dropped. 'Don't you want it?'

She managed a smile. 'It's always useful. More omelettes. They're good for you.' She unclipped the apron on the pram and popped it in.

He asked her whether she was still going to get a job. 'Of course! I've got Carol to support. It's not easy you know.'

Thoughtfully he shoved his hands in his pockets and nodded in agreement. 'I can see that. Still, at least you 'ad the guts to keep your baby and not...' He stopped dead, sounding as though he'd said too much.

She frowned and looked at him questioningly. He kept his head down. Billy was hiding something. It occurred to her that he might have a skeleton in the cupboard somewhere. Perhaps it was his own child he was talking about that some worried young girl had given away. But she didn't think so. Well, she would find out. She was good at finding things out from blokes like Billy. Smiling in a way that she knew men found irresistible, she slipped her arm through his. He was the one pushing the pram.

Holding her head pertly to one side, she asked, 'Is there something you need to tell me, Billy?' Then her voice and expression changed. 'If you've been cheating on me, Billy, if you've got some kid and some girl somewhere that you haven't told me about, then I want to know now!' He blustered at first. But Polly knew Billy wouldn't risk losing her no matter what. Once she turned those blue eyes on him and smiled as if he were the most important bloke in the world, he'd tell her anything. And when she threatened not to see him any more if he didn't own up... well... that would be suicide.

Polly could barely believe it of Edna. That mousy little creature! Fancy her having a baby. She looked such a little mouse. What glorious gossip! She couldn't resist passing it around – furtively of course.

Aunt Meg had never met Edna so Polly thought there was no harm in telling her about the baby in the orphanage. She told her how Edna's mother had sent her away so the neighbours wouldn't know. She also told her about the parcels that kept coming from America full of baby clothes.

'Poor girl,' said Meg. 'Sounds as if her mother's a right dragon. I'm glad you kept Carol,' she added.

'Yes,' said Polly. 'Lucky for me you were a good dragon!'

In bed that night she stroked Carol's curly fair hair. There had been times in the past when she wished Carol had never been born. Her birth and existence had curtailed her enjoyment for a while. But that time was all behind her. This was a new Polly and her dreams had changed. And tomorrow I'll get a new job, she said to herself. But not cleaning other people's places and not waiting on tables. I want something better. Something glamorous would be good.

There was a queue at the Labour Exchange the following day, mostly men in their demob suits or navy dungarees talking in loud voices but seeming slightly ill at ease. Some would be sent to factories or to 'wait-on' at the docks. Those most favoured might get in on the bonded warehouses down in the Cumberland Basin where casks of tobacco were already rolling in from Virginia, Rhodesia and Pakistan. A lot more would be sent to demolish buildings made dangerous by bomb damage or to clear sites ready for building – whenever that might be.

Polly queued outside the women's entrance. She listened as they talked about their lives. The single women talked of going to dances, the pictures or a pub and whether they were courting. Those having lately left school stood trembling, fearful to speak and fearful to move; their first foray into the world of work. A few were widowed or married. Someone mentioned it was a headache having her man home and she wished he were still away fighting.

'Yeah. I bet you 'ave headaches a lot now he's been 'ome for a while. Bet you didn't at first though, did ya?'

Raucous laughter followed.

Another said that hers was still out in Malaya receiving treatment in a hospital.

Polly kept silent. If anyone asked her about the man in her life she'd mention Billy. But her private business was her own and, in view of recent events, she preferred to keep things that way.

Eventually it was her turn to approach the clerk who sat in a small cubicle, a barrier between him and his job-seeking clients.

'Name?'

She gave it.

'Address?'

She gave that too.

'Married?'

'No.'

'Experience?'

'I have worked as a receptionist to a doctor...'

The clerk peered over his spectacles, which crept to the end of his nose.

'Have you qualifications?'

'No.'

'Then you'll have to make do with what you can get and be thankful for it!'

At one time he would have got a few choice words. As it was she was almost glad to be getting a job, re-joining the outside world no matter what the work was.

There were a few openings at the cotton factory in Barton Hill. It was within walking distance of York Street, but the thought of working in a building looking like a castle with turrets and stone blackened by war was somehow off-putting. The pay was reasonable but not outstanding.

Edwards & Ringers, a smaller cigarette factory than W. D. & H. O. Wills, were also taking on staff. It was a bit further to go than the cotton factory and was one of the few buildings left in Redcliffe Street, a main thoroughfare since medieval times and directly opposite St Mary Redcliffe Church.

She chose the latter. The clerk behind the counter gave her a card to take along on which was printed the name of the foreman she had to see.

The ugly brick building was only a little better than the cotton factory and had apparently replaced much older buildings in Victorian times. The fact that it was surrounded mostly by rubble did nothing to improve matters. Weeds, couch grass and swiftly growing buddleia were sprouting over what was left of the bombed-out buildings.

Inside was far worse than out. With each breath she inhaled tobacco dust. She could taste it on her tongue and smell it in her hair.

The man she had come to see was courteous and it seemed the job was hers. He held a cigarette in the corner of his mouth as he talked, telling her about the job, taking her to where she would be working, and explaining about bonuses and bank holidays.

At first she considered turning it down. She didn't mind smoking the odd fag, but raw tobacco was something else and in this place they were almost eating it. Then she thought of Carol and told herself she was lucky. Anyone else would jump at the chance. The job was hers and she should take it. The foreman seemed delighted and so was she. Starting date was in one week.

But things didn't go according to plan. The job would have been hers if one of the neighbours from York Street hadn't seen her. Iris Trent had five kids and a husband who worked as a drayman for the brewery. He'd been reprimanded for being drunk in charge of his horses after being reported by a policeman. But it was Polly who'd given him the abuse that day and he hadn't forgotten it.

Iris glared at her as if looks could kill. Polly just tilted her chin and looked the other way. They all had to work together. That was the way it was.

Two days later she received a letter stating that it had come to their notice that she had a child. It was not their policy to employ unmarried women with children.

'That bloody Iris Trent!'

It was the first time she'd cried in a long time. Meg held her close. 'Never you mind, Polly. Something'll turn up. You see if it don't. Now you dry your eyes and get yourself ready for Billy and the pictures tonight. I'll take care of Carol.'

Polly felt sorry that she'd taken Meg so much for granted. What would she do without her? Now when she looked at her she saw the worry lines, the tiredness of old age creeping over her forehead and around her eyes, the grey hairs sprouting profusely on her chin.

She felt better that evening, sitting there near the back of the pictures with Billy's arm around her. They went to the New Palace in Baldwin Street. It was in the middle of town and a real treat, despite having to pick their way carefully around the rubble that still littered the ground.

Since she'd been small, the picture house had been one of her favourite places. She remembered as a child being hypnotised by the shaft of blue-white light, the beam twisting and dancing with dust and cigarette smoke before it hit the screen. There was a liquid luminescence about it that had never failed to entrance her.

Of course she'd been to the pictures with plenty of Yanks during the war but couldn't recall a single one of the films. No wonder, she thought to herself. I was too busy fending them off. Hands like an octopus some of them had and the air had been blue with cigarette smoke and the unmistakable twang of their accents.

The magic of the movies, as the Yanks had called them, had never really left her. And it wasn't just about the film. The New Palace, like a lot of other picture houses, had a definite atmosphere. Everything to do with it was special. She realised while she was watching the film that the building itself had a special magic. Like a real palace it was, all red velvets, gold-painted plaster fancy bits around the walls and chandeliers hanging from the ceiling.

Then there were the people around her, the girls selling ice cream, but especially the usherettes shining their torches as they escorted people to their seats. There was something so glamorous about it all.

Suddenly she sucked in her breath.

Billy noticed. 'What's the matter?' he whispered, his breath warm on her ear.

'I'm going to be an usherette,' she said decidedly.

'Good idea,' he whispered back, and they both went back to watching Cary Grant and Ingrid Bergman.

* * *

There were times when Edna could feel Colin's eyes following her as she moved around the place. Getting home late from work had become something of an ordeal. He asked over and over again where she had been, why she was late. And again and again she told him that she'd worked late for a bit of overtime or that the bus was late. Colin was causing her concern. The workshop wasn't looking as neatly industrious as it had done. She badly wanted to ask him why, but was afraid of what he might say. She hated confrontation. Courage wasn't something that came easily. It had always been easier to let others have their own way rather than attract an argument.

The first inkling she had that something was truly wrong was when Billy came calling.

Billy was his usual ebullient self. 'Got a few more done, 'ave you chum?'

'Some!' Colin snapped, and nodded towards a workbench where four painted horses sat in a row.

Never had Edna seen him treat Billy in such an offhand manner.

Billy suddenly looked troubled. 'Is that all? Come on, Colin, you ain't gonna get enough for Mr Lewis for Christmas at this rate. You are going to speed up, aren't you? And what about employing someone?'

Billy left with a flea in his ear. Edna apologised as she accompanied him with two of the wooden horses. He carried the other two.

'I'm sorry, Billy. I don't know what's come over him. Mind you, he has been to the hospital a lot lately. He says they're doing a lot of tests but won't tell me why.' She frowned and clasped her hands tightly together because she couldn't help but fear the worst. Life without Colin would be unthinkable.

Billy looked resigned. He sighed and tipped his hat back further on his head. 'P'raps I shouldn't give you any more rides in me van,' he said. 'Making the old chap jealous, am I?'

Edna said nothing but looked down at the ground. Billy was probably right. Her mother had a lot to do with it. She wondered exactly what bitter seed she could have sown in Colin's head. The fact that Charlotte had asked Billy to give Edna a lift on a regular basis didn't help, but her hands were full trying to cope with David who had refused all medical treatment and had been lucky that Polly had refused to press charges.

Billy was looking deeply at Edna. 'You've got to do what's best for everyone,' he said to her as if reading her thoughts.

It was easier said than done. She'd never been very good at broaching a subject. Besides, she was terrified that Colin would find out her true reason for visiting the orphanage. She didn't want to hurt him. She preferred to bear the pain herself. And she was hurting because telling Colin about Sherman was becoming impossible. She loved them both. It was a terrible predicament and she couldn't see a way out.

17

Charlotte hated the night. The old Georgian house groaned around her as though settling down to sleep. Charlotte found great difficulty in settling down. There was too much turmoil in her head, thoughts concerned with recent events and whatever lay before her.

She had considered taking the children out of school and having them home with her, but David was difficult to deal with since the incident with Polly. However, she had been relieved that Julian's prognosis had been wrong. David had not committed suicide.

She had asked Julian to have him hospitalised but he had surprised her by refusing. 'He's come through it – more or less – and one has to think of his professional standing,' Julian had responded. 'I mean, you know how it is, this sort of thing only happens to other ranks, old girl.'

Old girl! She could have slapped his stupid face. What did one's professional or social standing matter if one's personal life was in a mess. Somehow she had to escape this situation whether by finding some legal way to get him treatment or, and this was something she found difficult to face, by divorcing him out of her life.

Marmaduke Clements, the family solicitor, had an office in Queen's Square. Charlotte went to him for advice as to what she should, or could, do. She was nervous about seeing him, flapping uncharacteristically as she got her bag and pulled her coat on before leaving home. The postman had been and usually she would have picked up the post and left it on the hall table. But there was only one pale blue envelope. She saw the Boston postmark and slid it into her handbag to be read later.

'Make yourself comfortable, Mrs Hennessey-White.' Marmaduke Clements indicated a large leather chair opposite his desk.

'I feel such a fool,' she said.

The leather was cool but its comfort was arguable. A few springs in the seat seemed in imminent danger of coming through.

'Why should you?' said Marmaduke. 'Matrimonial difficulties are not confined to the lower orders, my dear lady.'

It was the second time in a short while that an allusion to social status had been brought up with regard to David's condition.

She told him how things were. 'It seems to me that he has to kill someone before he gets proper treatment. I need to know if there is some legal way of getting him that treatment.'

Marmaduke sighed and sat back in his chair. 'Treating the mind after a person has endured frightening experiences is a relatively new science, my dear lady. And you are right, to some extent, when you say that nothing will be done until he kills someone. Now, if this young woman had pressed charges, something might very well have been done. But I will look into the legal aspects. In the meantime, of course, there is another option.'

She read his expression. 'Divorce.' He nodded.

'I've been offered a full-time appointment with the Marriage Guidance Council. It would seem more than a little surprising if my own marriage were dissolved.'

Marmaduke nodded sagely as though he was far older than his fifty years. She knew he was a bachelor, married to the law until death decreed otherwise. He hooked his thumbs into the pockets of his waistcoat, which only barely covered his girth, and looked at her kindly. 'I have to say that you are eminently suitable to take up an appointment with such an organisation. Only when you have experienced problems in a situation can you benefit others in that same situation, though of course,' he added with a raised finger and a shake of his head, 'I am commenting purely as a layman you understand.'

His last comment made her smile. She guessed it was supposed to. Marmaduke belonged to a dusty profession not known for its brevity but he had a definite twinkle in his eye. Perhaps it was imagination, but for her he seemed to make an exception.

She smiled appreciatively. 'Thank you anyway. I value your advice. Is there any more you have to give me?'

His chair, upholstered in leather like her own but more mobile, squeaked as he leaned forward and clasped his hands together on the desk in front of him. 'We can sue on the grounds of his adultery if you can prove any has occurred – or we can arrange for it to have occurred. Five years with his agreement and you'll be free to marry again. Seven if he doesn't.'

Five years! Five years would take them all forward into a new decade in which she would be a divorced woman and able to start all over again. And he was talking about fabricated evidence! There was no doubt about it. But was that what she wanted?

She got to her feet. 'I'll think about it.'

'Please do.'

It was beginning to drizzle outside. She pulled her coat collar up as she ran to the car, wishing she hadn't left her umbrella on the back seat. For a moment she sat in the driving seat thinking about what she should do.

David had a need to talk about things, but how was she to approach this? It occurred to her that he might have said more to Polly. It was a long shot but perhaps it might be worth approaching her.

Thinking of Polly made her remember the letter. The moment she began reading it her hands began to shake. After she'd read it she sat still, numbed by its contents. Polly had to know about this. Once she did, perhaps she would finally forgive her for meddling in her private life. Full of trepidation, she got into her car and circled the central oval of the Centre, heading back towards Victoria Street and Old Market.

* * *

It was on a weekend that Matron called Edna into the office to tell her that someone was interested in adopting Sherman.

Her heart almost stopped. Matron came round from behind the desk and gently patted her arm. 'It might be all for the best, my dear. If you can't give him a home, perhaps someone else can.'

Edna nodded. Of course Matron was right. It made sense for someone to give her son a proper home, to tuck him in at night, to read him stories, to watch him grow... Tears hung in her eyes. One blink and she'd cry and she didn't want to do that. She was visiting Sherman. The day was precious and she wanted to be happy for him.

Her other worry was Colin. He was working well enough again, but she'd caught him doing strange things, swivelling round in his wheelchair, raising what was left of his legs up and down eighty times or so, six times a day. His visits to the hospital were getting more frequent, but he was just as secretive about them as ever and it worried her.

Worries seemed to be piling up. The buyer of the toys was

pressing for delivery. He wanted an assurance that he'd get all that he'd ordered in time for Christmas.

Billy told her he'd done his best to placate him but Colin had to sort himself out. He had to get down to work if he was to make it in time.

Billy came calling later to see how things were getting on. He poked his head round the kitchen door. 'Any chance of a cup of char?'

She nodded, but her smile was weak. Billy came out into the kitchen.

'He'll get going again,' he said jerking his head sidelong at the door he'd closed behind him.

Edna gripped the edge of the kitchen sink. 'How much do we stand to lose if those toys don't get finished?'

Billy looked up at the ceiling as if the answer could be calculated up there.

'Now let's see. Five hundred at twelve and a tanner each is... well... over three hundred pounds.'

Edna looked at him wide-eyed. 'As much as that?'

He nodded. 'Less my ten per cent as the middle man.'

Edna sat herself down at the kitchen table, her thoughts racing. The order had to be fulfilled. And that was only one! What could she do to help? She eyed the old wooden dresser that she'd painted a warm cream. It was something she'd enjoyed doing. Something she could do!

Suddenly Colin called. 'Billy! Billy!' He sounded angry.

'Better go,' said Billy looking slightly embarrassed. 'Tell you what. I'll call in later with Polly. We do a lot of walking, do me and Polly.'

Edna remained seated after he'd gone, elbows on the table, her chin resting on her hands.

What was to stop her giving up her job as an invoice typist at W

D & H O Wills? She wouldn't miss it that much. But how would Colin view it? There was only one way to find out. Once the front door had slammed shut she took a deep breath and got to her feet. At first her courage threatened to leave her and she sat down again.

It's only Colin!

Again she got to her feet. If she couldn't talk honestly to her husband, who could she talk to?

She pushed open the door.

He was messing around with a half-finished aeroplane, turning it this way and that as if deciding what bit to do next. There was an unhealthy pallor to his face and he hadn't shaved.

'Colin.'

'Yes.'

It unnerved her a little that he still didn't look at her. Then it occurred to her that if he did, she might lose her nerve. Her heart was already threatening to jump through her chest, it was beating so fast.

'I'm giving up my job,' she blurted. 'I'm going to help you here in the shop so that you can fulfil your orders for Christmas.' Now he looked up.

'It might be nice,' she said quickly. 'We'll be together more often.'

He sat completely still as if contemplating what she'd just said. His shoulders were rounded, and he still hung his head.

She took a step closer.

'Did you hear what I said, Colin?'

Then she noticed his shoulders. It started as a slight shiver and at first she wondered whether he was cold. Then the shiver grew into a gentle shake. The first sob caught in his throat. The second did not.

'Colin!'

She threw her arms around his neck and kissed his forehead as he looked up into her face. His red-rimmed eyes brimmed over with tears.

'I'm sorry, Edna. Your mother made me feel so bloody useless! I wouldn't feel like that if I had some legs. Bloody Japanese!'

Edna grimaced. 'I've felt like that all my life.'

'She really made me feel as though I was only half a man because we weren't expecting yet. Then her insinuating, putting it into my head that you were going off with Billy...'

She hugged him tighter, his tears wet upon her cheek. 'You're a whole man, Colin. You were before you went away and you are now. I'll never think of you any different.'

* * *

It was a long walk from the Dings, an area of grimy brick back-to-back houses and dusty yards, to Bedminster. But, as promised, Billy showed up with Polly. To Edna's surprise they were pushing a pram in which sat a baby of about eighteen months old.

'This is Carol,' said Polly, face beaming with motherly pride. 'She's my daughter.'

'She's lovely,' said Edna and really meant it, despite the sharp pang of envy she felt. Polly had kept her child regardless of the father being miles away. Why wasn't I stronger, she asked herself, then imagined her mother's determined expression and sharp voice. Perhaps, if I'd told Colin about Sherman right at the start, things might have been all right. It was a frightening predicament. They were married and she still had not told him about her wartime romance. She had passed the point of no return. The opportune moments had come and gone.

She tried to control her emotions, but her resentment showed. 'And how's your friend David?'

Polly was taken unawares. The colour of her eyes seemed to change.

The scarf! Edna knew she had guessed about the day she'd gone back for her scarf. Never before had she seen Polly colour up like that.

But Polly found her voice. 'He's not well – so Charlotte says. She came to see me yesterday.' She then turned to the child and began to unstrap her from the pram. 'Come on then, darling. Let's get you out so you can see your Aunty Edna and Uncle Colin a bit better then.'

It was obvious that Polly was reluctant to discuss any further details of Charlotte's visit. Edna did not pursue it. She had her own problems.

But the visit of Billy, Polly and her child had done some good. Colin's mood changed over the weekend. As Edna got ready for work on Monday morning he rabbited on about how excited he was about her joining him, full of plans for the future. He spoke dreamily of how eventually they'd set up a proper business and employ people and lay out money for expensive machines.

'And besides helping you I can do more for Charlotte,' Edna added. She held her breath, half-afraid that Colin would revert to being suspicious about Billy. 'I can go with Charlotte or I can get a bus if need be,' she added in an attempt to calm his fears.

'And take me to the hospital?' He looked suddenly sheepish.

She agreed that she would and because it embarrassed him, she didn't mention the sores he got on his behind from sitting in the wheelchair all day. Bluff and jolly as he could be, Colin was also pretty sensitive about personal things.

It pleased her to give a week's notice. At the end of it she felt as free as a bird and by Saturday the workshop was stuffed full of wooden toys waiting to be painted or polished. All the same, Colin raised no objection to her visiting the orphanage, especially when he saw Charlotte pull up to take her there.

Unable to control her excitement, Edna babbled on about giving up work and joining Colin in his venture. Charlotte was mightily impressed.

'Does this mean you won't be helping me so much?' she asked.

Edna's mousy brown hair flew round her face as she shook her head. 'Try and stop me!'

Charlotte smiled knowingly.

The day was perfect as far as Edna was concerned. Whatever the future might hold, Colin was in a better mood and she was going to see her baby today.

Charlotte went to Matron's office with the clothes and Edna marched off to the nursery, patting the heads of small five- and six-year-olds as she went.

'Good morning, children!'

Humming happily to herself, she swept into the nursery and went directly to Sherman's cot.

It was empty.

She froze. There must be some mistake. Perhaps she had the wrong cot!

Whirling dizzyingly from one cot to another, she looked over the wooden railings at babies, some white, and some coffee brown, some almost black. None of them were hers.

'Where is he?' she wailed. 'Where is he?' A baby in a cold metal cot near the window started crying too: then another and another.

* * *

Polly was out at the sink in the kitchen scrubbing Carol's clothes. A galvanised tub full of water bubbled away on the gas sending white cotton garments ballooning to the surface. Hardly a welcoming sight and an embarrassment to Polly when Meg showed Charlotte in.

Polly blinked, wishing she was at least sitting in the living room and wearing a decent frock instead of the old blue cotton number reserved for doing housework. What a contrast to Charlotte's outfit: a black suit trimmed with white. White stripes started at the waist and ended just below her breasts. A white cockade decorated the right side of her hat. Black and white: Polly's own colours.

'Take a seat, Mrs Hennessey-White. Can I offer you a cuppa?' asked Meg.

'That would be nice.'

Polly pulled out a chair and Charlotte sat down.

Polly controlled the jealousy she felt over Charlotte's impeccable dress sense. This was a serious occasion. Was Charlotte going to name her in a divorce case? My God, but she didn't want that. She had Carol to think about.

But Charlotte didn't look spiteful, though looks could be deceiving. In fact, her face was paler than usual and she looked tense. Not that she was feeling much different herself. Charlotte had come to talk about David, of that she was sure.

'I'll come back when the kettle's boiled,' said Meg.

'There's no need to leave,' said Charlotte turning her face up to Meg. There were dark shadows beneath her eyes. Her cheekbones were more pronounced and there was a strangely remorseful expression in her eyes.

'All the same,' said Meg and left the room.

Polly stared hard in an effort to see through the woman, to somehow determine the underlying motive. Charlotte, the woman who helped everyone, now looked in need of help herself. So what had she come for?

Charlotte's soft, grey eyes met hers. It was difficult to meet her gaze so she got up, went to the dresser and got down three cups and saucers. One had roses on it. The others were plain and the saucers were assorted. Why aren't there any matching ones, she thought despairingly. Whatever would Charlotte think of them, this house, Aunty Meg with her sloppy slippers?

'I wanted to talk about David,' said Charlotte.

'Well! I didn't think you'd come here to ask how I was!' She purposely sounded flippant, her old cocky self, as she put the crockery down on the table with her own fair hands. Only they weren't fair. They were red from scrubbing and wringing. Quickly she rolled down her sleeves as far as they'd go.

'Obviously I've been terribly concerned,' said Charlotte. 'What he did to you was unforgivable.'

'Must have spoke out of turn!' said Polly as she sifted two scoops of tea into the pot. 'Anyway, why talk to me about him? You know him better than me.'

'David is ill.'

'It's not my fault.' Polly turned off the gas then poured the boiling water into the pot.

'I didn't say it was.'

Polly looked at her defiantly. 'So what have you come here for?'

Charlotte sighed and rubbed her forehead. 'Because he's still behaving the same. You might be able to bring some light to bear on the reason for him acting the way he does.'

Polly frowned. What would she know about David that his wife didn't?

Charlotte went on, 'Something happened to him during the war. He might have mentioned something to you. Do you remember?'

Polly stared at the woman she had wronged and a great surge of guilt flowed over her. But Polly hated to be cast as a wrongdoer. She wronged you in the first place, she reminded herself. It was her that got Aaron shipped back to the States. But it was no good. She couldn't hate her. She never really had.

'I don't think so...' she began.

The look on Charlotte's face was so intense it made her think harder. What sort of things had he said to her? Some of them, along with his rough behaviour, were best forgotten. But things he'd said about the war?

'Bodies with no heads!' She paused and waited for Charlotte's reaction. Her expression betrayed her hurt.

'Go on.'

'Legs being blown off. Arms being blown off.' Polly collected her thoughts. 'Oh, and carrying a man back to the hospital then realising when he got there that the man had no head. I nearly ended up the same meself the way he hit me about. But there you are. I kept me head and lost me man. Aaron. Do you remember him?'

They fell into an awkward silence. It was Meg who broke it.

'All right if I have that cup of tea now?'

Polly guessed that she'd been outside the door listening, waiting to see if things got ugly or if her presence was needed to lighten the proceedings. She felt more grateful to her than ever.

Charlotte looked nervous suddenly. 'I have one more thing to show you before I go.'

Polly watched as she opened her handbag. She took the letter that was offered. 'From Aaron?' she asked raising her eyebrows questioningly.

Charlotte shook her head and looked down into her lap. 'From his parents. Someone at the Prisoner of War camp got their address for me. He seemed concerned about Aaron. It appears from that letter that he had every right to be.' She had no wish to mention who had given her the address.

As Polly read it, her eyes filled with tears and a terrible anger rose in her chest. Meg's hand touching her arm made her jump.

'Read it out loud,' Meg said. 'If you can, luv.' Polly paused a moment, then did.

My dear Mrs Hennessey-White,

It is with great regret that I have to tell you that my son, Aaron Washington Grant, was sent home to us suffering from severe kidney damage, a punctured lung plus terminal brain damage.

These injuries were said to have been inflicted by a gang of enemy prisoners of war who he was, at that time, guarding.

Perhaps you could pass on our most sincere wishes to Polly and tell her we are glad he found someone who cared for him.

Although our son, a young man with a bright future ahead of him, was taken from us, we hold no malice towards those concerned.

Yours truly
John Smithson Grant

For a while all three women sat there, each trying to control the sobs in their throats. Eyes were misted. Fists clenched tightly.

'Bloody Krauts!' spat Meg.

Charlotte got to her feet and blew her nose. She had no wish to hear that kind of comment. Josef wouldn't do something like that. 'I'd better be going. I've got some clothes to collect from one of my sewing ladies. They're for the orphanage.'

'Poor little mites,' said Meg, her face sad with genuine sympathy before it brightened. 'But at least we kept our Carol. Wrong side of the blanket she may be, but then, there's no guarantee of happiness with a wedding band, is there?'

Charlotte winced. Meg seemed not to notice.

If Polly noticed she said nothing. Suddenly she had a great need to make things up to her. In one stupid moment she had almost alienated a true friend. She instinctively touched her arm –

a signal of reconciliation – as she took her to the door. Meg followed.

'Thanks for finding out what really happened.'

'It was nothing.' Charlotte frowned. 'I just wonder why the CO didn't tell me this had happened.'

Polly made a great effort to say some words that she'd rarely said before. 'I'm sorry I shouted to you about interfering. It wasn't right.'

'Never mind,' said Charlotte and walked out the door. The street outside was full of noise and activity. Kids with dirty faces and patched clothes were climbing all over Charlotte's car. The windows were a mass of sticky finger marks and scuffed boots were making squeaking noises as they scratched the roof and bonnet.

'Please! No!' Charlotte waved her hands as she might at a lone wasp.

Polly was more vocal. 'Oi! Get off of there, you load of lousy monkeys!' She got there first, pushing them off with a few well-aimed slaps on ill-protected behinds.

One yelled as she grabbed the back of his pullover and jerked him backwards. With her free hand she gripped the ear of another. He yelled even louder than the first kid. The rest ran off shouting insults and making faces as they went.

'Take yer bleedin' 'ands off my Eric!'

Polly recognised the voice and simmered with anger. Iris Trent was marching towards her, rolling up her sleeves and exposing brawny arms.

Polly turned to face Iris. 'Take the little bugger! This one too!' Spinning round on her heel she flung both boys away from her. One stumbled into the gutter. Eric collided with his mother's stomach.

'Local ragamuffins,' Polly explained to Charlotte who she had expected to look quite shocked at her outburst. Instead she looked amused.

But the boy's mother wasn't finished yet. 'Better than being a bastard!' shouted Iris Trent.

There was no way she would let her get away with that! Aware that neighbours were spilling out into the street and that kids were hanging out of bedroom windows, Polly turned to face the foe.

'You fat cow!' Polly clenched her fists. 'Cheap tart!'

'That's it,' growled Polly, taking slow steps towards her adversary. 'Just keep calling me names.' She felt excited! Ecstatic! Nothing would give her greater pleasure than to punch the fat face of the woman who'd stopped her from getting the job at Edwards & Ringers.

Polly took her measure. Iris was big but she judged she wasn't so quick.

Iris lunged. Polly sidestepped and Iris hit the floor. The crowd roared with delight. This was entertainment. Usually the wireless was all they had unless they could afford a night at the pictures. Because the houses were still gas-lit, everyone tried to conserve the batteries. Saturday morning was the time when the accumulators were taken up the garage for recharging.

'I'll 'ave you, you bloody whore!' spat Iris as she got to her feet.

She held her arms out from her sides. Her hands were clawed ready to tear at Polly's hair.

Polly crouched slightly. She had no intention of letting Iris get anywhere near her.

After a few catcalls, the crowd fell silent. Meg put a restraining hand on Charlotte's arm. Polly guessed she had suggested talking reasonably to the woman. Meg knew otherwise. Women like Iris Trent were not famous for being reasonable. They liked to feel they had some status all right, but it was the sort they got from opening

their big gobs and throwing their weight about. Iris Trent was
certainly guilty of the former and had plenty of the latter.

'Right,' growled Iris, 'I'm coming for yer!'

It was a stupid thing to say. Polly was warned and therefore was
ready. As Iris leaned forward and charged, Polly sidestepped again,
but this time left one foot behind.

Iris tripped but didn't fall. Instead she staggered forward, arms
flailing, head falling further down. And she was going too fast to
stop.

A gasp went up from all assembled as, like a bull dressed for
carnival, she went full pelt. There was the sound of a dull thud as
her head connected with the spare wheel case on the back of Charlotte's car. She staggered, then fell flat on her back, her body
wobbling like a well-set jelly as she hit the ground.

The crowd clapped and cheered. Even Eric Trent, the originator
of the problem, rested his hands on his knees, looked down into his
mother's face and said, 'Cor! She's out cold!' Then he looked up at
Polly, admiration shining in his eyes. 'How did you do that, then?'

Without answering she went to where Meg and Charlotte were
standing. 'Sorry about the dent,' she said to Charlotte.

A little shell shocked, Charlotte merely nodded silently. Never
seen anything like it, thought Polly. She asked her, 'Don't get posh
women in Clifton squabbling over kids, do you?'

'No,' Charlotte replied. 'They're mostly away at boarding
school.'

Polly wasn't so forgiving of Charlotte that she couldn't make a
comment.

'Posh women ain't got much to do then, 'ave they?'

Charlotte didn't rise to the remark. There were more important
things on her mind than scoring points. Her gloved hand folded
over her arm.

'That wasn't the first time David had hit you, was it?'

Polly shrugged. 'Sometimes I said things he didn't like. A bit like her really.'

She jerked her chin at her adversary who was still lying spark out on the ground. A crowd had gathered round, applying smelling salts to her nose and wet cloths to her forehead.

'But I wasn't going to have her call my kiddie names,' she added.

Charlotte smiled warmly and patted her arm. 'I don't blame you. A mother has a right to keep her child and a child is best living with his natural mother.'

'Shame that little Edna couldn't keep her baby,' said Meg who was standing with them, arms folded and a smug smile painted on her face. Polly *did* sometimes give her occasion to be proud. She went on, 'I know it might have been hard on Colin, but all the same, if the father had married her...'

Polly kicked her gently on the shin. Of all the things to say!

Charlotte smiled sadly. 'Mixed marriages are not allowed.' She looked directly at Polly. 'I'm sorry. I wasn't going to tell you that.'

Polly felt the full power of those silver-grey eyes, couldn't hold their gaze and had to turn away. Up until now she was the one who'd been wronged. The truth was hard to swallow. If only she'd thought things through a bit more and asked a few questions before blowing her top at Charlotte and getting involved with David. There must be some way she could make things up to her.

It wasn't thought through, but she had to do something.

'If you want me to give you a hand making these kiddies some clothes, Aunty Meg's got an old Singer in the front room. It's a treadle. Real nice it is.'

It was poor compensation for what she'd done. And she was about to start a job at the New Palace – chance of a lifetime she reckoned; wages a bit low but there was no paying to watch the film, was there? 'I could do the sewing during the day,' she added when she noticed the look of surprise on Aunt Meg's face.

Charlotte's face brightened. 'That is really wonderful. May I drop off some materials sometime this week?'

After Charlotte was gone and she'd closed the front door, Polly took a deep breath before turning round. Meg had to be faced, and there she was, arms folded and waiting for an explanation.

'Don't look at me like that. I can manage to do the sewing and go to work,' Polly said.

'It's not the baby clothes I'm thinking about. Polly, if you ever get married I hope you never have to go through what that poor woman's been through. You've got a lot to answer for and don't try to deny it!'

18

One of the typists employed by the Marriage Guidance Council had decorated the office with paper chains. They looked a little faded and Charlotte guessed they were pre-war but their presence was appreciated. They helped lift the sombre drabness of her office and fill the gaps between the scratched and dated furniture.

A four-drawer filing cabinet sat in the corner. Her desk and chair were of similar age and of the same dark oak as the cabinet. Clay-coloured linoleum, cracked with age, squeaked underfoot.

As if the office wasn't dark enough, the lower halves of the windows were painted in a dirty cream. Brush strokes and stuck bristles gave it an uneven, scruffy look.

'It's not very welcoming,' she'd said to the director of operations when first shown her domain.

He'd pursed his lips and drawn himself up to his full height so that he almost seemed taller than she. 'It's not supposed to be,' he said in a clipped voice. 'Divorce is a very serious business and should not be considered lightly!' His look of condemnation was enough to tell her not to press the point.

'Excuse me,' she had said, sweeping past him with dignified

ease as if she were one of those people who always were and always
would be in complete control of their lives. Little did he know.

She had an appointment at eleven, a Mr and Mrs Masters who
had married young in the middle of the war and were now having
problems. Charlotte was of the opinion that their marriage was
not beyond repair. It was just a case of rediscovering each other.
First she would need to take some notes. Tugging forcibly on the
right-hand drawer eventually persuaded it to open. Her pen lay
on top of a pile of unopened letters – unopened but for one,
that is.

Thoughtfully, and not without sadness, she took out the opened
envelope. Her thoughts immediately went back to the day when
Matron had told her that Sherman Burbage had gone out on a 'trial
adoption'. She had instantly known what Edna's reaction would be.

'Before you go to her,' Matron had said, her eyes full of concern,
'perhaps you could take these.' She had handed her the unopened
letters, about twelve in all. 'They were hidden beneath the clothes
in the parcels. I'm sorry about the first one having been opened.'
She blinked and Charlotte sensed her embarrassment. 'I didn't
know quite what to do with them – whether to hand them to Edna
or what. I thought I'd leave it to you.'

Charlotte had stared at them as if they were likely to burst into
flame and scorch her brown leather gloves.

They felt strangely heavy, heavy on the heart rather than on the
hands.

'It's from Sherman's father. There's a photograph,' Matron
went on.

The edge of the photograph poked out of the envelope. Like
Matron, Charlotte couldn't help being curious. Although she was
telling herself that it was none of her business, she pulled the
photograph from its covering. A smiling Edna, cheek to cheek with
a handsome young black soldier, looked up at her. They had that

certain expression in their eyes that she'd seen so often during the war years. *I want you today. Tomorrow may never come.*

'I'll take them,' she'd said.

Her footsteps had quickened as Edna's wail of despair joined with that of babies disturbed from their sleep, reminding Charlotte of an air raid siren as it resounded through bare corridors. She had to run to Edna, the pile of letters clutched tightly in her hand.

As Charlotte reached the nursery door a thought came to her. Sherman had been put out for a trial adoption. Hard as it was, it meant Edna's marriage would survive. No one could pretend it was easy to put the past behind them. Goodness knows she was trying to do it herself!

She had paused, considered quickly, then opened her handbag and shoved the letters out of sight.

Now they sat in the right hand drawer of her desk. The drawer itself was difficult to open because the office was damp and the wood had swollen. It was just as well. They would stay difficult to get at. She was as convinced as she could be that she had done the right thing. Once Sherman was adopted they could be destroyed. There was no point in handing them over to Edna. It would only give her further heartache and risk undermining her marriage and any chance of happiness. Wartime love affairs were best forgotten. Just like hers and Josef's.

So far she had received no word of what Josef was doing in Germany: a mixed blessing. There were enough complications in her life. But sometimes, usually late at night, she sat in her silent, empty house, staring at her bed and thinking of what had been.

* * *

Edna hated the hospital. At first it had been the smell of antiseptic. Now she hated it because it reminded her of the orphanage where she had last seen her son, now farmed out to potential parents like goods on approval. The thought was horrendous and she did her best to put it out of her mind. She kept telling herself that it was for the best, that Sherman now had the chance of a real family and a decent future.

Despite hating the hospital, she regarded it as her duty to go with Colin for his check ups. They had become much more frequent of late. On previous visits she had never been allowed to accompany him into his examination so she was surprised when a nurse asked why she hadn't gone with him. On this occasion it was allowed. 'It's just an investigation,' the nurse said.

'I don't think he wants me. He's a very private person,' she answered nervously. The nurse sniffed, took a swift glance at the chromium plate watch dangling against her chest and marched off to more important matters.

It was an hour before a student nurse wheeled her husband out, her bottom stuck out behind with the effort of pushing him and his chair back to Edna.

'Everything all right?' she asked with nervous hesitation.

Colin avoided looking her in the eye.

'Of course it is. Just get me out of here.' He slapped impatiently at the wheels.

Edna put her back into the job. 'I could have come in with you,' she said to him.

'I don't want you to! This is something I have to face by myself,' he snapped.

She opened her mouth to ask what he had to face that she couldn't face with him. Was he ill? Had some disease arisen out of his injuries? She thought of all the things it might be. Lots of dreadful conditions resulted from terrible war wounds. The list was endless. The worst thing was that she was frightened of finding out the truth, so she shut her mouth, but determined to keep her eyes open. Perhaps in time Colin would tell her what was going on.

* * *

Polly loved the pictures. The films were shown continuously, so she got to know the plots really well and could almost recite the dialogue word for word.

It was her job to shine her torch and guide the patrons to their seats once they'd shown her their tickets. Giving people information, such as where the toilets were and what time the ice cream girl came round, were also part of her duties. When at last the projector was switched off and the lights went up, it was her task to weave her way through each row of seats, upending those that were left down, collecting rubbish, and taking forgotten umbrellas, purses, shoes and handbags to lost property. Goodness knows how some people had gone home with no shoes!

Billy and his black van were always waiting outside when she'd finished and sometimes he treated her to fish and chips on the way home.

'I've got a treat for this Saturday,' he said to her one Friday night.

'I'm working,' she responded thinking it was the pub or the pictures – as customers, of course – and another slap-up meal of fish and chips eaten from newspaper. No airs and graces were needed to fit in with Billy's plans, that was for sure.

'All day?' Billy went on. He sounded excited, like a small boy who can't wait to show someone his first bicycle.

She sighed. 'I'm doing the afternoon and night shift, but I'm doing some more sewing for Charlotte in the morning.'

Billy remained silent. She sensed something about what she'd said had disturbed him. She glanced at him sidelong. 'Cat got your tongue?'

He shrugged his shoulders casually and tightened his grip on the wheel. 'I was thinking of Colin and Edna. Ain't 'ad much luck, 'ave they!'

She gripped his arm, eyes wide with alarm. 'You haven't told him about her baby, have you?'

He shook his head. 'No. Wouldn't dare. He'd go doolally. Adores Edna, 'e does. But I was thinkin' about 'er. Sad about 'aving to give 'er baby away. You ought to 'ave seen the look on 'er face when I took 'er to that orphanage. All brightness and light it was and when she came out, she was crying.'

Polly sighed. Through the grimy glass of the van window she casually watched couples walking arm in arm along pavements that were wet with drizzle. 'Well, that's something that's changed. She doesn't go out there now. Her baby's been put up for adoption is what Charlotte said when she came to collect my last lot of baby clothes.'

'Jesus! Poor cow! She'll never see him again.'

'It might be for the best. The father was black.' Suddenly Polly remembered Aaron, and the way he sang and played the piano; a bittersweet memory. Some of the bitterness turned to nasty words. 'Shouldn't have lowered herself like that, should she!'

'Polly! You ain't no bloody innocent!'

Polly felt her face colouring. Billy had made her angry.

She had to retaliate.

'And you can't read and write! So what?' It hurt, just as she'd known it would.

Billy took his attention off the road for the smallest of moments. The surface was slippery, his tyres not too special. The van skidded. The brakes squealed. Car headlights glared like twin suns, then were gone. Suddenly the van was careering onto the pavement where it spun once, righted itself, then smashed headlong into a lamppost.

* * *

When Charlotte went round to collect Polly's completed sewing, Meg was standing at the door, her face creased with worry and a crying Carol in her arms.

Since getting a permanent position with the Marriage Guidance Council, Charlotte had regained the confident air she had had before David had come home, but she was filled with apprehension when she saw Meg's face. Something bad had happened.

'What's the matter?'

Meg told her about the accident. 'It never rains but it pours,' she said. 'My sister's ill.' She went on to explain that she was off to look after her sister in Lancashire and would have taken Carol, but there was a risk of infection. 'Polly said to ask Edna to have her,' Meg said. 'She reckons she'd dote on her – considering the circumstances with regard to her own.'

'Would you like me to take her there?' asked Charlotte.

It didn't take Meg long to pack Carol's things and wash the sticky mess of dried jam off her face.

A fog was brewing, a foul mix of natural mist, the smoke from thousands of coal fires in living room grates, and yeast from Georges' Brewery. Chimney stacks towering above the city appeared to puff their effluent upwards when in fact it merely hung in the air, mixing with the smoke from streets of terraced houses.

Charlotte switched on her car lights. She'd left Meg dusting off a battered brown suitcase she'd taken from the top of a worm-eaten wardrobe ready for her trip to her sister's. She wrinkled her nose as she remembered the smell of mothballs when she opened it.

Carol's clothes were stuffed into two brown paper carrier bags, which now lay beside her on the back seat of the car. The child was sleeping, her cheeks still red from the crying she'd done earlier.

Charlotte guessed Carol was teething again. Every so often the
child sniffed back what was left of her sobs.

It was a slow journey. The fog was thickening and shadowy
figures shambled uncertainly through the gloomy streets, hat brims
turned down and scarves above noses. Charlotte drove slowly and
Carol slept until the car came to a halt.

Edna was surprised to see her and even more surprised to see
Carol in her arms. She listened patiently as Charlotte explained
what had happened to Billy and Polly. 'Billy's broken his leg and
Polly is concussed. She had a nasty bump on the head,' Charlotte
added, when she saw Edna's puzzled expression. 'She wondered if it
were possible for you to look after Carol until her aunt is back from
Lancashire.'

Edna seemed to freeze. Charlotte suddenly had visions of being
left – literally – holding the baby.

Would Edna refuse? It had never occurred to Charlotte that she
might. Polly had assured Meg that Edna would jump at the chance
of looking after a child. And Meg, in turn, had assured her. Because
of Sherman, thought Charlotte suddenly. My, but Polly was a crafty
one. She felt a fool. Why hadn't she realised that? Polly had
presumed, and Charlotte had taken the arrangement at face value.

Edna looked pale and was nervously rubbing her hands down
over her hips. Every so often she glanced apprehensively at Colin,
then at Charlotte and the child.

What do I do if she won't look after her, thought Charlotte? It
was not something *she* wanted to take on. She had a job now. One
hundred Marriage Guidance Centres had been set up nationwide
because of the soaring divorce rate. She was lucky to be in one of
them. Silently she willed Edna to co-operate.

It was Carol who prompted action. She was already staring at
Charlotte warily, leaning away at an awkward angle rather than
clinging to her with her chubby little hands. With her eyes full of

childish mistrust, her bottom lip began to quiver. The sobs of half an hour ago came back with a vengeance. Carol was choosy about who she loved and Charlotte was not favoured. No matter how much she tried to cuddle her close, the child leaned away from her.

'Poor little thing.' Edna's voice was full of sympathy. She held out her arms and the child almost fell into them. Carol, to Charlotte's relief, transferred to where she wanted to be and was soon burying her head in Edna's shoulder.

Charlotte placed the two carrier bags onto a workbench next to a bright red locomotive, which Carol also appeared to have noticed.

Toys! I don't think there's anything to worry about, Charlotte decided, and a surge of relief washed over her. She tried not to feel guilty about her dread of possibly having to take the child herself, then silently reprimanded herself for feeling responsible for everyone else's problems.

'I'm going to the hospital now to tell Polly that there's no need to worry,' she called, and headed for the door. She didn't look back and didn't feel she needed to. Both Edna and Colin were lavishing attention on their new arrival. Edna was swaying gently to one side, cooing babyish words of explanation as Colin pointed at the toys and told Carol what they were called.

Edna hardly noticed the closing of the door and the sound of Charlotte's car outside in the narrow cul-de-sac. She was too absorbed in entertaining the blue-eyed little girl with the tear-stained cheeks.

'I think she likes it here,' Colin said.

'I think she does,' Edna replied with a smile, relishing the warmth of the soft little body against her own.

'Makes you feel like having one of your own,' he added.

For a moment Edna's smile faded. She couldn't possibly meet his look. A sharp pain seemed to cut her in two and, for the briefest of moments, she felt like confessing about Sherman, begging him to listen to why it happened and to try and understand... But when it came to it she couldn't. The child she was cuddling close wasn't hers and yet, in some small way, she compensated for the child that should be there. If only she had the guts to tell Colin. If only she had had the guts to insist on keeping her own baby.

'How long have we got her?' Colin asked, stroking the child's black patent shoe that hung out from beneath Edna's arm.

'As long as it's needed I suppose,' said Edna a little hesitantly.

She cuddled Carol closer, her cheek sticky against her own. No. She could not tell him about Sherman just yet. Perhaps when Carol had gone home to her mother... perhaps then.

* * *

Polly lay glumly in the hospital bed. If she didn't get out of this place quickly she was in danger of losing her job. And she didn't want to do that. She loved it. Things just don't go right for me, she thought to herself. First there was Snowshoe who didn't come back. Then there was Al, then Gavin and being left with Carol with no wedding band on her finger. People looked down on you if you had kids without a husband and nothing was ever likely to change on that score. And after that there was Aaron. Then almost an affair with David. A list of disasters. Now Billy. Would she lose him too? She'd asked the staff if he was all right. He was. Just a broken leg. He knew about Aaron, she was sure of it. On top of that, she felt doubly guilty because it was her cruel words that had caused his beloved van to crash.

He loved that van, though she couldn't exactly imagine why. It was black, dull, and had funny little oval windows in the rear doors and a metal strip down the windscreen. After two days of being in hospital the manager from the New Palace came in to tell her that her job was safe. He liked her and so did the customers and that, to his mind, was all that mattered. Who knows? If he liked her that much, she might eventually get promoted into the ticket kiosk and get to leave earlier than everyone else. And she would be able to keep working just so long as Aunty Meg was still around. This going up to see Aunt Ada was only a temporary thing, she told herself. Aunty Meg would be back soon enough to take over looking after Carol again. All the same, the fact that she wasn't around was very unnerving.

* * *

That morning another letter had arrived for Charlotte. This time it was from Josef.

He told her the good news first. He was employed by the Pestalozzi Charity, erecting children's villages all over Europe for those orphaned by the worst war in history.

It did her heart good to read it. He sounded full of energy and so self-assured. Because of this he finally told her what had happened to Aaron Grant. Her eyes had narrowed as the terrible truth hit her.

Please believe me, I would have told you earlier, but my life too might then have been forfeit. Now there are many miles between me and those that could do me harm. Aaron was not killed by faceless enemy prisoners. He was killed by his own countrymen. Remember a man called Sergeant Noble? He was the ringleader. I have reported the matter to the relevant authorities. I could not leave this for you to do. I am home now. I feel safe and hope I am.

She remembered how worried he'd looked on the occasions she'd seen him before he left. She'd sensed that something was wrong but had told herself not to be a fool and had put it down to his going home. Guilt bordered on despair. She should have realised. She should have cared enough to press the matter further.

She thought about telling Polly. There were reasons for doing so and reasons against it. There again, what could they do about this miscarriage of justice? Who did she know who was so involved with the law and its workings that he would take pride in ensuring that true justice was done?

One name that she could trust leapt to mind. Before leaving home she made a decision, picked up the phone and rang Marmaduke Clements.

* * *

When Charlotte came in and confirmed that everything had worked out exactly as planned, Polly could have whooped for joy.

Knowing Edna's secret and how much she loved children, she had half a mind to wonder whether she'd ever get her daughter back. At one time she might not have worried. Someone else looking after Carol meant she could have gone out and thoroughly enjoyed herself. Meg had usually obliged, but things had changed. Polly had had time to think about what really counted. Carol was part of her and they'd got closer. Her life was changing. Billy was becoming more than a friend but she'd given him no encouragement to hope that things might get more serious. He hadn't tried anything on and, although sometimes she wished that he would, his respect made her feel special. But oh, she wished it wasn't her fault that he'd crashed his van. If only she hadn't belittled him with the fact that he couldn't read or write.

She wondered if he was still keen on her. She was certainly still keen on him.

On the day they said she could go home, she dressed in a black skirt teamed with a matching twinset that had a white pattern running around the neck and the cuffs. Before she left, she went around to see Billy. They hadn't allowed her to visit him when she was still a patient, wearing the white flannel nightgown Meg had brought in. 'I'm not going to get into bed with 'im!' she'd said to the ward sister.

The answer had been no. But now she was dressed respectably just like any other hospital visitor – except that the other men in the ward turned their heads to watch her walk by, the heels of her court shoes tapping determinedly on the highly polished floor.

She didn't acknowledge them, but she could feel their eyes on her and, Polly being Polly, her hips swayed that bit more in response to their obvious admiration. She stopped the moment she saw Billy.

Someone had given him a copy of *Picture Post*. He was frowning as he pretended to read it. Polly smiled to herself. Lucky it had pictures so he knew which way up to hold it! That was a mean thought. She compensated by planting a big kiss on his forehead.

'Hi there, honey,' she said in a vaguely, American accent.

'Polly!' His face was as bright as Christmas. 'I'm sorry about the accident. Are you all right? Are you hurt bad?' She couldn't believe it. He was saying he was sorry to her. Even though she enjoyed his adoration, taking the blame for the accident was something she couldn't let him do.

His jaw dropped as she took his hand between both of hers. Who could blame him? Never had she looked so intently into his eyes. 'It was my fault. I said something mean about Edna and the American soldier being black. Shouldn't have, should I? After all, that's what this war was about, wasn't it? His blood's the same colour as the rest of us.'

With bated breath she waited for him to mention what he knew about her liaisons with the friendly forces. The moment passed. Billy smiled and clutched both her hands in his. It confirmed what she already knew to be true. No matter how much of a wheeler and dealer he was, deep down he was a soft touch – especially where she was concerned.

'So! Will they be letting you home for Christmas?' she asked brightly. At the same time she wondered how far Meg had got with the scarf she'd been knitting him. Money was minimal in her job. Buying a present would come hard and knitting did not come easy to her fickle fingers – dropped stitches and more holes.

'I'm hoping to,' he explained excitedly, 'though I'd still be in plaster and on crutches. At the worst I might be in a wheelchair. Bit of a nuisance that, right on Christmas. I was going to pop along an' visit that Mr Lewis who's bin buying all our toys. Colin and Edna got everything delivered on time. Good job Edna packed 'er job in at Wills'. The bloke's already talking about ordering for next year. It's gonna take more than just Edna and Colin to make toys. Time to take on staff. Might even get a factory. What do you fink of that, then?'

'That's good!' Polly nodded vaguely, her thoughts on a more personal level of present giving. *I could sew something...* Then what Billy said sank in and she thought of Colin. 'But you ain't gonna be in a wheelchair forever, are you? That ain't what they mean!'

Billy grinned in that mischievous way of his and gripped her hands more tightly. 'Course not. Be up and about in no time.'

She told him about Meg going away and Edna looking after Carol. He already knew. His uncle, who ran a scrap yard in Sheene Road, Bedminster, had brought his mother in. She'd found out from Edna's mother who, of course, did not approve.

Polly stopped him from telling her exactly what Ethel Burbage had said. She could almost repeat it word for word. According to her, Polly should not have been out at the pictures with the likes of Billy. She should be at home. Her reputation was bad enough as it was without adding child neglect to her list of sins.

Billy's mother didn't know Ethel Burbage and had only heard the news second hand. 'Ma said Edna's mother sounded a right bloody cow,' said Billy. He said it loud, much to Polly's embarrassment. She'd acquired a few airs and graces from mixing with Charlotte and David. A few men heard and heads turned in their direction. Polly hissed and held a finger to her lips.

For her part, she adored what Billy had just said to her. It made her feel warm inside. Aggie Hill, Billy's mother, was a good sort, and although Polly hadn't met her yet she'd heard from Meg that her son's happiness was all that mattered. If he wanted Polly, then that would be all right by her.

'So where was this special place we were going on Saturday night?' she asked him, feeling better about the crash now and remembering their conversation about going out.

Billy grinned secretively and tapped the side of his nose. 'Nowhere! That weren't what I was going to say. It's what I was gonna do that mattered. But there you go. Have to wait for Christmas now, won't you?'

Polly promised to visit him every day, her job at the New Palace permitting. She reminded herself to take a look at that knitted scarf Meg had been working on. But first she had to go round to Edna and ask if she would take care of Carol while she was out at work until Meg came back, or until she could find someone else to help.

Twilight was settling on the city like a dusty veil when she left the hospital and began making her way to the bus stop. She checked what money was in her purse before the bus came. Not much. November had turned to December. Nights were cold and a crisp frost would send it colder. But she didn't mind. At least it wasn't raining and, besides, walking home past shops bright with lights and Christmas decorations made her feel pleasantly in tune with the season.

She set off down Colston Avenue where the concert hall was

advertising some orchestra. From there she cut across the large oval space that was still called the Tramway Centre. Since the destruction of the tramway lines by German bombs, only buses ran there now. It was dark by the time she got to Queen's Square, where the trees were bare of leaves and the grass was vaguely crisp underfoot.

As she passed St Mary Redcliffe, church of the parish since Tudor times, she glanced over at the piece of tramway line that stood erect among the ancient tombstones, like a sign pointing to heaven. It had been there since the night of 24 November. There'd been arguments about whether to remove it. Some had called it sacrilege for it to stay. Others said it should stay as a lasting memorial to the night when the medieval heart of the old city had gone up in flames.

On Redcliffe Hill the smell of cooked meats drifted out of the open door of a pork butcher just before the faggot and pea shop. He'd been there since the eighteenth century, according to the sign above the door. Her mouth watered. Closing her eyes she could visualise the Bath chaps, faggots, pork pies, chitterlings and pigs' tails oozing fat as they cooled off in the window.

Numerous buses went by, light from their upper and lower decks falling onto the slippery pavements. Car lights were less numerous and flashed by before they could get held up behind horse-drawn brewery drays or coal carts.

Because she was preoccupied with Billy's Christmas present and what to say to Edna, she hardly noticed the shiny black car pull into the kerb some way ahead. The door flew open unexpectedly just as the railway carriage had done a year ago. But this time she did not fall. The impact thumped her forehead. Were those stars she could see or merely the reflection of Christmas decorations on the damp tarmac? In that split second she was back in Temple Meads Railway Station, obsessed with looking for the father of her child until she was sent flying – almost as she was now.

Before the stars disappeared a strong arm lashed out and hit her across the back of the head. Harsh fingers gripped her arm.

'Get into the car!'

She tried to scream but he was too quick! Too strong! Like a rag doll she was pulled into the seat beside him, her head lolling back against the seat. The door slammed on the outside world. She shook her head in an effort to dislodge the bleariness from her eyes. Where was she? Who was she with? After rubbing her eyes she turned to look at the car driver. For a moment he was just a blur. Then she saw who it was and her legs turned to jelly.

David! Polly sank further into her seat and leaned against the door, needing to get as far away from him as possible.

'You won't escape. Not this time.'

19

Charlotte collected Edna's completed sewing for the orphanage. She'd fully expected her company as usual in delivering the little smocks, dresses and romper suits, but Edna had refused. Charlotte could see that her good humour was fairly fragile and she understood. Carol was helping Edna forget. Just like Christmas, Charlotte thought happily. Edna was coping with an unforeseen event! How very seasonal. It made her feel warm inside. Christmas was her favourite time of year. Soon Janet and Geoffrey would be home. She looked forward to it. Suddenly she wanted to absorb all the atmosphere of Christmas in one go – a bit like an alcoholic finding a full bottle of whisky.

On the way home she stopped off in East Street, Bedminster, the long sweep of shops that stretched for almost a mile from the London Inn at one end to the grim, grey police station at the other.

There were plenty of people about and, even though rationing was worse now than during the war, spirits were high though purses were light. Queues crowded the butcher's, the baker's and the greengrocer's, but one shop above all others had a mass of people pressed tight up against its window. Intrigued, and feeling childishly excited, Charlotte gently pushed her way through.

Peacock's Bazaar had scraped together a seasonal tableau display in its window. Cardboard houses with red and yellow cellophane windows stood among cotton-wool snow and, on the roof of the largest, a cardboard cut-out Santa Claus sat in a cardboard sleigh pulled by a red-nosed Rudolf. Colouring books, paint boxes, and baby dolls with staring eyes surrounded the scene as though the red-suited old man had flung them there with reckless abandon. Pride of place went to a rocking horse. A sign resting against one of the rockers read 'Orders taken'. Charlotte beamed with pleasure. Colin and Edna had been busy! They were doing so well so soon after the war. And all would go well. Hopefully Colin need never know about Edna's child.

Excited voices surrounded her and she quickly relegated sad thoughts about Edna to the back of her mind as she studied the display.

Small balls of cotton wool hung from threads that dropped down at regimented distances, feebly attempting to give the impression of falling snow.

Charlotte found the scene moving. It was hardly the best Christmas window display she'd ever seen. Shops in Castle Street, such as Jones's the large department store for instance, used to have some breathtaking displays in the pre-war years. Of course that was impossible now.

The store was no more than a pile of rubble. And then there was Regent Street. In the Thirties she had made a ritual of having one day of Christmas shopping in London. Even if she hadn't bought anything, which of course was never the case, it would have been worth the trip just to see the displays and, especially, the crowds of children observing them.

Small upturned faces glowed with happiness around her right

now. Their mood was infectious. 'Isn't it wonderful,' she said to one small soul, 'and what is Father Christmas bringing you?'

The child pointed to the rocking horse and Charlotte wanted to cry. The child's mother looked Charlotte in the face and furtively pointed to a much lesser present, a painting set. Not everyone could afford a rocking horse. And then someone said something that reminded her how things had changed since the war.

'Now the old man's 'ome, it's goin' to be a real family Christmas,' was the remark Charlotte overheard.

Her earlier high spirits had fallen to earth and, as her mood changed, so did the display. She could see it now for what it was. Cheap, tawdry, made from spare bits and pieces of cardboard and paper. The cotton wool was probably from First Aid stocks handed out during the war but never used.

What would David be like over Christmas? A shiver coursed down her spine. She made a momentous effort to regain her self-control. Never mind. What is a family Christmas? A lot of husbands didn't come home at all.

Suddenly the lights went out. Yet another power cut. A groan rose from the crowd around her because the world was less gay and winter darkness had descended again.

* * *

Polly's head hurt but her vision gradually cleared. They'd come to a standstill and it was pitch dark outside. For a moment she half imagined she was back in the blackout, necking in a staff car up along the sea walls, an area of wilderness on the edge of Avon Gorge.

Once her eyes had focused she realised that was indeed where she was.

David was sitting silently beside her. She wondered how long they'd been there and what his intentions were. Obviously they weren't here for necking. He wasn't making the right overtures for that.

Her whole body seemed to have frozen. She was desperate to escape. If she could just catch him off guard...

As her fuzziness began to clear, the urge to take flight became stronger.

She looked at David, his eyes staring out at the darkness, the film of sweat lightly coating his face, the shaking hands. Why the hell had he brought her up here? What was in his mind?

They were at the very top of the Avon Gorge. A few feet away there was a sheer drop to the bottom. A terrible thought came into her mind and she trembled. She closed her eyes and swallowed as she imagined her body bouncing against the rocks, falling head-long through the bushes, and finally shattering like a rotten apple on the ground three-hundred feet below.

Another car went by, its headlights picking out the angular jaw and deathly white features of David's face. The beam was bright but quickly gone. Yet in that moment she'd seen the wetness on his cheeks. David was crying.

It occurred to her that he had forgotten she was there and relaxed slightly. Her chance had come. Slowly and silently she reached for the door handle. For a moment its precise position eluded her. She felt her way, determined not to panic. It had to be done slowly. He mustn't notice. The fact that David began sobbing audibly filled her with fresh fear. Despair is pretty deep when it causes a man to cry. She went rigid as he wrapped his arms over the steering wheel then banged his head against it again and again and again.

Her fingers touched something cold. The handle! It moved. One push, the door was open and she was out, running, running for her life.

'Come back here!'

Polly ran, fear propelling her legs faster at the sound of his running footsteps. Closer and closer! The tips of his fingers brushed her shoulder. She screamed, scared of the darkness but more scared of David and the fact that the gorge was so close and so deep.

Then suddenly it wasn't dark. Headlights, perhaps the same ones that had passed earlier, pierced the night. They approached quickly. There was a squeal of brakes. The car doors opened even before it came to a standstill.

Two men got out. She ran past but heard their footsteps joining those of David.

He got to her before they did. His fingers gripped her shoulder. She screamed and stumbled. Then suddenly he was dragged off her and she could get to her knees and then to her feet.

'Now then, what's going on here, sir?'

Even though they weren't wearing uniforms, Polly knew the police had arrived. But there was no way she wanted to be asked awkward questions like who she was and what her relationship was to the man chasing her. It was all in the past. She didn't want it intruding on her life.

Without a backward glance she took to her heels, mindlessly running into the darkness, dipping to take off first one shoe then another, continuing to run faster than ever, the grass frostily cold beneath her stockinged feet.

* * *

After the call came Charlotte phoned Julian and begged him to meet her at Bridwell Police Station.

She was shocked when she entered the cell. There was David,

his face the colour of cold ashes, his eyes staring and seemingly devoid of emotion.

She whispered his name.

He continued to stare, his fingers entwined in front of him.

She said his name louder.

He looked at her then looked away.

Charlotte raised her hand to her face. This was just too much to bear!

Julian stepped forward, pulled at his trousers just above the knees then hunkered down, looking upwards into David's face as he spoke. 'What were you doing up on the sea walls, old chap? Can you tell us that?'

David blinked. Charlotte's hand dropped to her breast. Her heart was thundering along like an express train. Nerves fluttered in her stomach.

Julian tried again. 'Who was the woman you were chasing?'

Again he merely looked into Julian's face and blinked. 'Probably just a lady of the night,' said the station sergeant, who had danced attendance on them since the minute they'd walked through the station door. Suddenly remembering there was a lady present, and a very upmarket one at that, he blushed and mumbled his apologies. 'Sorry, ma'am.'

Julian got up, cupped Charlotte's elbow in the palm of his hand and guided her to the door.

'Charlotte, will you hand David over to my guardianship entirely?'

She stared at him, fearful of hearing the awful facts she knew he was leaving unsaid. Marmaduke Clements and his advice sprang to mind. He'd said something to the effect that nothing would be done until violence had occurred and the law became involved. Well, now the law was involved.

'Are we talking about a mental institution, Julian?'

He paused as if for breath, but she wasn't fooled. She saw the hesitation in his eyes.

'Tell me the truth,' she said.

'I'm pretty certain it's a breakdown. Everything's been leading up to it. Bottling things up – all the experiences he suffered overseas.'

Charlotte thought about some of the difficult marriages she'd been dealing with lately. Women complained of men coming back from the war as strangers; the same in body, but different in mind and behaviour. She'd heard terrible things in her job. Children neglected while their mothers were out drinking, new-born babies found in dustbins, wives beaten to within an inch of their lives. And I'm one of them, she thought. It was the first time she'd fully admitted it to herself.

Eventually, taking her courage in both hands, she took a deep breath. 'If you think you can cure him, then I agree.'

'I'd like to try,' he said gently.

'I would have liked him home for Christmas,' she said with a hopeful smile. But in truth she already knew what his answer was likely to be.

He shook his head and smiled sadly. 'I can work wonders but I don't do miracles. I'll do my best, Charlotte. I promise I will.'

She asked what she could do to speed things along. He only asked her to promise not to visit for a while until David had made some obvious progress. She promised she wouldn't. There was no time for her to brood on what he would do. It was three weeks to Christmas. The children would be home from school for the holidays and would take her mind off things.

She was determined to give them a good Christmas. One thing she had no intention of giving them was the news that their father was in a mental institution. If adults were likely to be openly intolerant to those with mental problems, children could be downright cruel. Janet and Geoffrey would be hurt and ashamed. Neither they nor David deserved that. She would tell them he was abroad working. 'Something to do with the army.' Christmas festivities for the Hennessey-Whites began with a day out. Charlotte took Janet and Geoffrey to the same teashop she'd gone to with Edna up on Redcliffe Hill. The children, thankfully, had seemed to accept

David's absence and the reason she'd given for it.

At the teashop the waitresses were still offering digestives to compensate for the ongoing sugar rationing. In addition to the brass bits and pieces that festooned the wall, there was an Office of Information poster which suggested – though ordered might be a better word – that bread should only be asked for if you couldn't possibly do without it. A war followed by a bad harvest and a lack of dollars. It was certainly hard work being the victor in a modern war!

'So tell me about school and your plans for university,' Charlotte asked enthusiastically.

Janet's attention was fixed on the teaspoon she was presently dangling over her teacup. Charlotte immediately sensed she was going to hear something she didn't want to hear. Not pregnancy, she prayed, but thought it unlikely. Janet's beloved Americans had mostly gone home.

'I've decided not to try for university,' Janet stated defiantly. 'I haven't got a hope in hell.'

Charlotte was taken aback. 'Janet! How can you say that! Things are going to change for girls. Just you wait and see. If you work hard...'

'Working hard has nothing to do with it,' Janet snapped.

Charlotte pushed her cup of tea towards the centre of the table and said more severely than she had intended, 'Then I suggest you explain yourself!'

Janet sighed and slouched in her chair. Charlotte resisted the impulse to tell her to sit up straight in public.

'I simply do not see the point,' Janet said airily.

'Your future depends on your studying as hard as you can,' said Charlotte.

Janet turned her big brown eyes onto her mother's face. 'What future, mother? Peace has been declared but everyone's still arguing. And it's all to do with the bomb. What chance will I have when the Third World War starts?'

Charlotte searched for something to say. 'I simply refuse to think such a thing will ever happen.' It sounded lame. What right had she to make such a statement? In her heart of hearts she knew that Janet was making a valid point. Since the Americans had dropped the atomic bomb on Japan, talk about another world war had accelerated. But it won't happen, she thought to herself, then looked across at her daughter and son. At least, she hoped not.

'No one thought this war would happen,' said Janet.

'Now, Janet,' Charlotte said adopting a brightness she certainly didn't feel, 'you mustn't be a pessimist. Perhaps you'd like to tell me what you do intend to do with your life.'

Janet's eyes gleamed. 'Enjoy myself and perhaps get married while I still can.'

Charlotte frowned. Was her daughter talking about sex? She caught herself blushing at the same time as feeling concern. Was this a glimpse of the future? Goodness, she saw enough marriages contracted in haste. She found herself speaking as though to one of the innumerable couples she saw in her work. 'One does need to consider the possibility of children coming along. One does have responsibilities.'

'And precautions,' responded Janet in a low, furtive voice.

Charlotte turned away, embarrassed that she was blushing again. It was difficult to accept that Janet was growing into a woman. In an effort to hide her confusion, she turned to Geoffrey. 'So how are things at school, Geoffrey?'

At that moment the waitress came over to refill their cups. 'Milk? Sugar?'

Charlotte nodded, her eyes fixed on her son who, up until now, appeared disinterested in what she and his sister had been talking about.

He began tapping his spoon against the side of his cup. 'All right,' he muttered. Yet she could see he was not all right. Since arriving home yesterday afternoon he had mooched around the house with his head down and his usually lively chatter oddly absent.

Growing children! Charlotte sighed. What could she do with them? And then there was David. It hurt to think of him, not because of what he'd done, but because of what he'd gone through. She felt guilty for not having read the signs correctly; regretful that she hadn't had the courage to ask him about the appalling things he'd seen.

Dispirited, but still determined that the run-up to Christmas would be as happy as possible, she left the teashop, the children tagging along behind her. The pavement was two steps higher than the road where the car was parked.

Having unlocked the passenger door for Janet and Geoffrey, Charlotte started round to the driver's side when a woman guiding a pushchair carefully amongst a host of trousered and stockinged legs caught her eye.

'Edna!'

Edna stopped and looked down. Charlotte bounded up the steps.

She peered in at Carol, pleased to see that being parted from her mother had done her no harm at all.

'So when is Polly coming out of hospital?' she asked.

'She already is,' answered Edna. 'But she's doing the matinee today so she asked me to look after Carol.'

Charlotte forgot everything else when she was making a fuss of a child, which is why she said what she then said. 'Golly, Edna. You are most certainly going to miss her when she's gone. It must almost be like having your own.'

The moment it was out she could have bitten off her tongue. Edna looked crestfallen.

'Oh Edna, I am really so sorry!'

She saw the sadness in the young woman's eyes and knew immediately that, despite looking after Carol, Edna still hankered after the child her mother had forced her to give away.

* * *

It was a terrible wrench for Edna to give Carol back to Polly, but Aunty Meg was back and Billy was home. Despite his needing some assistance from crutches, Edna fully expected to see Billy back on the van, flogging anything he could get his hands on. Until then someone had to go and see Mr Lewis, the toyshop manager, about sorting out some proper contracts – with deposits up front – for next year. Billy had sent a message that he was too ill to go. His legs were playing him up, and he suggested Edna go on their behalf.

'We've got to see the bloke,' said Colin. He held out his hands helplessly. 'Or rather you will. Shops ain't made for wheelchairs.'

'But Mr Lewis will be expecting a man,' said Edna, awash with nervousness at occupying the important position she'd been suddenly thrust into.

Colin took hold of her hand. 'Go on! You can do it.'

Edna was not the sort who said no. She preferred to please people. There were fewer arguments that way. But she wished Billy were around to do the job. The sooner he was mobile again the better.

Colin had another hospital appointment just before the meeting with Mr Lewis and Edna had no option but to go along.

The waiting room seemed to be full of men who, like Colin, were missing limbs or suffering severe disfigurement.

She sat nervously, not even bothering to take one of the tired copies of *Picture Post* or *Good Housekeeping* that lay in untidy piles on the table. She noticed Colin didn't either. He seemed absorbed in what everyone else was doing, especially those that were walking with crutches. Jealousy, she thought, and wished that things could be different.

'Colin Smith!'

The abruptness with which his name was called out made Edna jump.

Her throat was dry with apprehension. The words came out in a nervous rush.

'Let me come in with you.'

'It's my body. My business.'

He turned away abruptly. She never saw the look in his eyes and didn't need to. He had to be hiding something really awful, something else to worry about.

'You'd tell me if you were ill, wouldn't you,' she asked, hopeful at getting the truth but so prejudiced by her fears that she was certain he would be lying.

'I'm all right,' he answered impatiently and brushed her aside as the nurse wheeled him off down the dull cream corridor.

Edna watched him go in, still afraid for his health but also hopelessly ashamed that there was another problem weighing her down. Regardless of anything else, she was going with Charlotte to the orphanage on Saturday. She had been happy enough looking after Polly's child, but all the time Carol had been in her care she had secretly fretted about whether Sherman had gone off to his new parents, or whether they'd perhaps brought him back – a bit like people did a wireless set gone wrong or a dress that they'd suddenly realised was not quite their colour. The latter seemed the most sadly apt.

But her life was full at present. Colin's home-based business was going from strength to strength. Few toys were coming in from the United States because of exchange controls and a severe lack of dollars, and people were prejudiced against German toys. It was they, Colin and she, who had gained.

Again, just like before, it was an hour before Colin re-emerged from his appointment.

'Have you got anything to tell me?' she asked as she wheeled him away from the hospital towards Gloucester Road, a busy thoroughfare which still had some shops standing.

'He says I'm as well as can be expected – for a man with no legs.'

Again Edna felt cold fear clutch at her heart. It was likely that she was shortly to lose Sherman. Surely she couldn't lose Colin as well? And if he was ill, then there was no way she could tell him about Sherman.

Her heart was racing at the other problems she had to face. Mr Lewis, the man who wanted to buy so many of their toys. She fell into silence.

'His name's *Lewis* not *Lion*,' Colin said, as if reading her thoughts. 'He won't eat you.'

Edna's sigh shook her from head to toe. 'I know,' she said, attempting to sound confident.

Of course, Colin couldn't come with her to see the man. Apparently his office was situated at the top of three flights of stairs. Other arrangements had been necessary. 'Are you sure your friend Charlotte doesn't mind?'

Colin asked as they made their way towards the local offices of the Marriage Guidance Council.

'She said it's all right to stay there until I get back. Anyway, she's got a meeting, so you'll have her office to yourself. You could work on that new toy design while you're there.'

'That was my intention,' said Colin and patted the wedge of papers he had tucked under his coat. 'Now you know what to say to Mr Lewis, don't you?' he asked her.

'Yes.'

After dinner last evening Colin had sat her down and drummed into her head exactly what he expected from the new contracts. 'Nine shillings and eleven pence and not a penny less for the scooter. He's got to bear in mind I've got wheels to buy and no doubt he'll be selling them out for nineteen shillings and eleven. Have you got that?'

'Nine shillings and eleven pence. Yes. I've got it.'

Like a carousel that never stops, the words whirled round in her head. By breakfast time she knew them off by heart. I have to be strong, she said to herself. I mustn't come over all queer and get it all wrong. It was too important, Colin – and Billy – were depending on her.

Charlotte was dressed in a royal blue woollen dress with a bow at the neck. Her hair was wound over a blue velvet ribbon, the ends forming another bow at the nape of her neck. She welcomed them profusely and offered them tea or coffee.

She also apologised. 'I'm sorry I can't serve it to you myself, but I have a meeting to attend.' She looked so calm, so self-assured, that Edna almost felt like asking her if she'd like to go along and see Mr Lewis while she stayed behind and made the tea.

'My secretary will get it for you,' Charlotte said to Colin as she grabbed a bundle of files from her desk and her handbag from the right-hand drawer, which promptly jammed.

'Let me,' said Colin, always the helpful one.

'No!' Charlotte slammed the files she was carrying down on the desk. 'I can manage.'

Colin swiftly retrieved his hand.

'It always sticks like that,' said Charlotte apologetically. She smiled in an embarrassing way. 'Sorry for biting your head off, Colin. It's just that I'm used to it.' She indicated the cabinets and other things in her office. 'Most of it should have been chopped up years ago, I'm afraid. But there you are. We haven't got money to burn.'

A middle-aged woman with a severe hairstyle and horn-rimmed spectacles chose that moment to enter.

'Oh Miss Anstice. Could you possibly arrange tea for my guests?'

'Not for me,' Edna said. 'I've got to see Mr Lewis. You remember? I told you?'

'Just me for tea,' said Colin jovially.

Miss Anstice managed a smile.

Charlotte walked Edna back to the front door.

'I do hope Colin doesn't think me rude dashing off to this meeting like this,' said Charlotte.

'Of course not,' Edna almost laughed. As if Charlotte could ever appear rude!

Charlotte's face became serious. 'You're very brave, you know.'

Edna looked at her in surprise. Brave was not a word she would use to describe herself. 'I don't think...' she began.

Charlotte patted her hand. 'You've been through a lot. It takes courage to do what you've done. Everything will be for the best, just you wait and see. And one day you and Colin will have your own children.'

Without knowing it, Charlotte had imbued Edna with the courage to deal with Mr Lewis. She'd experienced many things during the last few years, and during the last few months she had experienced even more. After facing the trauma of marrying Colin and then giving her child away without him knowing, why should negotiating the terms written out on a piece of paper worry her? Nothing had ever been as hard to do as signing away her own child.

Mr Lewis was a large man who filled his leather office chair to full capacity. A free sample of one of Colin's scooters, painted bright blue, sat in one corner. There were filing cabinets and a large desk, all of pre-war if not pre-twentieth century vintage, but in much better condition than the furniture in Charlotte's office.

'Now,' he said, leaning forward and clasping his chubby hands together on top of a burgundy-edged blotter. 'I am prepared to offer you nine shillings and six pence per scooter...'

'Nine shillings and eleven pence,' Edna quickly interjected.

Mr Lewis's mouth remained open. He had one gold tooth. She could see it glinting among those that were more Cheddar cheese in colour.

His fat face slowly dispersed into a smile. 'Ah yes. Nine shillings and eleven pence. Please sign here.'

He pushed a pile of papers towards her. As instructed by Colin she read them quickly.

Once it was done, Mr Lewis got up from his chair, which scraped the floor as he pushed it backwards. As he shook her hand he said, 'You've struck a very good deal there, young lady. Do you realise how much that contract is worth?'

Edna calculated it quickly. One thousand scooters at nine shillings and eleven pence each. Even after making them, buying the wheels and painting, their profit would still be at least five shillings per scooter. 'Five hundred and two pounds five shillings,' she said avidly.

Mr Lewis raised his eyebrows. 'You're quite right. At least for the scooters. But I've also ordered the same of the rocking horses, the aeroplanes and the battleships. I think we'll owe you something in the order of two thousand five hundred pounds for the first order alone. You deliver by June and in July we order the next consignment. In the meantime...'

Edna couldn't find her voice. Her hand seemed to rise in slow motion as he handed her a cheque representing twenty per cent of the total amount for the first six months. Five hundred pounds.

Mr Lewis was saying something to her, but she was so stunned by her sudden fortune that she couldn't catch it at first.

'I'm sorry?'

Mr Lewis smiled. 'I was just saying, I understand your husband had his legs blown off during the war.' His voice was gentle.

Edna nodded.

'He's all right apart from that I take it,' Mr Lewis went on.

His words made her stomach jolt. Colin was keeping something from her about his health. She'd thought about talking to the doctor at the hospital herself, but she couldn't bring herself to do it. Colin, she decided, would tell her in his own good time.

'He's quite well,' she said quickly, and fancied she was blushing again. If only she could be elegant like Charlotte or bouncy like Polly. She was so bound up in her thoughts that she didn't at first catch what Mr Lewis was saying to her.

'I'm sorry?'

His smile was full of understanding. 'I said that if he should ever want a silent partner, one willing to put in money enough to buy a factory and enough machinery to go into export production, then bear me in mind.'

All the way back to Charlotte's office her feet hardly seemed to touch the ground. Colin, Billy, herself and possibly Polly, if Billy's intentions were definitely honourable, could look forward to a bright new future. It seemed too good to be true.

* * *

'So how did you feel when you first came home?'

The young man to whom Charlotte directed her question squirmed in his chair. He was twenty-four, but his face had the gaunt look of a worn-out fifty-year-old.

'I felt as if...' he paused, glanced ashamedly at his wife then looked back at Charlotte. 'Like a stranger.'

'*You* felt like a stranger?'

He nodded.

'And your wife? How did you feel about her?'

He shrugged and looked down at the floor. 'I didn't know her. I thought I did. Thought of her all the time when I was out in the Far East. But when I came back...' He shrugged again.

No answer was needed. This was the same script she'd heard a dozen times before. Men had been away to places they would never have dreamed of going. And women too had led different lives.

She didn't need to hear about the affair with a foreign soldier. That too was something she'd heard too many times before. At the end of their session she would sum everything up and give them some sound advice. The adultery side of things was always the most difficult to deal with. How could she condemn? She who had shared her marriage bed with an enemy soldier? It wasn't that easy to forget and rebuild.

After they'd left, Miss Anstice came in to ask if she would be taking tea in her office or in the interview room where she was presently.

'In my office with Mr Smith. I trust he isn't annoyed with me for leaving him there on his own.'

She got up from the chair, stretched and rubbed at the ache in the small of her back.

'Oh no,' said Miss Anstice, her sensible shoes thudding firmly on the brown lino as they both went out into the corridor that led back towards the front of the building. 'He said he needed to occupy himself and mentioned that he noticed you having trouble opening that drawer. He asked if he could fix it. So, I thought, what a wonderful opportunity. I immediately told him it was always like that but I did know that some workmen had left some tools.

'Oh no!' The letters!

Charlotte didn't wait to hear the rest of what her secretary had to say. Stupid, stupid woman! What a thing to do! Preparing herself for the worst, she ran along the corridor.

The moment she opened the door, she knew the truth had already happened. All the letters were now open, scattered around Colin's wheelchair like a host of dead bluebirds. He was staring at the photograph, his face a blank canvas of incomprehension.

'You knew,' he said quietly.

Charlotte opened her mouth to speak, but there was no sound. Never in her life had she felt at such a loss for words. Wasn't she the person everyone turned to when they had problems? Ever ready to dish out advice to others, yet unable to follow her own and stick to the straight and narrow. Consolation was easy enough to give to virtual strangers. But she'd come to know Colin. She'd come to know Edna. What could she say?

Stiff with tension, she leaned against the door, folded her arms across her chest and kept her gaze firmly fixed on the floor.

'Yes. I knew.'

She said it in a low husky, almost ashamed voice. The guilt was as much hers as Edna's, and shared with every woman who was lonely and in need of loving arms and a warm voice telling her that everything would be all right.

'Who else knew?' Colin asked.

His voice was hollow, supposedly empty of emotion. Yet she guessed that the opposite was true. For the moment he was shell-shocked, but not for long. This was merely the calm before the storm.

Suddenly it burst.

'But how could she? Edna! My Edna!' His cries of anguish brought people running from the other shoebox-sized rooms along the length of the corridor.

Charlotte marched towards the door. 'It's all right! Go back to your own rooms.' Amidst mutters and whispers, they went. Charlotte slammed her door shut.

The photograph crackled as Colin crumpled it in his hand. He threw his head back, the tears, a mix of despair and anger, streaming down his face.

Charlotte hugged herself and leaned back against the door. She felt so cold. So helpless. She forced herself to speak. 'Circumstances. She's a victim of war. You were apart a long time.'

'I still can't understand it. A decent, respectable woman wouldn't do that. You should know that.'

Charlotte saw a look in his eyes she'd seen so many times before. He was assuming she had been faithful. After all, with her clothes, her accent, and the accoutrements of her class, she was everything a lady should be.

'Like me, Colin? Is that what you're trying to say?'

Narrowing his eyes to keep back the tears, he managed a curt nod.

Charlotte sighed deeply, her shoulders slightly slumped. Sometimes it really felt as though the weight of the world had fallen on her shoulders. So far she had kept her own problems to herself. But now, she judged, was the time to drag out the skeletons in her own cupboard.

'Colin. This country, and a very large proportion of the world, have been through the most devastating of times. Everyone has been affected. I assumed that my husband, my family and myself had got through it relatively unscathed. But I was wrong.'

This was a hard speech. The hardest she'd ever made. She took a deep breath and hugged herself that bit tighter. Baring one's soul wasn't at all easy. Without him knowing it, Colin had become her priest. Because she had to save Edna's marriage she had to confess the truth about her own.

'I'm finding this very hard,' she said shaking her head and covering her eyes with one hand. 'Yet I feel I have to say it. My husband, as you know, is a doctor. You also know he came back from the war a changed man. You saw the bruises around my neck. Never! Never before had he ever done such a thing. My husband went to war and a stranger came home.'

'Yes, but to get shacked up with another bloke...'

'No! Listen.' Charlotte raised her hand to silence him. 'She's not the only one.' She turned and reached for the crocodile handbag that sat nearby on the desk and snapped open the clasp. 'I want you to read this.' She handed him the letter from Josef. He eyed it warily, then did as she said.

When he'd finished reading he stared at her. 'You?'

She smiled sadly. 'Yes Colin. Me. But I cannot truly blame the war as Edna can. My husband came home and appeared perfectly all right. But after a while I learned that it was just not so. The war took my husband and left me with a stranger. In my despair I needed someone to lean on. Then I met Josef.'

Colin looked at her. 'A German?'

He looked surprised when she didn't contradict him. 'That doesn't make me a collaborator, does it? And it may surprise you to know that I still love my husband, I still miss all the things we had together and, despite his violence and his philandering, I will still attempt to get back what we had.'

Many things had gone through her mind since the end of the

war, but this was the first time she had put into words what she really wanted. Through Edna's problems she had found her own strength.

Colin sighed and handed her back the letter. 'I thought I could count on her. I thought she loved me.'

'This is life, Colin, not a night at the pictures. You weren't there. Someone else was.' She paused, then asked, 'Did you love her all the time you were away?'

'I thought so.'

'And you got lonely at sea.'

He nodded. 'Yes. Of course I did.'

'And in port? What's that old saying I've heard tell of sailors? A sweetheart in every port? Now let's be honest, Colin.' Her voice was now that of the professional advisor.

Colin hung his head and nodded. 'I see your point. But I haven't got a kid.'

'As far as you know.'

He looked up then. Charlotte met his gaze. 'Millions have been killed, Colin. Millions more have been orphaned and others have been born out of this carnage. All those who participated have been affected by it. They acted out of character when the world was ablaze and it seemed as though death was near at hand. Our lives will never be the same again. All we can hope to do is to build something better on the ashes of the old.'

The sound of the outside door at the end of the gloomy corridor creaked as it opened. Charlotte felt her stomach tighten with nerves. Edna was back! What would he do now? What would she do?

Colin, too, assumed Edna was approaching. His whole body seemed to turn to stone. Not a muscle moved. His eyes held Charlotte's.

Footsteps echoed along the corridor, sounding unduly heavy.

What shoes had Edna been wearing? The tension was unbearable. Charlotte imagined Edna's face all smiles because she'd clinched the deal all by herself. It was no good. She had to say something.

'Try and understand,' she said in a hoarse, urgent whisper.

He looked up at her from beneath a heavy frown. There was no sparkle to his eyes, no hint of joy on his lips. She feared the worst.

The office door swung open and Charlotte gasped. 'Everything all right then, mates?'

The voice was unmistakable. Cheeky as a sparrow, there was Billy, trilby hat pushed to the back of his head, belted overcoat pulled tightly around his lean form. He glanced swiftly at the bits of paper scattered over the floor. 'Blimey. What the hell's been going on here?'

Colin spun the chair round. Charlotte watched, unsure of what to expect next.

'Got the van outside?'

'Course I have.'

'Are you feeling better?' Charlotte directed the question at Billy in an effort to inject some normality and calm into the situation. She remembered that the reason Edna had kept the appointment to read and sign the contracts with Mr Lewis was because Billy's injuries were supposed to be playing him up.

'Fit as a fiddle!' He flushed, and she guessed he remembered that he'd given an excuse that was far from the truth.

'I want you to take me home,' exclaimed Colin, turning the chair wheels himself, his face flushed with emotion as he made for the door.

Charlotte stepped into his path and barred his way. 'Colin! You can't!'

He said nothing but simply stared up at her, his eyes full of anger, his lower lip trembling with emotion. 'Get me out of here!' he shouted to Billy.

Billy frowned at Charlotte, expecting an explanation.

Charlotte put as much meaning as she could into the look she gave him back. She sensed immediately that he knew what the matter was.

She wanted to shout after him, ask him what she should tell Edna. But in her heart of hearts she feared his reply.

Exhausted by it all, she leaned against the desk and covered her eyes with her hands. God, what was she going to do about this? What was she going to tell Edna?

Her arms fell helplessly to her sides as she looked down at the scattered pieces of paper. Tears in her eyes, she bent down and picked each piece up from the floor, flattening them on her bent knee before putting them up on the desk. Words like *caring*, *wonderful*, *sweetheart* jumped off the paper at her and touched her emotions. Just as she picked up the last piece a shadow fell across her from the open door.

'I 'ope you don't mind, Mrs, but mind if I make a suggestion?'

Billy Hills was back. He had a witty, swift look about him, a spiv of sorts, the sort who sold tins of black market apricots on cleared bombsites then legged it when the police whistle blew.

Charlotte rose slowly from the floor. 'Why not?'

He pushed his hat back off his forehead, then hitched his thumbs into his braces like older men did. He looked serious. 'I fink it's a good idea to keep Edna away from 'im for now. Won't hurt, will it. He gotta get used to the idea first as last. And 'e will. Mark my words, 'e definitely will.'

Charlotte considered. 'You're probably right. Perhaps she should go home to her mother.'

Billy spluttered, then grinned. 'Oh I don't fink so. She's enough to make anyone suicidal. Besides, if she 'adn't forced her to marry without telling Colin about the kiddie, this might never 'ave 'appened. Anyway, you got a great big 'ouse. You could take her in.'

He beamed broadly as though everything in life was surmountable and nothing was too difficult to fix. 'Now, that's no problem, is it?' he added.

No, it wasn't a problem.

'Then that's settled then. I've dropped Colin at 'ome. I'll keep an eye on 'im and you can keep an eye on 'er.'

He had left her there to explain to Edna. Despite all that she was and all that she had been, the task she now faced filled her with the utmost dread.

20

The garden path at number eight York Street was narrow with hardly room for two. A few sprouts grew on one side of the path, and a cockerel clucked from a home-made cage on the other. Billy persisted in following Polly, unburdening his worries about Colin, the toy industry and what he would do if Colin did something stupid.

'Stupid? What do you mean, stupid?' Polly said quickly.

She had no intention of lingering over the problem. Sheets, pillowcases, and even underwear, were all as stiff as boards thanks to an early evening frost. She could feel the cold right through to her vest.

'Well, do you fink he might do 'imself in?' Billy asked.

Polly threw him a knowing look. 'Now you're the one being stupid!'

'But 'ow do I get him to understand that going astray during wartime don't make her a tart? Things were frightening. I was scared and so was everyone else around here. It's understandable. And you know as well as I do, Poll, you could get away with blue

murder in the blackout. But if you like someone enough, none of
that matters, does it?'

Mouth full of clothes pegs, Polly declined to answer. Each extra
peg she quickly passed to Billy and continued quickly to gather
more. Whether he knew it or not, he had just said the words she'd
been waiting for. He knew everything there was to know about her
past, yet still he wanted her.

She spat the pegs into the peg bag and said, 'Make yerself useful
while yer 'ere Billy and bring that fowl coop into the kitchen.
Rather me wring their necks than some thieving git out to make a
shilling!'

By the time they got indoors, Billy with his pockets full of
clothes pegs and Polly hidden behind an armful of stiff laundry,
Meg had the kettle boiled and three cups of milky cocoa stood on
the table. Carol was sitting in a laundry basket playing with a ball of
wool, soggy on one side from continuous chewing.

Lured by the thought of hot cocoa, they quickly forgot about
taking the chickens in.

Billy winced and clutched at his Adam's apple. Polly and Meg
laughed and the conversation turned back to Edna and Colin.

'It's a shame,' said Meg, as they discussed what to do. 'I'm going
to go round and 'ave a go at him,' Billy, stated, drained his cup and
got to his feet.

Polly followed him to the front door.

'You could invite him round for Christmas,' Meg shouted out
behind them.

'My God,' Polly exclaimed. ''Ark at her. It's only one cockerel
we've got and he's only got two legs, not six!'

Billy smiled like he usually did, but she sensed it was only a
front. He was taking it hard about Colin and Edna. From habit
ingrained during the blackout, Polly turned the light out. She
would normally have opened the door straightaway and told him to

get on with it, but the fact that they were together in the darkness seemed to influence her emotions.

On sudden impulse she cupped his face in her hands and kissed him passionately. He responded immediately, his technique influenced by enthusiasm more than experience.

'I want to marry you, Polly,' he said, his voice breathless but happy.

'So you should!' said Polly.

He beamed broadly before marching off down the street and Polly watched him go.

The curtains in the house opposite twitched suspiciously. Resting one hand on her hip and raising the other, Polly mimicked Churchill's famous 'vee' sign. 'Bugger you all,' she cried out loud. 'I'm gonna be married!'

* * *

Once Carol was back with Polly, Edna had no excuse not to go to the orphanage, though for now she hardly felt inclined to do so.

How could anyone understand how she felt? Seeing Sherman, if his potential parents had brought him back, would be like betraying Colin all over again. But Charlotte managed to persuade her to go. The babies and the older children looked forward to company. Janet and Geoffrey accompanied them, their arms full of discarded toys from their childhood that the orphanage could make good use of.

As they drove out of the city, Charlotte said to Edna, 'They may well ask you to sign the adoption papers.'

Edna nodded listlessly. 'Yes.' Then she turned away to look at the dreary scene outside the window. Christmas, the season of feasting and merriment, yet there were still queues at the baker's, the greengrocer's and, especially, the butcher's, where the chickens, ducks and geese were lean and turkeys non-existent. Goodness knows whether there'd be anything left at all by Christmas Eve.

The shock she had felt on the day that she'd clinched the deal with Mr Lewis was still with her. Charlotte had been terribly kind to take her in and she should feel grateful. But she felt only loss. First her child, then her husband. Like a rope of seaweed she was drifting on the tide with nothing to cling to and nowhere to go. Even making small talk was too great an effort. Only Janet had managed to get a decent conversation out of her. Janet had talked of the future and how they had entered an atomic age when, if another war occurred, tomorrow might never come.

Edna had listened patiently. Young as she was, Janet was earnest about her beliefs and what she intended to do. No more education; like those in the war, she wanted to grab what life she could, no matter what the consequences.

'It's my life. I can do with it as I please. If I want to get married, I will, and if I want babies, I will. But I won't be like my mother. My life will never ever revolve around the family and other people's problems.'

Edna was about to protest that Charlotte was a good wife, a good person, when she found herself wondering about her own family. Her mother had dominated her life and, to some extent, ruined it. Ethel had tried to mould her daughter to what she wanted her to be. Edna had never been allowed to be herself. Mothers, she now realised, had a lot to answer for.

The rest of the journey passed in a haze. What would she do with her life if Colin put her aside? The future looked empty. But there again, if Sherman wasn't adopted, perhaps she could make some sort of a life with him. After all, Polly seemed to manage, but of course, she thought with sudden despair, Polly had her Aunty Meg. There was also the distinct possibility that Billy would marry her judging by the look in his eyes and the fact that he let her walk all over him.

When they got to the orphanage, Charlotte insisted that the toys were taken to Matron's office first. Edna hung back, apprehension gnawing at her stomach. Once that job had been completed, Charlotte, Janet and Geoffrey prepared to go. Edna would have followed them, but Matron intervened.

'Miss Burbage. If I could have a word with you.'

The nervousness turned like a knife in her stomach. Charlotte patted her arm and gave her a smile as much as to say, 'Chin up. Be brave.' But she wasn't brave. She had never been allowed to be brave.

Matron got up from behind her desk, passed behind her and closed the door.

Edna wondered why she didn't ask her to sit down. Matron explained. 'I knew you were coming today.

Mrs Hennessey-White told me. You know what I'm going to say, don't you?'

Edna, wishing away her tears, merely nodded.

Matron opened a buff-coloured folder. 'I have the papers.' She paused. Edna held her breath, her whole body numb with the terrible finality of what she was going to be asked to do.

'Before you sign,' Matron went on, 'I have some people in the visitors' waiting room that I feel you should meet. It's not usual for us to do this; in fact, if I'm found out it may very well mean my job. But when I told them about you, Sherman's potential parents promised that they would keep our little secret. They're in the next room.'

Edna was speechless. This was a turn of events she had not expected. Quite what she would have done if asked merely to sign the forms, she wasn't sure. She might have signed quickly then run out of the door before the tears came. Or she might have refused altogether and insisted on Sherman being returned to her.

Weak with indecision, her legs shook as Matron led her to the waiting room. The door was slightly ajar. From within she heard the happy sounds of a contented baby. The sound clawed at her heart.

Sherman! Her pace quickened. She hadn't seen him for weeks! She rushed into the room, vaguely aware of a man in a well-cut suit and a woman in a dark red costume with black velvet around the collar and cuffs.

'Sherman's mother,' said Matron to the well-dressed couple.

Edna rushed past her. 'Sherman!'

He turned his big brown eyes on her and she smiled her warmest smile and held out her arms. To her great astonishment, his smile diminished.

'Sherman!' she said again. 'Don't you recognise me?' She took hold of him with both hands meaning to wrench him away from this woman if need be and cuddle him close to herself. Sherman's bottom lip trembled and, to Edna's surprise and sorrow, he buried his head in the shoulder of the woman who'd been mothering him for the last three weeks.

It was completely unexpected. First Colin and now this! 'He's my baby!' she said to the woman. She turned to the man. 'My baby!'

Matron gently touched her arm. 'Edna. These people' – she was careful not to reveal their names – 'have been looking after Sherman for the last three weeks. They've grown very attached to him, as he has to them.'

'We adore him,' the man said, his voice warm and gentle, his dark brown eyes glowing with sincerity.

Suddenly Edna felt very small and very stupid. The flaws in her nature burst into her mind like a newly cracked egg. She was indecisive, weak and cowardly. Her knees buckled slightly. She studied the couple closely, the man with his arm around the woman, the woman cuddling Sherman close and he looking up at her trustingly as babies do to their mothers. They cared for him deeply. She could see it.

Matron, sensing her feelings, took hold of her arm. 'Let me get you a cup of tea.'

She led Edna back to her office. Edna was forlornly aware of being steered somewhere, but unsure exactly where she was going. The vision of Sherman and the way he had looked at the woman was so vivid in her mind.

She was aware of Matron explaining that she was going to leave her for a few minutes. The final forms for adoption were duly slid in front of her, the last hurdle between her old life and the new.

Matron's voice was business-like but understanding. 'It's up to you at the end of the day. He's your baby and so, in my opinion at least, it's up to you to decide his future, not your mother. I'll leave you to think about it.'

The door closed softly, leaving her alone in a room where only Matron's certificates of professional qualification relieved the institutional blandness of the eggshell blue walls.

Time ticked by. She hardly noticed anything. Even the papers were no more than a blank whiteness on the desk in front of her as images of her life swam before her: her mother, always dictating, and her father, always placating; Colin, her friend since childhood who had slipped an engagement ring onto her finger before going off to play the hero. There'd been no talk of marriage before he'd done that, so why hadn't she protested?

Now she remembered bombs falling like dead birds and the scream of the siren as she ran to the shelters, the news of defeats, the fear of jack-booted armies marching through the city, then meeting Jim.

Someone to care for, someone to care about her; that's how she

remembered it. She'd found out she was pregnant. He'd been transferred to somewhere in the Pacific once his commanding officer
had found out how far things had gone. But through it all he'd been
adamant about writing and not shirking his responsibilities. And
he'd kept his word. The parcels were testimony to that, good quality
clothes from a country where there was no queuing for such luxu-
ries as fresh fruit, no arguing over uncut pieces of parachute silk, no
cutting down of blankets to make into coats.

But what about her responsibilities? Guilt, and that awful word
'if' accompanied that particular thought. If she hadn't met Jim, if
she hadn't felt lonely and frightened, if she had not allowed her
mother to pressurise her into having Sherman adopted.

The list of 'ifs' was endless.

She leaned back in the chair and closed her eyes. The biggest
'if' of all was Colin. If only she'd told him in a letter or the minute
he'd got home, things could have been different. No words had
been spoken and yet she was guilty of lying. Amends had to be
made – if it wasn't too late. Courage was never her strongest point,
yet she had to be courageous now if anyone was to benefit from
this. Above all else it was obvious that a bond had formed between
Sherman and his prospective mother.

By the time Matron's footsteps echoed in the corridor outside,
the tea on the table had long turned cold.

Matron entered silently, her expression both sympathetic and
anxious. 'Have you come to a decision, dear?' she asked.

Edna nodded. 'Yes,' she said falteringly, then coughed and
cleared her throat. 'Yes. I have.'

* * *

Charlotte had been so wrapped up in Edna's problems that, for a
little while at least, she had almost forgotten her own. She hoped

with all her heart that things would mend between Edna and Colin, not that having Edna around the house was inconvenient. It was certainly big enough, but the only time the distraught young woman's spirits lifted was when she was making paper chains with the children. Janet seemed to be the one able to reach her, and a smile would come to Edna's lips as Janet talked about school and her thoughts for the future.

Charlotte sincerely hoped that Colin would send word for his wife to come home, not that she wasn't welcome to stay for Christmas. Then Julian rang and her own problems once again became uppermost in her mind. He asked her how she would feel about David coming home for Christmas.

She hadn't been expecting this. At first she choked on her answer. 'I.... really don't...' then she sighed. 'I need to talk to the children first.'

She sensed his surprise. Julian had always been slightly Victorian where children were concerned: seen and not heard, that was his motto.

'I need to prepare them,' she said by way of explanation. As she put the phone down she knew it was only half the truth. It wasn't just the children she needed to prepare. The moment Julian had made the suggestion her whole body had tensed as if waiting for a threatening blow. That was the legacy David had left her with. But sticking to her marriage vows was important to her. She knew that now, despite her happy interlude with Josef. Josef had been there when she needed him and, for the first time, she no longer felt guilty about it.

But she feared telling the children that their father was coming home. Janet seemed so nonchalant about everything nowadays except her future being threatened by the atomic bomb. Geoffrey was less easily read. He had been morose ever since the day she'd collected him for the holidays. Something had been troubling him but she could not for the life of her work out what it was.

She made up her mind to tell them that evening.

A generous fire in the grate and the soft lamplight threw an amber glow over the sitting room walls.

Mrs Grey brought in mugs of Ovaltine on a tray along with bread and butter and home-made damson jam. She drew the curtains before leaving the room. A cosy scene, thought Charlotte, and judged the time was right.

She took a deep breath. 'I've got something to tell you.'

Geoffrey said. 'Is it about Christmas?'

'Yes.' She took a deep breath. 'Your father's coming home.'

Geoffrey leaned forward expectantly. 'Is it for long? Does he have to go abroad again?'

Charlotte paused. Now was the time to tell them the truth. 'I haven't been entirely honest with you. He hasn't been abroad, darling. He's been in hospital. He hasn't been well.'

Geoffrey looked relieved. 'He's bound to get better. He's a doctor.'

Charlotte felt the urge to explain further. 'None of us realised it, but his nervous system was injured in the war. It affected his mind.'

Janet had remained strangely silent. Charlotte eyed her nervously, seeking some reaction.

'Is he going to rant and rave at me like he used to?'

Charlotte adopted a calm countenance and a voice to match. 'He's taking medicine. There's really nothing to fear. Professor Sands assures me he should be all right, more like the man he used to be.'

She turned to Geoffrey. He was staring at her wide-eyed, his jaw less rigid and his eyes brighter than they had been in ages.

She asked him outright whether he was looking forward to seeing his father again.

He met her question with one of his own. 'Does that mean you and Dad are going to get back together?' She was surprised. Was he really keen to have him back home, the man who had strapped his backside with a leather belt? Surely there must be some reason for this.

'I think we have to try,' she said softly.

Geoffrey slumped back in the chair and for a brief moment she thought he was going to demand that he be put on the next train back to school. His response caught her completely by surprise.

'Good. When I go back to school I can tell them that my parents are *not* getting divorced. I shall be just like everyone else, with a father and a mother, and they won't treat me like Alistair Broadbent. His parents got divorced before the war even ended. Everyone avoids him. Their parents have told them to.'

Charlotte was shocked. 'I hope you are not one of those boys, Geoffrey. I would be very annoyed with you if you treated Alistair like that. It must be very sad for him.'

Geoffrey shrugged. 'He's okay.'

Okay! Charlotte clasped her hands together and studied the china cups resting neatly in their matching saucers. Like their lives, the English language had undergone a subtle change. Would it revert back now the Americans had left? She doubted it. Everything was different now.

'Oh, well,' she said, at least attempting cheerfulness, 'it seems we might have a family Christmas after all.'

After Mrs Grey had cleared away, Janet began reading and Geoffrey started a jigsaw puzzle. Charlotte took the opportunity to go to the study. She must write to Josef and explain what had happened. She knew she must suggest it might be better if he stopped writing to her.

She sat poised, with pen in hand. The paper sat on the desk, waiting for her words to fall across the page. It wasn't easy to find the right words to say without giving offence or causing hurt that was as unbearable to her as it would be to him. Of course, she could offer to keep writing on a purely platonic level, friends at a distance. She knew she had to put any other feelings aside if she were to cope with rebuilding her marriage. Like severing a limb, she had to cut Josef out of her life. It might indeed make her feel incapacitated, not quite a whole human being but, for better or worse, those were the terms under which she'd married back in the thirties. Things might be different in the future for Edna and Polly and her daughter's generation. The young ones might very well take a more casual attitude towards marriage. But she could not. The society she had been born into had made her that way.

So she wrote the letter and tried to forget how good it had felt when she and Josef were together. After that, she wrote Christmas cards and as she signed inside each snowy scene, each shining Madonna, she held on to the hope that David might indeed be on the road to recovery.

21

Edna would be staying with Charlotte over Christmas and she was grateful. Although she had heard nothing from her mother, her natural sense of duty took her to her mother's front door.

Bad feeling had persisted between them, most of it emanating from Ethel's side since the wedding when they'd moved into the house in Kent Street without telling her anything about it.

Christmas was a time of forgiveness, Edna decided, and anyway, she wanted to tell her mother that a loving couple had adopted Sherman and perhaps she'd been right in the first place. Even though she still grieved at her son's going, she could not forgive herself for leaving the poor child in an orphanage for months at a time while she searched for the courage to tell Colin about him. Things should have been different.

The front door was open, but the interior glass door with its white china knob was tightly shut. She opened it and called for her mother.

'Out here,' called her father.

She could hear her father coughing and clearing his chest in the living room, which opened out onto the kitchen at the back of the house.

A cold draught seeped from the living room door. Edna smiled sadly, guessing what her father was doing even before she saw him.

There he was in the middle of the room. The window was open and he was waving his arms around in an effort to get rid of the smell of pipe smoke. Smoking was something confined to the garden shed.

His face brightened. 'Thank goodness. I thought it was yer mother.'

'Where is she?'

'Gone shopping for a turkey or, if she can't get that, she's going to settle for a nice capon.'

Edna was surprised. There were few of those about except on the black market. 'That'll cost money.'

'Oh,' he said brightly, 'she's got plenty of dollars. You can get more with dollars than you can with pound notes, you know.'

Edna frowned. 'Dollars? I didn't know she had any...'

'Oh yes. There were dollars at the top of those boxes, you know.'

Mention of the boxes also brought the letters to mind. She'd only found out about them on the fateful morning that Colin had found them. They were gone now, nothing but ashes. In the past, her sin and any mention of the parcels had made her blush with shame. But her father had just disclosed that there was something else in the parcels. Dollars! Dollars that officially belonged to her or Sherman, and her mother, the guardian of law-abiding respectability, had kept them in order to buy food on the black market!

Edna stood as if frozen. Her father, suddenly realising the implications of what he'd just said, stepped forward. 'They were going to waste, Edna. I'm sure she'd have given them to you if she'd thought it was for the best.'

Sherman's dollars. If she had had them, perhaps she could have managed to keep him without a father and without having to work. She was vaguely aware of her father muttering things like 'it was all for the best'. But there had been an option she knew nothing about and now there were none.

He was her father and far softer than her mother, but she could no longer bear to look at him. In a matter of seconds she was out on the street, running down over the hill toward the main road. At the rate she ran it was no more than forty minutes before she was standing outside the house in Kent Street. The place was in darkness. She'd never known that before. She wondered where Colin might be. Perhaps he'd gone out with Billy to the Red Lion for a quick pint. Perhaps he was going to have more than one bitter in his present state of mind. And it was all her fault for not standing up to her mother.

She stood there staring until frost spangled her hair and froze her fingers. The only warmth came from the tear that escaped from the corner of her eye and ran down her cheek.

It was no good staying. This wasn't the time to face Colin and, besides, she didn't have a key.

Slowly and forlornly, she walked to the end of the street, quickening her steps as she reached the main road where patches of light fell from shop windows and made the pavements glisten.

She was hardly aware of the van pulling up alongside her until Billy gave a quick blast on the horn. She jumped. She'd been so deep in her thoughts.

'Need a lift?'

She nodded.

He didn't ask where she wanted to go but assumed it was back to Charlotte's.

Before getting in she looked back over her shoulder towards Kent Street and imagined Colin sitting alone in the darkness. It was too much to bear.

On the drive back to Clifton, Billy kept talking, telling her that everything would be all right. Colin would come round. But his constant chatter only served to convince her that the opposite was true. Her life was a mess. Under pressure from her mother she'd given up her child and because of that, her marriage too was over. All she felt was shame.

When she burst into tears Billy immediately brought the van to a halt and wrapped an arm around her.

'Come on, girl. Tell yer old pal Billy about it.'

It all poured out. She told him about meeting Sherman's new parents and signing the adoption papers. She also told him how she blamed herself for not standing up to her mother.

'If I'd been braver in the first place,' she said plaintively.

Billy patted her hand. 'Never you mind. Just leave things to old Billy and things will be fine.'

It was difficult to sleep that night, but in her dreams a Christmas angel put in an appearance and promised her that everything would work out for the best. It was a funny kind of angel: flowing white robe topped with a brown trilby tipped back on the head. When he said things would get better, he winked – just as Billy had done.

* * *

A few days before Christmas Billy gave Colin a lift to the hospital. Edna had already told him that he'd got very secretive about these visits and how she was worried he might be ill.

Billy told Polly how it was when he collected her from the pictures that night in a new van that was suspiciously khaki in colour. She didn't ask where he'd got it. She'd rather not know.

'Is Colin going to see Edna over Christmas?' she asked.

Billy shrugged. 'That depends.'

Polly looked at him long and hard, then she frowned. There was a twinkle in his eyes. He looked smug. 'Billy Hills, are you keeping secrets from me?'

He feigned surprise. 'You know me, Poll. Straight as a die!'

'Straight as a snapped twig more like! Now come on. Tell me the truth.'

'How much meat's gonna be on that old cockerel of yours? Enough to invite both Edna and Colin? Only I thought if we could get the two of 'em together, it might just sort things out.'

Polly smiled and pinched his cheek. 'My, but you're a crafty one, Billy Hills. No wonder I love ya!'

'Do you?'

Such was his joy that he started to turn his head.

Polly grabbed his chin and twisted it so he was looking straight ahead. 'Keep your eyes on the road! We don't want no more accidents!'

Meg and Carol were both in bed by the time they got back and, in the darkness of the hallway, Polly went out of her way to make Billy Hills think he'd died and gone to heaven. Her lips were hot, her hands were everywhere and she did things he'd never had done to him before. Everything else, including the ritual taking in of the chickens for the night went out of their heads.

On the following morning she smiled to herself as she made her way to the lavatory which was nestled up against the back garden wall.

Frost still clung to the pantiled roof of the small brick building that was barely big enough to sit down in. Hope the candle's still alight, she thought to herself. If it wasn't, the pipes would be frozen and it would be mid-morning or even late afternoon before they could flush.

Frost glistened on the top leaves of sprout plants and made them look, temporarily at least, like overblown cabbage roses. Still, the sprouts were almost ready for picking and once that was done she could chop up the remains, boil them, and mix them with potato skins and bran for the chickens.

Thinking about the chickens suddenly made her stop in her tracks. The cockerel had been strangely silent that morning. Usually when she ventured up the garden path all three would be clucking impatiently, demanding breakfast before anyone else had theirs.

Christmas! It wasn't the only word that came into her head when she saw that the wire netting was torn from its rude frame. The coop door lay in two pieces on the ground. If only she and Billy hadn't got so carried away! In the country foxes took chickens. In the city the thieves were human.

Billy kissed her passionately when he arrived in his ex-army van to take her to work.

She pushed him away. 'You can cut that out! If it weren't for you, Billy Hills, we'd still have our Christmas dinner having his head chopped off tonight. As it is, we don't even have Nellie and Martha. Even old boilers would be better than nothing.'

At first he looked hurt, but his expression brightened as she explained exactly what had happened.

'Is that all? No problem! Trust your old Billy Hills. Christmas dinner coming up.'

Polly gave him a warning frown and wagged her finger. 'Don't you go getting yourself into any trouble, Billy. It's prison and big fines for them involved in the black market.'

His cheeky grin was too much to cope with. She gave him a playful smack and in response Billy began to whistle.

What the devil's he up to, she wondered. But she didn't ask. If he was confident he could get them a Christmas dinner then that was all right by her.

* * *

On Christmas Day the sky hung grey and heavy as if threatening untold blizzards to come. Hopefully it won't be until the New Year, prayed Charlotte.

She got up early, partly because the turkey needed to go into the oven and partly because David was coming home for Christmas lunch. The whole house was warm with Christmas cheer. The paper chains and the greenery cut from the garden contributed to the look, the feel and the smell of the place.

Edna was not too far behind her. She came into the kitchen already washed and dressed – because she's expecting Colin to ask her to come home, thought Charlotte painfully. They'd heard nothing from him.

'The turkey smells nice,' said Edna without any real enthusiasm in her voice.

Charlotte agreed.

'It was jolly nice of Billy to get it for me. A little bigger than I needed, but I'm sure Mrs Grey will make use of the leftovers.'

Charlotte smiled secretively. If everything went according to the plan she'd discussed with Billy, the turkey would not go beyond Christmas lunch.

'I'll start the sprouts if you like,' said Edna, stooping to the raffia sack sitting on the floor.

'I'd like that very much, but there's no hurry.'

Too sad! She's too sad, thought Charlotte, and today is going to be a happy day not a sad one.

'First! A sherry!' said Charlotte, pushing the sprouts from Edna's hands and marching her through the door into the dining room.

She took a decanter and two sherry glasses from the cocktail cabinet. Then she had second thoughts, put the small glasses back and got out larger ones.

Charlotte gave Edna a full glass then raised her own in a toast. 'To a happy Christmas and a wonderful 1947.'

Edna sipped.

'In one go,' Charlotte instructed, indicating she should empty her glass and setting an example by swigging her sherry back first.

Edna grimaced as she swallowed. They both laughed, and Charlotte wondered how a girl like Edna had managed to get pregnant in the first place. It was unfair to judge, but she seemed such a timid little thing, hardly the type the GIs went after.

'I see Billy brought you a card from Colin,' Charlotte said in an effort to sound hopeful.

Edna looked embarrassed. 'I think Billy stole it. There was someone else's signature inside.'

Wordlessly, Charlotte mouthed an astonished 'Oh' and briefly wondered where Billy had got hold of the turkey. But she wouldn't question its origins. The enticing smell that was already wafting around the kitchen was enough encouragement not to.

'Here's to your health,' said Charlotte raising her glass.

Edna frowned. 'It's not mine I'm worried about. I think Colin's keeping something from me.'

Charlotte said nothing although she badly wanted to. Colin was not ill. Billy had told her exactly why he'd kept Edna out of the picture. Something else was about to change and soon Edna would know exactly what it was.

Please God it will be enough to give Colin the confidence he lost with his legs, thought Charlotte. And God, let our plan to get them back together work.

The children now joined them for breakfast. Both brought their stockings, full of chocolate and fruit, which Charlotte had attached to the bottom of their beds the night before. In the past David had done it, but since 1939 she had carried out the task.

Geoffrey thanked her for the books and the lovely sailing yacht

Colin had made. It was a three-foot-long ketch, rigged and with a sweep of pale blue sails.

Charlotte saw the pain in Edna's face as Geoffrey slid the boat over the dining room rug in the same way it might sail across a pond in the park.

Janet thanked her for the nylons, her first pair, and the make-up set that Charlotte had been assembling, piece by piece, over the past year.

The children had bought her a pen set between them, carefully saved for from their pocket money.

'And this is for you,' Charlotte said to Edna. 'There's precious little in the shops, but I bought this before the war. I'm sure it will look better on you than it ever did on me.' She handed her a small square present wrapped in pale blue tissue paper.

The gratitude in Edna's eyes was tinged with sadness.

'Thank you very much. And I made those for you,' she said proudly indicating the pale lemon napkins that sat beside each place setting on the table. 'You've got one each. I embroidered each family member's initial in the corner.'

'G for Geoffrey!' shouted Geoffrey while waving it in the air.

'And J for Janet,' added a smiling but less exuberant Janet.

Edna pointed at the one that was neatly tucked into a napkin ring in the middle of the table. 'That one's for David.'

Their eyes met. Charlotte patted her hand. 'You shouldn't have.' She turned away and said in as business-like a way as possible, 'Now let's get on with breakfast.'

Edna's eyes fastened on the yellowy morass of powdered egg.

Charlotte had hardly sat down when Edna was up from her chair. Her hand flew to her mouth. 'I feel sick!' Then she was racing for the door. Charlotte stared after her, listening as Edna's footsteps climbed the stairs and sped along the landing to the bathroom. Meanwhile the navy blue and yellow scarf had fluttered to the floor.

'Doesn't she like it?' Geoffrey asked pensively. 'Is that the problem?'

Charlotte smiled. 'No. That's not the problem.'

* * *

Polly was seething. The vegetables were all done and still no sign of Billy and the promised Christmas dinner.

Carol was gurgling with glee at a doll Polly had bought second hand and for which Meg had knitted matching pink baby clothes.

Meg was putting the kettle on to the gas for the umpteenth time.

'We'll make do otherwise,' she said. 'What with?' snapped Polly.

'I've got a tin of corned beef,' said Meg.

Polly sighed, folded her arms, then marched into the front room and stared out of the window. 'Just wait till he gets here,' she grumbled.

Just at that moment his drab little van hurtled into the street and pulled up with a sharp squeal of brakes.

Polly rushed for the door.

'Where the bloody hell have you been?' she shouted, elbows angular and hands resting on hips.

In his familiar way, Billy pushed his trilby to the back of his head.

'Getting your present ready.'

She almost fainted when he handed her a small cardboard box.

For once she was lost for words. Without opening it she knew instinctively what it was likely to be and what it signified.

If she hadn't been staring at the box she would have looked up and seen Billy's impatience. 'Aren't you going to open it?'

She did just that.

One single diamond sparkled in a ring of dark gold.

Billy's impatience and fear that she might have changed her mind got the better of him. 'Do you like it?'

Polly slipped it on her finger and admired it from a number of angles.

'Of course I do.'

'Can we get married in April?'

'Certainly not!'

Billy's face dropped.

'June. All the best brides get married in June.'

Billy grinned.

Just then the sound of Meg's footsteps echoed up the passageway behind her.

'Where's the bird?' she asked, food on the table always having a higher priority than pretty jewellery.

'Won't be long,' shouted Billy, rushing round to the driver's side of his van. 'I've just got an errand to run first. I've got to take Colin for a ride. I'll bring the bird back with me. Promise!'

'But what about cooking it?' shouted Meg.

It was too late. Billy was gone. Both women stared after him.

'Where's he going with Colin?' asked Meg.

Polly shrugged. 'Have you got that corned beef handy?'

* * *

David was strangely placid and there was a vacant look in his eyes.

'It's only the medication,' Julian explained. 'It calms him down until we know for certain that we can trust him.'

Julian went back to his home and his own Christmas dinner although Charlotte had invited him to stay. Being alone with David was frightening. How was she to know how he'd behave or whether she could cope?

They sat him in his favourite chair by the window. Despite his presence and the fact that his eyes followed her everywhere, Charlotte managed to keep her spirits up. This was a truly special day. She must not allow her husband or her fears to dampen her spirits.

Edna stirred the gravy while Charlotte carved the turkey. She sliced the meat from one side only. Janet watched. Geoffrey was in the living room doing a puzzle with his father, who had hardly spoken but watched everything everyone else was doing. Geoffrey chatted incessantly.

'Are we having the other half tomorrow?' asked Janet as Charlotte began hacking the carcass down the middle.

'It's too much,' Charlotte replied, but she didn't explain that Billy was on his way to collect the unused half and that they had cooked up more than a meal together.

The pendulum on the wall clock swung backwards and forwards with each even tick of its mechanism. Charlotte glanced at it far too often, expecting fifteen minutes to have flown and discovering that only five had passed.

So far Edna had suspected nothing: besides, Charlotte's nervousness could easily be put down to the fact that David was there.

She began seating everyone, David to her left, Janet and Geoffrey at each end of the table. Edna sat opposite with a spare place to her left and a laid setting.

'Who's that for?' Edna asked.

'Father Christmas!' Charlotte blurted. 'Isn't he supposed to call today? Must be hungry after delivering all those presents.'

Geoffrey laughed. Edna smiled.

Charlotte caught Janet's puzzled, amused look. No, I'm not mad, she wanted to say. But it was as well that everyone might think that. Soon, all would be revealed.

Wine was poured. Edna sipped it warily. Charlotte guessed she was not used to it at meal times, perhaps not at all.

David studied his wife intently as she poured. It unnerved her. She wondered what was going through his mind. She had a great yearning to look into his eyes, hoping once again to see a sign of the man he used to be. But she dare not – not yet. Early days, Julian had said. Do not hope for miracles. So she refrained from looking and concentrated on pouring the wine.

It occurred to her that she may have been unwise in agreeing to have him back for Christmas lunch, but then she looked at Geoffrey and decided she'd been right to do so. He was beaming at his father with undisguised admiration and talking nineteen to the dozen.

Janet glanced warily at her father at regular intervals. All was calm. Silent night, holy night, thought Charlotte. Again she checked the wall clock ticking the time away. Billy would be here soon...

One ten exactly and the doorbell rang.

'Father Christmas,' she said in answer to the enquiring looks.

She got up quickly before anyone else could offer to go, her heart racing and her heels clattering over the quarry tiles of the hallway floor.

'Hello there,' Billy said brightly as she opened the door.

She glanced questioningly over his shoulder.

Billy's voice was low. 'He refuses any help. He'll get out of the car himself and come to the door. I've said I'll come on ahead and that you're a potential customer, very eccentric, who insisted we have Christmas dinner with you before placing an order. Is the turkey ready?'

'Yes. Wrapped up and ready for you to take back to Polly. She must be frantic.'

'Livid,' grinned Billy. 'I told her I'd be back with something but she won't expect it to be bloody cooked already!'

Charlotte grinned, too, as he apologised for the language. 'Never mind that. Follow me and close the door behind you.'

Now it was his turn to look confused.

'He'll have to ring the bell,' Charlotte explained.

This was sheer subterfuge and she was thoroughly enjoying it. 'Into the kitchen,' she said and ushered Billy through the hallway, past the dining room door, which she had had the forethought to close, and into the kitchen. No one had seen them.

On the way she poked her head around the dining room door without allowing anyone to see that Billy was behind her.

'Will you answer the doorbell when it rings, Edna?' Edna nodded.

Charlotte willed Janet not to offer to do it. It had to be Edna who answered the door.

She stood in the kitchen with Billy, and handed him the half turkey, firmly wrapped in several layers of newspaper. They waited patiently.

'Hurry up, Colin mate,' urged Billy, his gazed fixed on the ceiling as if in prayer.

It seemed like an eternity before the doorbell finally rang.

Charlotte attempted to leave the kitchen, but Billy placed a warning hand on her arm. She counted to ten, glanced swiftly at Billy for approval, then left the kitchen first, Billy following behind her.

* * *

Edna sat silently at the table, totally engrossed in her own thoughts. It was like being dead. She was sure of it. And she deserved to die for not standing up to anyone about keeping Sherman and for not telling Colin. Things happened to her and she tended to let them. Well, she wouldn't do so any more.

She still shivered each time she thought of the day that she had kept the appointment with Mr Lewis. She had marched full of happiness into Charlotte's office only to find that Colin now knew her secret.

Her heart had broken in two when he'd left with Billy, who had then come back to say she wouldn't be welcome at the little house in Kent Street that they had striven together to make into a home and a business.

Charlotte had apologised for having kept the letters. Edna had burnt them, unread, on the very day she'd come to stay with Charlotte. The past was gone. She had a future to face. And Colin, too, must be faced. She missed him dreadfully and she was worried about him being ill. That was why she kept feeling sick and didn't want anything to eat. At least, that's what she told herself at first. Now she told herself that it was because they were living apart. But deep down she recognised the symptoms. Christmas Day and here she was sitting down with Charlotte's family, including her husband who looked terribly tired and was obviously ill. Charlotte, she knew, wanted to make the effort to mend her marriage. It was going to be a difficult job and she admired her bravery. But Charlotte had a majestic sense of duty.

It surprised Edna to hear the doorbell during the meal. She presumed that Father Christmas really was attending, that Charlotte had got someone to dress up for the sake of the children, although they did seem a little old for that sort of thing. When she heard it ring a second time she presumed he'd come in and gone out again. But she did as Charlotte had asked her and went to open the door.

She said nothing when she saw who it was. It was Colin, but it wasn't Colin. He was face to face with her, standing upright, his hands resting on two wooden sticks.

Her legs felt weak. Her heart danced in her chest. A deafening silence persisted between them.

She looked him up and down, unable to control the surprise

that was obviously plain on her face. At last she said, 'You've got legs!'

At the uttering of those magic words he seemed to grow taller. 'I was fitted for them a few weeks ago. I've been trying them out for a while. I'll need the sticks for a while yet, but after that...'

'You didn't tell me.'

'Seems like we've both been keeping secrets.'

Edna blushed and looked down at the floor in the meek fashion she always adopted when she wanted to avoid confrontation. But she had to tell him how she felt and how much she had given up to be with him. Somehow she found the courage.

'I love you, Colin. What happened was because of the war. I should have been brave enough to tell you earlier. Mother wouldn't...'

'I know.'

She waved him into silence. 'But I've made my own decisions since. My baby will have a good life with people who love him desperately. And I will have a good life with you and you with me – if you want me, Colin, if you still really want me.'

He shrugged, then smiled weakly. 'Someone thinks I must do.'

She sensed his emotions were mixed. So were hers. She didn't want to be rejected, but at the same time she badly wanted to throw her arms around his neck.

Her throat felt dry, the words dried like dust. Be brave, said a small voice inside, and, before the weaker, more pliant side of her could counteract her intention, she threw her arms around her husband's neck and rained kisses upon his cheeks. His sticks fell to the ground as he wrapped his arms around her, Edna partially taking the weight the sticks had taken.

The sudden sound of a car engine made them both look out onto the crescent. Billy's van was driving away.

Colin panicked. 'Where's he going?'

'Back to Polly with half a turkey. Come on in, Colin. Lunch is being served.' Charlotte was standing by the open dining room door. She was smiling and her eyes were misty.

Edna picked up Colin's sticks while he leaned on her for temporary support. He took both sticks in one hand, his other clinging onto Edna's.

'I'm going to learn to drive a car,' Edna blurted suddenly, for no other reason than it sounded incredibly brave.

Colin, still walking stiffly towards the dining room, stared at her quizzically. 'Why would you want to do that?'

'Because Billy is going to marry Polly and won't be around as much to deliver the toys. And besides, I'd prefer having a car to having a pram for the baby.'

Just before they went into the dining room she told him she ached inside for the loss of Sherman and always would. But another child was on the way – his child – and she had no intention of giving this one up.

* * *

Charlotte sighed with satisfaction as she sat down again at the dining table, aware that David was watching her. Once everyone was seated, they all watched as, with great patience, Edna helped her husband into a chair. He looked confused, hardly daring to take his eyes off Edna's face.

He knows about the baby, Charlotte thought. Without thinking she turned to David, smiled and said, 'I think they'll be all right. I think they may very well rebuild their lives.'

David smiled back, the way he used to do before the war. She looked into his eyes and studied them for some sign of the violence she had known. There was only a lost and lonely kind of look and, as her eyes filled with tears, she felt his hand slowly covering hers.

MORE FROM LIZZIE LANE

We hope you enjoyed reading *Wartime Brides*. If you did, please leave a review.

If you'd like to gift a copy, this book is also available as an ebook, digital audio download and audiobook CD.

Sign up to Lizzie Lane's mailing list for news, competitions and updates on future books:

http://bit.ly/LizzieLaneNewsletter

Why not explore *The Tobacco Girls* series, starting with *The Tobacco Girls*.

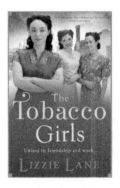

ABOUT THE AUTHOR

Lizzie Lane is the author of over 50 books, a number of which have been bestsellers. She was born and bred in Bristol where many of her family worked in the cigarette and cigar factories. This has inspired her new saga series for Boldwood *The Tobacco Girls*.

Follow Lizzie on social media:

f facebook.com/jean.goodhind
🐦 twitter.com/baywriterallat1
📷 instagram.com/baywriterallatsea
BB bookbub.com/authors/lizzie-lane

ABOUT BOLDWOOD BOOKS

Boldwood Books is a fiction publishing company seeking out the best stories from around the world.

Find out more at www.boldwoodbooks.com

Sign up to the Book and Tonic newsletter for news, offers and competitions from Boldwood Books!

http://www.bit.ly/bookandtonic

We'd love to hear from you, follow us on social media:

facebook.com/BookandTonic

twitter.com/BoldwoodBooks

instagram.com/BookandTonic

Printed in Great Britain
by Amazon

Printed in Great Britain
by Amazon